MÉLISA RYUN

Published in the United States by Create Mode Media, LLC. All rights reserved. Printed
in USA. First edition 2025. Cover design by Lisa Kubja.

Create Mode Media LLC
7925 W. Russell Road #401103
Las Vegas, NV 89140
eBook Edition ISBN-13: 9781947775121
Paperback Edition ISBN-13: 9781947775138

For permission requests contact:
info@melisaryun.com
www.melisaryun.com

DEDICATION

To the overthinkers, the ones who hold back... This is your sign. Take the leap. Chase your dream. The unknown is where the best stories begin.

CHAPTER ONE

KATIE

MY FISTS CLENCH LIKE they're crushing invisible stress balls.

With every crooked envelope Petra stuffs, I squeeze tighter. The dining room table—Jared's precious antique mahogany—is a war zone of calligraphy pens, address labels, and ninety-seven wedding invitations. My best friend seems hell-bent on destroying each cream-colored tissue insert. Her weapons of choice? Neglect and clumsy fingers.

This is what I get for thinking I could wrangle Petra "Chaos Is My Kink" Brinkman into conforming to my wedding standards. We're talking about the girl who turned her art history final into a radical, all-nude slideshow because—and I quote—"art should challenge the system."

I release my death grip and adjust my sensible button-down blouse. It's the blue one with tiny pink flowers that Jared loves and Petra calls my "sexy hall monitor" look. I've tied my golden-blonde hair into what I call a tactical ponytail, held by three hair ties—because backup plans should always have backup plans.

It's not paranoia, it's preparation. There's a difference.

Sign.

Seal.

Stamp.

Another invitation goes on the stack.

"For the love of all things laminated, what are you doing?" I lunge across the table to stop Petra as she attempts the next envelope assassination. "That tissue paper looks like it just survived a booger bomb. Did you use it as a Kleenex?"

"Seriously, Katie?" she responds, then twirls a strand of jet-black hair around her finger with mock concern. "Oh no. Someone better fucking call 911! We've got a full-blown catastrophe here." Her leather jacket creaks as she slouches deeper into her chair, the Harley Quinn to my Monica Geller.

Her smirk could start a rebellion—which, knowing Petra, is usually the plan. She's the human embodiment of a red flag wrapped in edgy ripped jeans, combat boots, and band tees. The silver rings on her fingers aren't just accessories—they're tiny brass knuckles waiting for an excuse.

Cam holds up her hands like a seasoned parent at a toddler playdate. "Petra, *¡concéntrese!* This is Katie's big day—you know how she feels about perfect corners." She pulls out her phone. "Ooh, we gotta film this moment. I'll edit it into your wedding video."

Camila, or Cam as we affectionately call her, is the sunshine that brightens up our little trio. Despite already working twelve hours as the personal videographer to a highly demanding YouTuber, this Latina powerhouse is here, supporting me—organizing envelopes with a smile. She's rocking her work uniform: cargo pants that could smuggle an entire film studio, her chestnut hair pulled up in a scrunchie, and a black hoodie that's seen more influencer melt-downs than a TMZ highlight reel.

We shouldn't work as friends, the three of us. On paper, we're a recipe for disaster. But somehow that random art history class freshman year at UCLA clicked everything into place.

"That's it." Petra slams both hands on the table. "Mandatory pizza break before Katie murders us over ink smudges."

"No! No food near the—" But she's already whipping out a CPK takeout box. "The crumbs! Think of the crumbs!"

The smell hits me like a roundhouse kick of deliciousness to the face. BBQ chicken pizza: my ultimate weakness. Well, that and a fresh pack of highlighters.

"I really shouldn't. I just watched my boss film a disgusting two-hour mukbang video, but..." Cam leans forward anyway, and Petra feeds her a bite with the tenderness of a mama bird. A very punk rock mama bird with a heart as big as her attitude.

"Crumbs!" I screech.

Fun fact: When we discovered our initials spelled CPK, I immediately created a PowerPoint presentation about friendship and destiny. California Pizza Kitchen became our headquarters for emotional emergencies, study sessions, and pivotal moments. Like the time we tried to convince Petra not to drop out of college and travel around Europe *(spoiler alert: we failed)*. Or when we celebrated Cam's first film festival win *(cue the ugly crying into avocado egg rolls)*. And for the past six months, where we've been planning my dream wedding on Wednesday nights.

Seven years of friendship built on pizzas, cheap wine, and obscene amounts of butter cake. We're talking late-night confessions, early-morning rescue missions, not to mention three-a.m. Target runs.

And then there are Ben & Jerry's therapy sessions and about a zillion group texts that start with "Quick poll."

I watch my BFFs laugh as they inhale another slice of pizza. Petra's sprawled out in her chair, not giving a single fuck. And Cam, even exhausted, radiates a passionate spark that makes you believe anything is possible. They both exist with such effortless ease—it's unfair.

Because I'm over here, sweating through my floral-blouse-and-cardigan combo, trying not to hyperventilate over improperly stuffed envelopes.

Oh God. The corner's bent. *THE CORNER IS BENT!*

My hands tremble slightly as I adjust one more invitation, the expensive paper crinkling under my unyielding grasp. My Excel brain is already creating columns: Signs of Imminent Breakdown, Panic Level, Number of Envelope Rearrangements in the Past Hour.

Thankfully, they don't see it. They have no idea the binder under my elbow is essentially my emotional-support animal. Inside, everything makes sense. Each carefully written to-do list, each meticulously organized tab, is a testament to my desperate need for control. Everything has its place.

Unlike my current mental state, which is best described as an avalanche of anxiety.

What if I forget something crucial?

What if I can't live up to the expectations?

What if I'm just... not enough?

The doubts creep in like shadows, threatening to overwhelm me. I've always been the one with the plan, the one who knows exactly what to do and when to do it. But this... this is different. This is my wedding, and everything needs to be perfect.

I pause my envelope quality control inspection to trace my fingers over the raised lettering on one of the invitations. Katherine Crawford and Jared Wagner request the pleasure of your company... Eight weeks. In eight weeks, I'll be Mrs. Jared Wagner.

Me. Married. First one of our little trio to take the plunge. It feels surreal, like someone took my well-constructed life plan and actually let me stick to my timeline for once.

According to my mom, marriage is the ultimate life hack.

Got anxiety? Get married!

Feeling stressed? Just say "I do!"

She's convinced putting a ring on it will finally help me stop feeling like I need to be the queen of perfection and just... relax.

BEEP.

BEEP BEEP.

BEEPBEEPBEEPBEEP.

Cam's phone buzzes like it's having a seizure. "*Dios mío, este hombre...*" She rolls her eyes. "Oh, surprise. The king of content has notes. He's doing that thing where he watches my video edits in real time and sends a gazillion texts about every single change. I gotta get a new job, like, yesterday."

Ah yes. Internet's favorite "prankster," Reece Dare. He's built an empire by playing the lovable risk taker. Online, he's all smiles, abs, and Silly String, but in reality, he's as pleasant as a porcupine soaked in hot sauce and wrapped in barbed wire. We have an ever-growing list of names for him, categorized by our level of annoyance and booze intake.

Pre-Wine: Dick.

Two Glasses Deep: Prickwad Douchewaffle.

Post-Tequila Shots: That Assbag Fuckhole Prettyboy Who Knows It and Needs a Lit Firework Shoved up His Perfect Ass.

Poor Cam. She should be out there making heartwarming documentaries about baby sloths, saving the rainforest, or elderly dogs finding forever homes. Instead, she's filming Mr. Mood Swing's "totally authentic" morning routine highlighting his "effortless wealth."

BEEP BEEP.

"Ugh! His fiancée is going full bridezilla. I have an award-winning documentary, and this is what I do with my life. She made me film seventeen versions of her proposal reaction. *Seventeen!* I had to schedule crying breaks."

"Amateur," I say, mentally adding "golden-hour tears" to my wedding photography shot list.

Petra barks out a laugh. "Guess we better get back to work so Cam can return to her personal hell." She licks her greasy pizza fingers and reaches for an invitation.

"Touch my envelopes with those greasy fingers, and you're gonna be the official wedding porta-potty supervisor," I warn.

"I'm kidding. Calm your perfectly coordinated tits," Petra says as she goes to the sink and washes her hands. "Who knew this was going to be the summer of back-to-back weddings and that Katie would be the sanest bride?"

"Speaking of weddings, Petra, how goes the Beverly Hills Barbie wedding planning? Is your future sister-in-law still doing the ruffly peach-colored bridesmaid dresses?" Cam said, teasing.

"God, don't remind me." Petra's voice goes tight in that way it does whenever she talks about her brother's fiancée. "She's hired some makeup artist to 'minimize the appearance' of my tattoos.

Heaven forbid anyone remembers the Brinkman siblings grew up on the wrong side of the country club."

I catch the flicker of hurt beneath her sarcasm. Petra acts like she doesn't care about fitting into her brother's world, but I recognize that look. It's the same one she wore in college when he stopped coming to her art shows.

"Hey," I say, momentarily forgetting about my invitation anxiety. "Your tattoos are more than welcome in my wedding photos."

"Which is exactly why *your* wedding is the only one I'm excited about," Petra announces, then ruins the moment by pulling out her phone. "Now, about your bachelorette party..."

She starts scrolling through a website full of stripper photos and profiles, featuring men who clearly lost their clothes in some tragic laundry accident—*hello, no shirts*! Each profile picture showcases another set of abs so perfect they seem airbrushed.

My fiancé Jared has his own distinct flavor of charm—he's a big old huggable teddy bear in dress slacks and a matching vest, always topped off with a colorful, patterned tie *(usually featuring dinosaurs)*. But these men... they could bench press all three of us while inducing orgasms with a sultry stare and some sexy whispers.

Why is everything suddenly so warm?

"No!" I squeak. "We'll have a nice dinner at CPK. Right, Cam?" I deploy my best pleading eyes.

"*Lo siento.* Sorry." Cam's betrayal comes with an apologetic smile. "I vote stripper! For documentary purposes, of course."

"Dr. Hard Body is officially booked!" Petra announces triumphantly.

"Look at you, already acting like the perfect corporate assistant," Cam says.

Petra groans. "This is my last week of sweet freedom before I enter my brother's corporate hell. Bro already sent me the employee handbook. It's like fifty pages of 'don't embarrass the family name.' As if I haven't made that my personal brand for the past twenty-five years."

"Maybe you'll surprise him," I say, slapping on some fake optimism. Truthfully, no binder of advice—no matter how thick—could get Petra get through her first week without disaster.

"I'll surprise him all right. Maybe I'll get a new tattoo to celebrate my entry into corporate slavery. Something really visible. Like... CAPITALISM IS A SCAM, on my cheek."

"Well, bright side, at least you'll get to see Bryce on the daily." Cam winces, instantly regretting her words.

Oh shit.

Red alert! Red alert! The B-bomb has been dropped! Initiate damage control protocols!

I watch Petra's face do that thing it always does at the mention of her brother's best friend—like she's trying to swallow a particularly bitter pill while maintaining her couldn't-care-less expression.

My heart twists. I've seen drunk Petra cry about Bryce Sterling exactly three times—once when she confessed she'd been in love with him since she was thirteen, another after she poured her heart out and he didn't return her feelings, and again when he and his girlfriend bought that perfect little house in the hills.

Here's the thing about Petra—she's got two settings when it comes to feelings:

1. Run away.

2. Run away *faster*.

That's the fucked-up thing about unrequited love—it hollows you out piece by piece. And Petra's been giving pieces of herself to Bryce Sterling since middle school. Now she'll be trapped in that corporate tower with him, watching him live out her dreams with someone else.

Every. Single. Day.

"It's fine. I just have to get through this summer," Petra mutters, picking at a hole in her ripped jeans. "Prove to my family I'm not the fuckup they think I am."

"You're totally gonna be the most badass assistant your brother's ever had," Cam says with that sunshine certainty of hers.

"Absolutely," I agree.

Something in that moment hits me. This is the first summer our little group of three won't be packing our bags and hitting the road together. Petra's adulting hard with a real job, Cam's busier than ever with her own career, and I'm about to tie the knot. I get it, marriage changes everything, but can't this little part of my life stay the same for just a bit longer?

"Guys, I know you'll both be really busy this summer, but..." I say, my voice getting embarrassingly wobbly.

"Oh God, she's getting sentimental," Petra groans. "Quick, distract her with a smudged wedding invitation!"

"Actually, I got you guys presents." I reach under the sturdy legs of the dining table and hand them my surprise planners.

"Dear God, she's breeding binders like rabbits." Petra's eyes widen in mock horror as she flips through the pages. "The woman's planned our entire lives. Quick, Cam! Check if she's booked your unborn children's teeth cleanings."

"Well, there goes your birthday present," I deadpan. "But seriously, we're each diving headfirst into these huge new chapters, and I don't want us to lose touch. Things might get tricky when we're not all together. Petra, that binder's gonna stop you from torching all of Mexico at your brother's wedding, and Cam, trust me, you're going need some chill time away from spoiled influencers in Hawaii."

They both go quiet, looking at the tabbed sections. Pages full of our memories, our inside jokes, our complete failure to maintain any kind of normal friendship dynamic.

"You made a Best Friend Emergency Protocol?" Petra's voice catches slightly.

"With cross-referenced crisis categories," I confirm. "And a rating system for when to call versus text versus initiate an emergency CPK intervention."

"Complete with pizza topping recommendations based on emotional distress levels," Cam reads, her eyes shiny. "BBQ chicken for general life crises, Hawaiian for guy problems—"

"And meat lovers for total emotional breakdowns," Petra finishes. "'Cause when crying wipes you out, you need protein."

"I can't believe you documented our stress-eating patterns," Cam says.

"Seven years of data doesn't lie." I shrug, trying to ignore the lump in my own throat.

Cam pulls us into a group hug. The apartment door opens with a soft click, and my heart does its usual happy dance as Jared walks in. He's wearing navy slacks, a tailor vest in the same shade, and a bright yellow tie covered in dinosaur fossils. His sandy-blond hair is perfectly disheveled, but when our eyes meet... something's off.

"And that's our cue to evacuate," Petra announces, standing up like someone pulled a fire alarm. "Nice tie, Indiana Jones. I've been wondering, are you forced to wear those at the museum, or do you just like blending in with the fossils you're always fondling?"

"Bold words from someone dressed as a Hot Topic manager with an identity crisis."

I take in their usual banter, mentally cataloging the micro-expressions on Jared's face. *Hmm. What's up with him?*

"Before we go," Cam pipes up, "hypothetically speaking, if someone in a polar bear costume was pranking people at the Ice Age exhibit, how much trouble would they get in?"

"Probably enough to warrant police involvement." Jared chuckles. "I don't recommend testing that theory."

"The museum could use the publicity." Petra shrugs. "It's not like 'forced field trip destination' is bringing in Gen Z."

Cam's phone explodes with an onslaught of notifications. "My boss's latest emergency awaits. Later, lovebirds!"

"Try not to organize the fun out of everything, Katie," Petra says, walking out the door.

"Text when you get home!" I call after them.

"Yes, Mom!" they chorus back.

Jared studies the dining room table with the same intense focus he gives to potential museum acquisitions. The one that means he's cataloging every flaw, every imperfection, every minute detail that's somehow not quite right.

But the explosion of wedding invitations, response cards, and my well-organized binders can't be what's bothering him. As a professional event planner, I regularly turn our Pasadena apartment into Command Central for everything from Hollywood wrap parties to product launches to celebrity sweet sixteens. Just last week, this room was buried under samples from some Gen Z influencer's tragic attempt at a streetwear line.

They'd managed to misspell *aesthetic* on every single piece of clothing. *Yes, really.*

Jared's always championed my spreadsheet-loving soul and my dream of someday owning LA's premier event-planning empire. So why is he looking at my chaos—*our* wedding chaos—like there's a forgery hiding in his precious museum collection?

My hands itch to straighten the already perfect stacks of envelopes, to fuss over the pile of response cards for the umpteenth time. Because that's what I do when I'm nervous—I organize the shit out of everything until the universe makes sense again.

"We're crushing these invites," I say, my voice hitting that manic octave that usually makes Petra hide my label maker. "Only thirty-two to go! And wait until you hear what I pulled off—I snagged us the ultimate cake-tasting appointment on Friday during your lunch break. Your mom's coming too, and—"

"Katiebug." The way Jared says my name makes my Type A senses tingle. And not in the good way. "Let's take this conversation to the living room."

Danger danger. Serious conversation alert!

Current status: Mild panic rising.

I follow him, mentally running through all the imaginable outcomes he could say. He plops down on the opposite end of the couch, his focus darting to my hyper-organized shelving unit. It's a masterpiece, really, with each wedding prep item neatly tucked into its own special bin or binder, like little soldiers ready for inspection.

"I'm just going to come out and say it. Something amazing happened today."

Phew! *Amazing,* I can handle. *Amazing* can be documented, categorized, and filed appropriately.

"The British Natural History Museum is doing this incredible special exhibit." His eyes light up like an excited puppy. "Lost Worlds: Fossils from the Dinosaurs' Golden Age. And they want to collaborate with us!"

I feel a little tug in my chest. This is my Jared—the guy who once created an entire video presentation explaining why a T. rex couldn't actually roar like in *Jurassic Park*. How can I not love him?

"That's fantastic! When is it? I'll jot it down in our joint calendar. I've got us scheduled through—"

"Actually..." He grabs the back of his neck. "Harrison broke his ankle this weekend. They want me to go instead, to oversee putting together the exhibit."

"Babe, congrats! I can add it to the Career Milestones section in our—"

"For the summer."

My brain stutters to a halt like a printer running out of labels.

"The... the whole summer?"

"I know it's a lot," he says gently. "But this is huge, Katie. The kind of opportunity that usually takes years to land. And since we haven't sent the invitations yet..."

"Haven't sent—" I sputter.

Panic meter: Reactivated.

"Hear me out. We could treat it as an early honeymoon. London this time of year is beautiful. We just postpone the wedding until—"

"Postpone?!"

Internal panic level: Maximum... Critical... *Oh my God, I forgot how to breathe!*

"But the timeline!" My voice hits that special octave reserved for organizational emergencies. "The caterer! The DJ! Do you know how many favors I owe my boss?"

"I get it. You put a lot of work into this," he says, reaching for my hand. "But sometimes the best things in life aren't planned—"

"Not planned?" I laugh. "Jared, I have contingency plans for my contingency plans. What if it rains? What if there's a heat wave? What if your grandpa chokes on a fish bone even though he requested the chicken? I've accounted for everything!"

"This is what I'm talking about." He sighs. "Life doesn't always follow a perfect schedule."

"That's precisely why we need one!" I grab my wedding binder, flipping rapidly through tabs. "Look, I've already mapped out each possible scenario. See? If we postpone, we lose our vendor deposits. The church's next available date is in two years!"

He doesn't respond. Instead, he reaches under the coffee table and pulls out my secret binder. The one labeled: KATIE AND JARED'S HAPPILY FOREVER AFTER *(Version 5.3 now with updated retirement projections)*.

My heart stops. Literally stops.

This isn't just any binder—it's my crowning achievement, my ultimate creation, my blueprint for a lifetime of marital happiness.

"What's this?" He flips it open to the Future Offspring section. His brows shoot up at my elaborately crafted timeline. "Katie... is this a personality prediction chart for our unborn children?"

"C'mon, what's wrong with preliminary research?" The words tumble out, desperate and defensive. "You can't just wing parenthood. What if they end up playing—God forbid—the trombone instead of joining the museum's junior curator program?"

Jared's eyes nearly pop out of his head with every page he turns. "A forty-year sex schedule? 'Sexy times Saturdays,' 'Will we or won't we Wednesdays'? Sex windows around the kids' activities? And when you think I'll need Viagra? Are you serious?"

I try to play it cool. "Yeah. No. Maybe... Hey, Wednesdays and Saturdays are basically our sex schedule now. We could always spice things up with 'Try for It Tuesdays.'"

"Katie." Jared's sigh feels heavier than my complete collection of binders. "I love your ambition. Your ability to look ahead, to plan for our future together—it's part of what made me fall for you."

I wince, bracing myself. This is not the first time friends *(and family)* have told me this.

Katie, you're a bit much.

Hey Katie, can you tone it down a notch?

Watch out! It's control-freak Katie!

"Okay, I admit I got a little intense with the planning, but think about how happy we'll be when everything goes exactly according to schedule!"

"This level of hyper-planning? It's suffocating. I can't spend the rest of my life with a person who can never be spontaneous."

"I scheduled spontaneity! Alternating Sundays between five and six—"

"See, this is what I mean!" He jumps up, raking his hands through his hair. "Every little thing, every tiny decision, every freaking breath has to be scrutinized, organized, and tucked away in one of your ridiculous binders. It's too damn much!"

My chest constricts. Each breath feels like swallowing glass. But I won't cry. I refuse to let him see me cry. "Because that's how you build a life together! How else can you make sure nothing goes wrong, nothing falls apart, nothing—"

"I'm sorry, but I can't do this." His voice goes soft, and holy hell, that's so much worse than the yelling. "We need to take a break. A total break."

He won't look at me. *Why won't he look at me?*

"And I... I need the ring back, Katie."

The ring.

My engagement ring.

The same ring I've cleaned every Sunday for the past two years. The ring I've built an entire future around. The ring that's supposed to have its own photoshoot at our wedding, perched perfectly on my bouquet while I stand in the golden sunset wearing ivory silk.

Oh.

Fuck.

The room tilts sideways. This isn't happening. This *can't* be happening. I have plans. Beautiful, detailed, laminated plans. There's no tab in my wedding binder for "Surprise! Your Fiancé Just Torpedoed Your Entire Future!"

I want to scream. To tell him my binders aren't just binders—they're promises. Every tab, every schedule, every color-coded note is just another way of saying I love you. I choose you. I want forever with you.

But he's already walking away.

There's no contingency plan for this.

CHAPTER TWO

KATIE

I BLINK RAPIDLY, HONEST-TO-GOD hoping I'm trapped in some kind of *13 Going on 30* body-switch dream. Nope. I am in my childhood bedroom. My gaze bounces between the pastel purple lilac wallpaper, the matching comforter, and the identical curtains *(okay, Mom, it was a phase)*. There's a box of unfinished wedding invitations staring me in the face, and it's a harsh reminder that this is, undeniably, present day.

My phone buzzes. Again. Then again.

GROUP CHAT: CPK FOREVER

Petra: Quick poll. Who wants to burn Jared's ugly-ass ties?

Cam: We can turn it into a party. I'll bring BBQ pizza! And tissues. And maybe those cute little paper umbrellas that make everything more festive?

Petra: Change of plans. We're taking you out and finding you a hot piece of ass. We need a full-on, revenge sex-travaganza!

Cam: Hell yeah, I'm in! And while we're at it, find me a man. It's been a hot second, and this girl has needs.

Me: Guys, I'm fine! Jared needs a little space, so I'm taking some me-time to reassess.

The lie tastes bitter on my tongue, but it's easier than admitting I'm falling apart. I view my reflection in the dresser mirror, and honestly? I look like I just survived a three-day music festival in the desert. Not cute.

Petra: *Bull. Shit.*

Petra: *No one's "fine" after their fiancé goes full dickbag.*

Cam: *We're here for you, babe. Whatever you need, we're on it.*

THE MISSION: LOVE AND MATRIMONY binder mocks me from my nightstand; its pastel purple cover is a monument to my teenage delusions. Empty wine bottles are littered all around it. *Those definitely weren't there when I headed to bed, were they?* After bottle number three, details are fuzzy.

Yikes, preteen Katie really went overboard with the Lisa Frank stickers. That unicorn's judgy eyes are tracking my every move. I flip open the binder, assaulted by the pure, innocent hope of fourteen-year-old me. Each page is OCD-level organized. Apparently even my teen hormones operated on a schedule. There's an entire section titled "Boyfriend Intimate Relations Timeline," complete with a step-by-step guide: hand-holding by week two and French kissing by month three—*if* his dental hygiene passes inspection.

Okay, so teenage Katie had never been kissed.

Sex was a mystery back then. Truth be told—it still kinda is. Jared and I do it, sure, but it's the kind of sex you could squeeze in between brushing your teeth and debating if tomorrow's outfit needs to be ironed. Routine—like Taco Tuesday. *Not that there's anything wrong with that.*

I see the "Future Husband Requirements" checklist, and I feel a sharp dagger in my heart. Jared nails every single one: Reliable. Dependable. Loyal. Lets me win at Uno.

I can fix this. I *will* fix this.

My fingers hover over the binder's pages. I want to rip them all out—destroy them with righteous vengeance. Instead, I calmly close the cover and set it back on the nightstand. Because what if he calls? What if this is simply a blip? A prewedding panic attack?

What if I'm lying to myself?

Cam: *Just remember we love you big-time. No matter what happens.*

Petra: *And I'm great at slashing tires. Say the word.*

A laugh unexpectedly bubbles up. God, I love them. This is why I can't drag them into my mess. I'm the stable friend. Miss Reliable... the friend who has her shit together so they can lean on me.

Me: *Love you too. But I promise, everything's under control.*

My phone buzzes one more time.

Petra: *Uh-huh, sure. When you're ready to stop living in la-la land, we'll be here. With wine. And matches, because those hideous ties deserve a Viking funeral.*

The smell of bacon and pancakes drifts into my room. Mom's stress cooking again, her way of saying "I love you" without having to navigate the messy world of actual emotions. The familiar scent of butter, maple syrup, and concern makes my eyes sting.

"Well, *winging it* has never made a quality husband fall into your lap." Mom's voice carries down the hall, precise as a metronome. "Real men want a woman with at least a five-year plan, Deborah."

I tiptoe toward the kitchen and freeze at the echo of Aunt Deb's raspy laugh. Picture a classic Hollywood movie starlet but with a voice roughened by decades of whiskey and sass. It's a sound that has church ladies scrambling for their prayer books three towns over.

"Oh Suzanne," Aunt Deb purrs. "Your daughter's planning obsession is not the problem. It's how she turns every simple decision into a military operation. The poor girl probably has a spreadsheet for scheduling optimal orgasms."

I choke on air. Really, I should expect it from her by now. Deborah Fox has lived without a filter for seventy-two years. There is no changing her.

"I'd rather have an intimacy schedule than your... what was it last month? A nude meditation retreat with those Swedish backpackers?" Mom says with a special tone reserved for when Aunt Deb's adventures cross into too-much-information territory.

"Darling, the culture's more enlightened there!" Aunt Deb defends. "And Gustav was a spiritual guru—realigning my chakras and my lady garden. But the point is: Katie needs guidance. No man wants a woman who requires a toolkit and assembly instructions for her vajayjay."

"I can hear every word, you know," I announce, shuffling into the kitchen.

Mom's wearing her LET'S GET WHISKING apron and pressed khakis. She wraps me up in a hug, smelling of vanilla extract and childhood comfort. Her shoulder-length blonde hair is styled in its usual practical bob, not a strand out of place.

"Katie-kins!" Aunt Deb exclaims from her perch at the kitchen island. "Looks like someone's been hit by the sad train and dragged through breakup town!"

She's one to talk. The woman looks like a peacock mated with a Stevie Nicks concert—her caftan an obnoxious rainbow of jewel tones. She's wearing enough jewelry to set off airport metal detectors, but, as usual, her strawberry blonde hair looks radiant against her flawless makeup. She's a ball of chaotic energy and unsolicited advice *(which she calls sage wisdom)*.

"Thank you for that *very insightful* observation," I say, dropping onto the kitchen stool with a sigh. "Exactly what I want to hear after my fiancé dumped me."

"Dumped?" Aunt Deb straightens up like someone just insulted her crystal collection. Her blue eyes flash with indignation. "Oh no, darling. Rule number one of being fabulous: we don't get dumped. We simply redirect our fabulousness elsewhere."

Mom slides a plate of bacon pancakes to me. "Jared's having prewedding jitters. You two are meant to be. But you really should go to the salon and fix up those eyebrows. You'll want to look your best when he comes back."

"Or. You wake up in a foreign country on top of an Italian hunk and neither of you remembers how you got there. That's how you heal a broken heart," Aunt Deb declares, pulling out her laptop. "Behold!" She waves her hands at the screen as if she's a game show host.

The computer display explodes with enough Italian eye candy to put a Dolce & Gabbana campaign to shame. Images of sun-soaked vineyards and ancient ruins that make my control-freak heart skip a beat. There are pictures of charming villas with terracotta roofs, winding streets lined with cypress trees, and views that belong on postcards.

"Got this amazing deal in my inbox yesterday." Aunt Deb clicks around on the travel website. "Monti Tours. Last-minute cancellation. It's a steal, baby girl."

I take a bite of my pancakes, trying to appear uninterested, but my eyes refuse to look away.

"We'll be on a luxury bus tour. Every day we wake up somewhere new, hop on our chariot, and boom—another Italian masterpiece." Her on-point manicured nail taps the screen. "Look at this itinerary—wine tasting in Tuscany, cooking class in Bologna, sunset boat ride in Venice. Even your spreadsheets would approve."

Whoever snapped these photos isn't just a photographer—they're a storyteller. Each image is alive—like you could reach through the screen and feel the warm Italian sun on your face, taste the wine on your tongue, and hear laughter echoing off ancient buildings.

That does sound amazing. I do have plenty of vacation days.

"Two weeks touring Italy for half price! Don't ignore the universe. It is personally demanding that you get your cute little uptight behind on that plane with me."

She vibrates with excitement, her bracelets jingling a chaotic melody. "We'll drink wine, eat pasta, and flirt with men named Giovanni. I tried to convince your mother to come, but she's committed to grandma duty. Criminal, really, if you ask me."

My mother sighs. "You know how it is with David—his job's too important. He can't take days off. Not when he's so busy saving lives. Besides, he asked me months ago to watch the kids while Emma is at that medical conference."

The mere mention of my older brother makes my skin prickle and break out in stress hives. Dr. David Crawford—handsome, successful heart surgeon—who of course comes with his doting trophy wife and two absolutely perfect children.

"The kids love spending time with Grammy," Mom adds, her voice carrying that special warmth she reserves for all things

David-adjacent. The same tone she uses when showing off his framed medical degrees to anyone who enters our house.

My mother insists she doesn't have favorites, but anyone with eyeballs can see—it's not me.

I stare at the travel website, at the joy and adventure playing out in sunlit Italian streets. My finger traces across an image of a couple laughing in front of the Trevi Fountain in Rome. That could be us. That *should* be us. I need to prove to Jared that I can be that person—carefree, spontaneous, everything he said I wasn't.

"Deborah." Mom sighs, flipping another pancake. "You just got back from Thailand. Don't you want to stay home for more than ten minutes?"

"Oh Suzy Q, if I could afford it, I'd travel every single day of the year. Life's too short to sit still!"

"I'll go!" I blurt out, surprising myself.

"Excellent!" Aunt Deb claps her hands together. "Smallish little detail—it's a seniors' tour. But honey, with your affinity for sensible shoes and early bedtimes, you'll fit right in! You're basically an eighty-year-old trapped in a twenty-five-year-old's body."

Mom's spatula clatters against the counter. "Katie, honey, this seems... impulsive."

"Exactly." I straighten my shoulders, feeling courageous *(or maybe it's the pancake sugar rush)*. "Jared wants spontaneous, so that's who I'm going to be!"

"That's my promising little protégé! We are gonna rage across Italy like gladiate-hers. We'll stumble back onto the plane two weeks later with full bellies, even fuller heart boners, and a contact list full of men named Stefano."

I did it! No turning back now.

"We leave in two days!" she adds.

Oh God. What have I done?

No. This is the plan. Jared will see my vacay pics and know that I've changed. He'll be begging for me to take him back.

Spontaneous Katie is going to Italy!

Now where is my passport binder?

***

"**THEY SAY IT'S HARD** to get into the mile-high club, but honey, I'm running a loyalty program," my aunt quips. "See any handsome devils?"

The elderly couple in 15D and E snap their heads around so fast their matching neck pillows wobble in perfect sync. I slump deeper into my premium economy seat, hiding behind my labeled Ziploc bag of artisanal snacks and disinfectant.

But Aunt Deb's already dumped her enormous bedazzled leopard-print tote over my what-was-organized tray table. My water bottle topples. My color-coded Italy itinerary scatters. And—what is that metallic pink thing rolling toward my—

Bzzzzzzzzzz!

The lipstick-shaped device buzzes to life in my lap, apparently triggered by the impact. Except no lipstick I've ever owned has come with multiple speed settings.

"What in the world is that!?" I yelp.

"Oh, that old thing?" Aunt Deb's strawberry blonde curls bounce as she beams. "She's my real travel companion. TSA barely blinked—I told them it was a facial massager!"

It slips off my lap before I can grab it. *Oh, come on!*

CLINK! It hits the ground and tumbles under the seat in front of us. The buzzing sound grows more intense as it rolls to the next row of seats, like it's actively trying to create the most mortifying situation possible.

I glance around. Maybe if I'm subtle about this...

Nope. The elderly couple is watching with horrified fascination as I slowly lower myself to my hands and knees. The airplane carpet is rough against my palms as I peer under the seats, looking for a flash of metallic pink among the forest of feet and carry-ons.

A small hand reaches out from two rows ahead, inches from the still-buzzing device. "Mom, look! A toy!"

"No!" I lunge forward, grabbing the lipstick-shaped vibrator. Holy crap, this thing is buzzing like a swarm of angry mama bumble bees. "That's... that's not a toy. Well, it is, but... it's that nice lady's toy." I gesture vaguely toward Aunt Deb.

The child—who can't be more than five—wrinkles his nose. "Old people still play with toys?"

"Kid, you don't wanna know," I mutter.

I make my way back to my seat and give Aunt Deb her overactive "travel companion." I think my hand might be permanently numb.

"You travel with a vibrator in your purse?"

Why am I asking? This is the same woman who once led a conga line through her retirement community, wearing nothing but a feather boa and a smile. The same free spirit who got banned from bingo for suggesting strip rules. She's my mother's polar opposite in every way. While Mom was playing it safe in suburbia, Aunt Deb was backpacking through Nepal with a guru named Moonbeam and learning rebirthing breathwork.

"You can borrow that if you want, Katie-darling." Aunt Deb winks, her bold blue eyeshadow somehow making her look both elegant and scandalous. "That's my backup in-flight entertainment, and it appears I won't be needing it tonight."

"We're on an airplane!"

"Exactly!" Aunt Deb's eyes light up like someone just handed her a shirtless fireman and a cheesecake. "You're free as a bird, baby girl. Time to spread those wings and maybe spread some other things too—know what I mean?"

She rummages more in her Mary Poppins naughty bag and pulls out a small flask masquerading as a water bottle, followed by what appears to be a Ziploc stuffed with suspicious herbs. Oh Lord, please don't let those be actual narcotics.

"Listen here, Katie-kins," she says, wagging her manicured finger. "Time for some ground rules for our trip. Rule numero uno: don't cramp my style! I'm here for the three F's: food, fun, and..." She glances at the scandalized couple across the aisle. "...becoming friendly with the locals. Not necessarily in that order."

I watch in horror as she pulls out an entire strip of condoms. "Oh my God!"

"Honey, at my age, you've got to be prepared for anything. These hips might be vintage, but they've still got some miles left on them! Just ask that charming Argentinian tango instructor from last month's cruise."

The elderly woman one row over clutches her pearls so hard she's about to have a bead-related safety incident.

"Now," Aunt Deb continues, completely oblivious to our growing audience, "if I want to stay out late or invite a Casanova in—and I do mean in—I'll need the room. *Comprende?*"

I'm reminded that this woman got escorted out of the Vatican for skinny-dipping in Saint Peter's fountain with her tour guide. Mom still hasn't recovered from that particular sisterly scandal—probably why she opted for babysitting duty.

"But other than that, this is our trip, darling!" She leans in close, and I smell her signature Chanel No. 5. "This is your sexual awakening! You need to go find the first Italian man who makes your lady parts tingle and let him rock your world."

"Aunt Deb!" I sputter, my face burning. "I'm here to win Jared back, not jump into bed with a stranger!"

"Oh Katie," she sighs. "Marriage is a prison of boredom and routines. You've been set free, yet you're trying to put the shackles back on like they're Cartier Love bracelets."

I'm about to explain that my idea of wild abandon is ordering dessert before dinner, when Aunt Deb spots something over my shoulder and practically levitates.

"Well, hello, silver fox," she purrs, adjusting her layers of necklaces. "If you'll excuse me, darling, I've spotted a rather distinguished gentleman in business class who could use some company."

"The seat belt sign is on!" I protest, but she's already sashaying down the aisle like it's a Milan runway. I'm left alone with her scattered belongings and what I'm pretty sure is enough contraband to get us arrested in several countries.

I pull out my binder and flip to my freshly written Win Back Jared plan, wishing I could ignore the fact that my seventy-two-year-old aunt packed more condoms than clothes.

Operation Win Back Jared is simple:
1. Post amazing Italian adventure photos.

2. Show how spontaneous I've become.

3. Make him see I'm the best thing he's ever lost.

4. Wait for the groveling to begin.

My pen hovers over the page as I consider potential photo opportunities. Maybe something with gelato or a shot of me laughing by the Tower of Pisa—

A burst of laughter comes from business class. Aunt Deb has somehow procured a glass of champagne and is now demonstrating her yoga skills in the aisle. *Damn, she's flexible.*

I turn back to my page, trying to focus. Jared's last words echo in my head: *"I can't spend the rest of my life with a person who can never be spontaneous."*

Once again Aunt Deb's laugh pulls my attention. This time she's leading an impromptu salsa class down the walkway, using her scarf as a prop while her aged Adonis pulls her in and dips her.

Surely there's some genetic material that Aunt Deb and I share—some morsel of carefree DNA that should make me effortlessly free-spirited like her. I mean, I'm on this trip without any advance notice, and that's pretty damn spontaneous, right?

I start listing potential Instagram captions: *Embracing the moment!* #whimsical #ItalianAdventures #UnexpectedVacation #Serendipity!

This scheme will work.

Nothing planned here, nope, nothing at all.

***

JET LAG? MORE LIKE travel-assault fatigue. My eyelids feel weighed down by tiny cement blocks, and my brain has turned into risotto. It's early, or late, or both—who the hell knows?

But wait—*Operation Win Back Jared* needs its first Instagram masterpiece. I struggle with my phone, attempting to snap that perfect *just arrived in Italy* glow. There's the selfie I want and the selfie I end up with, which has...

Total mugshot vibes.

My hair is staging a rebellion, and my saggy eye bags are the kind of knockoffs that even Canal Street wouldn't sell.

I stumble off the plane, barely registering the flight attendant's chipper "*Benvenuto* to Italy!" Meanwhile, Aunt Deb dances through the Malpensa airport like she's starring in her own travel show.

"Katie, darling, keep up!" she calls over her shoulder, as I struggle to maneuver both our carry-ons because she "simply must keep her hands free for greeting Italy properly."

This woman has *way* too much energy! It's all I can do to keep my eyes open and my feet moving. The Milan airport is a blur, a hazy mess of people and luggage, and not even a triple shot of Italian espresso can save me now.

The customs line snakes around like a drunk anaconda, but Aunt Deb somehow charms her way to the front. She's chattering away in Italian, but I don't know—every word sounds suspiciously made up. I hold my passport upside down against the plexiglass, my brain too foggy to function.

"*Per quanto tempo si ferma?*" the officer asks.

I stare at him like he's speaking in emoji.

He sighs. "How long you stay?"

"Fourteen days," I mumble. Actually fifteen, but day fifteen starts at four a.m., which is both inhumane and cruel, so I refuse to count it.

I'm overloaded with bags, struggling to keep up. Who knew sleep deprivation felt so much like being drunk?

I blink, and suddenly we're outside. I hear Aunt Deb shouting, *"Per favore, potete chiamarmi un taxi!"*

My eyes feel full of sand. *Just a quick rest,* I think, leaning against my suitcase. *Just five seconds...*

I jolt awake in a real-life game of Mario Kart. Our taxi driver is swerving like a lunatic, as he seems to think "speed limits" are mere suggestions and "lanes" are optional. He's zigzagging through cars, whipping around Vespas, and narrowly dodging floral roadside memorials *(RIP Alberto).*

"...and that's when I realized," Aunt Deb says from the front seat, "you don't need clothes for sunrise meditation! The monks were scandalized, but Kai—the divine Hawaiian Adonis that he is—declared me his muse for his book *The Kama Kai Sutra.*"

Oh God. Oh no. Is that her—

Confirmed: Her hand is definitely creeping up our driver's thigh.

I'm about to close my eyes and pray for death when I witness—

A miracle. Milan is gorgeous!

Wow! Just, wow.

Row after row of rustic buildings the color of sun-toasted bread line the streets, their terracotta roofs marching toward a sky so perfectly blue it looks computer generated. Tiny bridges arch over canals that sparkle like someone dumped a metric ton of glitter into the water.

Quick, get a picture for Jar—

The taxi swerves like we're dodging invisible missiles, then screeches to a halt. My phone goes airborne, performing a graceful triple axel before face-planting onto the floor mat.

"We're here!" Aunt Deb announces, giving our driver's upper thigh area *(okay crotch)* what I hope is a final squeeze.

As we enter the lobby, my jet-lagged brain processes the hotel's over-the-top grandeur. The entryway is what happens when a Renaissance palace hooks up with old money and their love child gets raised by Instagram influencers. Marble floors so polished I can see my disheveled reflection staring back. *Yeesh!* The stunning frescoed ceilings have had centuries of housing rich people's drama beneath them. And those cherubs painted on the walls? They're totally judging my appearance, but all I can think is *bedbedbedbedbed.*

We open the door to our room, and two queen-sized pieces of heaven appear. My body, mind, and soul gravitate toward the crisp tucked corners and drool-free pillows.

"Don't even think about it, missy. You're not giving in to jet lag. We power through!"

"We have six whole hours until the welcome mixer," I whine.

"Exactly!" She upends her suitcase into a clothing bomb on both beds. "Getting this level of pizazzzery takes time, preparation, and at least three different kinds of body shimmer."

Pieces of clothing fly through the air with impressive velocity. A sequined something catches the light, temporarily blinding me.

"Options!" she announces, holding up three dresses. "This black number screams 'seductress on the prowl,' the red suggests 'peel me off later,' and this leopard print..." she wiggles her eyebrows suggestively, "is a warning label that reads 'good decisions not included.'"

She zeros in on my suitcase full of snugly packed pastels like a heat-seeking missile. "Oh Katherine." She tuts, diving in and destroying hours of careful folding. "Are you interviewing to be a librarian? Is this a cardigan convention? Where's the sex appeal?"

"Jared likes the way I dress."

"Honey, Jared needs a fashion intervention."

"I'm not here to impress anyone," I repeat for the billionth time.

"Clearly." She holds up my modest one-piece swimsuit like it's radioactive. "Was this suit personally designed by the Amish?"

"It's practical!"

"So is a chastity belt, but that doesn't mean you wear one to an Italian beach."

She tosses the bathing suit aside with a dramatic shudder.

"I need a bath. Gotta get squeaky clean everywhere. These distinguished Italian gents aren't gonna seduce themselves."

I reach my hand into the pile and hold up a floral dress with a matching cardigan. "This is what I'm wearing tonight."

"Then don't stand next to me. I don't want people thinking I'm here with someone's grandmother," she says as she saunters to the bathroom.

Screw the jet lag advice. This bed's beckoning me like a lover's whisper. I don't care how I look for the stupid welcome mixer. To hell with everything except these heavenly sheets and—

"Don't you dare fall asleep!" Aunt Deb calls from the bathroom. "We haven't even started your underwear intervention!"

I faceplant into the pillow with a groan. Maybe if I play dead, she'll leave me alone.

A thong hits the back of my head.

Maybe not.

CHAPTER THREE

MATTEO

CAZZO. IT'S ALMOST NOON.

My phone vibrates relentlessly from my nightstand. Blazing sunlight assaults my face like judgment from above, my head throbbing in rhythm with my racing pulse. The weight of a warm, feminine body shifts against my side, and memories from last night flood back with crystal clarity.

My phone vibrates again—probably the twentieth time—and I know without looking it's Lorenzo ready to castrate me for being late to the repair shop. But *Cristo, what man could resist yesterday's midnight temptation?* This American redhead at Bar Basso kept eye-fucking me across the room while talking about her Italian romance bucket list. Who was I to deny—Rose? Roxanne?—the full experience?

Rolling my head to the side, I drink in the view. Sunlight paints her bare shoulder in warm hues, glowing softly against the white sheets. The kind of shot that gets my photographer's fingers itching. But cameras mean evidence, and evidence means memories.

I'm in the business of creating fantasies, not preserving them.

What was her name? Rebecca? Riley? My cock has developed a sixth sense for finding the perfect tourist—a woman looking for a story to tell back home, without a ring on her finger. A woman who understands that *amore* sounds better when it's just pillow talk.

I slide from the mattress with the stealth of a man who's mastered the morning-after retreat. Damn, our clothes look like we were ambushed by horny teenagers on spring break. One of my shoes is under the bed, the other—how the fuck did it get on top of the TV? My pants are tangled with her party dress by the minibar, evidence of how quickly things escalated after she purred "Come back to my room" in the worst Italian I've ever heard.

Stubbing my toe on her designer suitcase, I swallow a curse. *Amateur move, Monti. Get your shit together.*

This is exactly how I prefer it—quick, hot, uncomplicated. Let other guys chase the fantasy of forever. At a young age, I learned that love is like a grenade: the longer you hold on, the more damage it does when it detonates.

Her hotel room tells the same story I've seen a hundred times—Gucci shopping bags, an Italian traveler's handbook that's more Instagram prop than actual guide, and a cheesy souvenir statue of the Leaning Tower of Pisa.

Her phone lights up: "OMG did you really bang that sexy Italian tour guide??!"

My lips curl. Another satisfied customer for the Matteo Monti experience.

Where is my jacket?

"Mmm... Matteo?" Her sleep-rough voice hits me low in the gut, and my treacherous cock twitches with interest. For a split second, I consider crawling back into that bed, showing her exactly why

Italian men have such a reputation. But no. Lorenzo will actually murder me if I don't get to the garage soon.

"Last night was—" she starts.

"*Perfetto,*" I cut in smoothly, already backing toward the door. *Ramona? Ruby?* Better play it safe. "Like something from a movie, *cara mia.*"

Because that's all this was—a flawless, fleeting moment, not a real connection. I never get too close.

I grab my jacket from the back of the chair and bolt before she can suggest a sequel. It's a well-practiced exit, delivered with just enough warmth to prevent tears but not enough to encourage dreams. Tourists are perfect for my purposes—here today, gone tomorrow. No messy feelings, no complicated explanations, no awkward run-ins at my favorite café.

I have exactly one rule in this game: never sleep with women in my tour groups.

Milan slaps me awake as I step out into the bustling street, the sun annoyingly bright for my hungover eyes. My head is pounding like a techno beat, my mouth tastes like I've been French kissing an ashtray, and I've got... *how many hours?* I check my phone—shit, five hours until the welcome meeting.

Just another day in the life of Italy's least responsible tour guide.

You'd think after twelve years of leading tours, I'd have my shit together. Hell, I've owned Monti Tours for five of them. But no. Here I am, thirty-two years old, doing my usual walk of shame, trying to remember where I can score some last-minute welcome gifts.

A cherry-red Vespa nearly clips me as I dash across Via Dante. "*Occhio!*" she yells, her hand lifting to flip me off until... she gets a good look at me, and that hand morphs into a blown kiss. I wink back, the exchange leaving a spring in my step.

"Ciao, Matteo, you charming scoundrel!"

Carlo's voice crashes over me like a church bell. He's standing in his bakery doorway, arms crossed, wearing that who'd-you-sleep-with-last-night grin.

"Don't start." I scrub a hand over my face. "Just tell me you've got those little lemon cookies left. The ones that make American women write five-star reviews."

"Forgot the welcome bags again?"

"It's called winging it."

"It's called being a fuckup. One day all this 'playing it by ear' is going to bite you in the *culo*."

Carlo should know. Once upon a time, he was my wingman, until stunning Federica, with her sweet treats, stole his heart.

The smell of fresh cornetti hits me like foreplay. "That's what makes life interesting." I snag the paper bag he holds out, inhaling butter and sugar. "Those corporate tours? They're all printed itineraries and plastic souvenirs. My people get the real Italy."

"Is that what you're calling it now?" He smirks.

My phone jolts me with a buzz. Lorenzo. Probably wondering why his boss isn't at the garage yet, dealing with our dying bus. The AC's been making sounds like a cat in heat, and the transmission... best not to think about it.

"Take these." Carlo shoves another bag at me. "Extra cookies. For when that charm finally runs out."

I flip him off but drop extra euros on the counter. "Not possible. *Grazie, amico.*"

Next stop: Teresa's flower stand. While the big tour companies hand out cheap, mass-produced junk, I offer my guests something special—real Italian magic. Fresh flowers, warm cookies, and personal attention. That's how Monti Tours gets such killer reviews.

Well, except for that one woman from Ohio. But she was just pissed I wouldn't fuck her.

"Late again, *tesoro?*" Teresa calls out, already shaking her head as I walk up.

"You know you love me."

"I know one of these days your luck will run out." But her hands are already gathering blooms like she's conducting a flower symphony.

"Life's too damn short to be tied down by schedules and what-ifs. My parents taught me that much..."

Fuck. Even after twenty years, that wound's still raw.

Teresa's face does that thing, that soft, maternal look that makes my chest tight. She adds extra flowers without a word.

My phone erupts in another buzz. *Merda!* I still need water bottles and probably an actual miracle from the Vatican to fix my bus.

Running my own tour company means my reputation is everything. This is why I don't hook up with my own tourists. One pissed-off woman leaving reviews about the guide who screwed and screwed her over could tank my entire business. Plus three weeks is a long fucking time to avoid morning-after awkwardness when you're trapped on the same bus.

Thank fuck this is one of my seniors-only tours. Two weeks of blue-haired ladies pinching my ass and asking if I'm single. I'll take it. They're usually tucked in bed by nine, which leaves plenty of time for Matteo's After-Dark Tour—finding eager Americans who want their own Italian Stallion experience. And believe me, there's never a shortage of those.

I dodge a pack of Segways only to slam straight into a wall of red shirts and sensible shoes. A tour group—at least forty deep—shuffles past like a herd being led to slaughter, each one sporting headphones that make them look more ready for takeoff than a casual Milan morning walking tour.

At the front, some stiff in pressed khakis and red polo waves a flag bearing the Italy Express logo. His voice crackles through their headsets with all the warmth of a prerecorded message: "Ladies and gentlemen, you will have exactly fifteen minutes to view Leonardo Da Vinci's masterpiece, *The Last Supper*. Following that, we proceed to the gift shop for a mandatory two-hour shopping experience."

Cazzo. Two hours? That's not a tour stop, it's retail imprisonment. There's literally nothing to do but shop: fridge magnets of Milan, Italian flag key chains, plastic gondolas, and other crap made in China.

Italy Express—the complete opposite of Monti Tours. They're the Goliath to my David *(minus the impressive package)*, cranking out tours like factory-made pasta.

I should know. I used to work for them.

Same stops, same scripts, same soulless "fun facts" delivered with the passion of a dead fish. Their idea of experiencing Italy is checking boxes between bathroom breaks.

I watch the group shuffle past, bobbing along like pigeons chasing breadcrumbs. Not one of them even looks up at the actual city around them—they're too busy adjusting their headphones and checking their watches.

These corporate tours? They're Italy through a window—sanitized, scheduled, safe. My tours? We're Italy face-first in the pasta sauce. Every day is different. Every group brings new stories, new adventures.

I catch Corporate Ken's eye as I pass, flashing him my best I-actually-enjoy-my-job smile. He doesn't react—he can't. Not enough time in the schedule. He can keep his shiny red flag and predictable destinations. Because my people leave Italy with more than souvenirs. They'll bring home memories worth savoring.

I finally arrive at the garage. Lorenzo's hunched over the engine, newsboy cap askew, wispy white comb-over fighting a losing battle. His shirt's a canvas of coffee, crumbs, and oil stains, with his finger shoved up his nose like a five-year-old on a playground, and yep—plumber's crack on full display.

He hikes up his pants, turns, and gives me a stern look, his weathered face spelling out just how fucked the air-conditioning situation is.

In five years, I've seen the man smile exactly twice. He prefers communicating in grunts and shrugs. But he's the best driver in the business, and his ability to go entire days saying nothing but *sì* and *no* is worth more than any other chatty driver I've worked with.

I set my collection of supplies on a greasy workbench. "Give it to me straight."

Lorenzo holds up three fingers.

"Hundred?" I ask hopefully.

He shakes his head no.

"Thousand?"

A single nod yes.

My stomach drops faster than the time I tried to make my own limoncello.

"To fix the AC?"

Another nod.

"Can we—"

He gives a noncommittal shrug.

I've learned to fill in Lorenzo's verbal blanks. It's like playing the world's most expensive game of charades. "Okay, so a temporary fix?"

Nod.

"How long will it—"

He shrugs one shoulder. In Lorenzo-speak, that means "don't push your luck."

I peer into the bus's guts, as if I'll suddenly develop mechanical expertise and spot a miracle solution. Instead, I'm hit with a cacophony of metallic clanging and desperate sputters, as if a junkyard orchestra is warming up. "She's getting worse, huh?"

"Sì."

"What about the inside of the bus? Does it still smell?"

"Sì."

"So did something really die in there?"

He holds up three fingers again.

"Three... possibilities of what died?"

He rolls his head in frustration. "*Pulizie*."

"Three professional cleanings and the interior still smells?"

A single, solemn nod.

I climb aboard, flowers and cookies in hand, doing my best to breathe through my mouth. The interior of my beloved bus tells the tales of a thousand adventures—the floor scuffed by hundreds of shoes, the worn seats a result of countless dreamers rushing to see the next marvel of Italy. Sure, she's not the sleek, air-conditioned luxury liner the major players use, but she's got character.

And maybe mold... probably.

I make my way to the back, to my secret compartment where I keep the only things that really matter. My fingers find my mother's old Nikon digital camera, reliable as ever and effortlessly elegant—the last thing she ever gave me, before... well, before.

I flip through the photos from my previous tour group. There's that happy family at my best friend Enrico's vineyard, the kids purple-mouthed from stealing grapes when they thought no one was looking. Then there were the Sullivan teens, learning bocce from locals in that hidden piazza—they'd even kicked their ass by the end of the afternoon. That sweet couple from Maine sharing their porchetta with the fishermen in Puglia, not a word of Italian between them but somehow speaking the same language of food and laughter.

This. This right fucking here. This is what it's all about.

Too bad the bank doesn't accept "magical moments" as currency.

The repair costs are piling up faster than a Roman traffic jam, but looking at these shots—the pure joy on their faces, the way Italy transforms them—I can't give this up. The big-name operators might have their fancy buses and laminated itineraries, but they don't capture moments like these. They don't take tourists to the real Italy, the places off the beaten path. They don't make magic.

"Lorenzo?" I call, arranging the flowers in a vase I may or may not have stolen from a café in Turin. "Scale of one to ten. How fucked are we?"

"Otto."

"Eight? Come on, she's not that—" The motion sensor air freshener puffs out a cloud of Ocean Mist but smells more like Public Restroom Surprise. I choke back a gag. "Okay, maybe eight."

I hear a grunt from below that sounds suspiciously like "told you" in Italian.

"But she'll run?" I ask, straightening seats with practiced efficiency.

"Sì."

"Safely?"

A longer pause than I'd like. Then: "Sì."

"You're not making me feel better."

He peers up through the doorway, holds up five fingers, then points to the engine.

"We have five?" I wave my hand, encouraging more words. "Days?"

He makes a so-so gesture.

"Five days until what? Total breakdown? Explosion? The smell becomes sentient and takes over Italy?"

He almost smiles. "Sì."

"To which part?"

He shrugs and disappears back under the hood.

The thing is, I can handle a bus held together by dreams and duct tape. I can deal with mysterious smells and temperamental air fresheners. But what I can't handle? What keeps me up at night?

The thought of letting these people down. Of not giving them the Italy they've dreamed about.

Because that's the real magic of this job—not just showing them Italy but helping them fall in love with her. The way I do, every single day.

Even if she sometimes smells like feet.

I pull out my phone to check the time. *Shit.* I still need to shower, change, and become the charming tour guide version of myself that doesn't smell like bus mysteries and last night's bad decisions.

"Just... do what you can?" I pat the bus's side like an old horse. "She needs to hold together for two more weeks. Then I'll have the money to get her fixed up."

"Preghiamo." Lorenzo mutters it under his breath, but I catch it. We pray.

Coming from him, that's practically a speech. And not exactly reassuring.

"Any other problems I should know about?"

He raises a single finger.

"Just one? That's not so—"

Then another. And another. He keeps going until both hands are up, all ten fingers spread wide.

"You know," I sigh, gathering the rest of my supplies, "sometimes your silence is more comforting than your honesty."

That earns me an actual snort—the Lorenzo equivalent of belly laughter.

"Ciao, Lorenzo." I head for the door, already planning how many cookies each tourist should get to make up for the inevitable AC complaints. Maybe if I get them drunk enough on cheap wine—

"Matteo."

I turn back, surprised by the rare use of my name.

He points to my back pocket where a piece of lace is peeking out *(R-something's insurance policy for a second night).* It's a move I've seen so many times it should be featured in tourist guidebooks. They can list "Leave underwear in hot Italian's pocket" right after "Visit Juliet's Balcony in Verona."

I pull out the black lace and toss it to Lorenzo. "Souvenir?"

Without missing a beat, he wipes his greasy hands on the delicate fabric, probably ruining what was at least a hundred euros worth of La Perla. Then he tosses it aside like yesterday's trash and gets back to work, though I catch a flash of a grin.

Next up: meeting my new group. It's time to show them my Italy in all its imperfect glory.

***

THE WELCOME NIGHT CROWD starts filtering in—my new batch of senior tourists ready for their Italian adventure. The hotel bar fills with excited chatter as they find their name tags and cluster in groups, dressed like they're having dinner with the Pope himself.

Usually I'm excited about introducing myself to everyone. But tonight? Tonight I'm sitting at the bar, brooding into my third grappa and doing the math on a repair bill that's making my balls shrivel.

Three thousand euros. Might as well be everything I own.

"Would you look at this smorgasbord of man meat?"

Mother of God. That lady's voice has a spotlight and a mic. I follow the boisterous voice and see what appears to be a walking rainbow on two legs. But it's the woman trailing behind her that makes me forget all about my financial crisis.

Cristo, who ordered the angel?

Her golden hair catches the light like a halo, eyes green as emeralds and sharp enough to cut through bullshit at fifty paces, and a body that makes my mouth go dry. Her floral dress and prim cardigan scream, "I've never been late to anything," but there's something about the way she holds herself—back straight, chin lifted, and captivating curves barely restrained. It compels me to take a closer look at whatever she's hiding beneath that polished facade.

Everything about her is a contradiction—delicate features with a don't-fuck-with-me expression, sensible shoes on legs that are pure temptation, and minimal makeup with piercing eyes sharp enough to freeze hell over. I sense she's the kind of girl who could destroy a man—and who probably carries a playbook on how to do it.

"Aunt Deb!" Cardigan girl hisses at Rainbow Woman. "Could you be any louder?"

"Darling, inside voices are for people who haven't lived through disco." The aunt's attention locks onto me like a cat hearing a can opener. "Bingo! Three o'clock, by the bar. Tall, brooding, and yours-for-the-screwing."

I look around just to make sure she's talking about me. She is.

"Now that's an Italian Stallion." The older woman lets out a hungry sigh. "He's packing a zucchini that'll have you seeing stars and teach you things about your body you haven't discovered yet. You can thank me later."

I hide my smirk in my drink. Can't fault the lady's good taste.

The niece's cheeks flame red as her aunt slaps a name tag on her chest and pushes her toward the bar. "Fetch me a martini, sweetie. Extra dirty." A theatrical wink. "Like my intentions."

I turn back to my grappa, watching the blonde beauty approach in the mirror behind the bottles. Each step is precise, measured, like she's got a ruler hidden somewhere in that outfit. When she gets closer, her scent hits me and—merda. Sweet strawberries. My cock twitches—I've got a thing for strawberries.

The bartender is too busy watching the game on his phone to notice her increasingly aggressive attempts to grab his attention.

"Ciao, bella. Can I buy you a drink?"

She doesn't even glance at me. "I'm fine, thank you," she says with a voice so sharp it could slice prosciutto.

"Ah, American!" My smile deepens. "Welcome to my beautiful country. Perhaps I could give you a... private tour?"

She turns those green eyes on me full force and—fuck me—I wasn't prepared. That glare—it's like being stabbed by two smoldering emeralds.

"Let me stop you right there." Her voice could frost champagne. "Whatever line you're about to use? Save it for someone dumb enough to fall for the whole 'charming Italian' routine."

"But I had such a good one about my rock-solid Tower of Pisa."

"Gross." But her lips twitch. "Does that actually work? Do women just drop their panties because you have an accent and zero shame?"

"Usually, yeah. They do."

Which is exactly why this resistance is so fucking intriguing.

"Well, it's not going to work on me. I'm engaged," she snaps, shoving a very naked ring finger in my face.

"Looks like your fiancé really broke the bank on that invisible ring."

For a moment, real pain flickers in her emerald eyes. Then... gone, replaced by steel.

"I left my ring at home. Wouldn't want it stolen by some smooth-talking Italian con artist."

"The only thing I'm interested in stealing," I purr, sliding so close I feel the heat radiating off her body, "is a kiss from those beautiful lips."

Her laugh hits me like a kick to the balls. "Oh wow. That's... that's really bad. Like, monumentally cheesy. Do you practice these lines in the mirror? Or maybe you only recently learned English?"

Merda. My game is seriously off.

"Usually I save my best material for the second drink." I lean against the bar, trying to regain control. "But your eyes—they remind me of the mysterious depths of Venice's canals."

She presses a hand to her chest, mock swooning. "Did you just compare my eyes to water where tourists pee? That's so romantic. I'm dying. Really. Quick, call an ambulance."

"No, I meant they're green, like the algae—" *Cristo, what the fuck am I saying?*

"So now I'm canal scum?" Her eyes spark with amusement. "What's next? Going to say my hair looks like overcooked pasta? My skin reminds you of day-old mozzarella?"

My cock has no business getting this hard watching her demolish every move in my playbook. Women usually melt by this point, and God help me, I've never seen a tourist look so happy while gutting me with her words.

Enough of this amateur hour.

"Actually, bella..." I let my gaze drift down her body like a physical caress, lingering on the way her cardigan strains against her curves. A flush crawls up her neck like a sunburn. *Not so immune after all, are we?*

Her breath hitches when I step closer. All those cardigan buttons suddenly have my fingers itching to discover what's underneath. Is she wearing something practical? Or is there lace hiding beneath all that propriety?

Our eyes lock and the air between us thickens like honey. Her gaze drops to my mouth for a fraction of a second.

I lean in close, voice dropping low. "I was thinking more about how that dress makes me want to—"

"I dare you to finish that sentence."

She spins back to the bar, but a blush is spreading like wildfire across her cheeks. Her hands shake as she waves that credit card once again.

"Try your routine on someone else, Romeo. I've seen this Netflix movie. Hot Italian guy, American girl who lets her guard down... it ends with awkward texts that never get answered."

"You think I'm hot?"

"I think you're trouble."

"The hot kind of trouble?"

"The kind that should come with a warning label."

"Yet you're still standing here, tempting fate."

She's fighting a grin now, and I'm not even trying to hide mine. Cristo. I haven't had this much fun verbally sparring with a woman since... maybe ever.

And, damn. She's even more gorgeous when she smiles.

Then my eyes catch her name tag and... checkmate. *Fuck.* She's with my tour group. The one where I have a strict no-sleeping-with-tourists policy because the worst possible thing for my struggling company is that kind of complication.

Although why someone who barely looks old enough to rent a car is on a senior citizens' tour is a mystery that I'm suddenly desperate to solve.

"I'll get his attention. *Scusi!*" I reach past her to flag down the bartender just as she turns, and—shit—my open palm brushes across her breasts, sending her name tag fluttering to the bar top.

"What the hell!" She recoils, arms crossing over her chest as if it's armor. "Did you seriously try to cop a feel?"

"No! I was just—the barman—didn't mean to—"

Shit. I'm stammering like a virgin in a strip club.

"Use my boobs as target practice?"

"I would never—" I rake a hand through my hair, desperately trying to recover some dignity. "Katie, you're going to laugh when I explain this."

Her eyes narrow to dangerous slits. "How do you know my name?"

"It's on the name tag." I hold up the sticky label—my peace offering.

She keeps those arms locked across her chest, glaring at me like I might make another attempt. Which, fair enough. But also? I'm not usually this fucking clumsy. Something about this woman has my game completely sideways.

"Let me make it up to you with dinner?" The words come out smoother than I feel, which is a fucking miracle considering my brain's still short-circuiting from that accidental handful.

"If you're that desperate to get laid, the gorgeous strawberry blonde over there currently holding court with half the men in Milan is single and very ready to mingle." She jerks her chin toward the crowd. "Fair warning though—she's got some wild theories about cosmic orgasms and sacred body exploration."

My smirk slides back into place. "Maybe I prefer my women with a little more... challenge."

"Goodbye... whatever your name is."

"Matteo," I supply, thoroughly amused by her righteous indignation.

"Goodbye, Matteo. It was *not* nice meeting you. Don't worry, I'll forget you existed by breakfast tomorrow."

She spins away, all offended dignity and swaying hips that are doing absolutely nothing to help the situation in my pants.

I signal the bartender for another drink. Miss Uptight doesn't know it yet, but she's going to be seeing a lot more of me over the next two weeks. *Should I warn her?*

Nah. Where's the fun in that?

CHAPTER FOUR

KATIE

Mom: *What about sending Jared a quick text? Something casual like, "Hi, hope you're doing well!"*
Me: *Mom, no.*
Mom: *Or, "Hey, saw this and it reminded me of you." Maybe a pasta dish? Men love food.*
Me: *I'm not using pasta as an icebreaker.*
Mom: *Okay, just trying to help. Team Jared 4ever!*
Me: *Did you seriously write "4ever"?*
Mom: *The grandkids say it's cool.*

"SIX MINUTES LATE!" I squint against the harsh Italian sunlight, scanning the bustling street for a sign—any sign—of our tour bus. Seven minutes... Seven and a half... *Ugh!*

Yeah, they're late, and yeah, I'm annoyed. But the real problem is last night's bar encounter—living rent-free in my head all morning.

And by "problem," I mean that walking snack of a man.

My body thrums like a low note struck on an unfamiliar instrument. Good Lord, that Matteo guy was unfairly gorgeous, lounging against that bar counter like he was doing everyone a favor by existing. His dark brown eyes were undressing me, taking in every inappropriate thought *(I swore I wasn't having)*. And that mouth—full and sexy—curved into a smirk that hinted at all kinds of dirty promises.

His coffee-colored hair was a tousled masterpiece—total sexy bedhead—like he rolled around in some high-thread count sheets all night. And my God, that accent—a warm, gooey chocolate lava cake melting in your ears, turning whatever he said into pure panty-dropping poetry.

Not to mention his rugged, capable hands that look like they know their way around a lady's body. Hands connected to powerful biceps and commanding shoulders. That man could easily hoist me up, wrap me around him, and send our hips crashing into each— Oh geez. *STOP thinking about his hips.*

The nerve of him. Is this how Italian men are? Charming their way into women's panties between espressos.

I snap open my binder, fanning myself frantically. I'm here for Jared. Sweet, agreeable Jared who'd never compare my eyes to murky canal slime. I glance down at my outfit of the day—a pastel blue floral top that always made Jared smile, paired with my most flattering jeans and sensible ballet flats. The ensemble screams, "naturally beautiful without trying too hard."

Focus, Katie. I'm here with a plan—a very specific plan to win back my fiancé. Not to daydream about some insufferably handsome Italian man who throws ridiculous pickup lines at every tourist he meets.

I scan our group of travel companions huddled outside the hotel entrance, and it's like someone raided all the retirement communities in America—a literal sea of grandparents. The elderly couples are so adorable it makes my heart squeeze—weathered fingers clasped together and matching walking shoes. But the senior singles? *Not so much!* They're living their best golden-years-gone-wild lives, flirting with a shameless enthusiasm that says, "Screw the 401(k), I'm gonna live it up!"

And then there's Aunt Deb, a dazzling peacock amid the flock of pigeons, draping herself around some dapper man who could pass for George Clooney's older brother. Her hands are wandering places I really, really don't want to think about this early in the morning.

I refocus, finding myself suddenly giddy about the upcoming two weeks. A grand adventure across Italy, hopping from one city to the next—riding in the lap of luxury on a tour bus with windows so big they might as well be picture frames. This is why I'm here.

Like any respectable event planner, I've come fully prepared for the day ahead.

Laminated itinerary is tucked neatly into my binder. Check.

Phone at the ready to capture perfect photo ops. Check.

Trusty water bottle. Check.

Combine those with an oversized tote of essentials and a makeup bag, and I'm ready to battle any and all chaos the Italian sun decides to unleash.

Different country, same organized Katie!

Today I have a clear objective: Shadow Aunt Deb and study her every move. I'll wait for those perfect, "spontaneous" moments that'll make for killer pictures and pounce. After a quick snap, I'll post them with adorably teasing captions, and watch as Jared takes the bait.

We're visiting the Leaning Tower of Pisa before noon, so I've got my sexy pose already figured out. However, for the rest of the time, I'm counting on Aunt Deb to inspire whatever whimsical posts will keep my feed fresh.

Twelve minutes late. Where's the stupid bus!

"Gather round, my lovelies!" Aunt Deb's powerful voice rings out over the murmurs of the crowd. "While we're here, let's awaken our inner zen with a morning yoga flow!"

She waves me over, undeterred. "C'mon, Katie-kins! Join your favorite auntie for some rejuvenating stretches."

Aunt Deb leads her silver-haired disciples in a basic tree pose. Holy downward-facing disaster! The mortifying scene looks like a herd of overly enthusiastic, hopelessly uncoordinated flamingos playing Twister. It's equal parts *hard to watch* as it is *can't look away*.

But then— Oh. *Oh!* This is exactly the kind of "candid" shot my Instagram feed needs.

I whip out my phone faster than you can say "namaste," searching for the perfect angle that screams "unplanned tranquility." I push my inflexible self to bend and arch, lifting my leg in some mystical blend of sexy and spiritual. The cobblestones dig into my sensible shoes as I hold the pose, my breath catching, my heart hoping...

Three...two...one...

CLICK!

Yikes. The photo makes me want to die a thousand tiny deaths. *Is that a triple chin?* Plus I look like I'm doing the potty dance in the middle of Milan. It's less *Eat Pray Love* and more Eat Pray, Oh-God-I-Need-to-Pee.

"Katherine Blair Crawford, put that contraption away!"

My spine stiffens at the use of my full name.

"Is your entire generation incapable of experiencing life without filming it?" She untangles herself with the grace of someone who definitely wasn't doing tequila shots at breakfast. *(She was. I saw her)*. "Life's not about snapping photos, darling. You gotta dive headfirst and live in the moment."

The seniors' enthusiastic cheers save me from her next round of wildly inappropriate advice. Our "bus" has arrived, and it's pretty underwhelming. Calling it a bus is a bit of a stretch. I'd say more *wheezing relic* with its duct-taped mirrors, a muffler that coughs like a chain-smoker, and tires so bald they're shiny.

The ancient driver opens the door and nods to our group. I contemplate whether walking across Italy might be the better alternative. Because this is *not* the luxury coach I saw online. This thing is old, dingy, and the windows are so smudged I can barely see into the bus. The elderly passengers slowly board, and I join them, accepting my fate. One step inside and— Dear God, what is that smell? It's like something crawled in here to die but instead decided to throw a fart party with its dumpster-diving pals.

I snag a seat near the front, praying that the source of the stench is somewhere in the back. No such luck. *Is it worse up here?*

"*Buongiorno*, my lovely tourists!"

No. Sweet baby caprese salad, *NO!*

My body recognizes that voice before my brain does, and every inch of my skin tingles with awareness.

"For you, *signora.*" He presents a flower to Mrs. Thomas. The seniors swoon like he's just invented sliced bread and social security on the same day.

I'm about to make a beeline for the back of the bus when Aunt Deb shouts, "Oh, Matteo! I must introduce you to my delightful niece, Katie. She may not be a senior in age, but trust me, she's a senior in spirit."

Matteo's eyes meet mine, and a smirk crosses his lips. "We actually met last night. And you're right. She has all the charm of an irritable, crotchety schoolmarm."

My jaw drops as Aunt Deb cackles uncontrollably. "Oh, you've got her pegged! Our Katie does take herself rather seriously."

I stand there, fists clenched, as they bond over their shared amusement at my expense.

"Don't you worry, dear Deborah," Matteo coos into a microphone. "I'll make sure your delightfully uptight niece doesn't put a damper on our fun. Now, who's ready to kick things off?"

The seniors cheer like they've just been offered an early-bird special at half price.

"Katie?" He holds the mic up to my face, eyes dancing with challenge. "I can't hear you."

"Woo," I deadpan.

"We'll work on your enthusiasm, *principessa.*"

I hate him so much.

His overconfident swagger, those cheesy flirtations, and that cocky attitude—it's like nails on a chalkboard to my organized soul. Worst of all, I hate how my body remembers exactly how close he stood last night and how his cologne, warm with hints of leather and vanilla, lingered in the air.

Two weeks. I'm stuck with this jackass for two goddamn weeks?

"Your Wish Cards, per favore!"

Matteo makes his way down the aisle, gathering the papers with a theatrical flair. He puts on a big show of reading them. "Oh, this one is absolutely brilliant—and—we're gonna have a blast making this happen." When he gets to Aunt Deb's card, he gives her a wink. "You sneaky vixen. I'm not sure the Vatican would approve."

My aunt purrs. "That's what makes it fun, darling."

What the hell are Wish Cards? Did I miss some kind of senior citizen memo?

"And for today's wish..." Matteo waves a single card in the air. His biceps flex with the movement. "Should I tell you now or keep it a surprise?"

The seniors scream "Surprise!" so loud I think I lost hearing in my left ear. But I'm too busy watching Matteo lean over the bus driver, murmuring a phrase in Italian that has no business sounding that good.

It's only words. Regular words. So why does my skin feel too tight?

"Everybody repeat after me—*guida l'autobus*, Lorenzo!"

I press my lips together, arms crossed, while our group massacres the Italian language. Matteo catches my eye, and the challenge in his gaze makes my pulse skip.

"Perfetto!" His praise rolls through the bus, and the seniors glow. "You've just learned to say 'Drive the bus, Lorenzo!' Your first step to becoming Italian!"

The seniors applaud like they've already mastered the language.

"Now, tour tradition time!" He pulls out a camera. "Day one photos! Show me those beautiful smiles. Even you, Miss Grumpy Face."

He winks at me.

I glare.

He grins wider.

Once again, Matteo murmurs something to Lorenzo in Italian, and I'm about to protest when music blasts through the speakers. Not soft, cultural background music. Oh no. This is full-on Italian festival music, the kind that makes nonnas drop their knitting and start dancing in the piazza.

The seniors instantly come alive—clapping, swaying, stomping chaotically. Even Lorenzo bobs his head to the infectious beat.

I've boarded the party bus from hell.

I grab Matteo's arm as he strolls by, then immediately let go like I've been zapped by static electricity. Odd. That zing was probably... bus friction.

"Hold on, hotshot." I channel my best don't-mess-with-me voice. "Where exactly are we going? And what's with the Wish Cards?"

"Ah, bella. If you hadn't been so busy insulting me last night, I could have explained everything."

I hit him with my death glare. "I'm not finding any of this amusing. At all. Zero amusement happening here."

But instead of cowering like any sensible person would, he sits next to me. "You made it very clear last night that fun isn't part of your... vacation itinerary."

I'm ready to deliver a scathing comeback, but he leans in and—my heart starts racing—suddenly I forget how to form words.

"And about that little hand slip?" He gestures toward my chest with zero shame. "Total accident. Though watching you get all fired up, breasts heaving like that... makes me wonder if you're secretly wanting an encore."

He's dead. Right after I stop blushing like a tomato having a hot flash.

Looking extremely pleased with himself, Matteo leans back in his seat with maddeningly casual confidence.

"You did not just go there!" The shriek escapes before I can subdue it.

"Relax, I'm having a little fun. No need to get those sensible cotton panties in a twist."

"Bold of you to assume I'm wearing any."

Wait.

What?

Did I actually just—

His eyebrows shoot up. For one glorious moment, I think I've rendered Mr. Smooth speechless.

Then he laughs.

Not a chuckle. Not a giggle. A full-bodied, rich-as-tiramisu laugh that does things to my insides I refuse to acknowledge.

"There she is. The firecracker hiding behind all those proper buttons."

The way he says *buttons* should not sound that suggestive. Should not make me hyperaware of exactly how many fastenings stand between his gaze and my skin. And his eyes—those stupid, gorgeous, bedroom eyes—rake over me like they're undressing my cardigan one button at a time.

"Oh yes, this tour is going to be *molto interessante*."

I clutch my binder like it's a shield against his Italian charm. No man should be allowed to make basic English words sound like audible foreplay.

"Wish Cards. Explain. Now," I grit out.

Matteo holds up his hands in mock surrender. "All right, all right. On my tours, everyone gets one special wish—something they dream of doing in Italy. And I?" He taps his chest. "I make those dreams come true."

"Wait. *Your* tours? As in, you own this company?"

"Sì, bella." His smirk reaches dangerous levels. "I'm *il capo*. The boss."

"But how do you grant wishes and stick to the scheduled itinerary?"

Matteo shrugs. "The schedule is merely a suggestion."

No fixed itinerary?

No carefully planned timeline?

Just two weeks at the mercy of this man's whimsical Wish Cards?

I'm going to pass out.

"Here." He slides a blank card across the armrest, his fingers brushing mine deliberately. "Show me what desires are buried beneath that... cardigan."

I snatch the card away, but I can still feel the ghost of his touch. "My only desire is for you to follow the schedule."

"So you want things predictable... no surprises. Sorry, that wish is a no-can-do." He leans in, his voice low and seductive. "But if you ever get in the mood for a little trouble, I'm totally game."

With that painfully smug little mic-drop moment, Matteo stands up from his seat, casting one final scorching glance over his shoulder before casually strolling away.

I stuff the ridiculous Wish Card into my binder. I'll be damned if I let this insufferable, chaos-loving man ruin the vacation I've spent hours perfecting.

***

Clunk. Screech. Wheeze.

My hands shoot out to grab the seat in front of me, narrowly avoiding face-planting into the decades-old upholstery. The ancient vehicle shudders to a stop, and I swear I just heard something important fall off. And by *thing* I mean the whole freaking transmission.

Through windows that appear to have been cleaned with a dirty sock soaked in olive oil, I stare at what has to be the most underwhelming building in all of Italy. The brown brick facade could be a prison. Or maybe a DMV?

It's not the Leaning Tower of Pisa that's for damn sure.

My event-planner senses are tingling, and not in a good way.

Ah. Now it all makes sense.

This isn't a wish-granting detour. This is Tourist Trap 101. Any minute now, he'll claim his "dear friend" owns this "authentic" establishment and offer us a "special private tour" for the low, low price of fifty euros each. I've seen more polished acts from magicians at kids' birthday parties.

He better get ready for a scathing review because I'm documenting every single way this con artist is destroying my vacation.

Reasons Matteo Monti Is Definitely a Scammer:

1. Late pickup.

2. Bait-and-switch transportation.

3. Mysterious unscheduled stop.

4. His smile *(too perfect)*.

5. Those forearms *(distractingly suspicious)*.

6. The way his ass looks in those pants that makes my thighs clench (*wait, no. Scratch that one*).

"Signore e signori!" Matteo's honeyed voice fills the bus. "Prepare yourselves for something *magnifico*!"

He dances down the aisle, all calculated charm and well-rehearsed finesse. The seniors are eating it up, but I see through his performance. Every gestured flourish and flawless grin—it's Tourism Theater, and he's going for a Tony.

"Principessa." He appears beside my row, hand extended in an invitation that I have no intention of accepting. "Allow me to escort you to your first Italian adventure."

"I can manage," I inform him coolly. "But thanks for the transparent attempt to separate these nice people from their money."

His eyes darken dangerously. "You think I'm running a scam?"

"If the suspiciously overpriced shoe fits..."

"Such little faith. What must I do to have your trust?"

"Sticking to the schedule would be a start."

"Patience, bella. Good things come to those who—"

"Let me guess. To those who pay inflated prices for 'authentic experiences'?"

An emotion flashes in his eyes—hurt? guilt?—before his mask of charm slides back into place.

"Let's get this surprise over with. I have an important picture to take at the Leaning Tower of Pisa, and I'd like to get there while there's still sunlight."

"Katie, darling!" Aunt Deb clutches my arm, her bangles jangling. "Isn't this absolutely thrilling? The mystery! The romance! The view!" She makes a show of fanning herself while openly ogling Matteo's retreating form.

The seniors spill out of the motorcade, and Matteo motions everyone forward, then claps his hands sharply, demanding the group's attention.

"Please meet the star of today's adventure, Otto Peterson!"

Otto looks like every sweet grandpa in every heartwarming holiday movie ever made. His wire-rimmed glasses sit slightly crooked on his nose, and his silver hair forms this perfect fluffy halo.

"Can you please tell the group about your Wish Card?"

"Been playing violin since I was small," Otto begins. "Back in Idaho, my father and I, we'd play together. Some of my best memories." He adjusts his glasses with trembling fingers. "The Stradivarius violins... they're more than instruments. They're pieces of history. My father dreamed of seeing one. He never got the chance."

"My friend." Matteo places a hand on the older man's back. "This is the Museo del Violino. Today you live that dream for both of you."

The seniors explode into applause while Otto hugs Matteo.

"Didn't that just wrap your heart in the coziest little hug?" Aunt Deb gushes beside me, squeezing my arm as a dreamy sigh escapes her lips.

"I guess?"

"Oh, Katie-darling, that heartwarming moment was poetry in motion! We are living out the grandest of bucket list fantasies on this trip. Let the magic wash over you, my dear!"

This has to be an act. *Has to be.*

Even if Otto's tears are real enough to drown in.

Even if Matteo's joy seems to light him up from within.

We trail through the museum like ducklings following their mother. The air hangs heavy with history and wood polish. Our footsteps echo off marble floors as we trail between glass cases that stretch into forever, each one housing another priceless instrument bathed in amber lighting.

But this boring museum has me thinking about Jared and his fossil lectures—not that he's boring of course, just, like, the fact that it's a museum.

"And here we have a masterpiece by Giuseppe Guarneri," drones our ancient museum guide. "Notice the revolutionary varnishing technique—"

The seniors predictably "ooh" and "aah" on cue while I stifle a yawn. *Violins, check. Now let's go.*

"The way your eyes glaze over really adds to the museum ambiance," Matteo murmurs, suddenly right beside me. His presence startles me, an unexpected pull I can't ignore. "I didn't know anyone could look so desperately unimpressed."

"Oh yes, riveting." I gesture at the display. "I particularly enjoyed the part about"—I squint at the plaque—"spruce versus maple. Life—changing."

"Most engaged women find this romantic." His voice drops lower. "They see the beauty in tradition, the passion in—"

"The brown?"

His laugh rumbles through the space between us, too intimate for strangers. "You work so hard at being cynical."

"Not as hard as you work at being charming."

"Who says I'm working at it?"

"Your whole"—I wave my hand vaguely at his everything—"performance is an act."

He shifts closer. "I find your skepticism oddly attractive."

My mouth goes dry. "Your flirting needs work."

His grin turns wicked, predatory. "Oh, *piccola tigre*, when I'm flirting with you," he says, his low voice setting my ear on fire, "you'll know it."

He walks away before I can respond, leaving me burning and breathless between the displays.

Damn him.

We finally reach the Stradivarius display after what feels like seventeen years of varnish appreciation. Otto snaps pictures next to the display cases. I'm mentally calculating how far behind schedule we are when Matteo steps forward, grinning with seasoned showmanship.

"I could not convince them to let you play a Stradivarius," Matteo says, presenting Otto with a polished violin. "But this beauty is one hundred and fifty years old. Would you honor us with a song?"

I settle in for what is sure to be a creaky, off-key squeaking session. Otto closes his eyes, breathes deeply, and draws the bow across the strings. My jaded expectations... are shattered.

The first note hits me like a physical blow. Rich and deep and devastating. He plays a dramatic concerto, and the rich, resonant notes echo off the walls, saturated with longing and passion. Otto sways, fully consumed in the rhythm, and the music swells. Tears shine on his cheeks. Each note carries weight, carries memories, carries... so much more than just the notes.

Against my will, the power of Otto's performance triggers a wave of emotion. Jared's face flashes through my mind.

Jared. The man who was supposed to be my future, my everything.

I dig my nails into my palms, fighting back the lump forming in my throat.

No. It's going to work out. This is not our farewell tune. Rather, the melody of our bright new future.

I have a plan. I have a schedule. I have a fiancé to win back.

***

"**THAT STUPID LEANING TOWER** of Pisa is ruining my life!" I mutter.

Behind me, that world-famous hunk of slanted marble looms mockingly, as if to say, *Nice try, but even I can tell how painfully unsexy you are.*

Thanks to Matteo and his relaxed sense of time management, I have less than ten minutes of sunlight to capture a thirst trap sultry pose that'll make Jared's jaw drop. I hold out my phone and sum up every ounce of seductive femininity my body can muster.

Butt out.

Head tilted.

Lips pursed.

CLICK!

I compare the photo to the pose I've preselected in my binder. *Grr!* I can't get the right angle. And why does my face give off serious constipated vibes? There's no time to go back and get my selfie stick. *Maybe if I lean the phone against this chunk of rubble on the ground?* I set my timer and hurry into position.

Arch back.

Chest out.

Open mouth.

CLICK!

I cringe at the image. My sultry wish-you-were-here photo has turned into something straight out of a porno. My hands look like I'm molesting the tower while trying to give it a blow job!

"Very seductive, bella," a deep, gravelly voice rumbles in my ear, a rush of warmth sweeping across my neck.

I nearly jump out of my skin as Matteo materializes, his maddening smirk plastered all over that annoyingly handsome face.

"Go away," I snap, angling the phone away from him. "This is not for your pervy eyes. I'm trying to take a picture for my fiancé, Jared."

Matteo grabs my phone and swipes through my pictures. "Your angles are all wrong. You do know I'm a photographer, right? Let me help you."

I snatch back my phone. "I'd rather endure a twelve-hour root canal without novocaine than let you take my photo."

"I think drilling you for twelve hours sounds like an incredible way to spend a day."

Flames dance across my skin. "You're—"

"MATTEO, darling!"

Oh, thank goodness.

Aunt Deb shouts through the crowd like a bedazzled foghorn. "We simply *must* discuss the impressive length and girth of this phallic masterpiece!"

"Duty calls, *bellissima.*"

I watch him saunter away, trying very hard not to notice how well his pants fit *(for purely professional reasons).* I'm documenting suspicious tour guide behavior.

Right. Focus.

I can do this. I am a strong, independent woman who can take one damn sexy photo without help from Mr. Italian Stallion over there.

Channel your inner vixen. Work those angles. Make Jared eat his heart out.

CLICK!

"Nailed it!" The caption is perfect: *Ciao! From Italy!* Simple. Elegant. Not at all desperate.

POST!

My phone explodes:

Petra: *YOU'RE IN ITALY???*

Cam: *Um... surprise vacation?*

Petra: *Have you been kidnapped by the Mafia?*

Cam: *You look gorgeous!*

Petra: *Total smoke show. But who's the clueless senior citizen spelunking in his nose?*

The what now?

I zoom in and—

Oh dear God no. There's Lorenzo. Our veteran bus driver. Standing behind me with his finger so far up his nose he's touching his brain.

This cannot be happening.

I just posted soft-core tower porn that features a geriatric nose-picker to my Instagram feed.

I give up. This day is a total bust, and there is only one person to blame... Matteo.

CHAPTER FIVE

MATTEO

Pro tip for running a dying tour company: Nothing says safe travels like your elderly bus driver/mechanic conducting open-heart surgery on the engine while everyone pretends not to notice as they board.

"Buongiorno my bold explorers!" I pass out Carlo's lemon cookies like they're golden tickets, praying the sweet distraction works its magic.

My beloved seniors shuffle aboard, their warm smiles and enthusiasm make my insides all mushy. They deserve better than this hazard on wheels.

I pat the bus's worn exterior, our daily ritual. "Just a little longer, old girl. I applied for the business loan and once it gets approved, we'll get you a full makeover. New transmission, fresh paint job, and how about one of those disco balls for impromptu dance parties?"

The bus responds with a concerning gurgle that sounds suspiciously like a death rattle.

And then, here comes trouble in a fitted floral top. It's pulling at her curves like a magnet, and let me tell you, my personal compass is pointing due north. I shift my weight and straighten up as Katie climbs the bus steps like she's marching up to her throne of judgment. She looks fully prepared to ruin my day, my self-esteem, and my will to keep things professional.

"Are we actually touring Milan like it says on the schedule?" she asks, all clipped consonants.

I stroke my jaw, catching how her eyes track the movement. "Eventually. Probably. Maybe?"

The way her nose scrunches when she's annoyed shouldn't be adorable, but damn if it isn't.

"So we're at the mercy of wherever your horny brain takes us?"

"If you're craving a private tour with me, bella, simply say the word. I'll show you pleasures you never knew existed."

Oops. There goes my professionalism.

A rosy hue spreads across her cheeks, and Cristo help me—watching her get flustered is my new favorite hobby. She drops into the seat beside me with a huff that gives her chest a sexy little bounce.

Not that I'm looking... much.

"The bus smells different today. Less dead animal, more toxic fart bomb."

I bark out a laugh without thinking. She's got a mouth on her, this one. Makes a man wonder what else that sharp tongue can do. And she's not wrong. The smell is another reminder of how far Monti Tours has fallen. Running a travel company takes a lot of business skills, something I am not exactly known for.

But that's a problem for future Matteo.

"You are aware," she starts, "that customer expectations are everything in the service industry, right? You need proper protocols, quality assurance standards—"

"Trust me. My customers always leave very, very satisfied." I let my voice drop an octave on the last word.

"That is not what I meant and you know it."

"Perhaps." I wink, enjoying how her blush deepens. "I want you to understand how dedicated I am at providing... full service."

I snatch the mic before Katie can dive into what I'm sure would be a riveting lecture on the importance of schedules and punctuality. Maybe she'd even give me a sneak peek at her... binder.

Okay, fine. I meant her breasts.

"My friends!" My voice fills the bus. "Time for the moment of truth. Should we stick to our safe, already planned schedule..." I pause, aware of Katie's knuckles going white around her binder, "...or should we let another Wish Card guide us to something magical?"

The response is instant and deafening. These seniors appear to be sweet, but they've got rebel souls. "Wish Card! Wish Card!"

"The people have spoken." I look directly at Katie, and sure enough, those beautiful green eyes of hers are ablaze with irritation.

"Get ready, everyone! I'm taking you on a surprise trip to a secret destination. You'll see that the best memories are made when you least expect them!"

I flash her a victorious smirk, and she responds with an over-the-top eye roll. For a second, I wonder why seeing her all riled up is making my pulse race. But I'll have to dissect that thought later—right now, my audience awaits.

"Time for your morning Italian lesson!" I scan the eager faces. "Who remembers how to tell Lorenzo we're ready to roll?"

"Guida l'autobus, Lorenzo!" they shout in their best attempt at Italian.

Lorenzo, that magnificent creature of few words and questionable hygiene habits, stomps the gas like he's crushing his enemies. The bus shudders to life, and we rattle out of Milan like a can of loose change. Within minutes we've left behind the chaos of the city for the breathtaking backdrop of northern Italy. The road unfolds like a love letter to my homeland—dramatic mountain peaks, endless sky, while patches of wildflowers paint the hillsides in bursts of color.

"Let's spice things up with some essential Italian phrases," I announce. "First up—*dove è il bagno?*"

My exaggerated pronunciation elicits giggles from the tourists as they slowly echo, "Doh-vay eel bahn-yo?"

"Congratulations! You've all unlocked the key to survival anywhere: 'where's the bathroom?'"

Chester, the group's resident comedian, stands up in a T-shirt that reads WITH A BODY LIKE THIS, WHO NEEDS HAIR? "Bathroom schmathroom! At our age, we've upgraded to portable plumbing!" he declares, patting his hip with a wink. "We've got the luxury of adult diapers!"

Laughter explodes across the bus, followed by more loud, raunchy jokes that would scandalize a proper tour guide. Good thing I've never been proper.

Katie stares out the window like she's determined to be miserable her entire vacation. It's a challenge, I realize, to break through her walls and get her to loosen up. Lucky for her, I'm a man who doesn't back down easily.

"Next phrase! *Mi scusi, non parlo italiano*—"

"Hang on, handsome!" Deborah's bold voice cuts in. "Forget the tourist talk. How do you say 'your place or mine'?"

I swallow a laugh. While Katie's got herself wrapped tighter than a nun's habit, her aunt's basically Betty White at Mardi Gras—beads optional.

"Trick question," I say coolly, playing along. "An experienced woman, in any language, knows the way to speak this... is with her body."

Deborah pushes out her chest and shimmies, her movements eliciting hoots and hollers from the laughing crowd. Her carefree spirit is contagious.

A distinguished Texan by the name of Howie Dixon rises to his feet. His tall, muscular frame makes him an imposing sight, especially for someone in their seventies. His gray mustache adds to his rugged charm.

"How do y'all say 'Sorry about my large erection,'" he blurts out with a laugh, his strong Southern drawl adding to the absurd situation.

"Scusami per la mia grande erezione, I say, making an exaggerated hip thrust gesture that I'm not proud of. Okay, maybe I'm a little proud of it. *Hell, who am I kidding? I nailed it.*

I catch a tiny quirk of Katie's lips before she wrestles her features back into disapproval. It's like gazing at a rainbow trying to peek through storm clouds.

Bring it on, bellissima. Before this trip is over, I will have you laughing so hard that your whole body will be shaking. You'll throw your head back, your cheeks will be sore, and your mouth—ah, I better stop thinking like that.

Glancing out the window, I realize we've reached our destination. "All right, my wild crew, we're here. Rose, come up here and join me—today is all about making your wish come true!"

Rose glides to the front of the bus as if she were walking on clouds. She's petite—barely reaches my shoulder—but her presence fills the entire space. Her striking blue eyes hold a world of wisdom and experience. Her white hair, styled in a classic, short cut, frames her face gracefully, highlighting her timeless beauty.

She takes the mic from me with trembling fingers, but her voice is steady as a heartbeat when she speaks. "Stan and I came to Italy for our honeymoon." I swear the entire bus is holding its breath. "We were young and broke, but so in love. Now here we are, sixty years later..."

I catch Katie shifting in her seat, her grumpy expression softening. Heck even Lorenzo stops picking his nose to listen.

"My Stan, he loves the water," Rose continues. "Every weekend, rain or shine, he's out on his little boat. But there's one lake he's always dreamed of seeing." She shifts her gaze to the back row where Stan sits. "Lake Como."

I glance over at Stan, this stocky guy with eyebrows bushier than a Tuscan pine tree, and he's not even trying to hide the tears behind his Coke-bottle glasses.

"Well, Stan," I say. "Your lovely wife has used her wish to make your dream come true. Everyone look out your windows. Behold the famous Lake Como and all its breathtaking beauty."

The bus erupts in cheers and whistles, but Stan only has eyes for his Rose. He's throwing kisses, his weathered face glowing with the kind of love that makes cynics believe in happily ever after. It's raw, unfiltered love—pure as it gets. I soak it in.

This is why I do it. This feeling—this high—I fucking love my job.

***

"WHAT DO YOU MEAN the main tour is booked?"

"Complete-ah-mente full, Matteo Monti," Signora Ricci announces. Her penciled eyebrows arch. "All large boats, reserved. Weeks ago. By people who plan ahead."

That last bit comes with enough judgment to fill Saint Peter's Basilica.

Of course, this is on me. I had to wing it, confident my charm could pull off the impossible. And now? I'm standing here with my dick flapping in the breeze while thirty-two seniors—Katie included—are expecting a once-in-a-lifetime tour of Lake Como.

Parked alongside our bus is the giant red Italy Express motorcoach, looming like a middle finger in my peripheral vision. Its glossy paint reflects my shame. A swarm of tourists in matching red shirts pours out like ants from a hill.

My jaw tightens as I glance at the lake. Sure enough, the massive tour boat I'd been hoping to reserve is boarding now—its spacious decks ridiculously packed with those same red shirts.

I drag my gaze from the grand sightseeing ship to the small wooden vessels bobbing against the dock. They're gorgeous, sure—classic Italian craftsmanship with vintage elegance—but they're also... tiny.

"Okay, what about the small boats?"

She makes a show of consulting her ancient ledger. "Sì. Six people maximum per boat. Very romantic." Her eyes narrow. "Very expensive."

Of course they are. Because the universe loves to remind me that "making it up as I go" is not an actual business strategy.

Merda. At these prices, I might have to sell a kidney. But one look at Rose and Stan, holding hands by the water's edge, and I refuse to let my poor planning ruin their sixty-year dream. This is exactly the type of financial decision-making that has Monti Tours circling the drain.

"Per favore, Signora Ricci." I lean across the dock's ticket counter, deploying my most charming smile. "Surely we can work something out? These are special customers."

Signora Ricci peers at me over rhinestone-studded glasses, immune to my charms after decades of dealing with fast-talking tour guides.

"How many you need?" she asks, though her tone suggests she already knows I can't afford it.

I do some quick math. Thirty-two people, plus me and Lorenzo, divided by six per boat... "Six boats."

She names a price that causes my balls to retreat into my body. *"Dio mio!"* I choke out. I'm going to have to sell both kidneys. And maybe my left testicle.

"Pardon me, folks."

A voice smooth as aged bourbon cuts through my panic. Howie, our resident Texan, strides up to the kiosk like he owns it—hell like he owns the whole damn lake. Everything about him screams old money, from his pressed linen suit to his Rolex that's worth more than my entire bus.

His sharp eyes survey the boats, then drift to where Aunt Deb is currently scandalizing a group of fishermen. She has one hand on the man's chest and the other suspiciously low on his hip, grinding to the rhythm of a tango that she's clearly improvising on the spot.

"I reckon"—Howie strokes his impressive mustache thoughtful-ly—"a fellow with enough grit and gumption might secure himself a private vessel... for two?"

I clear my throat. "The private boats are quite expensive."

"How much we talking, son?"

"For everyone, including your extra boat, it's seven thousand eu-ros."

Without missing a beat, Howie pulls out a black credit card and sets it on the counter like he's playing a royal flush. "Sold. There's one li'l detail we gotta work out."

His gaze shifts to Katie in the background, who's intently study-ing her binder. As the sun catches in her hair, illuminating those bouncy blonde waves, I imagine running my fingers through it. *Fuck me sideways. I need to stop noticing these things.*

"The lovely Miss Deborah's niece," he continues, mustache twitching with pure mischief. "I'm gonna need you to keep her... otherwise occupied. Can't have her puttin' a damper on our good time."

"Done," I say before he can change his mind.

Howie turns to Signora Ricci. "Now tell me what kinds of love-bird specials you got."

The change in Signora Ricci is like observing a piranha spot a wounded fish. That black credit card disappears faster than wine at an Italian wedding. "For you, signore? We have many *special* roman-tic options."

Never pit charm against money... money always wins.

***

"**Everyone, find your assigned** boats!" I shout, consulting my hastily scrawled passenger list.

Naturally, Katie ignores the command. Of course she does. She marches up, all sharp green eyes and clipped steps, like she's demanding to speak to the manager—oh wait, that's me.

"Why aren't we renting a bigger boat like that Italy Express tour group?" she asks, pointing at the ferry in the distance crammed full of red-shirted tourists.

My patience snaps. "Because that's not a tour. That's a human filing cabinet. Intimate boats like ours give you the real Lake Como experience."

"Or maybe you're justifying your lack of planning."

"You think I don't plan?" I step closer, tilting my head to meet her challenging gaze. "I plan *magic*. I plan moments people remember their whole lives. You want a checklist? Fine. Here's mine: laughter, bliss, unexpected beauty, and memories so good they make you cry in the airport on the way home."

She blinks, momentarily caught off guard, before her defenses snap back into place. "Some people appreciate structure," she fires back—daring me to argue. "Not everyone wants their vacation to feel like an episode of *Survivor*."

"Your boat's down that way, principessa," I say, pointing toward the far dock. "Let's not scare the captain with that death glare, okay?"

She huffs, brushing past me, but not before her shoulder bumps mine too hard to be accidental. As she and her attitude walk away, I catch the sway of her hips and my grin stretches wide.

If she thinks she's getting the last word on this, she's got another thing coming.

Rustic brown wooden boats gently bob in the crystal-clear water as the sun paints the lake's surface with sparkles like scattered diamonds. Mountains in the background frame the postcard-worthy view, releasing my frustration.

"Mrs. Thomas, careful with those steps." I steady the elderly woman as she boards.

"Lorenzo!" I bark at my driver, who's excavating his nasal cavity again. "Get a damn Kleenex and help Mr. Jenkins."

A burst of laughter draws my attention to where Deborah is dragging Howie toward their private boat. "Time to make some waves, my Southern stud!"

"Comin', sugar!" Howie's grin could light up Rome as he follows her.

I check my list again. One boat left—me, Katie, and the Dawson sisters who are currently... *leaving?* Why are they walking away from the dock?

"We've decided to skip the seasickness adventure," Agnes Dawson announces. "Margaret and I spotted the cutest little shops in town. Those Italian leather bags have our names on them. They just don't know it yet."

Her sister nods enthusiastically. "You two have a ball! We'll be back before the bus leaves, scout's honor."

Before I can protest, they're power-walking toward town.

Which leaves me with—

"Absolutely not," Katie says, arms crossed. "I am not getting on that tiny boat alone with you."

"Scared of a little one-on-one time, principessa?"

"You're so full of yourself. Does your giant ego have a hard time fitting into your pants? Wait, no, don't answer that."

"Relax." I gesture to the elderly captain arranging cushions on our boat. "We'll have a chaperone. *Due persone*," I tell the captain. "Just two."

A knowing grin stretches across his timeworn face. "Ah! *Gli amanti!*" With renewed enthusiasm, he sets to work, transforming the back section into a floating love nest—presumably for our benefit. Plush cushions arranged like a bed, complete with soft throws and—*Cristo—are those rose petals?*

Katie opens her mouth to argue, but the captain is already urging us forward, his forceful hospitality something only Italian men over seventy can pull off. "Presto! The romance package, very special!"

"Romance package?" The pitch of Katie's voice could shatter glass. "Tell him no thank you!"

"Perhaps next time you'll pay attention in my Italian lessons so you can tell him yourself."

"Vieni!" The old man pushes us toward the boat. "Love waits for no one!"

I step on board, instantly unsteady on the cushion paradise. "Take my hand before you fall."

Katie lifts her chin, defiant as always, and attempts to board without assistance while maintaining her death grip on that binder.

"I'm perfectly capable of—"

The boat lurches.

Katie's eyes go wide. She pitches forward with a yelp. And then she's airborne.

WHAM!

She lands on top of me. Her breasts press against my chest, her thighs bracket my hips, and that strawberry scent that's been driving me insane since the night we met floods my senses. My cock immediately stands up to introduce itself.

Those green eyes meet mine, darkening with awareness. Her lips part with a soft gasp that does dangerous things to my self-control. A strand of her silky, sweet-smelling hair brushes my cheek, and I swear I feel her heart pounding against me.

Katie jerks back as if stung, but Signore Meddling Romantic, the captain, decides it's the perfect time to gun the engine, catapulting her precious binder into the air.

"No!" She launches herself after it with zero self-preservation instinct. She's halfway off the boat with a death grip on her binder, unaware of how momentum is dragging her dangerously overboard. One more inch, and she'll be gone.

"Fanculo!" My hand snaps out, catching her wrist before a splashy disaster. The boat hits a wave as I yank her back and—

CRUNCH.

Her hefty planner smashes into my nose with the force of an angry nonna wielding a rolling pin. Spots dance in my vision as hot pain blazes across my face.

"Oh God, your nose!" Her hands flutter near my cheeks. "I swear I didn't mean to—"

WHOOSH!

The boat lurches violently as a massive wake from a passing ferry hits us broadside. Katie screams—not a dainty yelp but an all-out shriek—and launches herself into my arms like I'm her personal lifeguard. My arms instinctively lock around her waist, and I pull her close.

Fuck me. The feel of her curves melting against my body sends all the blood from my nose rushing back down south.

Cristo, she feels good. Too good.

Our eyes lock, and I get hit with that captivating contradiction again. Fear flickers in her gaze, but it's the defiant spark beneath that sends a thrill through my veins.

We're so close I'm seeing amber-colored flecks in her irises and counting each perfect eyelash. Her lips part slightly, and my body reacts with a jolt of pure want. She relaxes into me, and my arms tighten, holding her steady. Safe.

"Perfetto!" Our captain's joyful shout shatters the moment. "The lovers cannot be denied!"

He breaks into song. Not just any song—a full-throated, passionate rendition of "That's Amore" complete with dramatic hand gestures that make me seriously question how he's still steering the boat.

Katie jerks away, straightening her clothes like she can iron out the sexual tension crackling between us.

"You know, cara mia," I say, sitting up on the seat. "I've been with many complicated women, but you—you're a fucking masterpiece of mixed signals."

Our enthusiastic captain stretches out his arm, presenting me with champagne and chocolate-covered strawberries, his eyebrows doing a playful waggle.

"Does everything have to be a seduction with you Italian men?" Katie huffs.

"We're irresistible and unmatched in bed—it's in our DNA."

"Wrong on both counts." Her eyes light up. "And trust me, women can get very good at faking it."

"Is that what you do with your man?"

"Don't talk about Jared." Her eyes flicker.

I lean in, unleashing my bedroom eyes. "Interesting how you don't deny it. Tell me, principessa, has anyone ever taken their time with you? Tasting and touching—making you fall apart piece by piece until you're desperate, writhing, and begging for release?"

Her breath hitches. "Sex is overrated."

"Tesoro, you wouldn't say that after one night with me," I say, my voice turning dark and promising. "I'd destroy you for any other man's touch, and you'd never settle for mediocre again."

Her thighs press together—a tiny tell that shoots straight to my groin. "If you think I'll be your personal plaything just because you're the only man here who doesn't need Viagra, you're out of your damn mind."

"For a proper girl, you have a very filthy mouth." My lips curl. "But I only tease. I am not serious. You need not worry because sex is off-limits."

"It was never an option! I'm engaged." She holds her binder up, hiding her breasts.

"Plenty of engaged women go looking for one last wild night." I let my gaze drift over her curves. "And bella, I bet you're magnificent when you let go. But I have one rule I never break—no hooking up with tourists on my tours."

Something ignites in her emerald eyes—*disappointment?*—before she masks it. "Never?"

"Never."

"Perfect." Her chin lifts in defiance, but I detect the slight quiver of her bottom lip. "Finally we agree on something. No sex."

Fucking hell. I never should have told her about my goddamn rule. The words just tumbled out, and now I'm sensing that tiny spark of possibility fade from her eyes. Why does her quick agreement feel like a kick to the gut?

And why the hell do I care?

Katie sets down that soul-sucking binder and picks up a strawberry. Watching her lips wrap around the chocolate-dipped fruit has me swallowing hard and shifting in my seat.

"So what's in there anyway?" I nod at the binder, trying to distract myself from inappropriate thoughts about her mouth. "I think I earned a peek, considering I saved both your lives."

She swallows, leaving a smudge of chocolate at the corner of her mouth that I desperately want to lick away. "Ideas and poses for pictures to show my fiancé what I'm doing. Different vacation itinerary things."

"And where's Prince Charming while you're touring my beautiful country?"

"London. He's opening a new exhibit at the Natural History Museum." Her voice falters slightly.

"Must be hard being apart." *Why am I pushing this?*

"Yes, but that's why I'm documenting everything."

"Always prepared, aren't you, principessa?" I study her profile against the lake. "Bet you've never forgotten a birthday or missed a deadline in your life."

"Being organized helps me feel grounded." She blinks, as if she startled herself with the admission. "I don't know why I just told you that."

"Maybe you're finally succumbing to my Italian charm." I wink.

She rolls her eyes, but I catch the hint of a smile.

"Have you filled out your Wish Card yet?"

"No, honestly, I haven't given it much thought."

Something tells me that's a lie. I get the sense that she's overthinking it, but I drop it. We fall into a comfortable silence, the kind that feels as natural as breathing. Katie leans back, drinking in the view, and I do my best not to stare at her... I'm failing miserably.

Lake Como is showing off today. It's like being in a lover's dream—all sparkle and seduction under the golden sun. The water now parts smoothly for our boat, as if welcoming us into its embrace. Majestic mountains shoot up around us, their peaks kissing the sky. The air is clean and crisp with a hint of pine. This is no ordinary view; this is an experience that seeps into your soul.

What the tourism websites don't mention, however, is that this stunning water is ice-cold and will have your teeth chattering and your... parts shrinking, no matter what month it is.

Katie takes a big breath, and it's the first moment I've seen her unwind. This is why I do this—unveiling Italy's beauty and watching people fall in love with it the way I have. Even when my bank account's crying and my bus sounds like it's saying its final goodbyes.

But right now? All I can focus on is how the light plays across Katie's features. She gazes out at the lake—lips curving ever so slightly—eyes reflecting the calm waters. The quiet wonder on her face hits me square in the chest, and before I know it, I've got my mother's old Nikon in hand.

CLICK.

Her head whips around, eyes flashing. "Did you just—"

"Sì." I check the preview screen. Perfect. The light, the composition—the way her profile angles against the backdrop of mountains, she's fucking gorgeous.

"Delete it." But there's curiosity in her voice.

I hold out the camera, close enough to feel the warmth radiating off her skin. "Look first. Then decide."

She takes it carefully, and I notice her face as she studies the image. I've caught her in a rare unguarded moment.

"This is..." She trails off, touching the screen gently.

"Breathtaking?" I lean closer. "That's because you are, principessa. Even when you're trying to kill me with your binder."

A blush creeps up her neck, and damn if I don't want to trace it with my tongue. She keeps her eye on the camera, but I see her pulse jumping at her throat.

"You are actually talented," she says softly. "I mean, really talented."

"Don't sound so surprised. I'm more than a pretty face and the best tour you've ever had."

The boat's engine sputters, jerking us to a sudden stop. Without warning, the jolt sends Katie's precious binder hurling across the cushions and off the side of the boat.

"No!" Katie lunges for it, but she's too late.

I don't think. I dive.

One thought blazes through my mind as I launch myself over the side: *That binder is her everything.*

SPLASH!

Holy mother of frozen fuck.

The water hits me like ten thousand ice daggers straight to the nuts. My lungs seize as Lake Como reminds me why it's meant for admiring, not swimming.

The binder twirls in slow motion below me, pages starting to spread like wet butterfly wings. My muscles scream as I knife deeper, fighting the cold that's trying its best to turn my dick into an innie.

Got it! My fingers close around the plastic cover right as it's about to become fish food.

The captain swings the boat around as I break the surface, gasping and sputtering Italian curses. I haul myself back aboard, water streaming off me as I hand Katie her sopping wet binder.

"Merda, it's freezing!" I strip off my shirt, then attack my pants, not even caring that I'm putting on a show. The wet clothes are pure ice against my skin.

I catch Katie's eyes going wide as I stand there in nothing but clingy boxer briefs. Her gaze travels from my chest down to my abs, then lower, and—

"Ah!" The captain's laugh booms across the water. "The great Lake Como, she makes even the mighty Italian Stallion look more like a tiny pony, no?"

Katie's eyes snap to my groin and—oh Cristo—she's definitely noticing the current... situation.

"It's *cold!*" I protest, grabbing for the towel the captain throws at me. "Shrinkage is a perfectly normal male response to freezing water!"

And then it happens.

Katie Crawford—Miss Organization, Queen of Control—loses it. She doubles over, howling with laughter. The sound bursts out of her like she has been storing it up since birth, pure and unrestrained and fucking beautiful.

"The water..." I try again, but my mouth twitches. "It's very, very cold."

"Oh sure," she gasps between giggles, wiping her eyes. "I'm sure you're usually very..." Another laughing fit hits her. "...impressive."

"I'll have you know that under normal, non-Arctic conditions—"
But her laughter is contagious, and before I realize it, I'm howling
too—half-naked, freezing my ass off, and fully humbled by Mother
Nature.

I want to make her laugh every day for the rest of this tour.

And fuck me. That thought is more dangerous than hypothermia.

CHAPTER SIX

KATIE

Mom: Look at this article I saw! "Ten Romantic Ways to Surprise Your Ex in London."
Me: No way this is real.
Mom: IT IS! Found it on Pinterest! #7 involves balloons and roses—so cute!
Me: Thanks, but I know what Jared wants, and it's not balloons and over-the-top clinginess.
Mom: Why not? Picture it. He opens the door, realizes his mistake, and BOOM! Happily ever after.
Me: Hard pass. I've got this handled, Mom. Love you.

MATTEO'S WORDS ECHO IN my head: *No hooking up with tourists from my tours.*

"This is good," I tell my reflection in the hotel's bathroom mirror, aggressively brushing my teeth. "Totally good. Great, even."

The lie tastes worse than morning breath.

I've been up since five a.m., absolutely not thinking about the way Matteo's wet boxer briefs clung to his thighs yesterday when he rescued my binder. Or how his voice dropped an octave when he described how he'd ruin me for other men. Or the fact that his no-tourist stance felt like both a relief and a personal attack.

Which is ridiculous. I'm *engaged...* Sort of. *Taking a break.* Whatever.

The point is, Matteo's rule means I can stop reading into his outrageous flirting.

Stop imagining his strong hands sliding up my thighs...

His stubble scratching against my neck...

His sinful mouth whispering filthy Italian promises in my ear—

"Jesus." I splash cold water on my face. "Get it together, Katie."

Somewhere amid my artfully displayed toiletries, my phone chimes—another Instagram "like." I've gotten approximately eight million since posting that Lake Como pic *(photo credit by Matteo).*

It's the one where I look... different. Softer. Like a woman who doesn't fold her underwear into separate piles based on type. *(Everyday undies in front, period panties in the middle, and scheduled sex nights in the back.)*

I pull up the post, ignoring how my pulse kicks up at the sight of all those notifications. Jared? Nope. Scroll, scroll. Family. Scroll, scroll. Friends. *C'mon Jared!* Scroll, scroll... and nope!

Petra: *WHO IS THIS WOMAN AND WHAT HAVE YOU DONE WITH OUR KATIE?*

Cam: *That light! That angle! Excuse me but what magazine is this photo for, miss supermodel?*

Mom: *You look so relaxed, honey! But let's button up that top one more...*

Still no sign of Jared.

My thumb hovers over his profile. His last Instagram picture—a slightly blurry shot of his favorite triceratops skull—stares back at me, mocking my neediness. He's probably too busy with his new exhibit to check social media. That's all. I am absolutely not going to text him the photo directly like some desperate ex.

Even if technically I am his desperate ex.

No. Stay strong. This is all part of the plan. He'll see these photos eventually and realize I've changed. That I'm spontaneous now. That I don't need to schedule our sex life through 2065.

Speaking of scheduling sex...

My mind drifts back to the boat. Okay, yes, Lake Como might have temporarily diminished Matteo's... assets, but that just makes me wonder about their non-frozen state. Would his little maestro match the rest of him? Of course it would. I mean all that hard, sculpted perfection comes standard issue with Italian men, right?

Heat floods my cheeks as his words rush back: *"Has anyone ever taken their time... tasting... touching... making you fall apart... begging for release?"*

Holy. Mother.

Jared would never—has never—said anything that brazen. Our dirty talk consists mainly of "You wanna?" followed by "Sure, let me brush my teeth first."

Which is fine. Normal. Safe.

I recall the image of Rose and Stan wrapped around each other on their boat. Sixty years together and still acting like lovestruck teenagers. That's what Jared and I could have. Dependable, forever love.

"Katie-kins!" Aunt Deb's voice rings out. "Put down whatever list you're making and help me pick a dress that'll make these Italian boys pop a button—and not from their shirts!"

My hands mechanically pack my toiletries while Matteo's rule plays on repeat.

No hooking up with my tourists.

Why can't I quit thinking about it? And worse... Why won't my heart stop racing?

***

Our group clusters outside the hotel entrance, the air thick with excitement and a cloud of floral perfumes that scream, "I've got a purse full of Werther's Originals."

Matteo's oozing rugged charm, carrying himself in a way that's both relaxed and commanding, like he owns the world. I'm doing my best not to notice how his white T-shirt clings to his chest like it's painted on or how his dark pants hang low on those hips.

Oh my God, his ass. I bite my lip.

"My beautiful travelers!" Matteo's voice projects across our group. "Today is our last day in Milan, which means"—his eyes find mine with a knowing glint—"we will be sticking to the schedule."

I snap my mouth shut so fast my teeth click. *Damn him for anticipating my question.*

"Well, mostly," he adds with a grin. "We have a special shopping detour planned, because today's Wish Card comes from our fashionable Dawson sisters."

Agnes and Margaret saunter forward like seasoned socialites. Their matching paisley-print scarves should be a crime against fashion, but somehow they're working it.

"You see, sweeties," Agnes announces, adjusting her oversized Gucci sunglasses, "Margaret and I have dreamed of thrift shopping in Milan since we first saw *Roman Holiday*."

"Wrong city, sister dear," Margaret cuts in.

"Details, details. The bottom line is, we're here to hunt vintage treasures! Because just like us, vintage never goes out of style!"

"And a designer purse," Margaret adds, "always fits, no matter how many cannoli you eat."

A savory smell wafts over from a café's dessert display where chocolate biscotti and sugar-dusted pastries sit behind the glass, begging to be devoured. Several faces in the group light up, stealing glances at the tempting treats.

Matteo beams as he lays out the plan, his excitement pulling us in. "We'll blend classic Milan landmarks with shopping at my favorite hidden gems—the ones tourists never find. And if you need a break, Lorenzo will have the bus waiting nearby!"

As we cross the street, Matteo's voice carries like music, painting Milan as a living, breathing entity. He doesn't just describe the city—he conjures it, turning stone facades into whispers of history and hidden courtyards into secret gardens waiting to be discovered. The city feels less like a tourist trap and more like an old friend eager to meet us.

The group pauses for photos at the base of an ornate building, its carvings glowing in the sunlight. Suddenly Matteo is beside me.

"No binder today?" His voice teases.

"Still recovering from its brush with death in my suite," I say, keeping my tone cool. "Thanks to my forethought to have the pages laminated, and your little lake rescue, it will survive."

"Heroic deeds are my specialty. Besides, we can't have your fiancé missing out on the fantastico adventures of Binder Girl, now can we?"

Something about his easy tone makes me brave... or possibly insane. "How's your, um, love wand? Still suffering from frostbite?"

Oh my God. Did I actually say that out loud?

Matteo throws his head back and laughs. "Fully recovered, principessa. Care to verify?"

"In your dreams, Romeo." But I'm grinning, and it feels... natural. Like maybe his no-tourist boundary is exactly what we needed. We can simply be fun and flirty with zero chance of those abs convincing me to do something stupid.

We follow him through streets that wind like spaghetti noodles until we arrive in Navigli. The district hits all your senses at once—the soft splash of canal waters, the sweet scent from a gelato shop, and the rainbow of vintage clothes spilling from doorways. Beautiful old buildings slant over the canals, their faded paint and crooked shutters only adding to the charm.

"Welcome," Matteo announces with a theatrical sweep of his arm, "to where fashion goes to be reborn."

The Dawson sisters are already speed-walking toward the nearest shop, and what's left of our group disperses like confetti, drawn to different window displays and outdoor racks.

I clearly missed the dress code memo because Milan's sidewalks are a never-ending runway show. The parade of women that strut by seem genetically engineered by some top-secret Italian lab. A girl eating pizza looks like a Gucci ad. Another casually applies lipstick while strutting in weapons-grade heels, and a brunette, weighed down by shopping bags, moves like she's floating on a cloud.

Even the tourists have mastered that casually glamorous I-woke-up-in-Prada vibe. A group ahead of us is taking selfies, and they've got that head-tilt-hair-flip-laugh combo down to a science.

Meanwhile, I'm over here in my clearance-rack blouse and practical flats, feeling about as runway-ready as a Pizza Hut breadstick.

"They're all so... intimidating," I mutter to Matteo, watching another goddess float past. "How do they make it seem so effortless?"

"Ha! It's more of an illusion," Matteo says, a faint smirk on his lips. "You'd be surprised how much effort goes into looking effortless."

"Well, whatever they're doing, it's working."

"Depends on what you think 'working' means." Matteo tilts his head, assessing me on a level that makes me feel vulnerable. "Some people like to be seen. Others... don't feel the need to try so hard."

"Are you saying I don't try?" I shoot back, defensive now.

His eyes lock onto mine with an intensity that steals my breath. "I'm saying, true beauty comes from the soul and you... look beautiful with or without clothes."

"Excuse me? Are you, like, a local?"

Before I can respond, a blonde American bombshell, who surely owns stock in push-up bras, stands there eye-fucking Matteo so hard that her stare is rounding third base.

"Born and raised, bella." And there it is—the panty-melting smile I was stupid enough to think was mine alone.

"We're staying at Hotel Milano." Her equally stunning friend appears like they're tag-teaming their prey, all perfect hair and practiced pout. "Maybe you could show us the kind of intimate spots we want to see?" She glances between Matteo and her friend. "We're very... open-minded about sharing authentic Italian experiences."

Wow. About as subtle as a neon sign advertising DOWN FOR A THREESOME.

Matteo soaks up their attention like it's his life force. Reality check delivered: I'm not special. I'm just another tourist getting the standard Matteo Monti experience, complete with smoldering looks, casual touches, and flirty nicknames.

"Ah, *bellissime*. You're painting a very... enticing picture. Under different circumstances, I'd give you both a thorough Italian education." He winks. "But sadly, ladies, I'm working. Enjoy your trip."

They slink away like pampered princesses denied their prize, and I'm trying hard not to think about what kind of "lessons" Matteo offers in his spare time.

"What happened to your no-tourists rule?" I arch an eyebrow.

"I said no tourists from *my* tours." His mouth curves into an infuriating smirk. "Other tourists? Much simpler. Here today, gone tomorrow. No complications."

Right. Matteo treats relationships like Airbnbs. Meanwhile I'm over here planning joint cemetery plots. Add that to the list of Reasons Why the Hot Tour Guide Is Eye Candy Only.

"That's kind of sad. And lonely." I gesture toward Stan and Rose, who are sharing a gelato as if they're starring in a romance movie. "I want that. Sixty years with someone who still looks at me like I'm their whole world."

Something dark flashes across his face. "Sure. Until the day it's all taken away."

The raw pain in his voice surprises me. Before I can ask what he means—

"Darlings!" Aunt Deb's voice cuts through the air. "I simply must have your opinions on some scandalous purchases."

She hooks her arms through ours with surprising strength and drags us toward a high-end boutique that screams "Your entire paycheck won't cover the tax."

"The vintage can wait," Aunt Deb declares.

Howie trails behind us. "Lead the way, sugar."

The moment we step inside, I know I'm in trouble. This isn't Target. It's not even Nordstrom. This is what you get when money and fashion have a passionate affair and send their love child to the most prestigious school in Paris. The lighting is designed to make you forget about trivial things like rent and food. The air smells like a bouquet of fresh flowers, but also the sweet scent of financial recklessness. The clothes hang on minimal racks like precious artwork, each piece spaced far enough apart to suggest they're too elite to mingle with the others.

A price tag peeks out from a "simple" black dress. "Holy shit. Maybe I could start an OnlyFans for my binder collection."

Matteo's laugh rumbles beside me, but it's drowned out by the sound of Aunt Deb's full-on chaos. Three saleswomen flutter around her, their arms straining under the weight I swear is half the store's inventory. She selects pieces rapid-fire, like a fashion-obsessed orchestra conductor.

"Katie-kins. Dressing room. Now!"

My stomach drops. I know that tone. It's the same one she used when I was eleven and refused to participate in her "junior burlesque" dance recital. OMG, the feather boa incident...

I still have nightmares.

"Strip!" Aunt Deb announces as she corrals me into the dressing room. It's less of a room and more of a small palazzo, where the mood lighting could rival a *Vogue* photoshoot.

"I can't—" My protest dies in my throat as my aunt's outfit drops to the floor. Underneath, she's wearing a crotchless lace bodysuit in sapphire blue to match her eyes.

"Darling, how do you expect to seduce anyone if you can't undress in front of the woman who pulled a highlighter cap out of your left nostril when you were five?"

Fair point.

Faced with the unstoppable force that is my aunt, I slowly start peeling off layers.

She gasps. "Oh, honey. Are those... are those beige?"

"They match everything!" I defend, though even I have to admit the color could best be described as sad oatmeal.

"Darling, those cotton panties are forcing your vagina into early retirement." She circles me like a stylish shark. "A stud like Matteo wants to unwrap you like a saucy Christmas gift, not tear open a boring Amazon Prime box."

The thought of Matteo unwrapping anything of mine sends heat surging through my body.

"It's not your fault. Your fashion faux pas come from your mother. She struggled with perms, puffy sleeves, and pantyhose. I couldn't save her, but you, you still have a chance. Here." She tosses something silky at my head. "Try this."

I hold up the dress. *Not sure if this flimsy bit of material qualifies as a dress.* The neckline plummets to my belly button, and are you kidding me... "It's see-through!"

"That's the point!"

"There should be some imagination left for an outfit."

"This is going to be more work than I thought," Aunt Deb says, studying me like a particularly challenging puzzle. "First clothes, then lingerie. Rome wasn't built in a day, and neither was sexual confidence."

Ten minutes and several minor wardrobe malfunctions later, we're doing our best runway walks for an audience of two. Howie's drooling as Aunt Deb twirls and shimmers under the boutique's strategic lighting.

"Sweet tea, you are stunning! You could make a paper bag look like haute couture," Howie drawls.

I would sell my soul for a paper bag right now. It would provide more coverage than this so-called dress. Note to designer: Less isn't more and fabric is *not* a suggestion. My hands are playing a game of tug-of-war, trying to keep everything from popping out.

And then there's Matteo—leaning against the wall like an Italian dessert menu.

"Matteo, darling! We need your masculine perspective."

His lips curve into that stupid, cocky smirk. "It's... fine." He shrugs with indifference. "But not quite sexy enough to catch a real man's attention."

Oh, you arrogant Italian ass. I see right through him—five minutes ago, he was Mr. "Beauty is on the Inside," and now he's purposely provoking me.

"No trouser tingles? Challenge accepted! Katie-kins, back in the changing area. We're going to turn you into a model or die trying!"

"I. Hate. You," I mouth at Matteo, narrowing my eyes.

"More skin!" Aunt Deb demands, tossing dress number two at me. "A little cleavage never hurt anyone, baby girl. Now put on this push-up bra, and try a size smaller."

Each dress Aunt Deb chooses is progressively more scandalous. And Matteo keeps playing his part to a tee—the bored, unimpressed critic whose disinterest only fuels my auntie's determination to reveal more Katie lady parts.

Dress number six welcomes everyone into my VIP section.

"Boring," he drawls.

Dress eight exposes my entire left butt cheek.

"Perhaps something tighter?" he says.

Dress nine could double as dental floss. I refuse to leave the room. And then.

Oh.

Then.

The red dress happens.

Not just red—this is make-the-devil-blush red. The sort of red that could trigger an international scandal.

The fabric doesn't just hug my curves—it's serenading them with love songs. The neckline is downright illegal, the back is nowhere to be found, and the slit? Well, my mom took baby pictures of me in the tub that were less revealing.

This. This is the one.

Jared won't see me coming. One glimpse of me in this dress, and he'll be screeching into my parents' driveway, begging for those wedding invitations. He'll go into Door Dash driver mode and blow through stop signs in every zip code just to hand-deliver those wedding invites himself!

"You look breathtaking," Aunt Deb says with a genuine smile and glassy eyes. "Now let's fix these tragic undergarments. You can't put Target under Valentino."

"This is way too expensive," I say, but I can't look away.

"Consider it my gift, Katherine." She adjusts my neckline slightly, somehow making it even more lethal. "This trip is about your transformation, your sexual awakening! Speaking of which..." Her eyes sparkle with mischief. "Be a dear and tell Howie I need help with a stubborn zipper."

And that's my cue to leave. I step out of the fitting room. "Um, Howie? My aunt needs your... assistance."

He almost levitates from his chair, moving quicker than any man his age ought to. His mustache twitches with excitement. He zooms past like a silver-haired bullet.

That's when I notice Matteo's gaze. Fixed on me. He's enamored.

His mask of indifference has cracked, replaced by something that makes my pulse race. The way his dark eyes roam over me is so potent, so intense—it's as if this silk dress is charged, like I'm wrapped in a thunderstorm. I saunter over to him, amused by his eyes that keep ping-ponging between my face and my neckline.

"So?" I twirl, channeling my inner goddess *(who apparently has been hiding under cardigans all this time)*. "Think Jared will be into this?"

"You look..." His voice comes out gravelly.

He swallows hard. Twice.

Trying to recover his cool, Matteo attempts to lean casually against what he thinks is a wall.

Spoiler alert: It's not a wall.

Matteo's body slams into a mannequin display.

CRASH!

The domino effect is spectacular—mannequins fall like, well, dominoes, and Matteo goes down in a heap of plastic limbs and Prada. He's managed to get his head wedged between a mannequin's legs while another's arm is stuck down his pants. Each attempt to stand up only makes things worse.

"Merda!" *THWACK.* Another mannequin attacks.

"Cazzo!" *SMASH.* A display rack goes down.

"Porca miseria!" BOOM. Drowned in Gucci bags.

"Matteo?"

An American redhead in stilettos storms over, her heels as lethal as her glare. Matteo, still wrestling with his plastic companions, looks up and smacks his head on a fallen display.

"I've been texting you nonstop for three days!" she screeches. Matteo's a hot mess, wrestling the plastic arm out of his pants as he stands to face her.

"Ah, Rebecca—"

"Sadie! My name is Sadie, you pig!" She turns to me, nostrils flaring. "Run while you can. He's not even that good in bed. I didn't even come the third time."

Something possesses me—temporary insanity maybe? Or it could just be the sight of Italy's hottest tour guide being attacked by department store fixtures.

"Wait," I gasp, summoning my best over-the-top telenovela star. "He's my boyfriend! Are you saying you slept with my *boyfriend*?!"

His eyes go wide.

"Matteo, how *could* you?" I dramatically press the back of my hand to my forehead. "After all those promises of forever!"

SLAP.

Sadie's palm hits Matteo's cheek with a smack that registers on the local seismic monitors. She storms out muttering, "Sexy Italian fuckboy."

I absolutely lose it. The laughter bubbles up uncontrollably as Matteo stands clueless, surrounded by fashion carnage and sporting a bright red handprint on his cheek.

"Oh, this is funny to you, principessa?"

"Your face!" I wheeze, doubled over. "When I said 'boyfriend'—while you were—with the mannequins—" I can't even finish—I'm laughing so hard.

"Enjoy laughing now." He moves closer. "But revenge is like good wine best served... unexpectedly." He tries to sound menacing but stumbles over a silk scarf and lands back in the pile.

The boutique now resembles a murder crime scene—legs everywhere, decapitated torsos in a pile, and heads scattered on the floor like trophies. Somewhere, Guccio Gucci is rolling in his grave.

Best. Shopping. Trip. Ever.

CHAPTER SEVEN

MATTEO

THAT DRESS ISN'T RED—IT's molten temptation, liquid sin poured over her body.

Ever since Katie stepped out in that dress, my dick has been in full-scale rebellion. Hours later, she's still wearing it, and I can't concentrate. I'm supposed to be guiding this walking tour, highlighting the wonders of Milan, but the way that fabric caresses her curves and swirls around her legs with every step—Cristo, all I want to do is feel that silk beneath my fingertips.

"Direct your attention to the stunning nineteenth-century glass arcade—the Galleria Vittorio Emanuele II," I say, pointing toward the ceiling. "They made this renowned passageway to connect the sacred walls of the Duomo cathedral with the cultural heart of the opera house..."

My mind won't stop rewinding to the boutique when Katie's eyes gleamed with playfulness. That moment when she claimed me as her boyfriend and laughed that warm, infectious laugh. It filled the room, and I was basking in it even as I was left squirming in my mannequin orgy.

Thank God for Howie and his credit card with no limits. The bill from my mannequin massacre would've bankrupted Monti Tours faster than Lorenzo can pick his nose.

"Notice the intricate mosaic tiles beneath your feet—" I say in my best guide spiel, only to break off mid-sentence when Katie stumbles. Her shiny new heels, clearly designed by someone who hates feet, turn against her.

"Young man!" Stan's voice booms in the busy space. "Where are your manners? A gentleman always offers his arm to a lady in heels."

"Oh, that's not necessary—" Katie starts.

"I'm sure she can manage—" I try.

But Stan's not having it. Neither are the other seniors, who've stopped and are now staring, with very clear expectations. They hail from a different generation, with different standards for chivalry.

"Now, now," Stan insists, his bushy eyebrows wiggling like caffeinated caterpillars. "That is no way to treat a beautiful woman." The rest of the group nods in synchronized judgment.

Fanculo. There's no escape.

I extend my arm, trying to ignore how my heart's already racing. "Shall we, principessa?"

Katie slides her hand into the crook of my elbow, and every nerve ending in my body dances. Her skin, soft and sensual, brushes against mine, and suddenly I'm swimming in her intoxicating scent—sweet, tantalizing, forbidden strawberries.

Every step through the Galleria is a mix of pure bliss and absolute agony. The way she presses against me when tourists pass, how her fingers dig into my arm when her heels wobble, the soft catch in her breath when I help her dodge a rogue selfie stick.

Focus, idiota.

"Amici miei, meet Milan's most celebrated stud—and his impressive family jewels."

I gesture to the colorful design on the floor. Thousands of tiny black and cream tiles fit together like a satisfying puzzle, creating the unmistakable shape of a muscular bull. The bull stands proudly on a blue coat of arms that sparkles like a giant sapphire.

"You see that hole?" I point to the worn spot in the mosaic. "That's where generations of people have spun three times for luck in love. Right on the bull's *testicoli.*"

That gets me a laugh from the seniors.

"Katie, darling, give those bull balls a spin!" Deborah cheers.

I wink at Katie. "Care to test it out, bella?"

"Is this a real tradition, or are you trying to make a fool of me?"

"It's an important ritual in my culture," I defend, as I guide Katie to the spot. "Very historic. Very lucky."

"Fine. But if I break an ankle spinning on ancient bull testicles, you're carrying me for the rest of the tour."

Merda. Now I'm imagining carrying her, that red silk sliding against my—*stop.*

Tour guide. You're being a tour guide.

The seniors burst into applause as Katie starts to turn.

One spin. Her dress flares out like a rose blooming.

Two spins. Her smile lights up the whole gallery.

Three spins. Her laughter ricochets off the historic walls, bright and unfiltered, like it's got a direct line to my chest. It's a sound that almost makes me believe in miracles.

Something's shifting inside me, and no, it's not just my very insistent hard-on trying to weigh in. This is different. More substantial.

And damn if it isn't making me want to catalog every single one of her genuine, unguarded smiles.

***

BEHOLD, THE HEART OF Milan herself, the Duomo di Milano!"

I spread my arms wide, showcasing the colossal cathedral, like I'm unveiling a masterpiece—which, to be fair, I am. The way those Gothic spires pierce the sky, how the marble glows pink and gold in the setting sun—pure fucking magic.

"Tonight I have arranged something special. A private tour that will take us through the cathedral's secrets, ending with the most spectacular evening view in all of Milan—the Duomo's rooftop terrace."

I detect a subtle spark of approval in Katie's eyes.

"The city lights will spread out below you like scattered stars," I continue, letting my natural enthusiasm flow. "The marble angels watch over Milan's sleeping streets. Trust me, it's a once-in-a-lifetime view."

The excited murmurs from my visitors hit me like a drug. This never gets old. Watching them fall in love with Italy in real time? That's the real payoff. Not the euros, not the reviews. *This.*

And let's be clear—this is *not* the kind of experience Italy Express would ever offer. Hell no. Those corporate robots put their tourists to bed by six p.m.—seven if they're feeling generous—and God forbid anyone sees Milan after dark. They need their puppets bright-eyed and bushy-tailed for the *riveting* experience of visiting souvenir shops at sunrise.

"We will meet back at this spot." I check my watch. "One hour till go time! The piazza is yours to explore."

I came up with the phrase "One hour till go time" during my first year of guiding. It was back when I learned the hard way that "Meet back here at 13:00" means *WTF-o'clock* to jet-lagged tourists who can barely remember what continent they're on.

The seniors instinctively check their watches, phones, and those weird digital things hanging around their necks. It works every time. Something about the countdown gets their attention better than other instructions I've tried. Plus it's catchier than "Please don't wander off and get lost in a foreign city while I have a panic attack trying to find you."

"Oh dear." Mrs. Thomas tugs at my sleeve. "My blood sugar's getting a bit low. Is there somewhere nearby I can get a snack?"

"Giuseppe's. He'll be pulling his signature pistachio cannoli from the oven right about now."

I whip out my handy little notebook and pencil from my pocket. It's not as fancy-schmancy as Katie's binder, but it does the trick. Being a tour guide means helping people find their way. I draw her a quick map and hand her the paper. I've done this a thousand times.

"Tell him Matteo sent you. He'll wrap up something special."

"Any chance there's a bathroom near that bakery?" Bob asks, doing an emergency-level potty dance.

"Even better. The café two doors down from Giuseppe's has the cleanest restroom in the district. Just buy an espresso first"—I slip him a two-euro coin—"and tell Sofia behind the counter you're with Monti Tours."

"Well now," Howie's voice booms above the crowd. "Miss De-lightful, I do believe there was a sapphire necklace with your name on it back at the Galleria. I must say it would complement your eyes."

"You Southern Casanova, you had me at delightful." Deb entwines her arm with his, and they stroll back toward the elegant archway.

The next ten minutes is a frenzy of me doing tour guide triage.

Chester can't read the street signs? Take this map with my signature stick-figure landmarks.

Stan's knee acting up? I bust out a folding chair stashed on the bus for exactly this scenario.

One by one, my seniors disperse into the gathering dusk, armed with personalized directions and my cell number "just in case." And then it's just Katie and me.

"Matteo?" She fidgets with the red fabric around her neck, twisting it nervously between her fingers. "Would you... would you take my picture? In front of the cathedral?"

"Of course, principessa." I take the cap off my camera lens, the familiar weight of it grounding me. The late-afternoon light bathes the square in a golden glow, highlighting the full glory of the cathedral. And looking at Katie, with her body filling out that sumptuous dress—it's a scene that demands to be captured.

So why do I feel like this is a terrible idea?

Katie steps into position, glancing over her shoulder at the towering structure behind her. Her first attempts at posing make me wince. She stiffens, tilting her chin too high, her arms hanging awkwardly at her sides like she's not sure what to do with them. Then comes a forced smile—tight and unconvincing, like a kid at school picture day. Everything about her screams discomfort.

I show her the initial shots. They're... nice. Not exactly 'Gram-worthy but still cute.

"Could we maybe...?" She swallows hard. "Try for something... sexier? For Jared?"

His name is like ice water down my spine. *Right. The fiancé.* The lucky jerk who gets to unwrap this breathtaking present every night.

"Tesoro, you're thinking too much. You're posing like someone's holding you hostage. Let me help you."

"I just..." Those green eyes dart away. "I don't know how to be sexy."

"That dress says otherwise." I deliberately drop my voice to that register that makes women's knees weak. "Turn around. Face the cathedral."

When she hesitates, I add, "Trust me, per favore. I will bring out la tigre that you are in this dress."

The moment she turns I start shooting, but this isn't about the photos anymore. This is about making Katie Crawford realize exactly how fucking gorgeous she is.

"Now imagine hands sliding up those perfect curves, touching all the places you dream about late at night..."

Her breath catches. *Perfetto.*

"Good girl. Let your head fall back. Like you're remembering the best orgasm of your life."

"Matteo!" But her body betrays her, arching like she's already feeling phantom touches.

"That's it, bellissima. Look over your shoulder at me—like you're deciding which part of me to explore first."

The sound she makes—this tiny, desperate whimper—does dangerous things to my self-control.

"Fantastico." *CLICK.*

"You are temptation itself in that dress." *CLICK.*

"Those legs make men beg for mercy." *CLICK.*

"And that mouth... Dio mio, the filthy things I'd teach that pretty mouth to do."

Each word strips away another layer of her inhibitions. Her hands glide up her sides like a lover's touch, slow and seductive. Those exquisite breasts beg to be freed with each breath, straining against the fabric. She's radiant in the fading light.

"Show me what you're thinking about, principessa. Let me see those dirty thoughts you hide behind those innocent eyes."

"I'm not—" She bites that full bottom lip, and my control snaps.

"No?" I move closer, drawn by a primal force I can't fight anymore. "So you're not imagining rough hands replacing that silk? A wet tongue licking every curve you keep hidden?"

Her pupils dilate until those green eyes are nearly black, her body edging toward mine like it knows exactly where it belongs. When I speak again, I deliberately let my accent thicken, watching her shiver in response.

"Ammettilo, ti stai immaginando di scoparmi."

Admit it, you're imagining fucking me.

"I think that's enough." Her voice comes out breathless. "I need to post some pictures for Jared."

And there's that name again, slicing through my growing arousal.

Fuck. I need to get my shit together before I do something monumentally stupid. Like press her up against these sacred walls and show her how an Italian man worships a woman. But she belongs to someone else—invisible ring or not. And despite my reputation, despite how much I want to ruin her for any other man's touch, I don't cross that line. Not ever. No matter how much my cock wants to.

I pass her the camera, ignoring the thrill of her fingers brushing mine.

"That's... that's me?" She blinks rapidly like she's trying to reconcile the seductress on-screen. "I look..."

"Like a woman who doesn't just catch a man's attention—she chains him to her presence. You look like a weapon of desire—like the reason priests question their calling."

"Stop!" But she's grinning that real smile—the one that splits me open and disarms me in a single heartbeat.

"I'm serious, Katie. This—" I lean closer, pointing to a shot where the sunset turns her into liquid gold. "This is the woman who's always there, burning beneath all that control, begging to break free."

Our eyes meet in the screen's reflection and holy fuck—the heat between us could power all of Italy.

The second the photos transfer, she's typing and posting like her life depends on it.

"Tag Monti Tours?" I keep my voice casual, like I'm not desperate to see what kind of man gets to call her his.

"Of course!" She doesn't look up, probably crafting the perfect caption with the same precision she applies to everything else in her life.

My phone pings, and I hit *Follow* before I can stop myself. *Porca miseria!* My feed explodes with pictures of her and some *professore* who looks like he gets turned on by pictures of dinosaur feet. It's a fucking shrine to perfect coupledom. Photo after photo of her in tasteful cardigans, him in ugly ties with stupid fucking dinosaurs. In every one, Katie wears that polite smile that doesn't quite reach her eyes.

No wonder she made that comment about women faking their climaxes. I'd bet my last euro Jared's never made her come so hard she gripped the sheets until they tore. He probably pencils in their missionary position encounters between ironing his ties and polishing his fossil collection.

But who am I to say anything? Of course she's into reliable guys with put-together lives and careers. Girls like Katie don't dream of a man who can barely keep his tour company running.

Why the hell am I spiraling over Katie Crawford's all-American life as if it's any of my business? She's a tourist who needed photos. That's it.

I took the pictures. I did my job.

Even if watching Katie finally unleash her sultry side made my cock harder than marble.

I've got my rule; she's got her fiancé.

Time to focus on being the charming tour guide—not someone imagining how she'd taste or how she'd sound screaming my name.

I need to get my head straight and focus on something else—like tomorrow's Wish Card.

The seniors start filtering back, right on schedule, and I begin my head count. Katie beams at her phone screen *(which I ignore... unsuccessfully)*.

Last to arrive are Deborah and Howie, and *cazzo*—that sapphire around her neck could fund a small country.

"Deborah, that necklace is almost as stunning as you." I whistle low. "Though you should see the gorgeous photos I just took of your niece. She wanted something special for her fiancé—"

"Fiancé?" Aunt Deb chuckles. "Darling, Katie doesn't have a fiancé. Jared broke things off, and we hightailed it to Italy."

Katie freezes. Her phone slips from her fingers, hitting the cobblestones with a crack.

I look down at her face, watching the color drain from her cheeks, and suddenly everything—those staged photos, the constant mentions of Jared, that empty ring finger—clicks into place.

***

"**AND TO YOUR LEFT,** you'll see…" I trail off, staring at the ornate altar, hoping it will magically beam the words into my brain. *Nothing. Niente.* "An incredibly… shiny thing. With, um, angels and… stuff."

There's nothing quite like the Duomo at twilight. The way candlelight flickers across soaring pillars and ancient marble, turning everything soft and golden. The air is thick with a mix of incense, history, and the whispers of countless prayers. Even the stones are pulsing with secrets, eager to divulge the most scandalous tales from the past half millennium.

But tonight? Tonight I'm the world's shittiest tour guide.

I completely blanked on showing off the sundial on the floor—the one that tracks perfect time with a beam of sunlight from a tiny roof hole. Forgot to bring up the statue of Saint Bartholomew holding his own skin like a superhero cape, which always gets a mix of ews and awesomes from the crowd. And I don't think I even shared that it took six centuries and seventy-eight architects to complete this marvel—and here's a mystery for the ages—no one knows who the original architect was.

All because Katie Crawford lied to me.

Her arm is locked through mine—the seniors still insisting on proper gentleman etiquette—but she feels like a ghost of herself.

The confidence she had earlier? Vanished.

The playful banter? Ciao.

The way she owned that red dress? Gone.

It's like she pressed pause on herself, leaving behind only a fragile shadow of this Katie of mine.

Katie of *mine*? Why the hell did I call her *mine*?

"And here we have…" I gesture vaguely at a massive painting I could normally describe in my sleep. "Jesus. Doing… Jesus things."

Brilliant commentary, idiota.

That damn binder keeps flashing through my mind—the one I risked hypothermia and permanent testicular retreat to save from Lake Como. One night, no strings, clean getaway, no fucking feelings—that's my world. That's what makes sense. So why can't I stop thinking about this woman who loves so deeply—planning every detail, every moment, every breath?

No one's ever wanted me with that kind of intensity.

The sheer dedication of it stuns me.

And why does watching her hurt feel like I'm the one breaking?

"And now, my friends," I announce to the group, "we climb to heaven itself. Just three hundred and twenty-five steps to the most spectacular view in Milan."

The collective groan from my seniors could drown out the bells of a Sunday mass.

"Just kidding," I say with a wink. "We'll take the elevator."

Twenty minutes later, Milan glitters below us like someone be-dazzled the entire city. The view is pure Italian magic—modern buildings playing peek-a-boo with ancient towers, streets woven to-gether in a beautiful, orchestrated mess. The air is perfumed with the scent of blooming jasmine, and a gentle breeze carries the warmth of a summer night. The city seduces each and every one of us, one sparkling light at a time.

I'm doing my usual tour guide thing, highlighting all the best landmarks. Rose and Stan are holding hands, the Dawson sisters are taking gargoyle selfies, and I spot Howie and Deborah sneaking away from the group with muffled cackling.

For fuck's sake, please have them make it back to their hotel room before clothes start flying. The last thing I need is my senior citizens defiling sacred ground. Though knowing Deborah, she'd probably high-five the saint statues on her way out.

"I've decided what I want for my Wish Card."

Katie materializes beside me, but something's off.

She thrusts the Instagram feed on her phone in my face. "Look at this!"

I squint at a poorly lit photo of a pasty hand next to an empty display case with the caption: Fossil exhibit coming soon.

"Jared didn't like my photo, but he posted this exactly seven minutes and twenty-three seconds ago." Her words come faster than I've ever heard her speak. "Which means he's online. Just... ignoring me."

She's pacing now, her heels click-clacking against the timeless marble in a frantic rhythm. "But it's fine. I'm fine. I just need to adjust the timeline. Create a new plan. Because that's what you do when plan A isn't working—you don't give up, you make a plan B! And a plan C! And maybe a plan D through Z just to be safe!"

She trips over her own heel, catching herself on a gargoyle. She immediately apologizes to the gargoyle, then continues her manic pacing.

"Careful, principessa. The church frowns on shedding blood on holy ground."

Cristo. I've seen many sides of Katie Crawford. The uptight princess with her death glares. The hidden vixen in a red dress who makes my dick hard. The vulnerable woman whose sadness breaks my heart. But this Katie, with anxious energy crackling off her like a lightning storm? This is uncharted territory.

"Still not hearing a wish in this presentation."

She stops dead, those green eyes locking onto mine with laser focus. "Be my fake boyfriend."

My cock actually twitches at the word *boyfriend*. *What the fuck?*

"Help me make Jared jealous. We'll take pictures—"

"Ah, so now you want to take sexy photos with me?" I waggle my eyebrows, trying to lighten the moment.

"No!" She looks horrified. "I want... flirty pictures, not sexy ones. You know, the kind that make someone go 'Oh, what's going on there?' Just enough to make him realize what he's missing. I can't seem like I've moved on, but I have to get his attention now. I have a very specific timeline—"

"Tesoro, that's not how jealousy works." I step closer, drawn in by her magnetic force. "A man only feels jealous when he can't have what he wants."

Like how my stomach burns every time she says Jared's fucking name.

"So..." That pink tongue darts out to wet her lips, and my entire body notices. "Will you help me? Grant my wish?"

"No." Her face crumples and it physically hurts. "I will be your fake boyfriend, but this doesn't count. Your wish is something just for you to remember this trip. Promise me you'll think of a real wish."

"Yes!" She bounces on her toes, and suddenly she's hugging me, all soft curves and strawberry scent and—

Merda.

Reality crashes into me harder than Lorenzo's emergency braking. I just volunteered to be Katie Crawford's fake boyfriend. To help her win back her fiancé.

Why the hell did I say yes?

And why does my dick keep twitching at the word boyfriend?

CHAPTER EIGHT

KATIE

GROUP CHAT: CPK FOREVER

Cam: *Red alert! Your mom made a Pinterest board: "Katie+Jared= Destiny."*

Petra: *I already followed.*

Me: *Please God, tell me you're kidding.*

Cam: *467 pins and counting.*

Petra: *"Why Museum Men Make the Best Husbands."*

Me: *Don't worry, I have a plan.*

Cam: *Like mother like daughter.*

"TAKE A DEEP BREATH, everyone. Can you smell the history?" Matteo's voice carries over the harbor.

I'm currently vibrating at a frequency that could power a small Italian village. So what I smell is *EVERYTHING*. Fish. Sea. More fish. Coffee beans from that café six blocks away. Did someone crack open a jar of marinara back in Milan? Because I swear, I can pick up on that too.

Is it me or is Matteo moving in slow motion while the rest of us are in fast-forward?

Note to self: Maybe twelve espressos before eight a.m. was overkill. But I needed to stay alert after my all-night binder-making session. *Operation Make Jared Regret Everything* required fresh tabs, color-coding, and at least fourteen contingency plans for every possible fake-boyfriend scenario. Including, but not limited to, what to do if Matteo gets abducted by pirates. Hey, we're at a port. It *could* happen.

My leg won't stop bouncing. *Should I be concerned?*

We hit the road from Milan early this morning, and after a two-hour bus ride, we arrived at the harbor. It's a painting come to life *(minus the god-awful fish stench)* with its pastel buildings and vibrant-colored fishing boats bobbing up and down. The sound of distant ship horns fills the air while seagulls circle overhead, eyeing their next gelato target.

"Today I will show you my favorite places in Genoa." His accent wraps around each word, and my ears soak in every syllable. "Starting with this port, which was once the maritime capital of the world for over seven hundred years until 1797. Take in the salty sea air."

The stinky sea air can kindly go screw itself. I didn't squeeze into my most photographable sundress to smell like the dumpster behind Red Lobster.

"Genoa was once the richest city on earth," he continues, as I count seagulls at hyperspeed. Seventeen. No, eighteen. That one just split into two. *Wait.* "And a little locals trivia... Genoa is also referred to as Genova."

"You mean Genovia, like from *The Princess Diaries*?" I snort-laugh, amused at myself.

Crickets. Dead silence. Even the seagulls stop mid-swoop to judge me.

Clearly these people do not know the rom-com genius of Garry Marshall. I guess they don't share my dream of being transformed from an awkward teenager into a princess overnight.

I clutch my binder, taking comfort in my brilliant, laminated plan for success. It's the product of last night's caffeine-fueled mania—a step-by-step guide to making my ex jealous. Inside? Over nineteen pages of inspirational couple poses, complete with notes that definitely *don't* feature Matteo's perfect jawline.

My eyes dart to Matteo as if they have a mind of their own. My heart races even faster, which should not be possible given the pure caffeine coursing through my veins. Sweet espresso beans. He's pretty. Like, illegally pretty. I should add a tab about that.

WHERE'S MY BINDER? Oh right, I'm holding it. Ha!

"Today we will visit palazzi, which you would call palaces," he says, and my mutinous mind replays our photoshoot last night. Backlit by cathedral lights, Matteo's dark eyes burned into me as he commanded my body and thoughts. And then the velvet in his voice when he described how he'd worship every inch of me. *Yes, more please.*

As if he can hear me thinking, Matteo catches my eye and winks. Good Lord, his chest in that fitted navy T-shirt could make the devil himself jealous. My entire body flames up like a furnace. I've apparently developed a serious weakness for Italian-accented dirty talk.

I think I might spontaneously combust.

Or maybe that's the caffeine.

EVERYTHING IS REALLY INTENSE RIGHT NOW.

"We will end the day with Barb's Wish Card—taking an authentic Italian cooking class and making delicious pesto. And guess where that was invented? Here, in beautiful Genoa!"

Barb reminisces about the Italian restaurant she owned in the Bronx while I flip through my agenda at warp speed. I'm no longer paying attention because I'm now pondering how to casually measure Matteo's biceps with my hands in the photos without looking like it.

"Speaking of Italian cuisine," Aunt Deb purrs, "we should practice the other exciting ways you can use olive oil. I did a retreat with Hercules, this massage instructor in Greece..."

Oh God, no. My last functioning brain cell begins playing Aunt Deb's Greatest Hits of TMI, featuring her Greek trainer's equipment *(which apparently required its own zip code)* and creative applications of extra virgin olive oil to places that ensured nothing remained virgin.

Nope. Abort that thought.

"How long will the class take?" My words tumble out fast and jittery. A muscle under my left eye keeps jumping like it's trying to escape my face.

"Relax and enjoy the adventure, principessa."

I'm about to tell him where he can shove his "relax and enjoy" when—

WHOOSH!

A kamikaze seagull dive-bombs out of the sky, its beady eyes locked on target—my face.

I shriek and leap straight into Matteo's arms; my binder turns into a rectangular frisbee and flies through the air. He catches me with ease, and now all I'm focusing on is how his muscles bunch beneath my fingers. *Why do our bodies fit together so perfectly?*

The seagull circles back, eyeing my precious binder where it landed. Without setting me down—his fingers tightening possessively on my hips—Matteo strides toward it like some kind of avenging knight in fitted trousers. The fact that he's rescuing organizational supplies instead of slaying dragons is the hottest thing ever.

Matteo scoops up my binder one-handed, the other arm still keeping me firmly pressed against him. The seniors burst into applause as if he just scored the winning touchdown at the Super Bowl.

"That's three times I've saved your binder. You owe me." His breath fans against my ear, sending lightning down my spine.

"Not like how you're thinking, I don't." But my body betrays me, pulsing everywhere we touch. Or that could be the caffeine. *Everything is very warm and very fast and does anyone else hear colors?*

I reluctantly peel myself off his broad frame, and the moment his touch is gone, I feel... empty. I'm beginning to worry this fake relationship will be my undoing. Death by sexual frustration and too many espressos.

Here lies Katie Crawford, taken too soon by an Italian tour guide's ripped forearms and filthy mouth. May she rest in organized peace.

I should probably make a tab for that.

Right after I figure out why my tongue tastes like a sparkler exploded in my mouth.

***

TWENTY MINUTES AGO, MY caffeine crash knocked me flat, leaving me with a heap of regret and a skull-splitting headache. On the bright side, I can finally form sentences and I stopped trying to translate every street sound out loud.

I hang back at the rear of our group, plotting out today's photo ops, while up ahead, our lively crew of seniors huddles around a fleet of rickshaws.

Matteo announces, "Today we will travel on three wheels and experience endless adventure as we see all the highlights of Genoa."

"Take my queen to her palace!" Howie says.

Howie helps my aunt into a rickshaw, and she's milking every second. She never misses a chance to be overdramatic, working those rickshaw steps like they're the Met Gala stairs. *Damn, Aunt Deb! You're wearing enough jewelry to sink a cruise ship.*

Hold up. Is that *another* new diamond necklace?

I'm totally scrutinizing these death traps on wheels. The bikes can't be more than one pothole away from falling apart, and they each have a rustic cagelike canopy with a seat attached to the back. *Cute, maybe. Safe, not a chance.*

Then Matteo helps Rose into her rickshaw. There's a tenderness in the way he gently holds her arm, crouching slightly to meet her gaze. It feels unhurried and genuine, as if she was his own grandmother.

Next thing I know, he's cleared the crowd, and it's just the two of us.

"Cara mia, mettiamoci comodi." His voice slides over me like warm mozzarella.

"What's that mean?"

"My dear, let's get cozy."

"Oh no," I say, ignoring his sinfully dark eyes. "That's not how this fake relationship is going to go. Photos only. That's the deal."

He doesn't reply, just hits me with that lethal half smile before effortlessly hopping into the rickshaw. I'm left to awkwardly climb in after him. I'm halfway inside when I feel my sundress riding up my thighs and then—

BAM! Gravity lurches the rickshaw, and I'm suddenly pressed up against his body, my face buried in his chest. I rocket upright so fast my spine cracks in three places.

These ancient cobblestone streets are determined to torture me. Every bounce sets my breasts jiggling. At this rate, a wardrobe malfunction is not a matter of if, but when. I cross my arms over my chest, praying he can't see how my nipples have hardened beneath the thin fabric.

Palazzo after palazzo blur past like a candy-colored fantasy, with mint-green shutters and sunflower-yellow walls. Unfortunately, I can't appreciate any of it because I am too focused on avoiding becoming a human pancake on the pavement from this seat belt-less rickshaw.

WHAM! Another bump. My binder flips open on my lap to reveal—please God no—my comprehensive guide to fake boyfriend touching zones, complete with anatomical diagrams.

"Approved physical contact zones, eh?" Matteo peers at the image, his breath tickling my ear. "Is this a chart of where I'm supposed to put my hands?"

I snap it shut. "It's a systematic approach to fake-relationship photography."

His arm drapes behind me. "What does your diagram say about this?"

SLAM! The rickshaw hits the Grand Canyon of potholes, and suddenly I'm sprawled halfway into his lap. Lord, even through his pants I can feel how hard he is. *His muscles, I mean. His muscles.*

"This is not in the chart," I manage to squeak out.

He firmly places his hand on my hip, his thumb tracing small circles, and my skin ignites beneath my sundress. "But what if I need to keep you steady?"

"I keep myself satisfied... Steady! Gah, you know what I'm saying!"

My voice reveals how flustered I am, which is embarrassing since I'm the queen of keeping things under control. Everything except my heart rate thanks to this infuriating Italian.

"Of course you do." His laugh rumbles through his chest. "Romance doesn't come with a planner, even if it's a fake one."

"Hate to break it to you, but I will not take organizational tips from someone who blows up his schedule every day."

I slide off his lap, reclaiming my side of the seat, but my skin still tingles. His scent—smooth vanilla and smoky leather—clings to me, rich and intoxicating. I frantically pull up Instagram on my phone.

Snap out of it, Katie. You are supposed to be using him to mess with Jared's head, not to start swooning over his... everything.

"I've strategically planned our photo opportunities for maximum impact. We have three important posts today. First, a casual shot at a fountain—it has to look spontaneous to introduce us as a couple. Then, during the cooking class, I'm thinking flour on the nose, maybe a playful food-fight moment? And finally, at sunset, you'll gaze at me and pretend I'm the most beautiful thing you've ever seen. I've analyzed the optimal angles—"

"Put the phone down." Matteo's warm hand covers my screen, his fingers dwarfing mine. "Katie, enjoy the beauty around you. I promise we'll get your photos later. I know the perfect spot."

"But my timeline—"

"Trust me." His voice softens with genuine enthusiasm. "Genoa isn't like Rome with its tourist traps and endless lines. Here you can *feel* the real Italy. You must not miss it. See this building in front of us? That is the Palazzo San Giorgio. Observe the beautiful Renaissance painting of Saint George slaying a dragon."

The fresco stretches across the palazzo's facade, colors impossibly vivid against the weathered stone. A dragon writhes beneath Saint George's spear, scales glinting like emeralds in the afternoon sun. It's breathtaking—captivating—in a way my phone camera could never capture. Still...

"A dragon?" I arch an eyebrow. "Really?"

"Legend says the dragon terrorized the city," Matteo explains with gusto. "Saint George slayed it on this very ground. Some say the dragon's bones were found in a cave not far from here."

"Let me guess—the bones mysteriously disappeared?"

"Mock all you want, but the legend lives on." His eyes dance with amusement. "Oh, and Marco Polo was imprisoned there."

"The explorer or the pool game?"

"Both. Tragic water sports accident. Very sad."

I snicker, then something flutters deep in my chest, like a trapped bird frantically beating its wings against my ribs. I watch Matteo's face come alive. The smooth-talking tour guide act disappears when he speaks about the city's treasures. His brown eyes spark with passion, which is doing dangerous things to my insides.

The realization slams into me like a cold shower: my body has never reacted to Jared this way. Six years of diligently nurturing our romance, not once did I experience this kind of electric spark.

How can Matteo light me up with only a look or accidental touch?

The rickshaw bounces again, and I grip the seat tighter. I try to admire the buildings around us, but I'm fixated on him—how his accent gets thicker when he's excited—how obscenely attractive he looks in that navy fitted shirt—how his hands would feel on my—

No. Control yourself. Focus on the mission!

Get photos. Make Jared jealous. Win him back.

Don't get sucked into Matteo's infectious joy. Ignore how his whole face transforms when he shares stories of his beloved Italy. Do not, I repeat do not, let it stir something inside you.

Matteo's voice trails off mid-sentence about some medieval scandal. *Oh shit.* He's caught me staring. His eyes become darkened storm clouds, but he clears his throat quickly. "The Palazzo Lomellino. Most tours skip it, but inside..." My view is blocked, but I see him shift and point to a building on his side. "There are secret gardens that feel frozen in time. Like stepping into another century."

Before I can veto this monumentally bad idea, I lean across him to get a glimpse of the palazzo—my hand pressing on his thigh. The building stands tall and proud like a wedding cake—all pastel blue and cream with carvings so intricate they must have been crafted by Renaissance angels. Cherubs and flowers dance across the facade, their delicate designs weaving a love letter to a bygone era.

I tilt my head back, following the ornate stonework up to where it meets the sky, marveling at how the palazzo's blue perfectly matches the heavens. The rickshaw keeps moving forward, and I'm not ready to lose sight of this architectural marvel. I turn my head to keep watching. I turn even farther, and—

Oh.

Oh.

My lips are a breath away from Matteo's, and every nerve ending in my body short-circuits at once. I'm stretched across him, my palm now firmly gripping his thigh. The reality of our position hits me. His eyes drop to my mouth—the lust in them could trigger a nuclear meltdown.

One tiny movement and we would—

I surge forward, crashing my mouth into his. His lips are impossibly soft, parting instantly for me. My head is a whirlwind. I push closer, hungry for more, craving more. He tastes like espresso and trouble and everything I've spent my whole life avoiding.

The first slide of his tongue against mine makes me gasp.

Matteo's rough exhale vibrates against my lips as he deepens the kiss. Some primal, unknown part of me takes over. My tongue strokes against his, demanding, exploring. The soft groan he makes ignites me, urging me on.

His tongue plunges hot and deep into my mouth, scraping against my teeth, and my brain completely whites out. No thoughts of Jared, no plans, no timelines. Just the overwhelming sensation of Matteo's mouth moving against mine.

His hand grips the back of my neck, fingers tangling in my hair. The slight tug sends a cascade of fireworks racing through me. I arch into him, begging for more. He responds by tilting my head and nipping at my bottom lip before beginning his tongue exploration all over again.

I have to get closer. Must feel more of him. My body moves on pure instinct, breasts pressing against his solid chest. The deep moan that rumbles through him makes me throb in places that I didn't know existed.

I want—no, need—to hear that sound again.

My fingers dive into his thick hair, gripping the strands while his mouth devours mine. I've never been this reckless, this out of control. This isn't me—I'm the girl who plans out her underwear choices a week in advance. The girl with a label-maker collection. I don't do reckless. I leave for the airport four hours early just to be safe. I don't *wing* it. I staple it, highlight it, and file it away.

His mouth finds a sensitive spot on my neck and he sucks hard. This embarrassing sound escapes me—half whimper, half plea. Something wild flashes in his eyes, turning them nearly black. His hand slides between us, cupping my breast through my sundress while his lips move to my ear. His finger dips beneath the fabric, rough and hot against my bare skin, and just as he brushes my hardened nipple—

We.

Have.

Stopped.

Moving.

Our rickshaw driver has paused mid-pedal and is shamelessly watching us through the rearview mirror, clearly enjoying the show.

I scramble backward so fast I nearly topple onto the street. Heat floods my face as I take in Matteo's thoroughly ravished appearance—hair wild from my fingers, lips pink and swollen, chest heaving with each breath. The intensity of his expression makes my insides clench all over again.

"Thank you for getting that eyelash out of my eye!" The words come out strangled and high-pitched. Before he can respond, I launch myself out of the still-stationary rickshaw, my legs shaking beneath me.

Shitshitshit.

What have I done? My lips are tender from his stubble, tingling with the ghost of his kiss. My skin burns everywhere he's touched, like he's branded me. I'm dizzy, and there's an ache between my thighs that has absolutely nothing to do with the rickshaw's bumpy ride.

This is meant to be a fake relationship. Not... whatever that just was.

I cannot want this. Cannot want him. He's merely a pawn in my master plan—a way to make Jared realize what he's lost. He's not supposed to make me feel things. Not supposed to kiss me like he's been craving it for eternity. Not supposed to have me forget why I flew all the way to Italy.

One kiss. One unplanned, impulsive, breath-stealing kiss and my world has shattered like a dropped wine glass.

CHAPTER NINE

MATTEO

MORNINGS ON REGULAR TOUR days are chaotic but on checkout days? Pure mayhem. I've been up since dawn, racing between the front desk and the breakfast room like a goddamn Ping-Pong ball. Thirty-two guests and their luggage is no joke.

If there's one universal truth about senior citizens on tour, it's that they will absolutely forget tI'm heir medications in hotel rooms. Every. Single. Time.

"Last call. Anyone missing chargers, pills, or"—I spot a denture case on the floor and pick it up—"chewing equipment?"

"Those are mine!" Chester, the resident jokester, calls out with a laugh. "First they escape, next they apply for a work visa."

The Hotel Miracolo isn't exactly the Four Seasons. Hell, it's not even a Travelodge. The floors creak, the wallpaper's seen better decades, and the elevator makes sounds that suggest it remembers World War II personally. But the place is clean, family run, and most importantly—cheap. This is how you operate a travel company when you're one transmission repair away from bankruptcy: hook them with the fancy Milan resort, then slowly transition them to places where rustic charm means the hot water's more of a suggestion.

By week two, my guests are too in love with Italy to notice where they sleep. They're living on pasta highs, chasing sunsets, and drowning in wine-soaked memories. After a decade at this job, I've learned no dodgy mattress can dampen the spirits of someone in a constant carb-induced coma. Plus, I get to support small business owners like myself.

Stepping into the breakfast lounge is a total time capsule—like traveling back to the sixties. Yellow walls faded with age, plastic flowers with decades-old dust, and hospital-worthy landscape photos. No one cares because everyone's attention is on the Italian comfort food—baskets of pastries, local cheeses, sliced meats, and some American cereals that look suspiciously expired. But the coffee? Perfetto! By day seven, that's all anyone needs.

Cazzo. I'm thinking about coffee again. And of course, that makes me think of *her*.

My mind basks in yesterday's rickshaw kiss. When Katie's lips met mine—with an intensity that matched my own—I couldn't control myself. She tasted like a blend of espresso and mints that left me dizzy and wanting more. Her mouth was hungry for me. Desire coursed through me like a shock wave; the sensation was fucking electric! When my fingers felt the warmth of her breast, it was all I could do not to—

"MATTEO! The toaster is on fire."

Merda! I sprint to where Agnes Dawson is performing an interpretive dance of panic around what is definitely not a fire, just charred toast with enough smoke to signal the Vatican.

I grab the blackened bread and, with a swift motion, toss it out the window. "And that, my friends, is how you send our little burnt friend off to toast heaven." I say, making the sign of the cross with a grin. "Might I suggest cereal? It's simple, tasty, and won't burn the place down."

Agnes nudges me with a playful elbow and pours herself a bowl of rainbow ring-shaped circles, basically giving her diabetes medication the middle finger.

My eyes dart around the room—no hint of Katie. She hasn't said a word since bolting from that rickshaw. She even skipped the pesto cooking class and dinner last night. Used jet lag as an excuse despite us being six days into the trip.

Some fake boyfriend I turned out to be—I couldn't make it one day without screwing everything up. Not a single photo was taken. One kiss and the whole charade imploded. Probably for the best. I'm simply no good at relationships, real or otherwise.

I shouldn't have lost control, but Cristo, I wasn't prepared for her heart-pounding, reality-bending lips! I've never experienced such sweet surrender. That kiss was like skydiving, realizing midair you forgot your parachute, then getting struck by lightning on the way down.

Exhilarating. Intense. Absolutely fucking unforgettable.

Must be because I was sober. Usually when I pick up tourists at bars, there's enough alcohol involved to make even Lorenzo's driving seem smooth. That's gotta be why it seemed so intense. Has to be.

But the sensation of her melting against me, that little moan she made when my tongue—

"Matteo! Is this cheese supposed to be this color?"

Right. Focus. One more week. I can't have Katie hiding in her hotel suite or flinching every time I speak. I've got to find her... Clear the air.

My no-tourist rule exists for a reason. One mind-blowing kiss won't change that.

"Sì, Mrs. Thomas, that's the normal color for aged pecorino. Think of those spots as cheese freckles."

I'm doing my morning head count when Katie walks in. A spark of excitement ripples through me, uninvited. I swear—it's getting out of hand.

She spots me and tries to escape. *Not today, principessa.*

"Running away so soon?" I call out. "I thought you would play nice after our little rickshaw... bonding."

She freezes mid-step, turning back with an authoritative scowl that dares me to argue. "I wasn't running. I was... strategically relocating."

"Attenzione!" I address the group before she can 'strategically relocate' herself out of the building. "Once everyone's finished with breakfast and bathroom breaks, Lorenzo's waiting with the bus. We're heading to Florence for Chester's wish to see Michelangelo's masterpiece—the original statue of David."

I keep Chester's second part of his wish to myself. That surprise is going to be either brilliant or a disaster. Knowing Chester, probably both.

"Join me?" I gesture to an empty table. "I promise to keep my hands where you can see them. Unless you prefer otherwise..."

She sits anyway, pointedly ignoring my smirk. "What I want is a time machine... to erase that mistake."

"Do you mean when you accidentally attacked my mouth? Very traumatic. My lips are still feeling vulnerable and afraid."

"I didn't—" Her cheeks flush that dangerous shade of pink. "Will you keep it down! We both know that rickshaw was bumpy and that gravity—"

"Gravity made you grab my hair and moan into my mouth?" I lean closer.

"I was trying to strangle you," she hisses, glancing around nervously. "And you kissed me back!"

"Self-defense. My lips were fighting off a very aggressive tourist."

Her eyes narrow. "Don't you have a rule about tourists in your groups?"

"Ah, yes." My phone nearly slips from my suddenly clumsy fingers. "Which is why I made plans. To prevent any more of your sneak attacks on my face. I, uh, mapped out some photo locations in Florence. For the fake-boyfriend thing."

I pull up screenshots of some incredible backdrops, then switch to my Notes app where I have the whole plan laid out. The schedule is über-organized *(especially for me)*, with detailed directions and the best times for natural light. *Yeah, I should have been sleeping instead of obsessing over how to get her to smile again, but here we are.*

She takes in the detailed planning. Her playful defensiveness melts away. "You made this? For me?"

"Couldn't sleep," I lie. "I know you like things organized, and after yesterday…"

"Matteo." The way she says my name makes my heart squeeze and my cock twitch all at once. She reaches for my phone, her fingers brushing mine as she studies the screen.

"No one has ever made a schedule for me before."

The vulnerability in her voice... I'm floored. For a moment, we're not the uptight American and the playboy tour guide.

Her finger traces delicately over my knuckles as she scrolls through the plans, and my entire body hums. The casual touch feels more intimate than any full-body contact I've ever had. My heart pounds against my ribs as if it's trying to escape.

This is dangerous. This is exactly what I can't let happen.

WHAM!

I shoot up from my chair so fast it crashes backward, making several seniors clutch their hearts.

"Right! So that's the schedule. Very scheduled. Much planning. I should—bathroom! Because you really don't want to use the one on the bus. Lorenzo's driving makes aiming impossible. Not that you need to aim, obviously, because you're a woman and you sit and—*Madre di Dio*, why am I still talking about pissing?"

My brain is screaming *shutupshutupshutup*, but my mouth keeps moving. "It's physics really. Motion and trajectory and—and I should... go... now."

Katie's lip is caught between her teeth like she's fighting hard not to laugh, but there's something else in her eyes. Something that makes me want to sit back down and see what other sounds I can draw from that smart mouth of hers.

Instead, I back away so fast I nearly take out Mrs. Thomas and her questionable cheese.

What is wrong with me?

I'm the guy who once convinced an entire bachelorette party I was a long-lost Italian prince. Why am I babbling about bathroom logistics because Miss Organized grazed my knuckles?

Dio mio. Is this a panic attack? Am I finally cracking under the pressure of managing my travel business? There can be no other explanation. This woman's not even my type.

I think I'm having a medical emergency.

***

AFTER A GRUELING THREE-HOUR bus ride from Genoa to Florence, I've come to three conclusions: (1) Lorenzo needs to invest in better deodorant; (2) stealing glances at Katie Crawford nine rows back feels as tragic as a middle school crush; and (3) my brain's officially on vacation and it's my dick that's running the show.

But I am determined to regain that control... starting now at the museum.

"And here we have one of the Galleria dell'Accademia di Firenze's finest examples of Renaissance artistry." I point to the massive painting before us.

The seniors crane their necks, eyes wide, taking in the oil canvas depicting saints draped in rich, jewel-toned robes—their faces serene in martyrdom. Our footsteps echo sharply off the polished marble floor. We pass rows of sculptures, each carved muscle frozen in time, alongside paintings so detailed they seem to breathe.

From every direction, saints stare down at us in judgment as if to say "You're headed straight for hell, sinner." Of course, it could just be my imagination—or guilt—since I'm struggling to keep my eyes *(and hands)* off another man's woman for more than thirty seconds.

Katie stretches up on her tiptoes to read the artwork description, that sundress doing unholy things to my concentration. The woman is taking notes with surgical precision in not one, not two, but six different museum guides.

The way she dives into each page with such laser focus, as if the little details are the most important things in the world and she wants to capture them all.

"If you need a better view," I murmur as I pass behind her, "I'd be happy to give you a lift. Though I should warn you about my wandering hands. Professional hazard."

"I'd rather use Alice's walker," she whispers back with a ghost of a smile.

"Documenting your fascination with me?"

"No, I'm gathering evidence for a refund."

"Ah, but my tours are priceless. Like that blush creeping up your neck."

She quickly flips to a new page but not before I spot her fighting another smile.

"And here," I announce to the group, maintaining my rhythm, "we have a masterpiece that's pure seduction of form and light. The artist captured intimate details with breathtaking precision, using the tempera technique—pigments blended with egg yolk. Think of it as the early Renaissance's version of Photoshop."

Katie's scribbling away, and I can't stop staring. Those delicate fingers wrapped around that pen turn even the act of note-taking into something inexplicably sensual. And when she brings that pen to her lips, lost in thought? *Fuck.* I've never been more jealous of an inanimate object in my life.

But it's not just her body that's got me tied up in knots; it's the way Katie Crawford organizes everything around her with such careful attention. After seven days of observing her, I'm learning her tells. Like how she taps her left foot when she's processing information. I've started to recognize her *problem-solving* face—lips pressed together, head tilted slightly, and that little crease between her brows that's always there because her brain never takes a break.

Her intensity is hypnotic. I'm finding it impossible not to be fascinated by her. She approaches each moment with the same unwavering determination, whether taking notes on Renaissance art or positioning her water bottle so the label faces perfectly forward. The world is one giant puzzle she's determined to solve.

Fanculo. I need to stop obsessing over her. Stop letting myself get caught up in the secrets behind those mesmerizing green eyes. Stop imagining how her soft, commanding hands would feel on my—

"Matteo!" Chester's voice cuts through my Katie-induced haze. "When do we get to see the giant naked guy?"

"Um... ah, yes. It's showtime, my friend."

Time to focus on someone else's dick instead of my own—Chester's wish!

I lead our group through the crowded halls of the Accademia, where Michelangelo's iconic statue of David is surrounded by a sea of selfie sticks and fanny packs. The crowd noise swells around us—a symphony of "Wow" in twelve different languages, incessant camera clicks, and at least five different tour guides trying to out-lecture each another.

"All right, my beautiful people, gather round," I say, gently maneuvering Chester to the front. "Before we admire David in all his marble glory, Chester has something to share about his Wish Card."

Chester straightens his I'M WITH STUPID T-shirt *(the arrow points up at his own face)* and clears his throat. "You know me—always cracking jokes, being the group clown." The usual mischief in his eyes dims. "But today I want to tell you about my Gladys."

I give Chester a comforting pat on his shoulder.

"This trip to Italy? It was her dream. She talked about it constantly—wanting to see the art, savor the food, experience it all." Chester's weathered hand presses against his heart. "She's still with me, right here. And let me tell you, she would've loved every single minute of this adventure with you all."

Katie edges closer, and I catch the shine of tears in her eyes.

"Gladys, she always laughed at my jokes," Chester continues. "Especially the bad ones. God, she had this snort-laugh that could wake the dead, but it was the most beautiful sound on the planet. Even when I told the same terrible pun for the thousandth time, she'd giggle like it was the first time she'd heard it."

I scan the group, and my seniors all wear the same glassy-eyed expression. Stan's arm tightens around Rose's shoulders. The Dawson sisters clutch hands. Even Aunt Deb has stopped making eyes at Howie long enough to dab her cheeks with a silk handkerchief.

I look at Katie again, and the longing on her face guts me. After that dickhead Jared left her, she still wants this soul-crushing kind of love. Can't she see? She's lucky to avoid wasting half her life before realizing love's cruel truth. Before the inevitable, that love always fucking ends in loss. Someone is left behind—left trying to solve an impossible problem—left to have their heart bleeding out for eternity.

Which is exactly why I have a system. My life, my way, my rules—it's all flings and early-bird exits because I'm not strong enough to survive the devastation of that kind of love. It hijacks your entire existence.

Chester surveys our group, his smile wobbling but genuine. "This trip—since I lost my Gladys—has been one of the best times of my life. Traveling with you guys, swapping stories, and getting to know your wonderful personalities has been more fun than I could've imagined. You've become more than just travel companions; you are my friends."

"Oh Chester..." Rose lifts a tissue to her tear-streaked face, sniffing softly.

"So folks, I've got a little request, and I hope you'll humor me." Chester's familiar grin starts to return. "I want to have a silly photoshoot right here with David. That's right! I want each of us to take the funniest, naughtiest pictures we can with the giant ol' naked guy. Then I plan to put them all together in a collage and print them on one of my famous wacky shirts. That way I'll always have this memory close to my heart."

He gestures toward the towering statue. "Because if Gladys *was* here, this is precisely what we'd be doing. She'd be pretending to pinch his marble behind while making me take twelve different angles. What do you say?"

"For Gladys!" The cry rings out from thirty voices, echoing off the gallery's vaulted ceiling. Even the security guard, who definitely doesn't speak English, raises his fist in solidarity.

What happens next can only be described as elderly anarchy.

I watch through my camera lens in embarrassment and awe as my *(mostly)* dignified seniors transform into a geriatric flash mob of statue harassers. Margaret Dawson moves with shocking speed for someone who complained about her hip all morning, practically parkouring into position behind David's marble assets.

"Time for some hands-on art appreciation!" she announces, throwing down her purse and striking a pose where it looks like she's grabbing David's ass and motorboating his butt cheeks.

"You're a supermodel!" Chester cheers her on as he directs the shot. "You've got the whole world in your hands."

"More like the whole moon," her sister Agnes cackles.

Mrs. Thomas adjusts her bifocals, peering at David's anatomy. "Do you think Michelangelo..." She pauses for dramatic effect. "Polished everything himself?"

SNAP.

The photo catches her holding her glasses up to David's marble goods as though she's appraising diamonds at Tiffany's.

"Our turn!" Deborah announces, yanking Howie forward. Together they form a heart shape with their hands around David's package like they're framing the world's most inappropriate Valentine. "You know what they say. A hard man is good to find!"

"Good thing you found me, sweet tea. Two blue pills and I'm ready twenty-four seven," Howie says with a wink.

Stan nods wisely from his spot next to Rose. "I remember being young—didn't need any pills—my little soldier was always eager to serve."

"Stanley!" Rose cuts him off with a scandalized giggle.

Chester guides Rose, our sweetest group member, into position. "Okay stand right here..."

She cups her hands beneath David's exposed bits like she's about to catch holy water. "Is this right, Chester? Should I offer some support? Poor thing's been standing here so long out in the cold..."

"Perfect! Now look surprised, like you just got an eyeful of what's under his fig leaf."

SNAP.

Pretty sure I'm going straight to hell for that shot.

The security officer appears to be having the same crisis I am, caught between professional duty and the infectious joy of seniors treating art like a Magic Mike show. Right when I think he's shutting us down, he purposely glances the other way.

Chester pulls a feather duster out of his bag and poses as if he's dusting off David's package.

SNAP.

He distributes fake mustaches to our crew, who eagerly hold them up for a group pic. Chester whips out an extra 'stache and holds it up to David, forcing him to be part of the fun.

And then—sweet mother of tortellini—Katie steps up.

"How's this angle?" She tilts her head so David's marble bits appear to rest on top of her head like she's getting teabagged and loving it.

My jaw drops as she crosses her eyes and contorts her face—sticking out her tongue to complete the goofy photo.

SNAP.

Chester wipes tears of laughter from his cheeks. "Gladys would have loved this."

"To Gladys!" The cry goes up again, and this time even the German tour guide joins in.

David stands stoically through it all, probably wondering what he did to deserve this particular form of immortality. Though I swear that marble face looks more amused than usual.

***

THE LATE-AFTERNOON SUN BATHES Florence's cobblestones in warm hues. The piazza bustles around us—tourists snap selfies, street performers strum lively tunes, and impatient locals weave skillfully through the crowd. Katie's oblivious, positioning my camera for the hundredth time while I try not to stare at the light dancing in her hair and turning it into sunlit silk.

These staged fake-boyfriend photos are killing me slowly. Not even the spectacular view of the Arno River can distract me from the torture of having Katie so close yet so far. Every careful pose she arranges screams "siblings on vacation" rather than "passionate Italian romance."

"A little to the left."

She adjusts the tripod, that sundress riding up her thighs, and my hands flex with the need to grab her hips. To yank her back against me and show her exactly how unbrotherly my thoughts are.

"The composition has to be perfect."

Perfetto. Like the way her ass fills out that dress. Like how her nipples would feel under my tongue. *Cristo, I need to get my shit together.*

Every pose has been crafted to look as platonic as humanly possible. Hand-holding that could pass a Pope's inspection. Side hugs with enough room between us for Jesus and the seven apostles.

"How's this?" She positions herself next to me, careful not to actually touch me. Her hand hovers over my chest as though she's afraid I might combust.

Which, fair enough. My body temperature has been running about twenty degrees above normal since that rickshaw kiss. And if I touch her, I'm scared I won't be able to control what unfolds.

CLICK.

I've snapped thousands of photos of people lost in the thrall of Italy. There's a world of difference between posed shots and genuine moments—the ones where people forget the camera's there.

Mamma taught me that. She never staged a shot, only captured unfiltered life. Those photos of her and Papa are reminders of that—their love, raw and real, preserved forever. They're also a brutal reminder of what I've lost.

"Set the timer," Katie orders. "Then hover your arm near my waist while we stare at the fountain."

Damn. Her strawberry fragrance consumes me. I'm going to need a dozen cold showers to scrub her scent away, and even then, I'll be stroking myself raw to get her out of my system.

CLICK.

She rushes to check the screen. "Will this make Jared jealous?"

His name hits me like a sucker punch, reminding me exactly what this is. And what this isn't. I'm the stand-in. The prop. The guy teaching another man's woman how to make him burn with desire. The thought makes me want to put my fist through a wall.

Whenever she says his name, something deep inside me snarls. Because he gets to have her—really have her—while I'm here playing pretend. My body screams at me to corner her like an animal and kiss her until she forgets that anyone else exists.

She's not yours. She'll never be yours.

"No." My voice comes out harsh. "That wouldn't make a dead man jealous."

Frustration flashes in her green gaze. "Then show me what would."

Dio mi aiuti. I'm about to do something monumentally stupid.

"I'll have to actually touch you."

Her tongue darts out, wetting those lips I'm not allowed to sample. "Okay."

I set the camera to burst mode *(I can relate)*, hands trembling. "Now don't think. Just feel."

I act on impulse, grabbing her ass under her dress and lifting her against me. My hands grasp her firmly, and hell, she's wearing sensible cotton panties just as I thought. The confirmation only intensifies my urge to rip them off with my teeth and taste her.

The surprised gasp she lets out shoots straight to my cock, making me throb so hard I see spots.

I lift her higher until she's peering down at me, her hair falling around us like a golden curtain. Her arms wrap around my neck and Cristo, the look in her eyes. She wants to devour me whole. I think she'd let me devour her right back.

Her breasts press into my chest with each breath, and I'm dying to cross that line. But I can't. I *won't*. Because she belongs to him even if he doesn't deserve her.

Katie stills in my arms, uncertain. I see the moment guilt creeps into her face. She's loyal to a man who threw her away, and it pulls at me—makes me yearn more for her. I'm driven to understand this woman who loves so deeply and gives of herself so completely.

A tiny moan escapes her lips as my fingers dig into the soft flesh of her thighs, and what's left of my control shatters.

"Tell me you want my mouth on yours, principessa."

"I—" She trembles against me. "Everything in me wants... you to keep touching me."

That breathy confession is a torpedo to my restraint.

I slide one finger along her center, feeling the dampness through the cotton. "Cazzo, you're soaked." My cock throbs against my zipper. "Say that's for me."

She doesn't answer, but how she arches against my hand reveals her body wants this—wants me. But not her heart. It's already spoken for.

With strength I didn't know I possessed, I set her down. Every cell in my body protests, demanding I pull her back, fuck her right here against the fountain until Jared fades into oblivion. But I'm not the kind of asshole who takes what isn't freely given.

"That should get his attention," I manage to say, voice wrecked.

I turn before she's able to see how much this is killing me. But not before I see her face is flushed, chest heaving.

CHAPTER TEN

KATIE

Group Chat: CPK Forever

Petra: *Those fountain photos are fire.*

Petra: *If you're not letting Tour Guide Hottie re-arrange your organs, I'm disowning you.*

Cam: *The way he's looking at you!*

Cam: *Even my boss's staged "romance" shots for YouTube aren't that hot.*

Me: *It's not like that! He's just helping with Operation Win Back Jared.*

Petra: *Quick poll: Who'd give better orgasms?*

Me: *I'm instituting a new rule about inappropriate polls in group chats.*

Petra: *The fact you haven't immediately defended Jared's honor tells me everything.*

Cam: *GET IT GIRL!*

Me: *I'm muting this chat.*

Cam: *No you're not. You love us.*

Petra: Trust me—one night with an Italian and you'll forget Jared ever existed.

Petra: Your vagina will thank you later... Possibly in multiple languages.

DEAR GOD, I'M GOING to die.

Not in the good way, not because of the dreamy Tuscan landscape rolling past my greasy window. And not due to the madness of this rickety tour bus. And not even because of the shouting senior citizens who forgot their hearing aids.

I'm going to die because I'm trapped in a bus with a man who's intimately familiar with my eagerness-soaked panties, but is now acting like I'm invisible.

I won't let my thoughts wander there. Not a chance. I refuse to relive how his fingers felt outlining my entrance over my underwear, unveiling just how much my hoo-ha was on board. How my nipples tightened, crushed against his chest while every single nerve ending in my body screamed, *Yes. Please. More. NOW!*

I smooth my floral dress over my thighs for the twentieth time, not thinking about how I skipped over my sensible walking slacks this morning. The ones I'd already laid out. The ones that were the obvious choice for a day of wine tasting and touring vineyards.

But no. Here I sit in this breezy little sundress that keeps sliding up my thighs every time the bus hits a bump. I tell myself it's for the Instagram aesthetic. Just innocent photo ops. Not because I'm hoping for a repeat of yesterday. The ache between my thighs grows more intense, and electricity zips through my body as I recall how I was climbing for release in his arms. I swear a few more strokes of his finger and I would have had an orgasm. *Which is crazy. Right?*

I can't let myself climax for another man... and in public no less? I can't do that. It's not me.

Not that Jared ever... well. Why can't I recall a single time when Jared made me climax.

Another pothole sends my water bottle soaring. It lands, rolls forward, and stops directly at Matteo's feet. Without looking back, he picks it up and passes it to Mrs. Thomas. Who then returns it to me like I'm carrying the plague.

The bus sputters around another curve, and I start a new list.

Reasons I Need to Stop Fantasizing About Matteo Monti:

1. His touch turns my brain into sparkly mush.

2. His accent that does illegal things to my ovaries.

3. His smile makes me forget how to breathe *(this is very impractical)*.

4. That growly Italian thing he does makes me forget my own name.

5. The way he kisses me like he wants to devour me whole.

6. His stupid rule has made it very clear that I'm off-limits.

7. His chaos must be contagious because I can't think straight.

8. I'm supposed to be winning back Jared.

I underline that last one three times, just as Lorenzo slams on the brakes, sending my pen skittering under the seat. When I reach for it, I catch Matteo watching me in the overhead mirror.

The look in his eyes makes me forget every single item on my list.

Jared. Think about Jared.

I drag my attention back to my plan, my mission to make my ex realize what he's missing. I refresh my Instagram feed again—hopeless.

Either Jared hasn't seen these photos of me draped over six feet of pure Italian temptation, or worse... he has and doesn't give a damn.

The bus coughs and hacks as we climb the hill, and I'm totally hypnotized by the way Matteo's forearms flex while he holds on to the overhead bar.

"These hills"—Matteo's voice carries through the speakers—"were carved by centuries of— LORENZO! Both hands on the wheel!"

Our driver reluctantly abandons his quest for the elusive diamond in his nose, and the bus swerves slightly.

HOOOOOONK!

Like everyone else on the bus, I twist around in my seat to look out the back window. A sleek red Ferrari is practically dry humping our exhaust pipe, close enough that I can see the driver's styled hair and red Gucci track suit. *Really dude?* Who coordinates their clothes with their car? A douchebag, that's who.

It seems our bus's turtle-like pace is a personal affront to Mr. Midlife Crisis in his red Ferrari, because he's pounding on his horn like a serial masturbator. After years of LA traffic, this barely registers on my road-rage radar, but our bus full of senior citizens are not having it.

"The nerve of some people!" Margaret Dawson shouts like he can hear her.

The hill steepens, the hairpin turn mocks us from up ahead, looking more treacherous by the second. Our ancient bus wheezes with an ungodly sound... like a chain-smoking grandfather at mile twenty-six of a marathon.

Lorenzo rolls down his window, flips him the laziest bird I've ever seen, and motions the Ferrari to pass. The instant the red car starts to pull out— *Oh God*. A yellow Fiat comes screaming around the corner ahead.

The Ferrari swerves back behind us—just in time—his enraged horn blaring. Our bus belts out a dying groan, really selling the drama, before the engine calls it quits.

For a suspended moment, we're frozen in time. Then gravity remembers it has one job.

We start rolling backward.

"LORENZO! Do something!"

Matteo's shout is barely heard as the screams of the elderly tourists fill the bus. We're rolling back down the hill and picking up speed.

Lorenzo just grunts and takes his hands completely off the wheel in the most dramatic "not my problem" gesture I've ever witnessed.

"Porca miseria!" Matteo lunges for the emergency brake, his muscles straining against his shirt as he yanks it with all his strength. The metal screams in protest.

SCREECH!

The bus jerks to a stop so hard that my belongings—purse, water bottle, binder—each pick a different direction to launch in and I'm suddenly airborne. I catch a glimpse of Matteo's panicked face before I tumble into the aisle, my sundress giving everyone a show.

When the dust settles, I'm flat on my back, staring at the ceiling as a sharp pain radiates through my chest, each heartbeat pounding like a sledgehammer. My whole body is trembling with leftover adrenaline.

HONK! HONK!

I hear the Ferrari zoom past without even slowing down. If I wasn't currently sprawled on this sticky bus floor contemplating my mortality, I'd be more offended by the lack of human decency.

"Everyone okay?" Matteo calls out, doing a quick head count.

A chorus of groans answers him as my fellow passengers untangle themselves from various positions. Somehow, our geriatric crew seems completely unfazed by our near-death experience. They're already cracking jokes like, "We've got more fun to have" and "Death will have to wait."

"Everyone out!" Matteo orders as smoke starts billowing from under the hood. "Into the field, per favore."

We step out onto a breathtaking Tuscan hillside, one that would make any Instagram influencer weep with jealousy. The grass tickles my legs as I pick my way through wildflowers, trying not to dwell on the fact that bugs are likely conspiring to nibble on my bare thighs.

"Emergency yoga time!" Aunt Deb announces, whipping off her designer sandals. "Nothing releases tension like stretching. Especially..." She waggles her eyebrows at Howie. "...the kind of stretching that requires a partner."

"Deb darlin', my new hip is ready whenever you are," Howie drawls.

I gag a little in my mouth.

Meanwhile, Matteo and Lorenzo are having the world's most fascinating nonverbal conversation by the smoking bus. Lorenzo responds entirely in facial expressions that range from "mildly constipated" to "deeply constipated."

"How bad?" Matteo asks.

Lorenzo grunts. "L'autobus è..." Shoulder shrug.

Behind me, Aunt Deb's voice carries across the field. "Now everyone, assume the position of the Lustful Leopard. Howie, demonstrate with me!"

Oh God.

Chester's voice rises from somewhere in the grass. "Is this position supposed to make my artificial knee sound like a popcorn machine?"

"Actually, that was my back." Stan adds with a chuckle.

I continue to try to focus on decoding the Matteo-Lorenzo show, but it's like watching a foreign film without subtitles. From what I can gather from their cryptic exchange, we're definitely stranded, and this bus is ready for its last rites.

Lorenzo makes a sound like a deflating tire and throws his hands up in what I'm learning is his signature move.

"Can I help?" I step forward. "I'm an event coordinator. Crisis management is literally what I do for a living."

Matteo's immediate "No" feels like a slap, but I press on, trying not to notice how his sweat-dampened shirt clings to his chest.

How big his hands are as they run through his hair.

How sexy he looks with that frustrated, furrowed brow.

Or how the sweat glistening down his neck makes my nipples stand at attention.

"Please?" I fidget with my phone. "I like feeling useful. And right now I'm just standing here watching Aunt Deb teach what she claims is yoga but looks suspiciously like moves from her exotic dancing days."

Matteo studies me for a moment. "Event coordinator?" His lips quirk up. "Like retirement parties and baby showers?"

"Try celebrity product launches and multimillion-dollar weddings." I lift my chin. "Last month I coordinated a Sweet Sixteen that had more security than the president."

"That actually explains so much about you."

"I'm choosing to take that as a compliment."

He chuckles, and then it turns into a full-blown laugh—low and rich and wonderful—a tidal wave to my soul. "It's a compliment for sure, principessa. You intrigue me. Your attention to detail is..." He trails off, his gaze dropping to my mouth before he looks away.

I'm processing the sudden shift in his expression, when the obnoxious roar of a massive red Italy Express bus barrels past, leaving a trail of exhaust and smugness in its wake. It makes its intentions clear of not helping by speeding up a little. Matteo's jaw tightens. And then... he explodes.

"*Cazzo! Che cavolo fanno, quei pezzi di merda arroganti!*" The Italian flows like an angry symphony, and I pretty much know *what* he's saying by *how* he's saying it. Especially that enraged middle finger.

If I thought he was stressed before, the tension radiating off him now could fuel a nuclear reactor.

A yelp from behind us is followed by "Don't worry! My new knee pops right back into place."

Matteo glances over my shoulder and winces. "Dio mio."

"Let me help," I say again.

"We're headed to my friend Enrico's winery, but after..." He glances at the smoking bus. "We won't make it to tonight's destination. I need to think about the Wish Cards, find a town with the right mechanic..."

I watch, fascinated, as he mentally sorts through options. His mind is racing, calculating, and something warm unfurls in my chest as I realize something. He's got every single wish memorized. This isn't just a job—he genuinely cares about making these seniors' dreams come true.

"Lorenzo," he says suddenly. "La Spezia?"

The old man performs what I'm starting to recognize as his yes shrug.

"La Spezia," Matteo tells me. "Eighteen rooms. Double beds. I'll handle the negotiating once you find somewhere."

"I can negotiate."

Matteo's voice drops low. "But can you do it in Italian?"

"I'm full of surprises." The words come out flirtier than intended.

"That I don't doubt," he says with a wink. "It doesn't need to be perfect, principessa. Just functional."

His casual dismissal of perfection hits differently than when others say it. There's no judgment in his voice, no expectations of flawlessness. Just... space to be myself.

But I don't have time to analyze why his acceptance makes my chest feel tight. We've got a crisis to handle.

After forty-five minutes of rapid-fire phone calls, my event-planner skills pay off. I find a hotel in La Spezia that not only has enough rooms for our entire crew but also working bathrooms *(crucial)*, complimentary breakfast *(score)*, and only two blocks away from the mechanic Matteo found *(lifesaving)*. My fingers are still smoking from how fast I've been typing notes and room configurations into my phone.

The rush of solving an impossible problem? Better than sex.

Well, better than any sex I've ever had.

The clip-clop of hooves pulls me from my list-making trance. Two enormous horse-drawn carriages appear over the crest of the hill, their wooden wheels crunching a rhythm against the gravel road. They look like they've rolled straight out of a fairy tale, all gleaming cherrywood and polished brass. The back sections are fitted with curved benches upholstered in leather, arranged in tiers so everyone can see.

"Matteo, you stubborn *cretino!*"

A man who could be a Roman statue come to life hops down from the lead carriage. He's tall and broad-shouldered with sun-kissed olive skin. His simple black shirt is rolled up at the sleeves, overalls splattered with dirt, and hands calloused from hard work. And his smile? It could outshine the Tuscan sun.

"Enrico, *mio fratello!*"

They collide in one of those aggressively affectionate man-hugs that involves way too much back-slapping. Enrico says something in rapid-fire Italian that has Matteo laughing with his whole body. I've never seen him like this—guard completely down, no smooth tour guide persona in sight.

"Your luck, she finally run dry, eh?" Enrico says, gesturing at our smoking bus. "First transmission go boom, now this?"

Something dark crosses Matteo's face—there and gone like a camera flash. "Not yet, amico. But days like this..." He shrugs, leaving the sentence hanging like the smoke still curling from our bus's hood.

"Amore. Wait!" Enrico suddenly shouts, his voice jumping two octaves. "You wait for help!"

A strikingly gorgeous woman, who could easily be mistaken for an Italian movie star, carefully steps down from the second carriage. One hand supports her very pregnant belly while the other grips the rail. She's petite but fierce with honey-gold skin and waves of dark hair cascading past her shoulders. Her dress stretches over her bump, and she looks more elegant than I do on my best day.

"Enrico," she says in accented English, "if you treat me like fragile bambina one more time—"

"Caterina." Matteo smoothly steps in to help. "Still haven't told him the bambino is mine?"

She lands a playful smack on his arm before kissing his cheek. "Keep joking, I tell him is true. Then you deal with crazy husband, sì?"

"The hormones!" Enrico's eyes go comically wide as he gestures behind his wife's back. "They make her..." He mimes what appears to be a brain explosion. "Is no joke."

"Like sleeping with grapes, amore?" Caterina's sweet smile promises murder. "That also no joke."

"Everyone"—Matteo's voice carries across the field—"meet Enrico and Caterina, owners of the best vineyard in all of Tuscany, La Dolce Vite—The Sweet Life. They're going to rescue us with some proper Italian hospitality."

"Ah!" Enrico's eyes land on me with delighted interest. "This must be your *fidanzata,* sì?"

Caterina translates with a knowing smile: "He asks if you are Matteo's girlfriend? If our wild boy has at last been tamed?"

"No!" Matteo and I yelp simultaneously.

"We're not—" I stammer.

"She's just a—" Matteo starts.

"Tourist!" I blurt.

"Temporary!" he adds.

"Purely professional."

"Completely platonic."

"Ah yes," Caterina's eyes dance with amusement. "This is why you both turn red like *pomodoro*? Because is so... how you say... platonic?"

Can I just vanish into this field and let the bugs eat me alive? Anything to avoid this humiliation.

Matteo rubs the back of his neck awkwardly. "Katie, I hate to ask, but could you work your event-planning magic with the group? I need to wait for the tow truck and then handle the hotel check-in. I promise we'll get your photos later—the vineyard at sunset is bellissimo."

The fact that he remembers about my pictures—that he's thinking about me when he's clearly stressed about fifty other things catches me off guard.

"Of course." I try to ignore how my stomach drops at the thought of him leaving. "Any special instructions?"

He rattles them off: "Mrs. Thomas needs hourly glucose check reminders. The Dawson sisters turn into wine vampires after two glasses. Chester's got a new knee—watch the stairs. And Stan needs bathroom breaks hourly but won't ask—Rose will signal by adjusting her hat."

A warm sensation flutters through me as I realize how well he knows them all. Every quirk, every need. I was so wrong about him. Behind that flirty facade and those ridiculous pickup lines beats the heart of someone who knows every single one of his tourists like family.

"Wait—" He pulls out his phone just as Enrico starts herding seniors into the carriages. "We should exchange numbers. For emergencies."

"Only emergencies?" I raise an eyebrow and offer him my phone.

He types. "Unless you can't resist texting me about how devastatingly handsome I am." That deadly smirk returns. "How much you miss my accent. My charm. My—"

"Your modesty?" I grab my phone back, glancing at the screen. "Really? You put your contact name as Italian Stallion with an eggplant emoji?"

"Just stating facts, bella."

The restless horses stamp impatiently. I climb into the carriage, suddenly very aware of Matteo's eyes on me. I glance back just once to see him staring, looking somehow both lost and determined. He grows smaller as the carriages pull away, standing next to our sad, smoking bus like some kind of gorgeous Italian action hero.

My phone buzzes.

Italian Stallion: *I saw the single tear in your eye. It's okay to miss me.*

I won't admit to him, but I already do.

***

THE TUSCAN SUN BEATS down on my head as I try *(and fail)* not to check my phone for the eighty-seventh time in the past hour. Not that anyone's counting. Except me. Because apparently I count everything now, including the minutes since Matteo disappeared with our smoking bus.

"Observe," Enrico commands, his calloused hands surprisingly gentle on the Sangiovese grapes. "In two months, these will become pure Italian magic. Like my bambino, and my wife, they cannot be rushed." He pauses, then smirks. "Our Famiglia Passione Rosso, it isn't just wine. It's legacy in a bottle. And legacy takes time."

Workers move through the vineyard like a well-choreographed dance, checking leaves and adjusting vines. The late-June heat shimmers off the hills, making everything look like a mirage. This can't be real.

"See how we trim?" Enrico demonstrates with careful precision. "Make room for air, for sun. Like relationship—need space to grow, sì?" He chuckles at his own metaphor.

I hang back from the group, pretending to take notes but actually watching the fascinating mix of people working the vines. Some speak rapid-fire Italian, others definitely sound American, and I'm pretty sure that guy over there just said *crikey*.

"You like?" Caterina appears beside me, both hands supporting her very pregnant belly. "The vineyard, she is beautiful, no?"

"Yes, very. The workers—they're from everywhere?"

"Ah, sì! Our volunteers." She waves at a group of twentysomethings hauling equipment. "They stay in dormitory, work the farm, learn real Italy. Not tourist Italy."

I watch the workers laugh together, their joy as obvious as their suntanned skin and dirt-stained clothes. "So they just... stay here? Work here?"

"One month, three months. We give them home, food, family. They learn Italian, travel on days off." She pats her belly. "Some never leave. Like me."

"I have a friend who did that," I say, thinking of Petra's fearless journey. "She traveled all around Europe, staying in places like this, trading work for room and board." My throat tightens with a mix of admiration and envy. "She's the brave one. I could never take on that kind of adventure."

"Ah, many young people find themselves here." Caterina settles onto a wooden bench, fanning herself. "Some running from something, some running to something. All find what they need."

I snap a quick photo of the sun-drenched vines and send it to Petra.

Me: Hey, I'm at one of those volunteer places you told me about.

Petra: Well, well, well... looking to ditch your binders and run away like I did? I know a great tattoo artist in Florence.

Me: No! Just... realizing how brave you were to actually do it. To leave everything behind.

Petra: Stop. You're making me feel things. I'm trying to look badass in my new corporate hell.

Petra: Wait, which vineyard did you stumble into? Need to make sure you're getting properly corrupted.

Me: La Dolce Vite.

Petra: FUCK ME SIDEWAYS. YOU'RE AT ENRICO'S?!!

Me: for reals?

Petra: I SWEAR TO GOD IF YOU'RE MESSING WITH ME, CRAWFORD. THAT'S MY FUCKING ITALIAN FAMILY.

Me: You're kidding.

Petra: Tell Caterina her favorite delinquent says hi. Oh, and ask Enrico about the time he tried to make "drunk chicken racing" a thing.

Me: You're not kidding?

Petra: See if he still smells like burnt feathers.

I pull up a photo of Petra and show it to Caterina. "Do you know—"

"Petra!" Caterina claps her hands together. "Our beautiful wild heart! So strong, so sad when she come to us. But this place?" She gestures to the endless vines. "It heal broken hearts."

I'm imagining Petra as I watch the volunteers, their faces alive with laughter. They seem so unburdened, so liberated. That kind of freedom terrifies me. My mind drifts to Petra's stories when she dropped out of college and chose the unknown path. I'd judged her for running away, but now I understand—she wasn't running from something.

She was running toward herself.

Meanwhile, what was I doing? Creating a PowerPoint on how Jared and I could align our fiber intake—charting our future children's college careers—designing a blueprint for the perfect life, as if list-making and ticking off boxes earned me the right to be loved.

I've invested six years into becoming Perfect Katie. The girlfriend who never made waves, the fiancée who knew what Jared needed before he did, the future wife who planned for every contingency.

And he still left.

Out here, where the vines grow wild and the air tastes like possibility, there are no schedules. No plans. No need to control every heartbeat, every breath, every moment. Just... living.

The opposite of who I've been.

The realization steals my breath. What if this whole *Operation Win Back Jared* thing isn't about him at all? What if it's about the one person I've been afraid to face?

Me.

Oh fuck. I'm going to need more wine.

My phone buzzes, and Matteo's name lights up my screen.

Italian Stallion: *Hotel secured. Missing your organizational skills. And your face.*

Italian Stallion: *Definitely your face.*

Pure need crashes through me, hot and demanding. Seeing his words makes me throb, remembering how his fingers felt against me in that fountain square. How he found places that made me gasp—writhe—forget everything. Everything except the craving for more.

I've never felt this before. Not once in twenty-five years of living. Not in six years with Jared. Never felt my body surge toward release like it did with just a few strokes of Matteo's skilled fingers. Never knew pleasure could build so fast—feel so intense.

What would it feel like to let him finish what he started?

Everyone else seems to know the secret. They dive into desire like it's a perfectly temperature-controlled pool while I'm here awkwardly checking the pH balance.

My fingers shake as I type. For once, I want to be reckless. I want something that makes my heart race, my skin buzz, and shuts down my brain's habitual reruns of worst-case scenarios.

Me: *Better hurry back. The vineyard isn't the same without someone making inappropriate grape innuendos.*

Italian Stallion: *Careful, principessa. Keep talking like that and I'll think you want me to be inappropriate.*

Me: *Maybe I do.*

I hit *Send* before I can overthink it.

For the first time in my life, I want to be the woman who takes what she wants.

Now I just need to make him break his rule.

CHAPTER ELEVEN

KATIE

CAN WE GET TO the part where I climax? The buildup is killing me.

This is what my life has come to—sitting at a gorgeous Italian dinner party thinking about orgasms. Not just any orgasms. Specifically the kind I want Matteo Monti to give me. Repeatedly. In various positions. Preferably while speaking Italian.

I should be soaking up every magical detail of Enrico and Caterina's backyard, not daydreaming about my tour guide returning and whispering naughty promises against my neck.

I force myself to pay attention, like a good event planner should. String lights crisscross overhead, creating a constellation of tiny stars. Rustic wooden tables stretch out endlessly, covered in linens so white they're judging my impure thoughts. Weathered wine barrels serve double duty as cocktail stations, complete with mason jars filled with flickering candles.

Even the setting sun feels like foreplay, caressing the vineyard with fingers of gold that make me think of other kinds of touching. The air is thick with the aroma of enough Italian food to feed a small army. Platters of handmade pasta glisten with olive oil, and fresh herbs have been scattered on the tables like edible confetti.

The vineyard workers and seniors have merged into one big, happy, wine-soaked family—sharing stories between bites of pecorino and prosciutto. Mrs. Thomas is glowing as she chats with a volunteer from her hometown in Michigan. "Your grandmother owns Romano's Deli? I eat there every Sunday after church!"

I wonder how these tablecloths would feel against my back if he took me right here?

Oh yeah, gone is Katie Crawford, Professional Event Planner Who Has Her Shit Together.

My brain keeps glitching to one thought:

MatteoMatteoMatteoMatteo.

And then he appears.

My muscles tighten, anticipation prickling across my skin as he approaches our table. His hair is still damp from a shower, curling at the edges in a way that makes my fingers ache to grip it. To pull it. To use it to guide his mouth to mine.

Jesus. When did I become this person?

His thigh brushes mine as he sits, and the contact makes a flush spread over my skin while my knees press together instinctively.

"Miss me, principessa?"

I dig my nails into my palms to keep from launching myself into his lap. "Like a paper cut."

Lie.

My lady parts missed him like wine misses cheese. Like pasta misses sauce.

Minutes tick by, and the dinner conversation flows around me in Italian. I can barely pay attention as I'm consumed by every whisper of contact between our bodies. When he reaches for the wine, his forearm touches mine. My body speaks up. *Everyone, stay calm. This is not a drill! Let's not mess this up.*

"English!" Caterina scolds. "Or Katie think we plot her murder, yes?"

I force a laugh, like I haven't been plotting exactly how to get Matteo alone and naked for the past hour. "Murder really would mess up my schedule tomorrow."

"Always so organized," Matteo says, his breath hitting my ear.

"Katie!" Enrico's face lights up. "Has Matteo told you about the time he steal my father's tractor?"

"Dio mio." Matteo drops his head into his hands. "Not this story. I was fifteen!"

"Picture this!" Enrico waves his hands. "Mr. Suave Matteo, trying to impress beautiful Valentina Bellini. He steals Papa's tractor—"

"Borrowed," Matteo says.

"—Steals Papa's tractor," Enrico continues louder, "thinking he will show off his farming skills. Instead—" He dissolves into laughter so hard he starts hiccuping. "Instead, he takes out three rows of century-old vines! Crashes into irrigation system! Creates mud geyser!"

I sneakily kick off my sandal under the tablecloth, becoming full-on seduction ninja. My toes find his ankle, and Matteo's body stiffens. *Challenge accepted.*

"Everything okay?" I ask sweetly. "You seem tense."

"Perfect," he grits out, then turns to Enrico. "But it wasn't like that—"

"Papa finds him," Enrico wheezes, "covered head to toe in mud, trying to push two-ton tractor out of ditch! Looking like swamp monster!"

"That's a very creative interpretation of events," Matteo says with forced calm, right as my foot slides up his calf. His knee jerks so hard it rattles the wine glasses.

Caterina shuffles forward in her chair, eyes gleaming. "These stories, I never hear! Was my Enrico such troublemaker too?"

"Me?" Enrico places his hand over his heart. "I was perfect angel!"

"If Lucifer had a twin." Matteo snorts, shifting subtly as my toes dance higher.

I take a slow sip of wine, locking eyes with him over the rim. "Let me guess—you were out there hitting on the locals with lines like, 'Ciao bella, are you Tuscany? Because I'd like to explore your rolling hills.'"

"They worked then, and they work now," he boasts with that smirk that does indeed make my lady parts tingle.

Time to step it up. Tonight I am not a woman with plans. I'm acting on instinct—embracing the unknown.

I let my hand wander under the tablecloth, settling firmly on Matteo's thigh. He spits out his wine, coughing and spluttering. I trace slow, teasing circles higher up his leg, enjoying the way his breath hitches.

Oh, he's flustered! The always-confident Matteo Monti is actually flustered—and I'm the reason. The power of it surges through me, and I press my fingers against him just a little firmer, relishing in his tension.

"The wine is excellent," I say innocently. "So firm—I mean, full-bodied."

Matteo's ears turn pink. "Speaking of bodies—*bottles*. Good thing your parents never found out about the wine cellar incident—"

My fingers creep up Matteo's thigh, and when his muscles twitch beneath my touch, it sends fresh heat pooling between my legs.

"Now that story I've heard." Caterina pats her belly meaningfully. "Because of you two, I hope we have a girl."

I avoid eye contact with him while I let my fingers explore the outline of his erection, and oh my God—he's rock-hard and so massive I'm like, *did he smuggle a baseball bat in there?*

"So what did Matteo's parents do?" I ask innocently. "When they caught him being such a troublemaker?"

The table goes silent. Enrico and Caterina exchange a knowing look. Something dark crosses Matteo's face, and I feel it. I've stumbled into forbidden territory.

I start to lift my hand off his leg, but Matteo swiftly grabs it, secretly interlocking our fingers together.

"My parents..." Matteo's voice carries an edge I've never heard before. "They knew to expect nothing but trouble from me."

"So the bus?" Enrico shouts, cutting through the tension. "How is our smoking beauty, eh?"

"Got a rental shuttle," Matteo says, his confident charm returning. "Mechanic thinks he can save her. Hotel worked out though—thanks to Katie's organizational superpowers."

My heart *(and other parts)* flutter at his praise. Seriously, I'm pretty sure they're performing a fully choreographed routine down there. Never in my life has being called "organized" turned me on so much.

"If you'll excuse us." Matteo's thumb strokes the pulse point on my wrist, and I want to whimper. "I promised Katie some photos before we lose the light completely."

He stands, and the loss of his touch is agony. I want those hands back on me, pronto.

"Are you sure?" I ask, my voice breathy. "The sun's almost set..."

"Trust me. I know how to work in low light."

The promise in his voice makes me clench. There's nothing professional in the way he's looking at me now. Nothing tour guide appropriate about the hunger I see in his expression.

Please don't let him be talking about actual photography. Please let "work in low light" be code for "push Katie into the shadows and make her forget her own damn name."

Please, oh please, let it be code for that.

***

MATTEO

I DON'T KNOW WHERE I'm going, only that I need to get away before I lose what control I have left.

My dick is so hard it could drill through concrete, thanks to Katie Crawford's teasing fingers. What the fuck is she doing to me? My pulse pounds in my ears, and every step away from that table feels like a battle I'm barely winning.

I need to walk this fire off. Away from the torture of watching her lips wrap around her wine glass while pretending I wasn't imagining those same lips wrapped around my cock.

"Matteo!" Her voice slices through the vineyard.

Don't turn around. Don't look at her.

"Slow down!" Katie's sandals click against the stone path. "Where are you going?"

I round the corner of the villa where the ancient vines cling to the walls. My feet betray me, halting mid-step. I spin around so fast she crashes into my chest with a surprised gasp. The contact is brief before she stumbles back, but it's enough to make my body roar to life.

Her scent overwhelms me—strawberries, always strawberries—wrapping around my senses like a silken noose. I drink her in: tousled hair wild from her sprint, cheeks flushed with heat, and those lips parted like she's daring me to close the distance. Her dress dances along her thighs in the evening breeze, taunting me. Testing me.

Madonna santa, I want her. The weight of it terrifies me.

"What's gotten into you tonight, principessa?" My voice is low, edged with frustration.

"Hopefully you." The words slip out before her eyes go wide and she claps her hand over her mouth.

Sweet fucking torture.

"Is this about Jared?" I grind out his name.

"No."

"Cristo, what was that back there, Katie? Another calculated move in your grand plan." I gesture toward my cock, which strains against my zipper like it's trying to break free and run to her. "Seduce the tour guide to get back at your ex? Because if that's your goal—*congratulazioni*. You succeeded."

She bites that full bottom lip like she always does when she's trying to stay in control. *Scopami*, I want to taste it.

No. Professional distance.

"What do you want from me, Katie?"

"I want to know what it feels like!" she shouts.

"Per favore, help me understand."

"To be wanted." Her voice falters, but she doesn't look away. "Really wanted. With Jared, I never... I mean, we did, but I never..." She groans, covering her face. "I've never had an orgasm."

Everything inside me goes deadly still.

The confession ricochets through my skull like a bullet.

She pulls her hands away just enough for me to see the flush creeping down her neck. "God, this is so embarrassing."

Embarrassing? My jaw tightens and hot, sharp anger floods my system.

Not at her. At *him.*

No pleasure? None? From a man who had the right to touch her every night for years? How dare he? How fucking dare anyone have this bellissima donna in their bed and not satisfy her? Not discover every sound, every sigh, every tremor of satisfaction she's capable of making?

My fingers twitch at my sides.

"Never?"

"No. It was always about his needs." She huffs out a bitter laugh. "I thought that's just how it was. Or maybe I thought I wasn't capable. Like maybe something was wrong with me."

Che fanculo!

Her vulnerability undoes me. I've had my share of women—nameless encounters, faceless passion, morning departures. *Love is a gamble I can't afford to take. Not after losing the people I loved most.*

So why does her admission feel like it's unlocking something I've kept buried since childhood?

Katie fidgets with her hands before meeting my gaze. "I want to feel... desired. I want you to give me an orgasm. Please."

My teeth grind. I bite my cheek so hard I taste blood. "Katie, you don't know what you're asking."

"Yes, I do." The pure conviction in her snaps the last thread of my control.

Because she's not just asking for pleasure. She's asking me to see her, to know her in a way no one else has. The thought of being the one to bring her to climax—her first time—makes my blood pound so hard I sense it behind my eyes.

Before I can stop myself, I reach for her hand. She stares up at me, pupils blown wide, and I long to kiss her. No, not kiss. Fucking consume her until she can't escape me.

"Where are we going?" Her voice shakes.

"Wine cellar."

"I've already seen—"

"Not this one."

I drag her down the hidden path, my fingers locked around hers. Every step feels like marching to my own execution, because the second she lets me touch her, I'm done for.

The ancient cellar door shuts behind us like it's sealing our fate. Darkness swallows us whole. I flip the switch, and the dim light reveals a private sanctuary. Rows of timeworn barrels line the walls, ready to witness whatever happens next. The air, cool and thick, is perfumed with the rich, musky scent of aged oak, sweet wine-soaked wood, and damp stone. It's a secret place where each breath feels decadent, and every shadow invites dark deeds.

Katie lingers at the threshold, her eyes filled with a blend of vulnerability and hunger. She looks like prey about to be captured, torn between the instinct to flee and the undeniable pull to stay.

"Is this where you murder me?"

"Perhaps. It'll be death by multiple orgasms. Are you ready to die?"

Her breath catches as I stalk toward her, giving her time to flee. She doesn't move an inch. Just watches me with those green eyes that haunt my dreams.

A voice in my head screams to tell her to run. To find someone better, someone whole.

But I'm too far gone. Hell, it's been like this since that first fiery glare in that hotel bar.

I stop when we're toe to toe. My thumb traces her jaw, tilting her face up. "Last chance, principessa."

"I trust you."

Three simple words. A bomb ignites within me.

"Say it," I murmur. "Admit what you want."

She swallows hard but meets my eyes. "I want you to touch me."

Cristo Santo.

The words hit me like a physical blow. Every woman I've been with played the game—made me chase, made me work. But Katie? She hands me her trust like it's the easiest thing in the world.

It's not. I know how much it costs her to surrender control. To let someone else take the reins.

"You've been thinking about this." I brush my thumb across her bottom lip, watching her pupils dilate. "Imagining my hands on you. My mouth."

Silence. The pink staining her cheeks tells me everything.

"Confess it—you want me to make you lose control."

"I want it." She's breathless but sure.

"Ti porterò all'estasi."

"What does that mean?"

I grip her hips, guiding her backward until she's pressed against the barrel. "I will take you to ecstasy."

"Matteo—"

I crash my mouth to hers before she can respond. There's nothing gentle about this kiss—it's all teeth and tongue and days of pent-up need. She tastes like wine and something so goddamn sweet I know I'll chase it until there's nothing left. Her fingers fist in my shirt, pulling me closer, and I'm lost.

I deepen the kiss, angling her head to get better access. My tongue slides past her lips, claiming every inch she offers. When I pull back to let her breathe, her lips are swollen, her eyes glazed with want.

"Have you ever been kissed like this?" I drag my mouth down her throat. "Made to tremble like this?"

"N-no."

My pride and possessiveness surge.

I shouldn't be this smug. I shouldn't *care* this much. But I want her to leave this cellar stricken with desire—obsessing about my hands on her body and my mouth on her skin.

Sliding my palms up her thighs, I push the hem of her dress higher, higher, until I feel her shiver beneath me. My knuckles graze the damp outline of her panties, and I groan, resting my forehead against hers.

"Already so wet for me," I whisper, my voice tight. "Aren't you?"

Her lashes flutter as she presses her lips tight together. I nudge her with my fingers, teasing the fabric until she breaks.

"Yes," she whispers.

"Dio mio."

I rip my shirt off, spreading it across the barrel before lifting her onto it. Her thighs part instinctively, making room for me to step between them. The sight of her spread out for me, trusting me to give her what she needs, makes my chest ache.

"What if someone—"

"No one's coming down here," I counter, smirking. "Except you. And when you do, *everyone* up there will hear it."

I brush my hands up the soft skin of her thighs, stopping just shy of where we both want me to go. "I wonder what kind of noises you'll make when you come. Are you going to scream my name? Beg me for more? Or will you feverishly moan when I break you?"

"You're so cocky. Maybe that Sadie girl is right, and you're not as impressive as you think."

I grin darkly, brushing my lips against hers in a teasing almost kiss. "Do you want the pleasure or not?"

Her answer comes as a shaky, breathless exhale. "Yes."

I hold her gaze as my fingers slide beneath the waistband of her panties. "Can I slip these off, bella?"

Katie nods and bites her lip as I drag the fabric down her legs, slowly, like I'm peeling back the curtain on a masterpiece that deserves to be savored, every inch a revelation. The second she's bare to me, I spread her thighs wider, and the air punches out of my lungs in one harsh exhale.

If this isn't heaven, then I don't know what is.

"Dio mio," I rasp, my voice so raw it doesn't sound like me. I drag my gaze over her. "Your pussy... so fucking gorgeous."

Her blush deepens, her thighs twitching like she's about to close them, but I grip her knees, holding her exactly where I want her. "Don't hide from me, Katie."

I kiss the inside of her knee sensually—slowly—deliberately. Her breath catches, causing my mouth to trail higher, dragging my lips up her thigh. I feel her quiver.

"Wait—" she says shakily. "So this is happening? We're... we're having sex?"

I freeze, my lips hovering just above where she wants me. I force my grin to stay in place as I pull back enough to meet her eyes. "No, bella. Rules are rules. But as promised, I will make you feel desired."

Her brows knit in adorable frustration. "So, what then?"

My grin turns wicked, my control slipping as I lean back in, pressing a kiss just above her core. "I've spent many nights imagining how you'd taste on my tongue. And now?" My fingers slide over her folds, tracing the outline of where she's aching for me. "I will find out."

I drop to my knees, hooking my hands under her thighs, lifting her slightly to bring her closer to my waiting lips. "Lean back, bellissima." The command in my voice leaves no room for argument. "And hold on tight."

She hesitates for a heartbeat... then obeys, her back hitting the makeshift blanket of my shirt as her hands grip the edges of the barrel for balance. Her trust in me feels dangerous. I shove it down and focus on the way she opens, so damn perfect.

I flatten my tongue and drag it against her clit in one slow, deliberate stroke.

Her reaction is instant—her body jolts, her thighs squeezing against my head. "Oh my God!"

"Yes, bella. Every woman carries an angel and a devil inside her," I murmur against her heated flesh, gently kissing her clit. "Unleash the fire of your passion. Embrace every sound. Let me hear how good you feel."

"Matteo!" Her fingers tangle in my hair, tugging like she's afraid I'll stop.

I grin against her center, kissing her sensitive bundle of nerves. "Don't worry, I'm not going anywhere. Not until you come screaming my name."

I lick her slow and deliberate, before sucking her clit hard between my lips. Her hips rise to meet my mouth like she can't help herself, and Cristo, she tastes like honey drizzled over sweet cream. With every flick of my tongue she gasps, and I relish in the way her breathing transforms into desperate whimpers.

"Matteo..." she pants. "I... I can't. You're too good at this."

I glance up, locking onto her wild-eyed gaze as I slip one finger into her heat. Sweet mother of sin, the way she clenches around me makes me shudder. "Too good?" I curl my finger, enjoying her lips parting in surprise. "*Tesoro*, we have only begun."

Her moan turns into a plea as I add a second finger, building her higher. "Oh God. Oh my— Matteo, I—"

"You can handle it," I growl, my voice rough, my other hand grabbing her hip as I keep her steady. "I know you can."

"There!" Her back arches off the barrel. "Right there— Oh God—"

"*Si*, principessa." I growl, my lips brushing against her. "Let go for me. I want to feel you fall apart."

She's close—I know it. I hold her tighter as I focus on driving her higher, letting her unrestrained sounds guide me. She's so responsive—so trusting—it's driving me mad. I thrust my fingers faster while I suck her clit harder.

Her body tenses, her cries breaking into desperate gasps as I take her over the edge. "Yes, oh God— Yes! Matteo!"

Her thighs squeeze against the sides of my head as she shatters, her body shaking with the force of it. She repeats my name, crumbling under her release as it hits her in waves, tightening around my fingers. I don't stop—not until her trembling slows, until her soft breathing turns to silence and she slumps back against the barrel, spent and boneless.

Her release coats my mouth and chin, and I savor one last lingering kiss to her center before sliding her panties back into place and rising to my feet. I pull her up against me, using my shirt to wipe my mouth, savoring her scent for later. She's even more breathtaking, utterly ravished and glowing. *Perfetta*.

Her dazed eyes find mine, still hazy. "Wait—what about you?" She gestures weakly at the very obvious, very painful bulge in my pants.

I kiss her temple, helping her wobbling legs find solid ground. "This was about giving you what you asked for."

I force myself to turn away, to stop myself from kissing her more—to prevent me from saying how fucking gorgeous she is after coming on my tongue—to avoid breaking every rule I've ever made.

"Meet me on the bus."

As I walk away, leaving her breathless in the wine cellar, one thought pounds inside me like a hammer.

I crossed a line.

I broke my most important rule—the one about keeping my heart locked away from everyone.

CHAPTER TWELVE

KATIE

GROUP CHAT: CPK FOREVER

Me: Help. Is it cheating if we're technically broken up?

Petra: The fact you're asking means you're already halfway to doing it.

Cam: Jared gave up all rights to your body when he returned those wedding invitations.

Petra: We support all your bad decisions... especially the naked ones.

Me: But what if he wants to get back together?

Cam: He should've thought about that before letting you go.

Petra: NOW GET SOME ITALIAN DICK!

MATTEO MONTI GAVE ME my first orgasm last night.

And we didn't even have full-on sex.

The morning sun glints off the spotless shuttle windows as I study the Mediterranean coastline, the turquoise waves sparkling like they're teasing me. And fine, I'll admit—seeing the gorgeous view without peering through a smudgy, crime-scene-level layer of grime is a treat. But at the same time, this sterile little bus with its new car smell and functioning seat belts... It feels wrong. Empty.

Is it weird that I miss that rolling death trap?

"Ready for some fun in the sun?" Aunt Deb says from the back where she's draped over Howie like a human scarf. "These Italian beaches won't know what hit 'em!"

Beach day. Aunt Deb's Wish Card. And Howie's, too, apparently. I don't know what I expected from my auntie—a live volcano expedition maybe or riding elephants through the middle of Rome—but the beach seems surprisingly tame.

Meanwhile, all that stuff Aunt Deb's been preaching about: pleasure, freedom, and living in the moment? Yeah, she was right. The kind of right that makes me want to erect a shrine in her honor—complete with an elaborate vibrator display—and set all my precious binders on fire as a sacrificial offering.

Because this? This feeling surging inside me like liquid lightning? *This* is what I've been missing. My body's still buzzing like it's auditioning for a role as Thor's hammer, and muscles I didn't know existed are giving a standing ovation for...

Matteo's ridiculously talented mouth.

And his hands.

And his dirty words...

Bravo, Matteo. Bravo.

A shiver works its way down my spine. I bite my lip to keep from squirming, but *Jesus, I can still feel him.* Like his touch owns me now, from my lips down to my curled toes. No matter how I try, I *literally* can't think of anything else. The sounds I made in that wine cellar—he drew them out, effortlessly, like he was uncorking a vintage chianti after years of pent-up pressure.

Is this how it happens? One earth-shattering orgasm and suddenly I'm ready to join a sex cult?

No wonder Aunt Deb travels the world chasing this high. How do people function after experiencing this? Like, are they just out there grocery shopping and answering emails while pretending they haven't seen God between their thighs?

I fidget with the hem of my beach cover-up, attempting to conceal my legs. Beneath it, the skimpy bikini my auntie forced me to buy is a scandal waiting to happen. Black. Tiny. Basically craft string masquerading as swimwear.

I am *not* the kind of woman who wears barely there swimwear on European beaches. Or so I thought. But Matteo Monti has officially corrupted me.

The man responsible for last night's fireworks is sitting four rows ahead, and he won't even look my way. Like, hello? Earth to Matteo? The woman you turned into a quivering mess is right here, trying not to spontaneously combust every time the shuttle hits a bump.

But nope. He's simply sitting there being all devastatingly handsome with his troubled eyes and clenched jaw, making me want to march up there and demand he tell me what's wrong. Maybe while sitting in his lap. *For emotional-support purposes only, obviously.*

Where's my insufferable tour guide? The one who flirts and makes inappropriate comments about "the harder the cork, the sweeter the wine." Matteo Monti doesn't *do* brooding. He does smirking, he does teasing, he does "Let me charm you out of your sensible panties." *Brooding* does not suit him.

I wish I knew what was bothering him.

The morning sun catches his profile, highlighting the stubble I remember feeling against my inner thighs, and I grab my hips remembering his caress. Last night, he looked at me as if I were his salvation and his destruction all wrapped into one.

God, I want him to *look* at me like that again.

My smile falters as I remember the way he left me in the wine cellar, gently putting my panties back on. No cuddling, no expectation of anything in return—just a quick getaway.

My brain—overthinking menace that it is—starts spiraling. Maybe last night was too much. Maybe he saw what Jared saw—that I'm exhausting. That my need to control everything, to plan every moment—

Stop it, Katie. Matteo is not Jared.

Matteo... he's different. He doesn't try to fix or change me. He called my organizational skills a *superpower*. And last night? For the first time in my life, I completely let go. No plans, no schedules, no analyzing what would happen. I let him take control, and I... I finally understood what it meant to be free.

The realization hits me like I downed a double espresso—I don't want more orgasms *(I mean holy cannoli, I do)*, but what I really want is more of that feeling. That moment where I'm not Perfect Katie with her life all planned out. I want to discover the unexplored parts of myself and who I can be.

I'm sure Matteo's stupid no-tourist rule comes from experience—probably dozens of clingy women who thought one night of passion meant locking him down. But I'm not asking for forever. I'm asking for right now. For a chance to explore this new version of myself who can take what I want without analyzing it to death first. To be spontaneous and maybe even a little bit wild.

I grin to myself, sliding a hand under my cover-up for a quick peek at the bikini. The old Katie would need three spreadsheets and a pros-and-cons list before even considering wearing this flimsy excuse for swimwear. But the old Katie never knew what it felt like to come so hard she saw actual stars.

The bus shudders to a stop, and Matteo rises from his seat, his deep voice calling out to the group. "*Signore e signori*, welcome to the waves!"

Lorenzo opens the bus doors, and our senior citizens deploy their beach gear as if they're storming Normandy. I take a steadying breath.

No more planning.

No more waiting.

No more rules.

Watch out, Italian Stallion. You're about to find out what happens when a perpetual planner throws caution to the wind and takes what she wants.

***

WHEN YOUR AUNT STARTS a sentence with "Gather round, my naughty darlings, let's get this party started!" immediately run in the opposite direction. Do not pass go. Do not collect $200. Just run.

But no. Here I am, toes curled in the sand, watching Deborah Fox perched on a driftwood log like some bohemian prophet summoning a congregation to witness a miracle.

"Today, Howie and I share the same wish," Aunt Deb announces, "to experience Italy the way God intended. Naked!"

My jaw unhinges so fast I might need surgery.

Did she say *naked*?

I grip my cover-up tighter, clinging to the only thing standing between me and sheer, unadulterated humiliation. I struggled to work up the nerve to wear this teeny bikini. Going fully birthday suit? Around other people? No. No, no, no.

I should have seen this coming. Of course it's a nude beach.

Howie steps forward, somehow already shirtless, his Southern drawl dripping with charm. "As my sweet tea here is saying, we've earned every single one of these imperfections. My artificial hip? That's from boogieing too hard at Zumba class. My knee replacement? Vietnam. And this gut?" He pats his round belly proudly. "My trophy of appreciation for good bourbon and better barbecue."

"After seventy-plus years of living, what do we have to be ashamed of?" Aunt Deb continues. "These wrinkles? They're our story maps. These sags? They're gravity's love letters. These age spots? They're beauty marks from Father Time himself!"

"And darlin', time's given you the marks of an angel," Howie says, pressing a kiss to Deb's hand.

The sexual confidence I woke up with? The one that had me planning to seduce Matteo with my daring black bikini? It has packed its bags and booked a one-way ticket to anywhere but here.

Deb fans herself dramatically. "We've spent our whole lives being contained, being... clothed. But not today, my dears. Today we're going to be as free as Italian seagulls! As naked as Roman statues. As natural as the day we took our first breath."

I can't decide what's worse—her speech or the fact that it's so effective.

The crowd cheers. Someone throws their hat in the air.

"Now you two"—Aunt Deb wags a finger at Matteo and me—"keep those perky parts covered. This is a celebration of vintage bodies only! We're talking fine-aged wine here, not fresh grape juice. If you want to be frisky in the wind"—she waggles her eyebrows—"you'll have to find another spot on the shoreline."

Matteo winks at her. "Don't worry, Deb. Your oh-so-proper Katie has already decided to stay covered. Though"—he leans in closer to me, his voice low and playful—"I was hoping to see what you were hiding. After last night, I already know how *delizioso* you are."

"Hmmm. What was last night? Oh, your performance?" I tease him, my voice coming out breathier than intended. "I'd say it's under review. I really have to draw up a flowchart and pie graph before I can properly assess your skills."

"Those noises you made say otherwise." His eyes darken dangerously.

Before I can explain that Wine Cellar Katie was clearly possessed by a sex demon, Howie claps his hands together.

"All right, folks! Let it all hang out! Remember, what happens on an Italian nude beach stays on an Italian nude beach!"

And then it happens. A flurry of movement. Shirts flying. Shoes kicking up sand. Belts snapping open. It's like a geriatric strip-a-thon, and I am entirely unprepared.

Chester starts unbuttoning his BODY BY BACON T-shirt, revealing a pale, hairless chest. "Time to let the boys breathe! You know you're an old man when the bells hang lower than the rope!"

That gets a laugh from every guy in the group.

The Dawson sisters perform a synchronized striptease that would make Chippendales blush.

"Freedom!" Agnes announces while Margaret adds, "The only fashion trend that never goes out of style!"

"Always wondered how a breeze feels... down there," Stan mutters, shimmying out of his khakis.

Skin. So much skin.

And then... *Oh. Sweet. Jesus.*

My eyes nearly pop out of my head as Chester casually starts doing lunges, buck-naked. He's surprisingly flexible, but his, um, "frank and beans" are just flopping around and hitting the sand when he goes into a deep lunge. I try to look away, but I'm helplessly glued to the sight. Next, Howie joins in!

Matteo chuckles at my astonished expression, thoroughly enjoying the show.

"It's not funny," I say to him. "Now they're doing jumping jacks! No. Those things flapping and swinging should not be testing the laws of physics."

He snickers, and I hate how charming he sounds. "It's merely gravity doing its thing. You know, everything that goes up..."

"Shake what you got, lovelies!" Aunt Deb's voice pierces through my meltdown, and there she is—my aunt, my blood relative—leading a conga line of naked seniors down the shoreline, her sun hat bobbing cheerfully as they all jiggle along in rhythm.

"If you squint," Matteo says, narrowing his eyes in mock concentration. "It's almost... art. Like one of those surrealist paintings where everything sags a bit too much."

My eyes dart frantically between naked bodies in the world's most disturbing game of Ping-Pong. "Please tell me this isn't normal for Italian beaches."

Matteo, looking way too entertained by my suffering, shrugs. "No, principessa. Usually there's less... enthusiasm. And more pants."

"I will never use the phrase *low-hanging fruit* again."

"Why fight it?" Matteo's smirk is infuriating. "They're living their best lives. Dancing. Laughing. Showing the world that age is just a number."

"My boobs are officially terrified." I fling an arm over my chest protectively. "They're wondering how many years they've got left before they're roommates with my belly button."

He leans in, his whisper dripping with mischief. "If it helps, I'm imagining your breasts are—"

"Do *not* finish that sentence," I hiss, jabbing him in the ribs but not before he unleashes some mysteriously filthy Italian.

"Matteo!" shouts Aunt Deb from across the sands. "Time to start the Beach Olympics! We need you to bring some dignity to the hot-dog-eating contest."

"Really? You're going to watch them deep-throat wieners. On a nude beach?" I ask.

He squeezes my hip, his searing touch burning through my cover-up. "Try not to miss me during the naked three-legged race."

I groan in frustration. *How can I still want to jump a man's bones when every other bone on the beach is swinging freely in the breeze?*

I spot our ever-silent bus driver perched on a rock *(clothed, thank God),* peeling a banana with the same level of intensity most people reserve for defusing bombs. The motion is oddly hypnotic but also deeply unsettling.

"Hey, Lorenzo." I sigh, slumping next to him. "I need to talk to someone, and you don't speak English, so congratulations, you're my new therapist."

He grunts, barely acknowledging my existence. God, I wish I had his zen. Instead, I've got an ache between my thighs that won't quit, even in the midst of this geriatric fever dream.

"Okay, so last night was monumental. I mean it, truly. You know how some people say they've had a religious experience? Well, I had one. In a wine cellar. With Matteo's tongue." I hide my blushing face in my hands.

I steal a glance at Lorenzo, still nothing. Just chewing his banana as he flicks a glance toward the volleyball game where Aunt Deb is now leading some sort of impromptu huddle.

"It's like he uncovered this whole other side of me that was hiding under all my binders with one flick of his stupidly talented tongue. Let me tell you something, Lorenzo—that orgasm, it was life-altering. Six years of scheduled intimacy with Jared and not once did I soak the sheets. But Matteo? One night and he's completely rewired my body."

Lorenzo starts peeling another banana. *Where is he even getting these?*

"The thing is... I've never wanted anyone like this before. Never felt this out of control, this desperate, this... horny. But he's definitely not on the same page because afterward he... straight-up left. Put my panties back in place like a gentleman and disappeared. Who does that?"

Lorenzo grunts—a low, almost pitying sound—as he gives a subtle shake of his head. I'm not sure if he's agreeing or feeling bad that Chester just took a volleyball straight to the nuts.

"But now," I continue, "I'm in panic mode. Because Matteo has this rule—this no-tourist hookups rule—and I'm worried he made it up to avoid me. He said it's to keep things professional, to avoid drama. But it could be his polite way of saying I'm too uptight, too... boring? What if I'm too much? Not sexy enough?"

The banana peel joins its compadre on the sand, and Lorenzo folds his arms across his chest. I swear his eyebrow twitches, as if he's finally paying attention.

"Or worse—what if last night was nothing but... customer service? Like, 'Hey, better give the uptight American a mind-blowing orgasm so she doesn't tank my Yelp reviews.'"

I stare at Matteo as he serves the volleyball. "God, that's it, isn't it?"

Lorenzo sighs deeply, his gaze fixed on the horizon.

"You're right, Matteo wouldn't do that." I sigh. "But how do I be *that* woman? The one who confidently goes after what she wants? Because... I want him. All of him. I want to know what else those hands can do, what other sounds he can draw from my body. I want—"

Lorenzo stands suddenly, his movement cutting off my rambling. Then, with military precision, he starts stripping.

"What are you...?" The words die in my throat as he tosses his clothes aside.

First the cap comes off, revealing his wispy silver combover. Followed by the shirt. Then, sweet merciful heavens, the pants. He turns to face me, stark naked and unapologetic.

"Piccola," he says, his voice rough as gravel. "When man make woman feel like that? He not thinking about reviews. He thinking about her. Only her." He picks up his cap and plops it on my head like some sort of surreal mic drop. "Matteo's rule? It's for himself. To keep people out. But you?" He smiles. "You are worth breaking it."

Without another word, he jogs toward the naked volleyball game, everything swinging and bobbing with the chaotic energy of a bag of marbles in a tumble dryer.

I'm frozen. Mortified. Beyond embarrassed. Everything I blabbed was out loud... to a stranger.

I just trauma-dumped my sexual crisis on our secretly-English-speaking bus driver.

And the worst part? I'm still clueless about what to do.

***

I NEED A CONDOM! Like, pronto. Not tomorrow, not in an hour—*NOW*. Because once Lorenzo finishes his naked volleyball game and tells Matteo about my complete mental breakdown, I'll never get my chance to experience his full Italian package. He'll take one look at me and run. *Hell, I'd run too.*

I scan the cove with the desperation of someone tracking down the last roll of toilet paper during a pandemic. But unless there's a secret 7-Eleven hiding behind all these glistening senior citizen bodies *(oh God, so much glistening)*, I'm screwed.

Think, Katie, think!

That's when I spot it—Aunt Deb's beach bag. She probably has a Costco-sized pack of condoms in there. But asking her for protection? Absolutely not. She'd organize a *Katie's Finally Doing the Nasty With an Italian Stud* flash mob with the seniors.

Nope, sneaky purse burglary it is.

Act natural. You're just a girl, standing in front of her aunt's bag, about to commit petty theft so she can get laid.

My hand slips inside and—

Bzzzzzzzzzz!

Why am I even surprised? Of course she brought her "travel companion" to the beach. The sudden vibration against my fingers startles me, but it's the memory of Matteo feasting on me that makes my breath hitch. My body is screaming, *Go to Matteo now!*

Down girl, we gotta get what we came for first.

After what seems an hour of fumbling past more "massagers" *(plural!)*, sunglasses, a water bottle, and some weird object that feels like military dog tags, my fingers close around the cool, foil packet. *Victory!*

But where to put it? This bikini has less fabric than a Band-Aid. With a resigned sigh, I tuck the foil packet into the front of my bikini bottoms, praying it stays put. Each step makes the foil crinkle as if it's announcing *This Girl is DTF* in morse code.

My entire body hums. I'm nervous and excited. I'm nervicited! Sex on the beach? Maybe this is too crazy.

But Lorenzo's words surge through me like liquid courage: *"Matteo's rule? To keep people out. But you? You are worth breaking it."*

"Matteo! I'm going for a walk," I announce, projecting Aunt Deb vibes.

He faintly glances my way. "Be safe."

"Um, which part of the beach is best for topless tanning?"

That gets his attention.

His head snaps up so fast I hear his neck crack. In three long strides, he's in my space, radiating heat and male possession.

"Katie, being alone and naked?" His jaw clenches. "That's asking for trouble."

"Perfect." I lift my chin. "Because I'm looking for trouble. And on a clothing-optional beach? I'm betting there's at least one guy willing to make some bad choices with me."

I turn to leave, but his hand wraps around my arm. The touch makes my lady parts pulse.

"Stay with the group."

"Can't. Aunt Deb's wish, remember? Don't want to rain on her naked parade."

I watch his control fracture, a muscle jumping in his jaw. Before he can object, I reach for the knot at my waist and untie my cover-up, letting it slide off my shoulders.

"Don't worry about me," I say sweetly.

His jaw goes slack. His eyes rake over me, darkening with every second that passes. I don't wait for him to recover. Instead, I turn slowly, making sure he gets a good look at what these thong bottoms do for my ass, and suddenly I'm a goddamn runway model strutting down the shoreline. My thundering heart mixing with the crashing sound of the waves.

"Katie!"

I keep walking. The condom wrapper crinkling against my skin like tiny applause.

"What would Jared think?"

I stop dead, spinning to face him. The waves crash around our ankles as I plant my hands on my hips. "I don't care what anyone thinks."

"Dio mio," he mutters. "What about what I think?"

"You're welcome to join me."

"So look but don't touch?"

"Your rule." I reach back, untying my top with trembling fingers. "Not mine."

I toss the fabric away and Matteo actually stops breathing. "Cristo," he murmurs. "Your tits are magnificent, cara."

I lay back on the sand, arching deliberately. "And now they won't have tan lines."

He drops to his knees beside me, his eyes wild. "Madonna santa. I want my mouth on you so fucking bad, bellissima."

"What's stopping you?"

"Katie." His voice holds that infuriating mix of desire and restraint. "I... I can't."

"That's fine." I aim for casual but my heart is racing. "I'm sure one of those surfers down the beach will come get a closer look."

"No one touches you, *tranne me*."

The next second, his shirt vanishes in a blur. Before I can blink, he's on me, pressing me into the sand. His kiss isn't gentle—like last night—it's desperate and demanding as if he's been holding back and can't anymore.

A wave surges over us, cold and relentless, but it might as well be pure lava for how it sets my body ablaze beneath his. The pressure of his lips, the scratch of his stubble—my entire being instantly craves its own undoing.

Then his mouth moves lower, his lips tracing my collarbone before he finds my nipple. There's no gentle exploration, no timid testing—he pulls me into his mouth, hard and insistent, his teeth grazing the sensitive nub.

The waves drown out my moan, and Matteo doesn't pause. His hands frame my breasts, his fingers pressing into my skin like he's starving for me. His mouth moves to my other nipple, his tongue delivering a wicked flick before sucking me hard. I'm already gasping for breath.

I've never felt this—never been so worshiped, so desired. I always considered my breasts to be average—practical, at best. But the way Matteo devours me makes me feel like an absolute goddess.

"Matteo. Oh my... yes." I pant, my nails digging into his back.

My hips buck up seeking friction. Every nerve ending is firing at once, and I can't tell what's sending me reeling—his mouth, his hands, the weight of him pressing me down.

I reach between us, slipping my hand into the waistband of his swim shorts. He props himself up on his arms, giving me space, and the lust in his eyes as I squeeze him is overwhelming.

Holy fuck, I finally get the eggplant emoji.

He's so thick and hard I can barely get my hand around him.

My confidence soars when he groans, the sound vibrating through my whole body. "Fuck, Katie," he growls, "you have no idea what you do to me, bella."

My lips find the sensitive spot on his neck, and I suck hard, hoping to mark him. His hips thrust in response, and I start to stroke him, my hand moving with slow, deliberate movements, enjoying the way he throbs in my grasp.

His curse cuts through the rush of the waves. "Dio, sì, principessa. Keep doing that."

The water crashes over us, soaking us both, but I'm completely lost in him. My world narrows to the man above me, the way his muscles tighten under my fingers, the way his lips part as his breaths grow urgent. The taste of salt water adds a raw, primal edge to our passion, driving me to stroke him more intensely.

Matteo leans close, his mouth brushing my ear. "Are you wet for me, Katie? With all this water I can't tell. Are you?"

"Yes," I gasp, the word torn from me. "God, yes."

His hand slides between us, pinpointing my clit with breathtaking accuracy. The first touch of his fingers sends my body into a frenzy, and I'm on the brink—balancing it all—clinging to the moment but aching to surrender.

Then he freezes.

He pulls out the condom hidden in my suit, staring at it dangling from his fingers. His expression turns to stone.

"Of course you planned this. Seduce Matteo to break his rule. I walked right into your little game."

"No wait. Please listen—"

He jerks up, grabbing his shirt and throwing it. "Put this on."

"Are you kidding me?" I struggle with the clinging fabric. "It's only sex. You have it all the time. What's the big deal?"

"Just sex?" His laugh is harsh. "You think I don't want it? Katie, I think about it—about you—every fucking second."

"Then why fight it?"

"Because I *like* you, dammit!" The words explode from him. "Cristo, I shouldn't, but I do."

"You *like* me?"

"Merda." He rakes his hands through his wet hair. "Sì, I do. That's why this can't happen."

I'm bewildered, holding his shirt to my body that's throbbing with need. How can something so simple feel so complicated?

I watch him walk away.

CHAPTER THIRTEEN

MATTEO

"Son of a—" I smack the light switch, like it's personally responsible for my current sexual purgatory. The fluorescent bulb flickers on in the cramped maid's closet. I'm a ticking time bomb of pent-up frustration, and I'm going to have to defuse it myself in the shower.

It's past midnight in this discount disaster of a hotel. The half-conscious clerk behind the front desk hasn't budged since we arrived. I'd swear he was dead if it weren't for the drool on his newspaper. That leaves me playing bellhop, handling every ridiculous request from "Can you make the Wi-Fi faster?" to "Why isn't there a bidet in my room?"

Chester needed three pillows for his "jazz knee." The Dawson sisters demanded fresh towels because theirs smelled like "black mold and broken promises." Then Stan and Rose discovered what they hoped was marinara sauce on their sheets, though given the state of this place, I'm not convinced it wasn't evidence of a murder. Sometimes good tour guides have to lie.

And then there was Howie's request for "massage oil with warming properties," accompanied by Deb's distinctive cackle through his door. Hard pass. You're on your own with that one, buddy.

Just like I'm on my own to try to will my brain to quit imagining Katie in that black bikini.

We've been avoiding each other since check-in. She grabbed her room key without sparing me a glance. I can't blink without seeing her stretched out on that beach, the water lapping at her skin, her body arching into mine—

"Cazzo!" I should be focusing on real problems. Like how the mechanic still hasn't given me a timeline on the bus repairs. Or how the bank is ghosting me about the loan. But no, my mind keeps circling back to waves crashing over us as I dove into her perfect tits as if they were the last two scoops of gelato in all of Italy. Those breathy little sounds she made when I sucked on her nipples. Cristo, those nipples—light pink and tiny, so firm and begging for my tongue. The feel of her hand wrapping around my cock, stroking me with those delicate fingers...

"Porca miseria!" I slam another box shut searching for soap.

My dick throbs painfully against my zipper, a brutal reminder of why I'm standing in this closet. I was too consumed by memories of our almost encounter on the beach to check my shower supplies. Now I'm shirtless and dripping, my skin still tingling from the hot water, and I'm left with this hard-on that won't go away.

"No sapone in my room? Dio mio! This hotel is shit."

The shelves groan under the weight of cleaning supplies and mini toiletries. A metal table dominates the center of the room, an island of chaos with assorted bottles and mismatched linens next to a shoddy stack of one-ply toilet paper rolls. *One ply, really?*

If Katie were here, she'd have this place alphabetized and labeled in ten minutes flat.

My chest tightens at the thought of her in *strategizing mode*.

But then I remember how she planned out today. Plotted to seduce and sabotage me into breaking my one rule. And fuck, I almost did. Almost gave in to that primal need to bury myself inside her.

The condom rustles in my back pocket where I've kept it since fishing it from her bikini—an impressive feat considering it was more skin than suit. Why didn't I just give in? She wanted it. I wanted it.

I know exactly why. Because sex plus feelings equals relationships. Relationships eventually mean family. And family means soul-crushing loss. Better to wonder what could have been than risk inevitable pain… again.

I'll have to avoid her for the next week. Make a plan and stick to it—*isn't that what Katie would do?*

Katie. Katie. Katie.

Apparently I'm no longer in control of my dick or my brain.

The door creaks open, and I shove the condom deeper into my pocket, turning to find—

Merda.

Katie stands frozen in the doorway, clutching a mini shampoo bottle. Her wet hair falls in dark blonde waves around her shoulders, and that tissue-thin hotel robe clings to every curve I had my hands on earlier. Water droplets slide down her neck, disappearing between her breasts, and my tongue pulses with the need to trace their path.

"Oh!" Those green eyes go wide as they trail down my chest, lingering toward the bulge in my pants. Her tongue darts out to wet her lips, and my cock makes sure I notice.

I'm aching to grab her, pin her against these shelves, and continue what we started on that beach. I want to drive into her and hear if she cries my name out in the same way she did when I first tasted her sweet pussy. Every inch of me is roaring to claim her.

Instead, I force my voice into curt professionalism. "What do you need?"

"I just... Shampoo was empty," she manages, holding up the bottle like an explanation.

I arch an eyebrow, letting my irritation mask the raw need pulsing through my veins. "Are you sure you're not here to seduce me with more strategically hidden condoms?"

Her eyes flash with that familiar fire. "Excuse me?"

"You heard me, principessa. Is this another planned seduction? Another item on your checklist?"

"We need to talk about what happened—"

"No, we don't." I snatch a bottle of shampoo from the nearest shelf, dislodging the mini soaps hidden behind it and sending them scattering *(so that's where they were)*. "Here. You can go back to plotting my downfall now."

But Katie plants her feet, that determined, confident look settling over her features *(here we go)*. Her chin lifts and that wet mouth of hers makes me want to kiss it, or at least nibble on it, and then direct those lips to my eager cock. I wish. Instead, I brace myself for impact.

"I'm sorry."

Che cazzo? She's apologizing?

"I was wrong to push you to break your rule."

She takes a shaky breath that makes her robe gap slightly, revealing a teasing glimpse of cleavage. My mouth waters.

Katie pivots to leave but pauses midstep. "But I still don't understand. Why wouldn't you have sex with someone you like?"

The truth rips out of me like a confession. "Because I never have."

Her brows shoot up. "Never had sex with a woman you cared about?"

"Feelings lead to other things, things like getting attached, things I'm not interested in."

"Oh my God," she groans, shoving the shampoo into her robe pocket. "I'm not asking you to marry me! I'm asking you for sex. You know, that thing you're supposedly very, *very* good at."

"Katie—

"Besides," she barrels on, her tone rising with frustration, "we live in different countries. Different continents. What do you think is going to happen? Nothing about this is permanent. Nothing can happen between us beyond this trip."

She doesn't get it. She doesn't get how dangerous this is for me. How dangerous *she* is.

"Why can't we just admit we like each other, have several *mind-blowing* orgasms, and go back to our regularly scheduled lives?" she demands, her hands on her hips now.

Of course she has a plan. Even for this.

Wait—did she say she likes me?

Her voice softens. "You make me feel free, Matteo. For once in my life, I'm not obsessing over every little detail. I'm not making lists. I'm just feeling. And I want to explore that... with you."

Her admission slices through me. Every instinct shouts, "Run!" urging me to put some serious emotional distance between us. It's been like this since the day I stood at my parents' graves. Avoid feelings. Casual sex is easy. Meaningless encounters don't leave scars. But Katie...

I want her—not merely her body but *all* of her. Her wit, her stubbornness, and her relentless drive. I want to consume her, piece by piece, until she's as much a part of me as I am a part of her.

Katie shifts, her confidence faltering. "Right," she mumbles, turning back to the door. "Sorry. I didn't mean to—"

"Wait."

I should stop myself. I grab her hand instead. Her skin is impossibly soft against my callused palm. A thrill arcs through me, powerful. Unstoppable.

What if this destroys you?

The truth is... she already has.

I shut the door behind her, gently pinning her against it. My thumb traces her bottom lip, and her sharp intake of breath makes my whole body throb with need.

"Sì, bella." My voice comes out rough. "Let us discover pleasure, together."

When I kiss her, it's not the same as before. This is slow, deliberate—savoring the sensations as if I'm tasting her for the first time. Her lips—soft and warm. She's responding, matching my languid pace.

Her hands slide up to my shoulders, her fingers digging into my skin as she pulls me closer. Katie's body melts against mine; every point of contact is a spark. I'm drowning in the sensation.

"Cristo," I breathe against her lips.

I've never kissed anyone like this.

I let my hands roam, caressing the curve of her waist and the delicate line of her spine. My fingers find the knot of her robe, and I tug it loose. She's gloriously naked underneath. An answered prayer.

My hands explore slowly, reverently—dancing along her hip-bone, sliding up her waist to cup her breast. The weight of it fills my palm perfectly.

"Talk to me, principessa." I brush my thumb across her nipple. "Tell me when something feels good."

Her eyes flutter open, her gaze locking with mine. "Th-that... feels good," she says breathlessly.

I drop to my knees, and her hands fly to the door behind her for support. Her body is trembling under my touch, and when I press my tongue against her clit, she moans like an angel gone rogue.

"Dio, the way you taste." I worship her with long, languid licks.

"The intensity—it's too much," she pants. "But... don't stop. P-please don't stop."

I keep my movements slow, savoring every gasp, every shiver, every broken plea. Her feminine folds press against my mouth and I'm consumed. Her hips chase the friction even as she quivers from the overwhelming sensations—she's unraveling under my tongue.

"I can't..." Her voice is shaky. "I don't think I can stand."

"I've got you, tesoro." I grip her hips tighter. "Let go. Trust me."

Her eyes slide closed, and she does. She lets go. Completely. I increase the pressure of my tongue. She releases the door to grab my hair, her fingers pulling the strands.

"Oh God. I'm so close," she gasps. "Wait—no. I want... I want you inside me."

I tilt my head to meet her gaze, my lips glistening, my breathing ragged. "Relax, bella. This is the first orgasm of many tonight." I lift her right leg onto my shoulder, opening her to me completely, and thrust my tongue firmly inside her.

She cries out, her hands flying to my shoulders as her entire body jerks. The sound is loud—unrestrained—pure animal. We're going to wake the entire floor. She moans my name and... *God help me. What was I saying?*

"Now," I groan against her. "Surrender to me, principessa."

I press deeper, my tongue moving with rough, deliberate plunges, driving her higher and higher. Her breaths are ragged, her pleas more urgent. "There," she gasps. "Don't stop. I'm almost... almost..."

When I slide my hand between her legs, my thumb finding her clit, her entire body goes taut. The moment I apply pressure, she shatters.

"Matteo!" she screams, and it echoes off the walls. Her release is hot and wet coating my face, her center trembling as wave after wave of pleasure crashes over her. I hold her steady, supporting her as she rides out her climax until... her cries fade into soft, breathless whimpers.

Her body yields and I rise to my feet, gathering her in my arms.

"Climax number one," I murmur against her ear. "I'm not done with you yet."

I grip Katie's ass and lift her into my arms, her legs possessively claiming my waist. Her skin blazes against mine, her breath coming in short, soft pants that tease my neck—my cock throbs. I see the metal table, a stage for our bodies to come together, and I carry her to it. With one decisive motion, I sweep my arm across the cluttered surface, sending toiletries, towels, and God knows what else crashing to the floor.

"Are you serious?" she says with a half-scolding, half-breathless laugh.

"Do I look like I'm joking, bella?"

Her lips twitch as she tries to hide a smile, but it's no use. I tenderly set her on the table, her robe open, exposing her to me. She's flushed, her skin glowing in the room's dim light. I take a step back and drink her in.

Her chest rises and falls with each shallow breath. Her nipples pebble, as if they can anticipate my intentions. The slight curve of her stomach, the softness of her thighs—where I know she's still slick and ready for me. She's perfection. She's mine for the taking.

"Dio mio," I whisper, my hands skimming up her sides, leaving goosebumps in their wake. "Katie, you're..." I pause, trying to find a word that could begin to describe how stunning she is. *"Un miracolo."*

"What does that mean?"

"A miracle."

She looks away, nibbling her bottom lip as my praise sinks in. Her sudden shyness is a complete contrast to the fiery, maddening, and incredibly confident woman who challenges me with her cleverness. Seeing these hidden depths of her is a shot of adrenaline. I want to dive in, explore every nuance, uncover every secret, and savor every part of her.

But then my dick chimes in—loud and clear—impatiently urging me on to the thing we've both been burning for.

"There will be time for adoration later. Now? I'm going to fuck you until you forget what day it is."

I step out of my pants. Her lips part as her gaze lands on my rock-hard cock. She just stares, saying nothing, as if she's trying to figure out how the hell this is going to work.

"Wow," she finally breathes. "I mean... wow. You're huge."

Heat floods my chest, a mix of pride and desire. "Careful, bellissima," I say, catching her fingers as they reach for me. "Your touch will finish me off before we start."

"That bad, huh?" she teases, her voice full of that playful edge I've come to crave.

"You are too much, way too sexy," I murmur, stepping back between her legs and running my hands over her bare thighs, spreading them to make room for me.

"Wait! We need a condom! I'm all for being reckless, but not that reckless."

My lips twitch into a grin as I reach into my pants pocket and pull out the condom, holding it up like a trophy. Her eyes zero in on it, widening slightly before flicking back up to mine.

"You kept it?"

"Of course," I reply, my grin widening. "You went to such lengths to keep it safe. Figured it must be valuable."

She groans, covering her face with her hands.

"I've been wondering where you got this. I've never seen this brand before."

"Don't make me answer that."

"Oh, I'm going to need an answer," I say. "Did you smuggle it into Italy the same way? Sneak it past customs tucked inside your *perfetta* pussy?"

"Let's just keep it a mystery and call it divine providence."

I nod, my grin turning wicked as I rip open the foil with my teeth. The sound slices through the air.

I pump myself a few times, the pressure almost unbearable, before sliding the condom on. My free hand moves to her center, my fingers tracing her slick folds, teasing her entrance.

"Time for your next orgasm, bella."

I pause for a fraction of a second to let the moment sink in, then push inside her... slowly. Every inch she gets tighter, slicker—Cristo, she was made for me.

"Oh God," she breathes out with longing.

"Are you okay? Tell me what you feel."

"So good... so full."

My restraint is hanging by a thread. I start to move, slow and steady—the friction is almost too much. Her moan—soft at first—morphs into a wanton growl. I thrust deeper, and it becomes something I'll replay in my head for the rest of my life.

"Yes," she gasps, her hands gripping the sides of the table. "More of that. Please, Matteo. Don't stop."

I'm teetering, edged to a cliff and fighting not to fall. "You're killing me, bella," I grit out, backing myself down to a measured pace.

But then she does something unexpected—her inner muscles tighten around me. I freeze.

"Oh," she says nervously. "Are you... done?"

The vulnerability in her voice, the uncertainty—it hits me. This is what she's used to. Quick, selfish lovemaking that leaves her wondering if she was enough. That won't happen with me. Not tonight. Not ever.

I cup her face, my thumbs brushing over her flushed cheeks. I force her eyes to mine. "Katie," I say firmly. "We're not finished here. Not even close. Not until you're screaming my name. Understand?"

She nods, and that's all the permission I need.

My grip tightens on her hips as I pull her flush to the end of the table. In one swift motion, I hook her legs over my shoulders, the new angle earning me a gasp from her lips.

"What are you doing?"

"What I've wanted to since the day we met."

I thrust into her, hard and deep, rocking our hips into a rhythm that makes our bodies sing together.

Her back arches off the surface, a cry tearing from her throat. "Jesus, yes!" she gasps between trembles. "I feel it. Please, more."

The sound of her, the way her body is responding—it's too much and not enough. My movements become faster, harder—my control slipping with every thrust. "You're perfetta," I say, my voice tight with restraint. "Sei bellissima. So fucking good."

"Harder," she pleads, quivering. "Right fucking there. Don't stop."

Dio, the noises of this woman. It's taking everything I have to hold on. I can sense it—how she tightens—the way her breaths grow ragged. She's close, and I want nothing more than to push her to her breaking point.

She throws her head back, her cries growing louder, more desperate. "Yes, yes! There, Matteo, almost... almost..."

And then it happens. She comes apart beneath me, her body bending with pleasure, her voice breaking as she's crying out my name. The sound of it, the sensation of her milking me, pulls me over the edge with her. My release crashes through me, white-hot and all-consuming, and I let out a roar, my body trembling with the force of it.

Paradiso in terra (heaven on earth)!

I move slower, each thrust prolonging the pleasure, unwilling to let this moment end. Her beautiful frame goes limp, collapsing back onto the table, her chest heaving as she gasps for air.

Her legs slide down from my shoulders, and I collapse against her chest, my heart thundering against my ribs. Every muscle in my body is liquid fire. "Cristo, principessa. You've ruined me."

She gives me a tired, sated smile. "You weren't so bad yourself, tour guide."

I can't stop touching her, tasting her—my lips forging a path of worship along her jaw, her throat, memorizing the salt-sweet taste of her skin. Words tumble out before I can stop them: "Stay with me tonight?"

"Will there be more of this?"

"My body is at your service."

Katie taps her finger against her chin, a playful smirk on her lips. "Hmm. Let me consult my mental spreadsheet. Pros: earth-shattering orgasms, sexy Italian accent, marathon-level stamina..."

I can't hide my bewildered expression. She laughs, the sound warm and genuine, and it rumbles through me, right down to where our bodies are still joined. She grabs my face, pulling me into a kiss that's slow and deep, her hands tangling in my hair.

She whispers against my lips, "I don't need a list, Matteo. I want you."

CHAPTER FOURTEEN

KATIE

GROUP CHAT: CPK FOREVER

Me: Help. I think I've become a sex addict.

Petra: FINALLY!! Details. Now. Every filthy one.

Cam: Our Katie? Getting some Italian action?

Me: Not just some. ALL the action.

Petra: YESSSS! Katie Sextravangza = SUCCESS.

Me: Multiple successes actually.

Cam: I'm officially living vicariously through your orgasms.

Petra: Jared who? More like Jared WHO CARES.

I CAN'T STOP SMILING.

My face is stuck in an I-just-nowon-the-Powerball-while-cuddling-puppies expression. I'm barely aware that I am sitting in the breakfast room of our Venice hotel—the croissant in front of me untouched—because I'm lost in the constant carousel of yesterday's memories.

Bologna? I think we went to Bologna yesterday. I vaguely recall something about famous towers? Tortellini? Everything's a delicious blur after that moment in the empty tour bus. While everyone else was admiring the architecture of some fancy church, Matteo was giving me a very different kind of religious experience in the last row.

He whispered, "Let go, bellissima" against my neck as I bit back a scream, trying not to alert the entire city to our escapade. And later, in his hotel room... well, let's just say my very definition of perfection has been thoroughly and delightfully upended.

My thighs still ache in the most delicious way, and I'm pretty sure my underwear is on backwards. But hey, at least I remembered underwear today.

"Good morning, Katie-kins!" Aunt Deb's voice cuts through my coitus-fueled haze like a trumpet. She floats into the eating area with Howie on her heels. Before I say anything, she squeals. "You had sex!"

"What? No!"

"Oh honey, I know that look. I invented that look." She leans forward, eyes twinkling. "It was our devastatingly handsome tour guide, wasn't it?"

My entire face ignites. "No! Of course not! What—why would you even say that?"

Deb gives me a knowing stare, then turns to Howie. "It was Matteo."

"I don't blame her," Howie drawls, his smile slow and easy. "The fella's like one of them models you'd see in a cologne commercial."

"Thank you!" Deb says, gesturing at him as if he's just proven her point.

"Oh my God," I groan, sinking lower in my seat. "Can we talk about literally anything else?"

"Fine," Deb says dramatically. "Let's talk about my sex life. It's more exciting than yours anyway."

I scramble to redirect, my voice squeaky. "Howie, what exactly do you do? Or did, before retiring?"

Howie chuckles, amused by my awkward pivot. "I'm retired, Miss Katie. Used to be the CEO of Dixon's Delights. Family business, four generations strong. We make those Butter Bliss Bars you kids grew up on and a few other sugary goodies."

I gape at him. "I would trade my whole lunch—even on pizza day—to get one of those bars! You're a candy legend!"

"Well, I don't know about that." His smile turns soft as he admires Deb. "These days, I take interest in the finer things in life. Like this magnificent lady right here."

Deb fans herself dramatically. "You'll have me swooning to death if you keep talking like that!"

"And then I'd have to invent a candy in your honor," he says smoothly. "Something sweet, a little spicy, and completely irresistible."

Okay, I admit it—my heart melts a little. They may overshare, but they're seriously cute.

I'm about to tease them when the atmosphere in the room shifts. My skin prickles with awareness as Matteo strides in.

He's a feast for the eyes in that navy button-down, sleeves rolled up, displaying those forearms that I now know demolish a woman's self-control. His dark hair is still slightly damp, curling only at the edges—his face freshly shaven.

"Buongiorno!" he says with a deep, accented voice, cutting through the breakfast chatter. The room immediately quiets. "Today we explore Venice on foot, so everyone must wear comfortable walking shoes." His eyes lock onto mine, dark with allure. "One hour till go time!"

Before the wink he shoots me fully registers, I am on my feet. "I'd better... um... change my shoes."

Deb's brow arches, but mercifully she says nothing as I bolt for the exit.

I arrive at the elevator where—surprise, surprise—Matteo's waiting, leaning against the wall like a walking, talking orgasm.

"Looking for me, principessa?" He smirks.

"Oh, didn't notice you standing there," I say, pressing the elevator button. "Gotta grab my binder—be fully prepared for your riveting, well-planned schedule today."

"My best plans involve *you* forgetting how to breathe." His fingers tease the bottom of my short floral sundress before pulling me into the elevator right as the doors open.

"Excuse me, but I have a very detailed itinerary that needs—"

"I will tend to every one of your needs, bella."

"Promise?"

The elevator doors close and his mouth collides with mine. We stumble down the hallway, a mess of wandering hands. Matteo fumbles for his room key.

"One hour," he growls against my throat as we finally reach his door.

The door clicks shut behind us, and all thoughts of schedules, seniors, and sightseeing vanish.

I only want him.

***

VENICE IS WASTED ON the sexually awakened.

Here I am, floating through one of the most beautiful cities in the world, and all I can focus on is how Matteo's knee keeps brushing mine every time our gondola takes a turn. His bare skin on my sundress-exposed leg is a live wire, zapping my brain and turning me into a puddle of lust.

The afternoon sun glints off the canal water, creating a mosaic of light that ripples against the effortlessly grand buildings surrounding us. The scent of the water—a blend of salt, moss, and the faint tang of history—fills the air, while the soft murmur of distant conversations mingles with the rhythmic dip of the gondolier's oar. Then there are the arches of stone bridges crisscrossing above, framing the sky in fleeting snapshots as we drift beneath them.

It's surreal, better than any dreamlike state you can imagine. At least it should be. But not when you're mentally undressing your tour guide. Which I am... Again.

"And on your right is the famous Bridge of Sighs. Named for the sounds prisoners would make as they caught their final glimpse of Venice while being transported from the Doge's Palace to the prison."

Matteo's voice carries that tour guide authority that used to make me want to shove a sock in his mouth. Now it makes my knees weak, remembering how only this morning he commanded me to bend over the desk in his room and—

I mean, seriously? Is this what it's like to be a man? Constant, overwhelming, can't-even-think-about-anything-else horniness? No wonder the world's a mess—everyone's too busy being thirsty to save the planet.

Stan and Rose are cuddled together in the rear of the gondola, resembling honeymooners. "Last time we were here"—Rose's eyes twinkle as she squeezes Stan's hand—"this one tried to stand up to take a picture and nearly capsized us! The gondolier cursed in Italian the entire ride back."

"Worth it." Stan plants a kiss on her temple. "Got a great picture of my beautiful bride."

My tears well up watching them. That's what I thought I'd have with Jared. That comfort. That certainty. That knowledge—of being right where you belong.

But Jared didn't want that. Not with my neurotic, overplanning self.

I get it now—why Aunt Deb lives how she does. When you can't have forever, all you have are moments of pleasure. That's why she chases climaxes across continents and collects memories instead of promises. Now is all we have, and maybe that's enough.

But am I built for that? Could I be satisfied with incredible sex and stolen moments in hotel rooms? Or will I always wish for more?

I wanted to be the woman who takes what she wants. Mission accomplished. But now what? The problem with deciding to be spontaneous is that there's no instruction manual.

Stan kisses Rose's hand, and instead of that old yearning for a perfect life plan, I catch myself wondering how Matteo's hand would feel in mine. Not during sex. Just... holding hands. Strolling through Venice. Making stupid jokes about pigeons.

The kind of thing he'd probably run screaming from.

And then Rose gently cradles Stan's cheek in her palm, kissing his lips with such tenderness. My heart cracks. The gesture holds sixty years of love, of choosing each other every day, of building a life wrapped in certainty and trust.

And fuck, I want that. I want the spark *and* the stability. The fireworks and the forever. The earth-shattering orgasms and the gentle forehead kisses.

I want it all.

But Matteo Monti doesn't do relationships. That's not a theory; it's a fact. Like gravity or the way my thighs instantly turn to jelly when he speaks Italian.

He's basically a tourist attraction himself—the hot tour guide who leaves a trail of satisfied women and steamy memories across Italy. The guy who's elevated the morning-after escape into an art form. His longest relationship is probably with his bus.

It's totally fine. Nothing but a vacation fling. This thing between us—it's hot and intense, and it'll burn out as fast as it started.

We both signed on for temporary.

***

A FEW HOURS LATER, our tour group is huddled together, gazing up at the iconic Rialto Bridge.

"Welcome to Venice's most famous shopping center," Matteo announces to our group, gesturing at the massive stone structure arching over the Grand Canal. "Where Venetians have been separating visitors from their money since the 1500s."

He's not kidding. The ancient arches are crammed with enough souvenir shops to make you wonder if the Romans had a thing for key chains and fridge magnets. The covered walkway is a maze of boutiques selling everything from "authentic" Murano glass *(probably from China)* to white carnival masks *(you know, the ones with serial-killer vibes)* to gondolier hats *(you too can be a Mario Brother)*.

The smell of leather and coffee mingles in the air, along with that distinctive scent of tourist excitement and impending credit card debt.

"You have one hour for shopping and exploring." Matteo shouts over the buzz of tourists and vendors. "We'll return here for lunch. One hour till go time!"

I hang back, half-browsing a rack of postcards as he deftly manages the chaos. The man handles crowd control like he handles... other things. With skill, patience, and goddamn finesse.

"Bathroom?" Mrs. Thomas does her signature pee-dance shuffle.

"Which stores won't scam us?" the Dawson sisters ask in stereo.

"Yo, fam!" Chester adjusts his hearing aid. "Where do I get some sick drip? My grandson says I need more swag."

"Sugarplum, let's get you out of those clothes..." Howie drawls, "and into some new ones."

"Why, Mr. Dixon"—Aunt Deb bats her eyelashes—"if you want to get your hands on my unmentionables, all you have to do is ask."

"Quite the contrary, my dear sweet tea. I say we find a lingerie store and dress up those unmentionables. Maybe find more of that warming massage oil."

"Ooh, yes! I do need new crotchless underwear... and maybe some handcuffs."

I spot a postcard with a grumpy cat in a gondolier's hat—absolutely made for Mom. I'm so buying it and sending a note: "*Wish you were here. Not texting me every five minutes about Jared.*"

Seriously, does she have some sort of *Meddle in Your Daughter's Love Life* app? Her constant stream of friendly reminders to reach out to my ex is hitting Guinness World Record levels. If I get one more "*Just thinking... Jared always liked lasagna!*" text, I will ghost my own mother.

Newsflash, Mom: Jared hasn't called. He hasn't texted. He hasn't even *liked* the red dress thirst trap I posted at the Duomo. He's not interested. And honestly? Neither am I. For the first time, I don't care about someone else's expectations. I'm living in the moment, having fun, figuring things out as I go. *Imagine that.*

The real question is... should I write this snarky note in calligraphy?

A warm hand wraps around mine.

Matteo.

His dark eyes, the color of deep Italian espresso, hold me captive for a moment. Then, without a word, he starts pulling me through the crowd. I follow because those hands do magical things to my body, which—apparently—now operates with a Pavlovian response.

Are we heading to some hidden alcove? Some secret spot where he'll do that thing with his tongue that makes me lose my mind and my panties *(not necessarily in that order)*?

Um. What?

The Hard Rock Cafe shop?

The windows are packed with neon signs, band T-shirts, and an overwhelming amount of merchandise emblazoned with the Hard Rock logo. Guitars hang like a row of storm clouds, silently grumbling above the heads of shoppers while goth jewelry, coffee mugs, and other touristy gifts litter every square inch of the store. The music in here is deafening, with screechy guitar solos blasting so loud I can feel it in my teeth. This is the loudest store, both literally and figuratively, I have ever been in.

"Matteo, what the hell are we doing here?"

He says nothing, walking us past a teenage employee in a ripped black T-shirt who has more facial piercings than face. There's a culture clash of customers—some are ready to headbang to AC/DC, while others look like they floated in from a yacht party.

Um, why does it feel like we're hitting up a Hot Topic at Mall of America?

I turn to him, trying to hide my WTF expression. "This isn't very... Venetian."

Matteo still doesn't say anything. He releases my hand just long enough to grab a few shirts off a rack, then he pulls me deeper into the store. My brain is still processing when he yanks open a dressing room door and tugs me inside.

The moment Matteo shuts the door, the click of the lock echoes like a starting gun, and suddenly his hands and lips are on me.

Fast.

Rough.

Wild.

My back hits the wall, and his body presses into mine as if we're two puzzle pieces not meant to fit, but we *definitely* do. Intimately.

I try to think, but Matteo's hands are all over my body. I sense his urgency, his need for me, and it's exhilarating.

"You have no idea how hard it is to resist you, Katie." His lips brush my ear, sending shivers down my spine.

I gasp between hungry assaults on my neck.

"Matteo," I whisper, not quite knowing if it's a plea or a protest. My pulse is pounding in my ears. Muffled rock music bleeds through the dressing room walls because... *we're in a freaking store.*

"We're—" I gasp as his hands slide under my dress, his fingertips brushing bare skin. "We're in public!"

He pauses, long enough to meet my gaze. "I don't see anyone else, principessa. Just you and me."

My brain's catching up as he grips the waistband of my panties. With one swift motion, he tugs them down my legs.

I'm bare.

Exposed.

Loving it.

I want him and he knows. His fingers find me instantly, sliding between my thighs and pressing against my clit with maddening precision. "Cristo, you're already so wet for me," he murmurs, his voice thick with approval.

"Oh God," I moan louder than I should.

That—that right there—is exactly why I shouldn't be doing this. It's a Hard Rock store, for crying out loud. There's probably a dad out there buying a Nirvana T-shirt for his kid while I'm here dripping all over my tour guide's fingers.

"Don't you see? You don't have to be quiet in here," Matteo breathes into my ear.

The loud rock music blares. The very loud music. Music so loud that it will muffle the sounds of our passion. I glance around the changing area, my breath hitching as I take in the high walls and solid door. No gaps, no cracks, and no way for anyone to see or hear us. And finally, a light bulb. That's why he chose here.

"Relax," Matteo whispers, his lips dragging across my jaw as his fingers pick up the pace, circling faster, harder. "We own this moment. You're safe with me."

Safe? Ha. If anything, I'm in danger—of losing my mind, my self-control, and whatever shreds of dignity I have left.

"Why are you—" I gasp. His thumb brushes over a spot that has me refocusing *all* my attention on him. "Why are you so good at that?"

His grin is lethal. "Practice."

Screw it.

I grab the hem of his shirt and yank it up, dragging it over his head with more force than necessary. He smirks, the sharp edge of his teeth glinting like a warning, and my stomach flips—it's no longer fear, just pure exhilaration from this impossibly, devastatingly sexy beast of a man.

My hands splay across his chest, sliding down over his abs—each ridge firm and flawless and completely unfair. My palms brush lower, and *(oh damn)* there he is. Thick and hard and straining against his pants.

"Dear Lord," I mutter under my breath, unable to stop myself from cupping him, enjoying him twitch beneath my touch. "Do you always get this hard this fast, or am I special?"

He chuckles, his hands tightening on my hips. "You're very special, cara."

I'd roll my eyes at his cocky tone, but I can't stop sliding my hand up and down, marveling at how his body is responding. The way his jaw flexes, his chest heaves, and his stare darkens tells me that my touch is the sole thing that can feed his need.

In the past, sex was... pleasant enough. Something I didn't mind. Honestly, I got some of my best meal planning done during those scheduled sessions. But this?

This is nothing like that.

I am breathless.

Shameless.

Unhinged.

"Matteo," I shout, my voice barely audible over the pounding rock music outside. "Are we really going to hook up in a store full of people?"

He reaches into his pocket and pulls out a foil packet, tearing it open with his teeth. "Does this answer your question, tesoro?" With a quick, confident motion, he pushes down his shorts, revealing his rock-hard cock *(or should I say his Hard Rock cock)* and then expertly rolls on the condom. His eyes never leave mine.

Damn. Well. Okay then.

For a split second, doubt creeps in. *Has he done this before? Is this where he usually brings women?* But then his mouth crashes onto mine, and every thought evaporates.

"I want to hear your pleasure," Matteo says.

"Then I better fucking hear yours."

His grip tightens, and his eyes darken. "This won't be gentle."

And then, in one smooth, powerful motion, he lifts me, pressing me higher against the wall, and thrusts into me... hard.

I cry out. My legs instinctively wrap around his waist as a surge of lust courses through my body.

It's intense. Brutal and fast and unrelenting. Every drive of his hips is a lightning strike, sharp and electrifying, lighting me up from the inside out. Each thrust forcefully plunges deeper. He's gripping my ass so tightly I love that I'll have bruises tomorrow.

"You feel…" His voice is ragged. "Cristo, Katie. Your pussy was made for me."

My head rolls back in bliss. "No one's ever— Oh my God—no one's ever made me feel like this," I manage between his relentless movements.

Every thrust is harsh.

Unforgiving.

Divine.

"Yes, Matteo yes! Rougher… harder!"

My God! I'm in public, literally screaming out this man's name and no one can hear. Mr. Monti, what have you done to me?

"Tell me you love my cock inside you!"

"It's fucking magic! I love it. God don't stop! Make me come!"

My words spur him on, his rhythm quickening. I'm clutching at his shoulders—my nails digging into his skin—Jesus, he's good.

Hard rock music thunders in the background, a chaotic symphony of drums and guitars, but it's nothing compared to the ragged sound of our breaths and the filthy, delicious words spilling from Matteo's mouth.

"Dio mio, Katie," he groans, his forehead dropping to mine. "You need to come. I can't—fuck—I can't hold back much longer."

The raw plea in his voice sets my senses ablaze. I've never had this kind of power over someone before, never felt so desired. It's beyond words, and I'll chase it to the edge and beyond.

The pressure between my thighs is building, coiling tighter and tighter—almost unbearable. I squeeze my legs around him, pulling him deeper, and I bite down on my lip on instinct, then let myself cry out.

This isn't making love. This is raw, unfiltered, unapologetic fucking. And I love every second of it.

"Fuck me harder. Harder. Yessss!"

"Oh Katie. God, yes! Principessa, bella, tesora, bellissima—"

His desperation drives me, and I find myself doing something I've never been brave enough to do in the presence of another person. I've always been too self-conscious, too timid. But now my hand dives between us, my fingers zeroing in on my clit. The instant I apply pressure, wild sensations explode through me.

Matteo's eyes flicker down, catching the movement. "*Sei così* sexy. That's so fucking hot, Katie... *Sto per esplodere*. Fuck, I'm—"

He cuts off with a guttural groan as his orgasm crashes through him. He's throbbing inside me—and we're spiraling over the edge together.

The release is overwhelming, all-consuming. Tremors wash over me in waves. I am moaning like a porn star, loudly proclaiming my pleasure in a retail store with strangers. I'm so alive it hurts. Matteo continues to move, his thrusts slowing but never stopping, as the sounds of my climax finally simmer.

Goddammit, this man's a genius.

When the final waves of pleasure subside, we collapse together, sliding down until we're a tangle of limbs on the floor of the dressing room. Matteo pulls me close, his lips finding my forehead, my cheeks, my lips, each kiss softer than the last.

"You are... *magnifica*," he says, his voice soft but laced with awe. "So *splendida*. So precious."

Precious? My heart stutters at the word. It shouldn't mean anything—it's simply a word. A word that doesn't belong in our world of... whatever this is. But it sneaks in anyway, and I melt into him, letting myself sink into the comfort of his touch and the tenderness of his kisses.

Reality reemerges. My dress is bunched up around my hips, and I'm pretty sure there's now a permanent Hard Rock logo stamped on my ass *(thanks, wall)*. I wriggle out of his hold, my legs wobbling slightly, and I reach for my bag.

I fish around my purse and thank God for my Type A personality—turns out, overpreparedness pairs perfectly with poorly planned sexcapades. Travel-pack Kleenex for the win.

His lips twitch into that infuriatingly perfect smirk. "Miss Katie Crawford, ready for every occasion."

"I call it being responsible," I say, tossing him a tissue. "Try it sometime."

Watching him clean himself up is almost as distracting as watching him strip in the first place. Almost.

"You say responsible," he says, balling up the tissue and tossing it into the tiny waste bin, "but I say adorable. And also, kind of sexy."

"Sexy? Jared always said my obsessive planning was too much."

"He's a fool not to see that all of you is sexy."

My heart soars at his praise, but I shut it down fast. *Don't read into it. Of course he's being nice after he rammed his rod so hard that I'll be walking funny for the rest of the day.*

We straighten our clothes with trembling fingers, trying to hide the fact that we just had the hottest quickie in retail history. The mirror reveals exactly what Italian-induced ecstasy does to a girl's previously styled hair.

I reach for the door. He catches my hand.

"Go on a date with me." He pauses, running his free hand through his hair. "I mean—I'm not forcing you to. I've never done this before. I'm asking. Per favore, go on a date with me, Katie."

"Yes." The word pops out instantly.

His smile lights up his whole face. He leans in, pressing a kiss to my cheek that somehow is more intimate than all the filthy things we just did against that wall.

He takes my hand again, and we're waltzing toward the entrance.

He tosses the shirts he'd grabbed onto the counter, telling the clerk, "She said it was too big. She really battled with it, trying to get it in, but it was a lost cause."

The clerk's eyes dart to me, and I bite the inside of my cheek to keep from laughing. Matteo glances at me, smirks, and then winks. A fully unrepentant, completely wicked wink.

We emerge into Venice's afternoon bustle, our fingers still intertwined. I stare at our joined hands, a knot tightening in my chest. It feels *right*. Like I've been walking around with an empty space in my life, and somehow Matteo has filled it. Effortlessly.

Oh shit.

This is more than sizzling sex. This is something far more dangerous. *Feelings.* Big, unruly, I'm-not-sure-I-can-handle-this feelings.

What kind of lust-filled lunatic falls for a man who doesn't believe in relationships? Apparently me.

Congratulations, Katie. You've officially lost your damn mind.

CHAPTER FIFTEEN

MATTEO

THE VENICE SANTA LUCIA train station is a fucking circus at eight a.m.

The massive iron-and-glass ceiling soars overhead like some grand cathedral dedicated to the gods of transportation. Here on the ground, it's all-out war. There's a storm of suitcases and obscenities as visitors charge each other like deranged gladiators. Oversized luggage takes out tourists' ankles while kids have meltdowns in French, German, and whatever language Satan's spawn speaks.

I stand with Lorenzo near Platform Three, where he checks his ticket for the fifth time. Guilt gnaws at my insides. "You don't have to spend your day off retrieving the bus from La Spezia. I should go."

The words taste bitter. Yesterday's call from the mechanic wiped out my savings. Monti Tours is now officially surviving on credit cards and prayers. If the bank doesn't approve that loan soon...

But I can't think about that because it's "Free Day," the one day that I build into my tours where I'm not playing tour guide slash babysitter slash human GPS. I schedule it in cities we've already explored so that the group has a better chance of making it back to the hotel alive.

"Seriously, I don't mind—"

Lorenzo's eyes narrow. He studies me with the intensity of a man contemplating either great wisdom or his next bowel movement. Then, in classic Lorenzo style, he delivers maximum impact with minimum words. *"Lo, autobus. Tu, lei."*

Me, bus. You, her.

He claps a hand on my shoulder, mutters "Idiota" under his breath, and walks away, leaving me to deal with the growing complication that is Katie Crawford.

I glance at her, and Cristo, my body responds like she's got me on a leash. Her golden hair dances in the morning breeze, her sundress lifting just enough to flash a peek of her perky ass. I want her. My traitorous mind teleports to last night—how she looked riding me, taking exactly what she wanted. I was under her spell. Still am, apparently.

Her perfect breasts bounced as she found that magic angle, her core squeezing me until I almost blacked out. The image of her head thrown back—when pleasure overtook her—she collapsed into my arms and fell asleep against my chest...

Stop. Now.

This is precisely why I declared the next twenty-four hours *No Sex Day*.

Last night—after round three—I told her today was about getting to know each other and showing her Verona, my favorite city, which seldom makes the official tour itinerary.

Today has one purpose—to prove that this thing with Katie is purely physical. It might be mind-blowing, earth-shattering, and the kind of sex that ruins you for all other women, but it's still just sex. Nothing more.

My mission: Find every flaw and stop these feelings from spreading. We started out barely tolerating each other—getting back there should be easy. *Right?*

My body's humming as I approach her. "Ready for Verona, bellissima?"

"I'm at your mercy. Let's wing it!" She takes my offered hand without hesitation, eyes sparkling with excitement.

Our fingers intertwine, electricity shoots through me, and—merda—this *No Sex Day* might actually kill me.

Five minutes into the train ride, I realize I have not said a single word. *Cazzo. An hour to Verona. What the hell do people do on dates?* Katie's hand is still in mine, and the silence stretches between us like an invisible wall.

Find flaws. Stop noticing how perfect her fingers feel in yours.

"So..." I clear my throat. "Scale of one to ten, how's my dating game going?"

"Hmm. If we're counting conversation skills? Negative three."

"What about hand-holding?" I counter, lifting our entwined arms. "I am *perfetto* there, sì?"

"Sure, if you're aiming for a participation trophy." She smirks, a teasing glint in her eyes, daring me to do something about it.

Dio mio. She's lethal.

"Okay," I say, straightening in my seat. "Rapid-fire questions. Let's go."

I don't give her time to process.

"Is Aunt Deb really your aunt?"

"Yes. My mom's sister," she answers smoothly with no hesitation.

"Where do you live?"

"Los Angeles."

"What's your favorite thing about where you live?"

"The weather."

"Do you enjoy your job as an event planner?"

"Most days."

"Do you have any siblings?"

"Older brother."

"Are you allergic to anything?"

"Nope."

Katie bursts into laughter. "Matteo, you just speed-ran through my entire life story like you're trying to win a game show. You weren't kidding about never dating, were you?"

I can't help it—I grin. She's impossible not to smile around. "Fine. Your turn then."

"All right." She taps a finger to her chin. "Where did you learn to speak English so well?"

"Watching reruns of *Friends*."

"Really?"

"School taught me the basics, but Jennifer Aniston's nipples were motivation for the rest. I wanted to hear her actual voice, not the Italian dubbing."

Her eyes widen. "Her nipples?"

"I'm a nipples guy."

Her cheeks flush pink. "Noted."

"What about you?" I ask, trying to find something—anything—to dislike. "Always wanted to be an event planner?"

"Yes!" Her whole face lights up. "I love it! Taking chaos and turning it into a perfect moment. I'm going to start my own company before I'm thirty."

"Maybe if I had you, I wouldn't have so many troubles with my—" I catch myself.

"Oh look, olive trees, bella!"

That was too close. The last thing I need is for Katie to find out what a shitshow my life is. Her effortless competence makes me feel like a damn amateur. A woman that sharp doesn't want to spend her time with a guy who can't run his own business. No, it's better if she keeps seeing me the way she does now—assuming I have my act together.

"Bella, cara...?" she asks. "Explain all your nicknames."

"Ah, bella means beautiful. Cara is dear. Principessa is princess."

"And what's an expression you never say?" Her voice carries a challenge. "A phrase you don't use on all your female flavors of the week?"

My mouth opens, then closes. This feels like a trap. But there's no point in lying. "*Mi amore*," I admit quietly.

"What does that mean?"

"My love. I've never said that to anyone."

The air between us crackles with tension. Katie's lips part slightly—

"*Prossima Fermata*, Verona!" The train speaker blares.

"We're here."

Thank fuck. Because one more second and *No Sex Day* would've ended right here.

***

"Is this your secret to seduction? Dragging women to hole-in-the-wall pizza joints that haven't had a makeover since the eighties?" Katie says, leaning back in her chair and scanning the room with a skeptical but amused expression. "I don't know what is sexier, the mismatched chairs or the peeling paint?"

"This isn't about seduction," I say, grabbing a napkin to wipe down the table. "This is about educating that American palate of yours. You're about to have the best pizza of your life."

"Let me set the record straight. You haven't lived until you've had a BBQ chicken pizza from CPK."

"BBQ... chicken? On pizza?" I say, horrified. "*Mi dispiace*, Katie. That's not pizza. That's a cry for help. And what's this CPK?"

Her jaw drops. "California Pizza Kitchen! You've never heard of it?"

I freeze, mid-clean, like she's insulted my entire existence. "California... pizza? You're joking, right? You're comparing California to Italian pizza? In Italy?"

"Well," she says, folding her arms on the table and leaning forward, "I'll have to see if this pizza of yours lives up to the hype. But I'll warn you—I'm a loyal woman. CPK's been there for me through thick and thin."

"You talk about pizza like it's an old lover."

"More like a therapist. My friends and I have regularly gone there since college. And not to brag, but our names spell out the initials CPK."

I tilt my head, intrigued. "Tell me about your friends."

"Petra and Cam." A small smile plays on her lips. "We met in art history class freshman year at UCLA. One minute we were strangers debating Renaissance paintings, the next we were sharing a pizza and our deepest secrets."

"And they were okay with you running off to Italy?"

She traces the rim of her water glass, a nervous tell I'm learning to read. "They were all for it. Petra said I needed to 'get some sexy Italian dick to cleanse my palate.'"

"Petra sounds very wise," I say with a grin.

"She's a force of nature," Katie says softy with affection. "Fearless and completely unapologetic. The kind of person who'd dig you a grave and be your alibi, no questions asked. And Cam... pure positivity in human form and so freaking talented. She can do literally anything. I'd be jealous if I didn't love her so much."

Her tone changes. "But after my wedding got called off, I don't know. I couldn't lean on them."

"Why not? They're your friends."

"Petra started this corporate job she's terrified of failing. Her brother owns the company, so she's trying hard to prove she's not the family screw-up." Her voice catches. "And Cam's dealing with this YouTuber boss from hell who treats her like a servant. They would have dropped everything. That's who they are."

"But you didn't let them."

"I've always been *their* rock," she says.

The confession tumbles out as if she's been holding it in.

"I'm the one with the plans, the answers, the solutions to every crisis. But this time..." She swallows hard. "This time I'm the crisis. And I don't know how to be that person."

She glances down at her hands, and I see fingernails digging into palms.

"I thought if I handled it alone, kept moving and planning and controlling everything—it wouldn't feel so real. That I could avoid the ugly truth that everything I knew about myself, about love, about my future—it was all bullshit."

She finally looks up, and the raw honesty in her eyes breaks me. "I've spent my whole life being the stable one, you know? But now I feel like I'm trying to build a puzzle with missing pieces."

My heart lurches—I need to protect her, to comfort her, to show her that sometimes the best things in life can't be planned.

"Maybe," I say carefully, taking her hand, "that's not such a bad thing."

Her fingers tighten around mine. "Why's that?"

"Because when you're falling... that's when you learn who's willing to catch you."

She looks at me then—really looks at me—and I see what she's hiding. The fear. The hope. The trust she's terrified to give again.

Today is about finding flaws, about pushing her away. But her insecurities and honesty have only made her more endearing. I want to help her discover the joy of the journey—the passion that comes from putting the puzzle together even if some of the pieces are missing.

This woman isn't just getting under my skin. She's exposing a part of my heart I thought was locked away forever.

CLINK!

The waiter sets two steaming pies in front of us. The smell of fresh dough, tangy tomato sauce, and bubbling mozzarella fills the air, and Katie's eyes widen in anticipation.

"All right, Mr. Tour Guide," she says, picking up a slice of her Margherita pizza. "Let's see if your precious Italian pizza can dethrone CPK."

"You're going to eat your words. And probably half my pizza too."

She takes a bite, and the moment the flavors hit her tongue, her eyes close, and a soft moan escapes her lips. My stomach flips like I'm the pizza she's devouring.

"Oh my God," she mumbles through a mouthful of cheese and sauce. "This is... this is life-changing. Matteo, I think I'm in love."

"With me or the pizza?" I ask, grinning.

"Let me finish the slice and I'll get back to you," she says, already reaching for another piece.

We fall into an easy conversation—about her family, her childhood with an overachieving brother, and her dreams of starting her own company.

Find her flaws, my brain screams.

She has none, my heart whispers back.

***

IN THE HEART OF Verona, the hotspot for romance is Juliet's Courtyard, and love is in the air. So is lust, which has made its way into my pants. Because I cannot stop obsessing about Katie in that dress. The fabric hugs her curves—my sanity is slipping—and every time she tugs at the hem, my zipper grows a little tighter. Each innocent adjustment hikes that skirt higher, flashing those thighs that were wrapped around me hours ago.

Focus on the statue, not on how Katie's skin feels under your finger-tips.

Juliet stands tall and proud, her bronze figure shimmering under the Italian sun, one hand resting gently on her chest. Tourists swarm about, eager to cop a feel of her breast, hoping the legend of true love will "rub off" *(pun intended).* The courtyard is a romance novel come to life, with ivy snaking up brick walls and that famous balcony where Romeo professed his love.

Love notes and padlocks adorn the walls, each a testament to the promises of visitors from across the world. Yet amid all this romantic chaos, it's Katie who commands my attention, and I'm wondering if she senses the same electric pull.

"You want me to just… grab it?" Katie hesitates, her gaze darting between me and Juliet's bronze breast. "This feels illegal. Is this illegal? It feels illegal."

"It's tradition, principessa. See how the right one shines?" I adjust Mamma's Nikon, looking through the lens. "Centuries of people seeking luck in love."

"From Romeo and Juliet? The teenagers who had the world's worst communication skills? Are you sure this isn't some pervy plot to watch women grope statues?"

"If I wanted to watch groping, bellissima, I'll continue replaying last night in my head."

She reaches out tentatively, then pulls back. "What if it's cursed? What if I touch it and suddenly start writing sonnets about your abs?"

"You don't write sonnets when you explore my body. You compose symphonies with moans of pleasure."

"God, your ego is bigger than Italy."

She makes contact, giving the statue's breast the world's most apologetic pat.

CLICK.

The shutter captures her adorably scrunched nose.

"That wasn't so hard, was it?"

"Says you. At least let me pretend to buy her a drink first."

"You need me to demonstrate proper technique." I reach out deliberately, but instead of touching the statue, I cup Katie's breast.

"Matteo!" she squeals, smacking my fingers away playfully. "Wrong breast!"

"Honest mistake. Yet strangely I'm already feeling luckier."

A nearby group of teenage girls erupts in giggles. Katie's face flames red, but then she surprises me by asking them. "Could you take our photo?"

One of the girls takes my camera with surprising care and lines up the shot.

"All right lovebirds!" she calls out. "Hands on boobies! Three... two... one!"

We slap our fingers on Juliet's breasts—me grinning like an idiot—but at the last second Katie pulls her hand away.

CLICK.

"Gotcha!" Her victorious laugh bounces off the timeworn stones. "That's what you get for copping a feel on *No Sex Day*."

"Worth it." I grab her waist, pulling her close.

"*No Sex Day*, remember?"

"This isn't sex. It's... appreciation."

I crush her lips with mine, and there's a chorus of awws from the teen girls.

***

"**Mercato!**" **Katie announces, surveying** the chaos of Verona's outdoor market. "I nailed that pronunciation."

I bite the inside of my cheek to keep from grinning. Watching Katie Crawford attempt Italian is my new favorite form of entertainment.

"If by 'nailed it' you mean 'made every vendor here cringe,' then yes. Perfetto."

She zeros in on a stall overflowing with silk scarves. "I am one with the *mercato*. The market and I... we are *simpatico*."

"That's Spanish."

She whirls around. "Don't ruin my vibe. I'm channeling my inner Italian goddess here."

"Your goddess needs subtitles."

"Shhh. Watch and learn, tour guide."

Oh, this is going to be spectacular.

She picks up a tan silk scarf with blue flowers, clearing her throat dramatically. "Bon-joor!"

"Wrong country, principessa. But please continue. This is better than cinema."

Her nose does that adorable scrunching thing that makes me want to kiss it. "Fine, Mr. Perfect Pronunciation. How do you say scarf?"

"*Sciarpa*. But clearly you don't need my help."

"Skee-arrr-pah," she says, rolling the R like a purring cat. The scarf vendor blinks, probably wondering if she's having a stroke.

I nod solemnly. "Flawless pronunciation. Want to try asking the price?"

"Please." She waves her hand dismissively. "I've got this. *Quanto costa la...* neck thingy with flowers?"

The vendor's face does some impressive gymnastics trying not to laugh.

"Quanto costa la sciarpa color cammello con fiori celesti?" I say quickly.

"That's what I said," she says, then attempts to repeat it. It comes out sounding as if she's having an allergic reaction while ordering pizza in Dutch.

"Venti euro!" the vendor says.

"Twenty euros! I understood that!" Katie claps her hands, radiant with pride. "I'm an expert now. Quick, teach me to say 'I speak better Italian than my smug tour guide.'"

"How about we start with thank you first?"

"Relax. I know what I'm doing." She turns to the vendor with complete confidence. *"Gracias!"*

"Still Spanish."

She forks over the money for the scarf, and the vendor grins from ear to ear as we walk away.

"You were supposed to haggle."

"Me no haggle-ah. I'm-ah happy with the scarf-ah." She wraps the scarf around her neck with a flourish. "How do I look?"

Like everything I never knew I wanted.

"Like someone who should stick to English."

She smacks my arm, but she's grinning.

"When it comes to my native tongue, bella, it's best if you just lie back and let me do it."

I steer us toward a small shop with a glowing green cross above the door.

She eyes the sign warily. "Is this... a pharmacy or a weed dispensary?"

"*Farmacia,*" I say, pulling the door open for her. "Time for your next lesson."

She crosses her arms, leveling me with a suspicious glare. "You're up to something."

"I am but a humble tour guide," I say, my tone the picture of innocence.

"That face," she mutters as we step inside. "That's your scheming face."

"It's also my incredibly handsome face. Very versatile."

An elderly pharmacist greets us from behind the counter, his smile warm and welcoming. Katie immediately relaxes. *Amateur move.*

I whisper a phrase in her ear.

"Okay, here we go." Katie straightens her spine and repeats the phrase *(sort of)*.

The pharmacist's eyebrows rocket skyward, nearly launching off his face.

"Nailed it, right?" She beams. "My accent was perfect. I'll have to show Aunt Deb my new skills."

"Very memorable," I say, struggling to keep a straight face as the man returns with an overflowing armful of boxes. Box after box of condoms spill onto the counter like an avalanche.

Katie's eyes go wide. "What did you make me say?"

I grin, unable to hold it in any longer. "You said. Excuse me. I am a sex addict from America. I need condoms. Lots and lots of condoms. I want to sample as many Italian men as possible."

The pharmacist winks at her, and I lose it.

I laugh so hard I keel over on the counter. Through tears, I apologize profusely *(to the man, not Katie)*, who laughs and waves me off like this is the highlight of his day. I buy a few boxes for his trouble. "Grazie!"

"This is *No Sex Day*!" she protests as we leave.

"Tomorrow isn't."

"Bold of you to assume you will have access after that stunt."

"You're still holding my hand."

She looks down at our joined fingers like they've committed treason. "That's... that's just because I need someone to carry all these condoms."

"Sure it is, principessa. Sure it is."

***

AFTER HOURS OF WANDERING and chatting, we're now at Ponte Pietra—a bridge so historic you'd half expect it to still demand a toll in Roman coins. We overlook the Adige River, and the water churns in a rhythm so perfect it's like it knows we're getting the ultimate romantic movie backdrop.

Katie leans her elbows on the stone railing, her wide, curious eyes taking in everything, as if she's trying to memorize it all. "I could get used to this."

She's breathtaking.

I thread my fingers through hers. "I love the feeling of your hand in mine."

She squeezes back. The simple gesture floods my body with warmth.

"So this is the famous Ponte Pietra," I say, focusing on something other than kissing her senseless. "Built by the Romans in 100 BC, which makes it Verona's oldest bridge. The Romans built it, of course, but it's been destroyed and rebuilt a few times since then. Kind of like Chester's new knee."

"That thing is indestructible! Did you see him doing squats on the beach?"

"Sì, sì, it's burned into my brain—one day, my boys will be taking a permanent vacation down south."

Her laughter fades as her gaze drifts to the river below. She's quiet for a moment, her expression thoughtful, almost hesitant. "Matteo," she says as her fingers brush against mine, "you don't have to tell me if you don't want to, but... what happened to your parents?"

My body stiffens, the weight of her question sinking into my chest like a stone.

Her face falls. "Oh God, I'm sorry. I shouldn't have asked that. Never mind. Forget I—"

"No." The word surprises me as much as her. "No, it's okay."

And it is. Somehow. With Katie, it feels... safe. Like maybe I can say the words without them breaking me all over again. There's a tone to her voice—genuine and gentle—that compels me to share this part of myself.

"They died in a car accident," I say. "I was ten."

Her hand tightens its hold on mine, her grip solid and grounding. "Matteo... I'm so sorry. I can't imagine not having parents growing up."

I nod, my gaze now fixed on the river's rushing water, catching the way the sunlight dances on the surface. "It's not something you really ever get over. You just... learn to carry it."

I brace myself for the look—the pity, the awkward head tilt, the well-meaning but hollow platitudes. But Katie doesn't give me any of that. Instead, she lifts her head, her voice gentle but curious.

"Will you tell me about them? What were they like?"

I didn't expect this. Most people ask about the accident—the aftermath—the pain. But Katie? She wants to know about *them.*

I breathe deep, the memories rushing back in vivid detail. "They were both history buffs," I say, a small smile tugging at my lips. "They met working as tour guides in Rome. My dad was obsessed with architecture, and my mom loved ancient mythology. They used to argue over which was more important—the buildings or the stories behind them."

"So that's where you get it from. The passion, the storytelling?"

"Yeah," I say, the ache in my chest easing a little.

"Is that why you became a tour guide?"

"It's my way of staying connected to them," I say, feeling a pang of sadness.

"Were they as fun as you?"

I chuckle. "My mom was. She had this laugh—loud and contagious. You couldn't hear it without smiling. She always smelled like lemons. Huh... I don't know why, but I forgot about that."

Katie smiles and asks, "And your dad?"

"Stern at times but also tenderhearted. My mom always said he was the most handsome, charming man she'd ever met. They were... affectionate. Always holding hands, sneaking kisses when they thought I wasn't looking. As a kid, it drove me crazy. But now... I think I understand."

Katie laughs softly. "That's every kid with their parents. My mom and dad weren't too mushy, but Aunt Deb makes up for it. She's a walking PDA."

I reach into my pocket and pull out my phone. "Would you like to see them?"

Her eyes brighten. "I'd love to."

I swipe to the folder I keep hidden. I only open it when I'm feeling lost... when I need to remember. I hand her the phone, watching her expression soften.

"Wow," she says with awe. "Your mom was right. Your dad is way better looking than you."

I laugh, snatching the phone back. "That's enough family commentary from you, principessa."

We fall silent, allowing the soothing water to lull us into a peaceful stillness. Katie wraps her arms around me in a hug, and I find myself accepting the comfort.

"You know," I say finally with a rough voice. "The Wish Cards were their idea."

She stays quiet, but her thumb strokes across my back, encouraging.

"Right before... before the accident, they gave me this stack of blank cards. Said every dream deserved to be written down and that no wish was too big or too small. We were going to do them together, one by one."

The memory cuts through me like a jagged blade. "After their funeral, I found them in my room. All these cards. Promises we'd never keep. I almost burned them." My voice cracks. "Years later I realized—what if their gift wasn't meant to end with me?"

"That's why you do it for the tourists." Understanding dawns in her eyes. "You're not only granting wishes. You're keeping their dream alive."

"Every card people fill out, every wish I grant—it's like they're still here, helping me create the magic they believed in." The confession burns in my throat. "Some days it's the only thing keeping me going."

"Matteo." She pulls back to look at me, her eyes glistening. "What a beautiful way to honor them."

I meet her gaze, my chest tight but warm. "They would have loved you."

She reaches up and kisses me gently, and for the first time in years, I feel something I thought I'd lost forever.

Home.

CHAPTER SIXTEEN

KATIE

Group Chat: CPK Forever

Me: Quick poll: Are we having a hot girl or a hot mess summer?

Petra: OMG NEITHER! My brother just held an emergency staff meeting about proper email etiquette.

Petra: He used the phrase "font crimes against humanity" six times. Apparently someone used Comic Sans...

Petra: It was me. And I'll do it again!

Cam: Can't talk. Boss is having an Instagram-induced breakdown. Currently googling "How to stage your own kidnapping for content" while I hide in his closet.

Me: Maybe I'll stay in Italy forever. Way less drama here.

Cam: Don't you dare!

Petra: NOT FUNNY!

LORENZO IS IN FULL beast mode—standing at the side of the bus, chucking suitcases like they've personally offended him. There's no rhyme or reason to his method. No Tetris-style stacking. It's sheer brute force, sweat, and aggressive handkerchief brow swiping.

THUNK. CRASH. BANG.

I wince as another designer suitcase takes flight, propelled by Lorenzo's surprising upper body strength. It ricochets off the vehicle's undercarriage like a deranged pinball before joining its fellow travel companions.

"Need help?" I ask Lorenzo.

He grunts, then shoots me a look that says, *No.*

"Got it," I say, nodding way too agreeably to get on his good side. "I wouldn't want anyone messing with my organizational system either."

The morning sun warms the cobblestones outside our Venice hotel, making them glisten like tiny mirrors that reflect the endless blue sky. Our faithful rust-bucket-of-a-bus has returned, and I hate how happy it makes me. Seeing it parked there feels strangely reassuring, as if the bus carries a piece of Matteo with it.

I lean against the motorcoach, scrolling through the same three apps on my phone without taking anything in. The truth is, I couldn't sleep last night. I tossed and turned like an overstuffed burrito being rolled by an aggressive Chipotle employee, replaying every second of our date.

And Matteo—true to his word—stuck to the whole *No Sex Day* thing.

Every time I close my eyes, the moments from our date come alive: our fingers laced together—wandering through hidden Verona alleys—how his eyes crinkled when he laughed at my terrible attempts at Italian. I especially loved the warm press of his shoulder against mine as I fell asleep on him on the train ride back to Venice.

My heart seriously needed the breathing room last night. These feelings inside me are growing faster than Aunt Deb's stash of pricey Italian jewelry.

WHOOSH. THUD.

A red hard-sided case pulls off an impressive triple axel before crash-landing upside down.

"I really need someone to talk to. My friends are drowning in work drama, my mom still signs all her texts Team Jared, and my auntie's relationship advice is always 'Don't buy the gelato shop... sample *all* the flavors!'"

SLAM. A designer duffel becomes one with the pavement.

"And, I mean, I trust you," I add. "You didn't rat me out to Matteo about my little beachside meltdown. So... you're my guy."

Another grunt. This one sounds like reluctant acceptance.

"I'm just gonna say it: I really like Matteo."

"Sì," Lorenzo says flatly.

"I'm not imagining it, right?" I press. "Matteo likes me too. The way he talks to me, the stuff he's shared... He told me about his parents."

This earns me a faint flicker of acknowledgment—a raised eyebrow maybe? Or it could've been sweat dripping into his eye... Hard to tell.

"Have you ever been in love?"

He pauses, a designer suitcase in hand. "Sì."

"What happened? Marriage? Little Lorenzos running around Italy?"

"No." He wipes his face again. "I was... foolish. She want marriage. I want... life to live. Young, idiota."

"Did she wait?"

His weathered face softens. "No. She marry. Have bambini. Very happy."

"And you never fell in love again?"

"With life and love, piccola, we not know what we have until..." He gestures vaguely. "Gone."

I'm about to ask if this sage wisdom applies to Matteo or Jared when—

"Lorenzo!"

The man himself appears. He's even more gorgeous today, wearing a fitted olive-green button-down shirt and tan pants that make his butt look extra yummy.

"How'd she drive yesterday?" Matteo asks.

Grunt.

"Any concerns about our three-hour trip?"

Shrug.

"You learn to speak Lorenzo the more you're around him," Matteo explains to me with a grin.

Lorenzo sneaks a wink my way when Matteo's attention is elsewhere. I flash him a smile in return.

"Everyone's loaded except one very important passenger." Matteo smiles, and it's a tsunami of warmth, crashing over me from head to toe.

Lorenzo mysteriously vanishes, and before I can blink, Matteo pulls my body flush against his.

"Sit with me today?"

I nod, my heart doing backflips.

"Tell me, were your sheets cold without me?" His whisper sends shivers down my spine.

"Actually, yes. My lady parts got lonely so I hopped a train back to Verona for a quickie with the pharmacist."

"*Farmacista*," he corrects. "And that's not funny."

"You seemed to enjoy the joke yesterday."

"Yesterday I hadn't spent an entire night without you," he says, cradling my face. "Without your soft breaths against my chest, and the way you curl into me like you belong there." His eyes go dark as espresso. "Now I'm starving for you, principessa."

His hand slides to the back of my neck, anchoring me in place as his mouth moves against mine, coaxing, demanding, tasting as if he's memorizing me. The kiss is devastating, consuming, and obliterates every thought in my head. My fingers grip his shirt, the soft fabric bunching beneath my palms as I try to steady myself.

But when Matteo kisses me like this—it's full-on vertigo.

And then, just as suddenly, he pulls back, his forehead resting against mine, both of us gasping for air.

"You're making this impossible," he murmurs, grabbing my hand like he owns it. Next thing I know he's hauling me toward the bus as if I'm some prize he won at the fair.

Impossible? What the hell does *impossible* mean? *The kiss? Me? Him?*

***

I SINK INTO MY bus seat, the worn fabric greeting my thighs like an old frenemy. Up front, Matteo and Lorenzo are performing their daily mime show of vehicular communication. Lorenzo responds to questions about fuel levels with eyebrow choreography while Matteo somehow translates "check engine light" from a single nostril flare.

"Katie-kins!" Aunt Deb's voice sings from across the aisle where she's cozied up in Howie's lap. "You'll never believe the evening we had!"

Her eyes sparkle, matching the massive ruby pendant hanging between her breasts.

"Club del Doge." She sighs dreamily. "Right on the water, facing the Doge's Palace. The most romantic dinner of my life. We drank so much champagne! Howie only orders the best, don't you, sugarplum?"

"Every minute with you deserves celebration, darlin'." Howie's drawl has gotten thicker, if that's possible.

I can't stop staring at what appears to be the Crown Jewels around my aunt's neck. "Is that—"

"Oh, this?" Aunt Deb casually adjusts the heart-shaped ruby, which is the size of a baby's fist. "Howie insisted."

"Miss Deborah Fox has stolen my heart," Howie declares. "Might as well make it official."

"I told him it was too much—over a hundred thousand euros!" Aunt Deb fans herself dramatically. "But then this naughty boy went and got the matching earrings!"

She swishes her head side to side like she's Beyoncé on stage, flashing ruby earrings so big they could fund an ocean-side mansion.

"It's only money." Howie waves his hand dismissively. "I spent my whole life making it, never had anyone worth spending it on.

Besides"—he takes Deb's bejeweled hand—"no gem could outshine my sweet tea's natural beauty."

"Oh you!" Aunt Deb playfully swats his chest. "You know what that nickname does to me!" She grabs his face and plants a kiss that makes several seniors wolf whistle.

"We painted the town red!" she announces, lipstick slightly smeared. "Dancing in the streets until three a.m.! Singing 'That's Amore' to confused street cats! I haven't felt this young since that weekend with Mick Jagger in Belgium—but that's a story for another time."

Howie chuckles. "Deborah, you make me feel twenty-five again."

Deb giggles, batting her eyelashes at him. "And you got me feeling... like a teenager but with fancier accessories."

My heart does this weird squeeze-flutter thing watching them. Italy has scrambled their brains like the world's most romantic omelet. Of course, who am I to judge?

But maybe that's all this is—the "Italy Effect." It's beer goggles with better carbs. Take away the gondolas, the sweeping vistas, and the sunset-stained canals—what's left? Credit card debt and buffet bellies.

"Speaking of romance." Aunt Deb's smile turns wicked. "How did *you* spend your day, Katie darling?"

"Oh, you know," I say, trying to keep my tone casual. "I went on the train to Verona."

"Alone?"

"Well... Matteo offered me a hands-on sightseeing experience... showing me tour guide stuff."

"Mm-hmm. Tour guide stuff. Is that what the kids are calling it these days?"

"Attenzione!" Matteo's voice rings through the bus interior. "Time to tell Lorenzo to drive! *Uno... due... tre!*"

"Lorenzo, guida l'autobus!" we all shout in varying levels of competence. Aunt Deb's version comes out as "Lor-enzo goo-da le bust!" while Howie sounds like he's chanting "Lord Zen, guide us."

I give it my best shot, but Matteo's eyes meet mine with a wink, and I know I've butchered it as badly as everyone else.

Lorenzo grunts in acknowledgment from the driver's seat and slams the door shut. The bus lurches forward, groaning like an arthritic elephant, and we're off.

Matteo pulls out a Wish Card with his signature flourish. "Today's wish comes from Mrs. Thomas!"

"Let me guess," Chester calls out. "Wishing for husband number three?"

"Fool me once, shame on you. Fool me twice, shame on me!" Mrs. Thomas shoots back. "There won't be a third sequel to those disaster movies."

The passengers erupt in laughter, and Matteo grins. "Actually, Mrs. Thomas wished to visit the Fountain of Youth. Now as much as I would love to promise eternal youth," Matteo says, his voice still tinged with laughter, "I must inform you that particular tourist attraction is in Florida. Perhaps that will be your next trip."

"Only if you're the guide!" someone shouts from the back.

"We better book it soon," someone adds, and the riders explode into another round of morbid jokes about burial plots, two-for-one cremations, and retirement communities.

"So instead of Florida, we are going to the Medieval Days Festival in San Marino!" Matteo announces with dramatic flair. "Where you'll all step back in time and become Lords and Ladies for a day."

"Do we get swords?" Chester yells.

"We already saw yours on the nude beach!" Howie drawls. "Not exactly Excalibur!"

The group erupts again. Wowza, these seniors are wild today. Maybe they were all out partying with Aunt Deb and Howie until three a.m.

"We'll feast! We'll dance! And guess what?" he pauses dramatically. "We'll even try our hands at archery."

As Matteo launches into his tour guide spiel about San Marino, I'm mesmerized by him—how his hands paint pictures in the air, his eyes sparkle with excitement, and yes, fine, the way his forearms flex when he gestures is giving my hormones a lap dance.

He's magnetic.

Alive.

Present in a way that makes my binders feel like security blankets I need to set on fire.

This isn't the smooth-talking player I first pegged him for—this is a man who gets genuine joy from making other people's dreams come true, even if those dreams need some creative reinterpretation and possibly liability waivers.

But does he care about me? Or am I just another notch in his tour guide belt? One more story he'll tell the next group while sipping wine and laughing about *that American girl who fell for the tour guide?*

It's only a fling. There's no logical explanation for this. We live on different continents, speak different languages—we want completely different things.

So why does my heart keep betraying me, whispering that I want him anyway?

"San Marino," his voice cuts through my spiral, "is the world's oldest continuous republic. Founded in 301 AD, never conquered, never ruled by a monarch. It's technically not even part of Italy—it's its own country with only thirty thousand residents. Like Vatican City but with better parties and fewer guilt trips."

Matteo finishes his big medieval-themed announcement with the kind of grin that makes everyone swoon—myself included—and hands the microphone back to its holder. The seniors burst into chatter as Matteo slides into the seat beside me, his hand finding mine with practiced ease.

"Sounds like a fun day ahead," I say.

"Sì, principessa." But Matteo's smile falters, just for a second. It's subtle, but I notice.

"What's wrong?"

He brings our joined hands to his lips, pressing a kiss to my knuckles. "Nothing to worry about."

"Tell me? Maybe I can help."

I bite my lip. *Have I crossed a line?* Just because he opened up yesterday about his parents doesn't mean he's ready to make vulnerability a habit. Some walls take more than a day—even a perfect one.

But then his shoulders drop slightly, and he lets out a soft sigh. "It's Stan's Wish Card. He wants to throw Rose a surprise party for their sixtieth anniversary. But there's no time. The tour... the tour ends in three days."

Three days? The words hit me and my stomach drops, but I push the panic aside.

"What about Enrico's winery?" The idea bursts out of me. "That terrace where we had dinner? With the views and the string lights? Add some food, decorations, music—it would be perfect!"

"There's no time, no money. The only opening in the schedule would be tomorrow evening, and—"

"I'll do it." The words come out firm, certain. "I can skip tomorrow's activities and set everything up. I want to do this for them. For you."

His eyes search mine. "Katie, you're on vacation. You shouldn't have to—"

"Have you met me?" I wave our joined hands between us. "Planning is literally my love language. My idea of foreplay is creating a detailed timeline with a dozen backup plans."

The minute the words leave my mouth, his eyes darken dangerously. Right. Maybe bringing up foreplay wasn't the smartest move when we're surrounded by seniors with questionable hearing aids.

"Just ask Enrico," I push on, trying to ignore the heat in his gaze. "Let me help. Consider it my gift to Stan and Rose. And to you."

"*Sei incredibile*. Thank you."

But then reality bitch-slaps me.

Three. Days.

Thanks to Matteo, I'm finally the main character in my own life. But... I've been so lost in this Italian fling—in wine cellar revelations and nude-beach shenanigans—that I completely lost track of time. How didn't I notice? I literally have seven different time-tracking apps!

Three days—that's all I have.

Not enough to figure out if this thing in my chest is love or carb-induced euphoria.

Not enough to know if I'm falling for Matteo or if Italy has pickpocketed my common sense.

Not enough to decide if I can go back... to my old structured ways... to before I felt so alive.

Am I falling for him or just the idea of him? *How can I know for sure?*

***

I'M HANGING AT THE rear of our group like a coward, pretending to study San Marino's fairy-tale skyline while actually watching Matteo through my phone's camera. Not taking pictures—just using it as cover so I can sneakily stare. Because apparently that's who I am now.

"Stay together, everyone!" Matteo calls out from the front of the group. "The tram will arrive soon, and we'll all board at once. No wandering off!"

I used to pride myself on my well-constructed life plans and my ability to anticipate every possible outcome. But here I am, melting into a puddle because Matteo just helped Rose adjust her sun hat and that sweet gesture makes me want to cry.

My fingers twitch, seeking comfort in what I do best—making lists. I open my notes app.

Reasons Why I Am *Not* In Love with Matteo Monti:

1. His smile. It's too perfect and ridiculously comforting *(Highly suspicious)*.

2. His endless patience with our group of chaotic seniors *(No one should be this calm around Aunt Deb)*.

3. The stupidly adorable way he mutters in Italian when he's frustrated.

4. How many orgasms he produces—no way that's sustainable.

5. My name on his lips—not just the accent but how he makes "Katie" sound precious.

6. How he actually listens when I ramble about spreadsheets, like my organizational fetish is endearing instead of weird.

7. The stories he tells about his mom and dad—not just the happy ones but the hard ones too—he trusts me with his pain.

8. The fact that he values my need for control, like it's not a defect, but an important part of me.

9. How he's my safety net and a trampoline all in one—making me feel protected even as he launches me into chaos *(and yes, I see the irony)*.

"Attenzione! The tram approaches!" Matteo calls out, and his eyes find mine across the crowd.

And there it is, reason number ten:

When I'm with him I know I'm exactly where I'm supposed to be.

My heart hammers as I look at the list. It's not denial; it's undeniable.

This is a confession.

A declaration.

A love letter. I've completely, utterly fallen for him.

The tram creaks up the mountain track, and my stomach drops—partly from altitude, mostly from facts. I have three short days to figure out if he feels the same way or if I'm another tourist passing through his life.

Is there a WikiHow for "Figuring Out If Your Hot Tour Guide Loves You Back without Dying of Embarrassment?"

San Marino steals my breath the second we arrive. Not just because we're literally in the clouds on top of a mountain, but because this place looks like someone took every Disney castle I watched as a kid and made them real. The cobblestone streets are so narrow they seem designed for goats. The air smells of wildflowers, roasted chestnuts, and the faint tang of sunscreen from all the tourists. Everywhere I turn, people are dressed like extras from a Medieval Times dinner theater.

Jared once took me to Medieval Times in Orange County, and I thought *that* was immersive with their plastic swords and bored horses. This is a gazillion times better.

My fingers trace the rough stone of a thousand-year-old wall as I try not to stare at Matteo. He's in his element, navigating our group through streets barely wide enough for crowds of humans, much less the parade of vendors hawking their wares. Every time he speaks—whether it's explaining a historical detail or giving directions—my body reacts as if he's whispering something scandalous for later, not just telling Mrs. Thomas to watch her step.

Because I'm so busy having an emotional crisis about my rapidly dwindling time with Matteo, I almost miss Aunt Deb's grand entrance.

She and Howie step out of a vendor's stall, looking like the medieval prom king and queen. Most of the group wears small souvenirs—a cone hat here, a knight vest there—but they've gone all in. Aunt Deb twirls in her velvet gown with gold embroidery and a tiara while Howie strikes a pose in a lord's cape and tunic. It's like they did Disney World's Princess Makeover but with a medieval twist—and zero restraint.

"I'm Lady Deborah of Pasadena!" Aunt Deb declares, her arms spread wide. "And this is my Lord Howie of the Butter Bliss Bars Kingdom!"

The group bursts into applause as Howie sweeps into an exaggerated bow, nearly losing his balance. It's so fabulously over the top that I whip out my phone and snap a picture to send to my mom.

The day is jam-packed, leaving no room to breathe, let alone have a serious conversation. We do everything: practicing archery, basket weaving, touring a castle with actors playing knights and ladies-in-waiting, plus watching a parade complete with dancers, drummers, and those extra-long trumpet players. It's glorious and overwhelming, but it's also leaving my heart unable to ask its tour guide for directions.

Through it all, Matteo moves like water—fluid, constant, everywhere at once. His hand finds mine in stolen moments, fingers tangling briefly before duty calls him away. Each touch whispers a promise, but of what?

There's been no time. No quiet breaks. No opportunity to pull him aside and talk. And as the day wears on, a sinking thought edges its way into my mind: Maybe that's the point. Maybe Matteo's keeping us all so busy so we *don't* have time to talk.

I offered to help earlier with tour guide triage—I mean, I wanted to—but Matteo just smiled and told me to enjoy the festivities. Which, fine, I have been. But I've also found myself wishing I could be useful. There's something oddly satisfying about helping these people, making sure everyone's okay, and solving the little problems before they spiral into bigger ones.

A realization creeps up slowly, then hits all at once. Like dominoes hitting one another with slow momentum before leading up to the big crash.

Matteo and I—we're two sides of the same coin. Both of us chasing that high of creating the best moments, of turning chaos into magic. Him with his natural charm and endless stories, me with my need to organize and produce results.

And suddenly I can't stop imagining what we could be together. *What if I didn't go back?*

The very thought should terrify me. Should send me running for my comfort zone of corporate events and predictable outcomes. Instead, it feels as if I've been holding my breath for years and now I'm finally exhaling.

We could work... together. I could handle the business side—the stuff that makes Matteo break out in hives—the schedules, the bookings, the spreadsheets. And he could keep being this force of nature that makes everyone fall in love with Italy. With him.

We'd make a hell of a team.

Mornings spent wrapped in his arms, trading kisses and itinerary changes. Late nights planning routes over wine and laughter, arguing about the best stops while his hands draw patterns on my skin. Working in harmony, knowing what the other needs without asking. Creating something bigger than ourselves.

Each tour would be unique. Each group would become family.

And the people we'd meet—the travelers from around the world, each with their own stories, their own dreams. We'd love watching faces light up as our guests experienced the unforgettable, knowing we made that happen. It's honestly what I love about my job now, except here? It feels... different, better, life-changing.

I can picture us both packing up the bus at the end of a long day, Lorenzo grumbling in the background. Matteo slipping his arm around my waist, pulling me close, and telling me I'm working too hard... again. I'll roll my eyes and respond, telling him he talks too much... again. Then he'll kiss me with a soft, lingering kiss that says everything words can't.

It's ridiculous, right? Totally, completely ridiculous.

I'm having an out-of-body experience while planning my own intervention. But for the first time, my life back home is not the only option. I can actually see myself here—with him.

"Everything okay, principessa?" Matteo says, breaking my fantasy. His eyes are soft, curious.

"Just thinking about party logistics," I lie.

"My beautiful planner," he murmurs, his fingers finding mine. "Always trying to organize the world."

That's when it hits me—the wake-up call I've been avoiding harder than my mother's constant texts about Jared.

Matteo doesn't do relationships.

There it is. The voice of Old Katie—perpetual planner, professional overthinker, and captain of the SS *Anxiety*—chiming in right on schedule. She's already reaching for her phone, ready to create a bulleted list titled Ways This Could Go Horrifically Wrong.

And honestly? She's got a point.

But then.

Something shifts inside me. This new version of myself—the one who's learned that sometimes the best memories come from unplanned moments and questionable decisions—just stands up and says: *Hold my wine.*

Am I terrified? Ab-so-freaking-lutely. But you know what? *Fuck that.*

Fuck the lists and the plans and the careful calculations. Fuck playing it safe and always knowing the outcome before you start. And especially fuck this idea that Matteo "doesn't do relationships." He's never tried one with *me*.

Old Katie is having an aneurysm right now, but New Katie? She's yelling "YOLO" and swan-diving into God-knows-what.

Because what's scarier than telling him?

Not telling him.

And if he doesn't feel the same? Old Katie echoes in my head.

But what if he does...?

CHAPTER SEVENTEEN

MATTEO

KATIE HAS TURNED MY hotel room upside down. My bed is now her personal command center, with plans spread across the white sheets like battle strategies. And I have to say... I'm into it. She's fascinating—the way she owns this space, my space, as if she belongs here. It's past midnight, and I love seeing her sprawled on her stomach, wearing nothing but my button-down shirt.

Dio, she's brilliant. Focused. Passionate. Her silky, golden hair still mussed from an hour ago when I laid her face down on that bed and she was begging for more *(or was that me?)*. That release was supposed to satisfy me, but watching her work now is revving me up again.

My laptop is overheating on my thighs while my inbox is mocking me. No word from the bank. No miracle solution for my failing company.

BING! BING!

Two new messages come in. One promising to enlarge a part of me that definitely doesn't need it *(trust me)* and another hinting that

I might have a long-lost uncle in Nigeria who's very generous with his Bitcoin. *Delete.*

Katie makes this little sound of triumph, solving whatever coordinating issue she was working on, and she's the best distraction I could ask for.

I love watching her mind work. The way she organizes—precise but passionate, controlled but creative—is captivating. Every note she writes, every diagram she draws, it's all infused with fierce determination to make tomorrow perfect for Stan and Rose. My little taskmaster has the biggest heart I've ever seen, and it's doing dangerous things to mine.

She rolls over in my oversized shirt, and I get a fresh peek at her cotton panties. My cock perks up like an overfed German Shepherd catching a whiff of bacon. *Down boy. We've already christened every surface in this room. Twice.*

I can't resist sliding my hand up the back of her thigh.

"Matteo," she warns without looking up, "if those magical fingers don't behave, this seating chart is going to end up with Chester doing the chicken dance next to the cake."

"Maybe your attention needs a little... redirection." I let my fingers trail higher, dipping under the waistband of her panties.

She turns her head, fixing me with that librarian-gone-wild look that makes my cock throb.

"Don't you have your own work to do?"

"You're too distracting. The way you write those little numbers? Very sexy."

She snorts. "Do not pretend you find basic addition erotic."

"Equations while wrapped up in my shirt? Mathematical foreplay."

I lean over, pretending to study her elaborate diagrams while actually breathing in her scent—strawberries and sex.

My eyes catch on a carefully measured rectangle in the center of her layout. "Is that a dance floor, bellissima?"

"Duh. It's a party. Obviously there will be dancing."

"Will you dance with me tomorrow?"

"Trust me, nobody wants to see my dance moves. I can organize circles around people, but dancing? That's a hard pass. And I blame Aunt Deb for that particular life lesson."

"Coming from your aunt, this has to be good." I shift closer, drawn to her like gravity. "Tell me."

"Fine. But this is trauma-level embarrassing. You have to promise not to laugh."

"If I laugh, I'll make it up to you with that thing you enjoy," I say suggestively. "You know, with my tongue?"

"Deal." She breathes in deeply, a playful twinkle in her eyes. "Okay, so imagine this: fifth-grade talent show and little Katie is all fired up to win. I thought, 'Why not dance?' One small issue—I don't dance. I'd never been taught. But who needs formal training when you've got sheer willpower?"

"That doesn't sound so terrible."

"Just wait. I've always been an overachiever, so I decided to study some dance videos. Specifically, from my auntie's collection."

"Oh no," I gasp, already feeling the laughter building.

"Turns out I was learning Aunt Deb's stripper routine from her exotic dancing days. I went onstage and performed her choreography—minus the actual stripping, thank God—in front of the entire school. "Pour Some Sugar on Me" blasted through the gym, and I thought I was killing it. When I started grinding against the microphone stand, they slammed down the curtain."

I burst into laughter.

"It earned me the nickname K-Tease for years." She's laughing now too, and the sound makes my chest warm. "My dad couldn't look me in the eye for weeks."

"Let me guess. Aunt Deb didn't apologize?"

"Are you kidding? She gave me pointers on my hip movements and bought me a mini feather boa."

"Of course she did." I pull her into my lap, loving how naturally she fits there. "Dance with me tomorrow anyway. I promise to keep you far away from microphone stands."

She wraps her arms around my neck, and—*Madre di Dio*—the trust in her eyes undoes me completely. "If you want me to."

"I definitely do."

I want everything with you. Every story, every laugh, every imperfect moment. I want it all.

"You laughed," she points out, "so you owe me."

"I feel I was set up. You knew that story was impossible not to laugh at."

"You'll never prove it," she challenges, then kisses me soft and sweet.

My hands slide to her hips, ready to pull her closer, when her phone buzzes against the nightstand like a sudden alarm.

She groans, breaking the kiss with a sigh. "It's my mom." She reaches over me and grabs it.

"Is she still texting you about Jared," I ask, trying to keep the jealous heat from my voice.

"Every day."

Jared. The name I thought we'd left behind. Katie doesn't meet my gaze as she powers off the phone and tosses it on the nightstand.

"Sorry," she says quickly, her voice too bright. "Let's forget it, okay?"

But I can't forget it. Not when the mention of him feels like a rock sinking in my gut.

Does she still think about him?

Is she planning on going back to him?

The questions gnaw at me as her head nuzzles into my neck. Her fingers trace soft, mindless patterns on my skin and I lie there, letting her quiet touch soothe the raging storm in my mind.

When the hell did I turn into *this* guy—holding on to her like she might evaporate if I loosen my grip? I've always been the one racing for the exit, keeping things surface level, uncomplicated. Now I'm lying here wondering how I'll survive when she walks away in three days.

She's quiet, her breathing steady as she keeps drawing what feels like hearts on my chest. I want to ask what's going on in that amazing mind of hers, but I'm afraid to break whatever spell we're under.

"So," she finally says, "what do you have planned tomorrow while I'm getting the party ready?"

"Several Wish Cards wanted to visit the hot springs," I say, keeping my tone light.

How can I stretch these moments into forever?

She hums thoughtfully, fingers lightly dancing across my sternum. A heart, then a circle. Cristo, her touch sends electricity zipping through my body.

"What happens after?" she asks quietly. "When the tour ends? Do you just... jump into the next group?"

"Usually I take a week off first." I run my fingers through her sex-messed hair. "Got to handle the thrilling paperwork. Your favorite."

Her laugh is soft but hollow. "Oh."

I watch her carefully—the way her mouth tightens at the corners, how her fingers pause before resuming their patterns. She's holding something back...

"Actually," I say, trying to sound casual. "I've got two weeks free after this tour. Business stuff to handle."

She goes still, then lifts those green eyes to mine. "Hypothetically," she whispers, "would you have time if I... stayed?"

My heart stops. Literally stops.

Every muscle in my body locks up. *Is she saying what I think she's saying?* I choose my next words with more care than I've ever given anything in my life. "Hypothetically, I could make time."

"And hypothetically, would there be somewhere I could stay? For those two weeks?"

I forget how to breathe. This has to be a dream. Some cruel dream where Katie Crawford is talking about staying. Even if it's only fourteen days, it's more than I deserve.

But I've waited too long to answer, and she starts backpedaling, words tumbling out in a panic.

"That's insane, right? I mean, now you're probably thinking I'm some clingy tourist, but I'm not. I promise. I just... I don't know, I thought maybe—"

"Katie," I cut her off, tilting her face up to meet my gaze. Cristo, those eyes. They hold everything I've been too scared to admit I want. "I will rearrange my entire life for you. Stay. Please. I've been going crazy wondering how I can ask without scaring you off."

"Really?"

"I don't know what this is," I confess, "but I want to find out. With you."

"I feel the same way. And then... after that? After those two weeks?"

"That's a problem for future us," I murmur, leaning in until our noses brush. "Right now if I don't make love to you, I will combust from happiness."

Her laughter bubbles up, bright and free, right before I capture her lips in a heated kiss. My hand slides to the small of her back, pulling her in, as my other hand carefully gathers her binder and papers.

"Oh my God," she breathes against my lips. "That's so fucking hot."

"My girl likes things neat and tidy."

"Your girl?" she repeats, teasing.

"Yeah," I growl, yanking her to me. "Mine."

Those green eyes go dark with want, and before I can blink, she grabs the binder and hurls it off the bed, sending papers flying everywhere. She tugs me on top of her, fingers pulling at my hair as her body arches into mine.

Honest to God, I've never been so devastatingly happy in my entire life.

***

"SMELLS LIKE SOMEBODY FED a dog a half pound of Limburger cheese," Chester says as he pinches his nose.

I swallow my laugh, having heard every variation of fart jokes possible at these springs. From "Fart-nado Falls" to "Bubble Butt Bidet" to "Satan's Bunghole," my tourists never disappoint.

"Signore e signori." I gesture to the cascading pools before us, steam rising like nature's own special effects. "Welcome to the Saturnia Hot Springs. That distinctive aroma? It's sulfur, straight from Mother Earth herself."

The pale blue waters cascade down natural stone terraces, creating steaming pools that look like something from a fantasy movie. Water flows from a small waterfall at the top, rushing down over smooth rocks, the sound soft and hypnotic. The scent? Okay, it's not exactly an ocean breeze, but the sight more than makes up for it.

My group of seniors are already suited up, ready to conquer these springs with towels and beach bags.

"These waters are heated by our local volcano. A constant temperature of thirty-seven degrees Celsius, maintained by..." I trail off, my mind drifting to Katie.

Katie. Her name lingers in my mind like a melody. She's at Enrico's vineyard with Caterina, preparing the place for Stan and Rose's sixty-year celebration. I can picture Caterina in one of her flamboyant rants about Italian men and Katie chiming in with an exaggerated story about me. Those two are probably making an assembly line of decorations and food while teasing each other about who's more of a perfectionist *(Katie)*. I'm sure Katie's working her organizational magic and turning the chaos of a last-minute party into a dream come true.

"Earth to Matteo!" Margaret snaps. "You were telling us about the magical powers of fart water?"

"Ah, sì, *scusate,*" I say. "These waters have been known for their healing properties for thousands of years. In fact, the Romans would journey here to heal their wounds."

"Well, hot damn." Chester grins, adjusting his swim trunks which are riding dangerously high.

"Maybe it'll fix my arthritis!"

"And my bum knee!" Agnes adds. "Years of teetering in stilettos—worth every twisted ankle!"

"What about fixing my second ex-husband's personality?" Mrs. Thomas says. "He's permanently glued to his La-Z-Boy, so we're gonna need a crane to get him in there."

The distinctive rumble of a tour bus engine cuts through our laughter. I don't even need to look. It's Italy Express—a rolling crimson reminder of everything wrong with modern tourism. Their massive bus gleams in the afternoon sun, pristine and soulless.

Their guide steps out in his pressed red polo, looking as if he irons it between mandatory gift shop stops. His herd of tourists follows, each sporting matching shirts and those ridiculous headphones, shuffling out like a horde of zombies.

"Fifteen minutes for photos and restroom breaks," Red Polo announces with the excitement of a flat soda. "Please maintain appropriate distance from the water; we don't have time to towel off and the buses have a strict no-swimsuit policy."

Any other day this would make my blood boil. But today? My heart is too full of Katie to care about these corporate puppets. Let them have their fifteen minutes. We'll stay here and soak up paradise until our fingers prune.

"Let's get wet!" I say and my group bursts into cheers.

"Cannonball!" Howie's war cry echoes across the springs as he launches into the water.

"Right behind you, my Southern stallion!" Deb says, her designer swimsuit a shimmer of stardust, before splashing in.

I help Rose navigate the slick stones, her small hand gripping mine with fragile strength. The water laps at our ankles, warm and inviting.

Katie would love this, the two of us floating in this oasis. Her lips would taunt me, drawing us closer, our bodies pressing each other until—

Cazzo. My cock just threw me a surprise party, and I'm suddenly very grateful for the water's cloudy properties. It's going to be a long day until I see her again.

Maybe tonight I'll take her back to that wine cellar, show her exactly how much I missed her...

Merda. Romeo's dagger strikes again. It seems my dick won't rest until it embarrasses me in front of all my seniors.

"Matteo!" Chester's voice breaks through my increasingly dangerous thoughts. "Watch this! I'm going to do a handstand!"

"Wait!" I shout. "Don't go—"

Too late. He's upside down mere seconds before he emerges from the water, spitting and choking.

"It's official." Chester gags. "This water tastes worse than it smells."

An hour later, Lorenzo appears at the edge of the springs, his face the color of overripe tomatoes. He's holding his breath, a handkerchief clamped over his nose like it's all that stands between him and death by sulfur. With a dramatic flair, he flashes five fingers.

I know why he's here, but today I'm feeling mischievous.

"Mi dispiace!" I call out in my most innocent tour guide voice. "Your hand signals are confusing me. Perhaps draw me a picture?"

His shoots me a look that says he's reconsidering his life choices, specifically the one where he agreed to work for me. His five fingers now wave frantically.

"What's that?" I shout, cupping my ear. "You want to practice your synchronized swimming routine?"

His eyes bulge out of their sockets. If this were a cartoon, steam would be shooting from his ears. He jabs his finger toward the picnic spot, and his face transitions from red to purple.

"Are you trying to tell me the bus is on fire again?"

That does it. He takes an involuntary gasp of sulfur-laden air and immediately doubles over.

"Merda!" *GAG...* "Puzza!" *RETCH...* "Fanculo!" He dry heaves, then straightens up just enough to spot my shit-eating grin.

The look of pure betrayal he shoots me could wither the richest man's vineyard. I start laughing hysterically. *Damn, I wish Katie was here to see this.*

"Sì, sì, old friend. Time to set up lunch." I wipe tears from my cheeks. "Your commitment to avoiding the fumes is impressive. Even better than that time in Rome with the broken sewage pipe."

"Idiota," he mutters, but the corner of his mouth twitches—the Lorenzo equivalent of rolling on the floor laughing. He shuffles back toward his beloved bus, occasionally stopping to cough.

I call out to the group. "Keep marinating in Mother Nature's hot tub! I'm setting up lunch on that hill. When you're ready, the changing rooms are to your right. Take your time!"

The hill gives a breathtaking view of the springs, like nature's own balcony seats. Wildflowers dot the grass in bursts of purple and yellow, dancing in the light breeze. The view stretches out forever—rolling Tuscan hills painted in shades of green and gold. The best part? Not a whiff of stinky sulfur, making it the perfect picnic spot.

I spread out the blankets that Caterina packed this morning. Despite her advanced pregnancy, she insisted on helping to prepare the picnic—fresh bread, an assortment of cheeses, cured meats, and twenty bottles of La Dolce Vita wine. Before I met Katie, I'd have told myself this is as good as it gets.

I slide my phone out of my pocket and begin typing.

Me: *How's the party planning, bella?*

Her response comes fast—she's been waiting.

Katie: *Everything here is incredible, but it feels wrong without you.*

Katie: *God that sounds clingy after only four hours.*

Me: *Keep talking that way and I might leave these seniors stranded.*

Me: *Worth it to get my hands on you sooner.*

Katie: *Already hid a blanket in the wine cellar.*

Katie: *The red dress might make an appearance tonight...*

Cristo Santo. My cock instantly twitches to the memory of that dress, of her curves wrapped in silk that begged to be peeled away.

Me: *You're testing my self-control*, bellissima.

Katie: *Maybe I like making you lose control.*

I can't wipe the stupid grin off my face. Two weeks. Two whole weeks of having her all to myself after this tour ends. My mind races with possibilities—places to take her, things to show her, ways to make her fall more in love with Italy. *With me.*

What about after that? I shove the thought down. We'll figure it out. She cares for me, I care for her. That's enough for now.

My phone buzzes again and my heart leaps, hoping for another teasing message from Katie.

But an unknown number flashes across the screen.

"Pronto," I answer cheerfully.

"Signor Monti? This is Luigi Vincetti from Banca di Roma."

My spine stiffens. The bank, finally. "Sì, buongiorno."

"I'll be direct. We've exhausted all options for refinancing. No one is willing to take on the risk. Your books simply don't show enough profit margin to justify a new loan."

The world tilts sideways. My throat closes up.

"Your existing loan payment is due in full by the end of the month. If you cannot make the payment, we'll have no choice but to begin bankruptcy proceedings."

"I understand," I manage, the word tasting like ash in my mouth.

"Mi dispiace, Signor Monti. I truly am sorry."

The call ends. I stare at my phone—at Katie's last message still glowing on the screen. I feel my world crumble.

***

THE EMPTY BUS REEKS of defeat. Or perhaps that's just me, sitting here alone while my seniors enjoy their picnic under the Tuscan sun. I sent Lorenzo away with some excuse about business calls. He knew I was lying—his left eyebrow said as much—but he went anyway. Loyalty I don't deserve.

The cloth seat beneath me is torn, worn bare by thousands of tourists who trusted me to show them the real Italy. Now the seat is mocking me. Every imperfection, every tear, every patch job—they're all proof of what I couldn't maintain.

I've been praying, bargaining, hoping this loan would come through. This company isn't just a business to me—it's my parents' legacy reimagined. Every Wish Card granted, every moment of joy created, it's all been for them.

But apparently passion doesn't pay the bills. My spontaneous detours and determination to give everyone their perfect moment have finally caught up with me. The numbers don't lie, even if I've been ignoring them for months.

I've run countless scenarios, searching for alternatives to this backup plan. But there's nowhere left to turn. Time to be a man and admit I'm exactly what I've always feared—a failure.

No more chances.

No more Monti Tours.

My fingers shake slightly. I dial the number I swore I'd never call again.

"Ciao, welcome to Italy Express. Your call is very important to us. If you know the name you wish to speak with, please say it now."

The recorded voice is as soulless as their tours.

"Antonio Toscano." My voice sounds as if it's been dragged through gravel.

"Buongiorno!"

"Buongiorno, Antonio—"

"Matteo Monti! I know that voice." His voice booms with fake cheer. "Your words still make the ladies swoon, no?"

I press my forehead against the window, the glass cool against my skin. Outside, wildflowers dance in the breeze, oblivious to my world imploding. "Nice to be remembered."

"Ha! You were my star! Best-rated guide ever. The tourists, they worshiped you!"

I close my eyes, remembering why I left. "That's good, because I'm calling with a proposition."

"Ah, let me guess—your little dream cards, they finally failed? I wondered how long before reality catches up with you. Though you lasted longer than expected."

"Wish Cards," I say. "And yes, they're popular but—"

"But expensive! This is what I always say—streamline! Tourists just want pictures for Instagram. In, out, cash in pocket."

The worst part is, he's right. I've been a fool, thinking I could build something special in this plastic world.

"So." His voice drips with satisfaction. "You want to come back?"

Through the windshield, I watch my seniors laughing together on their picnic blankets. Chester's telling another terrible joke. The Dawson sisters are sharing a bottle of wine. This—this is what touring should be. Real connections. Real joy.

But dreams don't pay bank loans.

"Yes. I'm stepping away from my company." The words are a surrender.

"You mean you're bankrupt."

My fingers curl into a fist. "No, it's... personal reasons. But I'd like to bring my bus driver with me."

"Ah, still sentimental! Well, you always had the best reviews. I do this for you, but just remember—no funny business. Stick to the schedule."

"I understand."

"Fantastico. You start in Rome in two days."

My heart stops. "Sorry, but I'll need more time to get my affairs settled."

"Now or never, Monti. I had a guide quit this morning."

Katie's face flashes through my mind—earlier today, wearing my shirt, her hair a mess from my hands, planning our next two weeks together with that expression of wonder.

But I'm chaos incarnate. A man who couldn't even keep his parents' dream alive. What could I possibly offer her now? She deserves better than a failed tour guide who can't fucking balance his own books.

She cares about you, my heart whispers.

She shouldn't, my brain answers.

I'm worthless. It's over. I lost.

"I'll be there." My voice sounds dead even in my own ears.

"Excellent! Welcome back to—"

I hang up before he can finish his victory speech. The phone slips from my numb fingers onto the seat.

Through the window, I spot Howie helping Deb adjust her sun hat, both of them laughing. They make it look so easy—choosing love, choosing joy.

But some of us don't get those choices. Some of us must accept reality and admit we're not good enough.

I shouldn't be surprised that it's over. Since I lost my parents, every good thing in my life eventually slips away.

Why should Katie stay?

If walking away makes me a coward, then maybe I am—because I don't know how to stand in front of her without breaking.

CHAPTER EIGHTEEN

KATIE

Mom: *Deborah says you'll be in Rome tomorrow. You should share that on social media. Who knows? It might be the nudge Jared needs to show up and win you back.*

Me: *Or I could toss my phone in the Trevi Fountain so you can't text me anymore.*

Mom: *C'mon, imagine: You turn around and there he is... holding flowers!*

Me: *You really need to get off Pinterest.*

Mom: *Don't be ridiculous! Rome was made for falling in love again.*

Me: *Jared falling back in love with me would require an actual miracle. Like, Vatican-level.*

Mom: *Good idea. If the Pope has an email, I'll find it.*

TODAY HAS BEEN A blur.

I barely remember breakfast or the bus ride to the vineyard. Time seems to have folded in on itself, moving both too fast and not quick enough. Caterina and I spent the day turning the terrace into a scene straight out of an Italian rom-com. Between the arrangements for the party, the chatter about Italy, and the sheer magic of the enchanting Tuscan sun, I've hardly had time to breathe—let alone think about what comes next.

And I kind of don't want to.

And then there's Caterina, the most badass pregnant woman I've ever met. She's been hustling in her tiny kitchen, producing enough authentic cuisine to feed a small army. At the same time, she's somehow orchestrating the arrival of decorations, a portable dance floor, and flowers—we're talking gorgeous custom floral arrangements. Apparently her friend in the village grows them specifically for events like this.

The woman has connections that would make a Mafia boss jealous.

She even tried to move one of the massive wooden tables herself. While. Seven. Months. Pregnant.

I swear Enrico materialized out of thin air, his tall frame blocking her path like a protective wall of Italian masculinity. He planted his feet and his casual smiling eyes went serious. "No, no, no. You sit, mi amore. Or lie down. Or eat something." His tone left no room for argument. "No lifting, *capisce?*"

Caterina's response was pure fire, phrases delivered in Italian so vulgar his eyes went wide. I couldn't understand the words, but the tone? Universal. It was the sound of a woman who's heard "you can't" one too many times. I thought she was going to prove him wrong, but instead, she rolled her eyes and relented, muttering something about how pregnancy isn't an illness.

I couldn't help but laugh. It's easy to see why Enrico is such a guardian of her—she's incredible. The kind of person who makes you pledge your loyalty to her after one conversation.

She's also the reason my brain has been spinning elaborate fantasies all day. It started this morning when she casually dropped the atomic bomb of "I can't wait for you to stay here" while arranging salami. *Hello? Did you just read my soul out loud?*

I nearly inhaled a piece of cheese. "I... I never said—"

"Pfft." She dismissed my protest with a wave of provolone. "Your heart speaks louder than your words. And I see you kiss Matteo before he leave."

From that moment on, she became a one-woman tourism board, painting pictures of my potential future. The seasons in Tuscany. The festivals. The wine harvest. The late-night dinners with food for days and endless laughter. Every dreamy, romantic detail rolled off her tongue like a sultry travel ad, and each one ticked off another box in my fantasy life with Matteo.

I've been secretly rehearsing how to tell everyone about my plans to stay.

My mom will need medical attention.

My friends will stage an intervention.

And Aunt Deb? Well, she probably won't even notice.

My current strategy? Ghost my return flight and deal with the fallout from a safe distance.

Nothing says "mature adult decision" like avoiding confrontation from another continent, right?

The seniors arrived an hour ago, bubbling with excitement and decked out in their finest clothes. Caterina and I worked together to get Rose ready, and I have to admit, the whole thing has been ridiculously sweet. Caterina borrowed a dress from a neighbor—a stunning ivory lace gown—and somehow found a local professional to do Rose's hair and makeup.

Rose stands in front of a mirror, and the room only gets brighter with her smile.

"Oh my," she whispers, running her fingers over the delicate fabric. "I haven't felt this beautiful since my wedding day."

"You look *stunning*," I agree.

Caterina sniffs beside me, dabbing at her eyes with a tissue. "Enrico always say a woman grows more beautiful with every year she is loved."

"I was such a nervous wreck at my wedding," Rose confesses, smoothing nonexistent wrinkles from the dress. "Poor Stan had to practically carry me down the aisle. My hands were shaking so badly he grabbed both of them to calm me down."

"You? Nervous?" I ask.

"Oh, Katie." Her smile is soft, knowing. "Love makes fools of us all. But here's the secret—the nerves don't matter. The dress doesn't matter. Even the wedding doesn't matter. What matters is what comes after. That is everything."

My heart squeezes as Rose turns to face me, wisdom etched in the deep lines on her face. "The real love story isn't in the grand gestures or perfect moments," she says. "It's showing up. Every single day. It's the coffee they bring you when you're exhausted. The way they hold your hand in the doctor's waiting room without being asked. The quiet assurance of 'I'm here and I'm not going anywhere' when life feels like it's falling apart."

I don't understand why, but the truth of her words is exactly what I need to hear.

"Love isn't about control," Rose continues. "It's about trust. About letting someone see all your messy parts and they love you anyway."

I swallow the lump rising in my throat.

"This is why I tell Enrico divorce is never option," she announces, breaking the heavy moment with a grin. She rubs her swollen belly. "Murder? Maybe. Divorce? Never."

Rose laughs. "He's a special man, your Enrico."

"Shh!" Caterina waves her hands frantically, nearly knocking over a vase of roses. "Don't let him hear you say that. His head is already too big to fit through doorways."

***

A SHORT WHILE LATER, the party is in full swing—the night alive with the sound of laughter and conversation. The courtyard is transformed with string lights twinkling like captured stars, casting warm hues over the weathered stone terrace. Candles flicker in the soft evening breeze, their flames dancing in rhythm with the music floating through the air.

My professional pride wants to catalog every detail I got right—the way the vintage crystal vases throw light across the tables, how the wildflowers soften the ancient stone walls with splashes of pink and white. The Forever in Love banner gleams in gold script above the dance floor, Stan's exact request brought to life. Simple. Elegant.

Tables groan under the weight of a feast fit for royalty: charcuterie boards overflowing with meats and cheeses, breads bursting from their baskets, and enough wine to drown a small village. There's a sweet scent of fermenting grapes in the air. I *should* be basking in this perfect moment; instead, my anxiety is doing backflips every time I see Matteo.

He's leaning against a wooden beam at the edge of the terrace, devastatingly handsome in his dark blue shirt with the sleeves rolled up to reveal those distracting forearms. The light catches the shadows in his eyes—the tension in his jaw. Something's wrong. The realization sits like lead in my stomach.

When I first arrived in this dress—the red one that usually makes his eyes go dark and hungry—he barely glanced at me. Just a quick kiss on the cheek and a murmured "bellissima" before he was gone again, slipping away to handle yet another mysterious call.

No smoldering looks.

No suggestive Italian whispers.

None of the electricity that normally crackles between us.

My brain is going into overdrive trying to figure out what I did wrong.

"Katie." I hear Stan's warm voice. He's beaming, his bow tie endearingly crooked and his cheeks flushed with happiness. "You did an amazing job. It's... perfect. My wish has come true tonight."

"Stan, you don't have to thank me. Your love for Rose is the reason this night is so magical."

Stan pauses, his hand reaching out to grasp the back of a nearby chair. I look at him, concerned, as he takes a deep breath. "Just a dizzy spell," he says with a chuckle, dabbing the sweat off his forehead with a handkerchief. "Comes with the territory when you're as old as dirt."

"Can I get you anything? Water? A cane?"

"Nah, I'm fine. I don't need any fuss." He straightens up. "I was hoping, if it's all right with you, I'd like to make my speech now?"

"Of course."

The seniors settle into their seats as I lead Stan toward the dance area—to his Rose, who's glowing in her elegant lace dress. I hand him the microphone, and the crowd falls silent—the magic of the moment enveloping us all.

Stan whistles at Rose, then starts his vows. "My darling Rose, it's been sixty years, and I still think you're kinda cute."

She giggles.

"I tell you I love you all the time, but it's never enough. Put simply, you're the one. My best friend. The girl I love above all else."

Rose smiles at him through her tears, radiant as an angel. They do a little shuffle toward each other and embrace—a forever hug. It's absolute heaven to be part of this.

"You're my partner in every sense. My confidant, my soulmate. We've had a beautiful life together, the best... Today I pledge to you my eternal love. Thank you for giving me the greatest honor of my life—the gift of being your husband."

Someone shouts, *"Saluti!"* and wine glasses clink together like bells as Stan leans to kiss Rose. I blink back tears, but my gaze is only on Matteo. For a split second, our eyes meet and the pain I see there steals my breath. He breaks away, and it feels like he's retreating to a place that I can't follow.

For a moment, I wonder if he's thinking about his parents, about the love they had—the memories they built together. I want to go to him, but I've got a job to do.

I take the mic back from Stan, forcing a smile. "Stan and Rose, I have a surprise for you."

Otto steps forward with his borrowed violin, polished to a mirror shine *(seriously, Caterina got everything on my list)*.

"Ladies and gentlemen," I say, addressing the crowd, "Stan and Rose will re-create the first wedding dance with the song that started it all sixty years ago. Otto, take it away."

This is the moment I've been waiting for. He begins to play "Can't Help Falling in Love," and the notes float through the air as if a spell is being cast. Stan brings Rose to the dancing space with infinite tenderness, and they move together like they've been practicing this moment for a lifetime.

Which, I guess they have.

The song ends, and for a moment, there's silence—then thunderous applause, loud and joyful, as Stan and Rose share another kiss.

I start the playlist on my phone, and couples pair up once more. Matteo's disappeared again, taking another piece of my heart with him. I wish I knew what was wrong—or how to fix it.

What has changed between last night and now? Between "stay with me" and whatever this is.

I'm interrupted by Howie's smooth Southern drawl. "If I could have your attention for just a moment!"

He timidly approaches the dance area, somehow appearing both bold and terrified. His white linen shirt is artfully rumpled, giving him the appearance of a retired billionaire on vacation—which he is. As he raises his wine glass, his hand shakes slightly.

"Please join me in a toast," he says. "First, to our lovely hosts, Katie and Caterina, for putting together the finest celebration I've ever had the pleasure of attending."

There's polite applause, and my cheeks heat up as guests look my way. Caterina beams in delight.

"But most importantly," Howie says, raising his glass higher, "to Stan and Rose. Sixty years of love, laughter, and partnership. What an incredible legacy y'all have built together. Here's to you!"

Glasses lift and a chorus of saluti rings out. I think that's the end of it, but Howie shifts his stance and locks his gaze onto Aunt Deb, seated at a nearby table. And then... he drops the bombshell.

"I never thought I'd find a love like theirs until I met Deb. She makes love seem timeless—still a possibility for us old-timers."

Aunt Deb is a ghost. My fearless, filter-less aunt who treats life like her own personal Broadway show watches Howie with an expression I've never seen before.

"Deborah Fox," Howie says, his voice filled with reverence, "you are a force of nature. A woman who lights up every room she enters. You make life more colorful, more exciting, more... everything. In a few short weeks, you made me experience things I didn't think were possible at my age. I feel young, alive... in love."

The terrace goes so quiet I can hear champagne bubbles rising from glasses. He takes the deepest breath of his life.

"I've had my share of adventures," Howie continues, reaching into his pocket. "But I know now they mean nothing without you. Deborah, my sweet tea, will you do me the honor of spending the rest of our days together?"

And then he pulls out a ring.

Not just a ring. A freaking boulder. A sapphire so massive it could anchor a yacht, surrounded by enough diamonds to make a chandelier jealous.

But Aunt Deb's face... is all wrong. Where's the drama? The flair? The embarrassing speech about cosmic connection and sexual awakening?

"I'd get down on one knee," Howie adds with that slow Texas smile that usually makes Aunt Deb purr like a satisfied cat, "but these old joints wouldn't forgive me. So let's pretend I did, darlin'."

Aunt Deb? She doesn't move. Doesn't speak, her bewildered face revealing that she's as surprised as the rest of us. I can't quite discern her look—she's thunderstruck.

This man is deeply in love with you Aunt Deb. What are you waiting for?

"Some people say you're a bit much, but for me... you're not enough. Marry me?"

Finally she stands, placing a hand gently on his arm. "Oh, Howie," she says softly, without her usual sparkle. "You're an incredible man. And these weeks with you have been... unforgettable. No, that's not the right word. Life-changing."

The room collectively holds its breath, waiting for Deb's answer.

Silence.

Deb's face...

Crumbles.

"But I can't marry you. I'm sorry."

Then, in true Deborah Fox fashion, she sweeps off the terrace like Cinderella fleeing the ball.

What the fuck?

The ring glints in the candlelight one last time as Howie lowers it, his face a masterclass in dignified devastation. It's the kind of heartbreak where you want to hug him before hunting down the offender—except in this case, that person is my aunt, and this situation is way above my emotional pay grade.

The crowd's collective discomfort ripples through the terrace like one giant social anxiety tsunami.

My event-planner brain kicks into crisis mode, pure muscle memory from years of handling disasters. I snatch my phone off the table, fingers flying as I pull up my emergency "save the night" playlist. The opening notes of an upbeat tune burst through the speakers.

"Let's keep this party going!" I sound like a cheerleader who's trying too hard, but desperate times call for fake enthusiasm. "Everyone back on the floor!"

Caterina, bless her pregnant heart, reads the room. "Enrico, mi amore," she shouts, "let's groove!"

The tension breaks. The music summons couples back to the dancing space like embers reignited by a gust of wind. I shoot Caterina a look of gratitude and slip away, following the trail of broken dreams and designer perfume that my aunt left behind.

I find her on the front porch of the vineyard house, a disco ball of sadness in her sequined dress. The moonlight catches every sparkle, but she's not her usual center-of-attention self.

"Aunt Deb? Are you okay?"

"Of course I am, darling."

The laugh she lets out sounds like it hurts. "At my age, forever is a little too close to the truth, Katie-kins." There's something in her voice I've never heard before—fear maybe? "You're young. Forever doesn't mean the same thing to you."

I keep my mouth shut. No spreadsheets or lists can fix this moment.

She releases a breath that seems to come from her soul. "This ain't my first rodeo, kid. Or my first proposal." Her smile doesn't reach her eyes. "Don't you worry."

"But—"

"Go back to the party." She cuts me off with a wave of her bejeweled hand. "You worked your butt off to make it perfect. Don't waste it on me."

I hesitate, my chest tight with worry. But there's something in her expression—a plea for space, for time to process. For once, the woman who's never met a moment she couldn't turn into a production needs silence.

"You threw one hell of a party, kiddo," she says softly. "Really. It's beautiful."

"Thanks, Aunt Deb." The words feel inadequate, but they're all I have. I leave her to her thoughts under the Tuscan moon, surrounded by the gentle chorus of crickets.

***

THE PARTY STRETCHES ENDLESSLY around me, a blur of twinkling lights and laughter. I can't take one more second of this—watching Matteo avoid me and pretending my heart isn't being shredded with every nonreturned glance. Each beat of the music feels like it's counting down to something terrible, and I'm done waiting for the other shoe to drop.

Tomorrow we'll tour Rome. Our last day. And I'll be damned if I'm leaving this country without knowing what changed. My body physically aches for answers, for his touch, for anything but this endless void between us.

My eyes scan the crowd, ignoring the happy couples swaying to the music. Then I spot him keeping a low profile off to the side of the crowd. Something inside me snaps.

No fucking way. He doesn't get to sulk in the shadows while I'm drowning in confusion and hurt.

Before my brain can convince me otherwise, I'm crossing the terrace with determination coursing through my veins. My fingers wrap around his bicep—*God, his skin is warm*—and I pull him toward the vineyard. "We need to talk. Right now."

He resists for a moment, muscle tensing under my grip, but then something in him just... lets go. His body deflates like a punctured balloon, the fight seeping out, and he lets me escort him away from the party. The vineyard sprawls out around us, with moonlight turning the leaves silver and the air thick with anticipation, ready for heartbreak.

"What's going on?" My voice comes out harder than I mean it to, but I'm past caring. "And don't you dare say nothing. You've been avoiding me all night like I'm carrying the plague in this dress."

"I've had things on my mind. Business things. Not every minute can be about you, Katie."

"Excuse me? Since when do I make it all about me?"

His eyes finally meet mine, dark and distant. "Since the moment you walked into my life."

"Why are you doing this?" My voice cracks like thin ice, betraying every emotion I'm trying to hide. "I see right through you, you know. Your eyes give you away."

"You don't know anything about me."

"That's such bullshit." I step closer, my heart thundering against my ribs. "I know when you're lying. I knew it the first day we met, when you tried to convince me your stupid Tower of Pisa pickup line actually works."

His laugh is bitter, empty. "You mean when *you* were lying about Jared?"

"What happened from last night to now? Because the man who asked me to stay with him, who held me like I was something precious—he wouldn't be acting like this."

He shakes his head, looking away. "It was a dream. A beautiful lie. We'd never last."

"Why?" I move even closer, forcing myself into his space. "Give me the real reason."

"Because we're too different. We want different lives."

"Different lives? I don't even recognize the life I wanted before you. Miss Perfect Plan, with her five-year goals and retirement portfolio, started at twenty-five. You wrecked that woman. Made me dream bigger. Want wilder."

"Katie." My name sounds like a prayer for mercy. "Please don't make this harder."

"No, you don't get the easy out." Another step closer. The pulse in his throat betrays him. "At least Jared was a man about it—he looked me in the eye when he said he didn't want me."

Pain flashes across his face so raw it sends my stomach plummeting. "*Cristo*, no. Katie, you're... you're perfection. It's not you—"

"Oh my God." My voice trembles like a wire about to snap. "Are you actually going to say 'it's not you, it's me'? Tell me, is that line just as pathetic in Italian?"

"Stop." He runs a hand through his hair. "Please just stop."

"Or what?" A tear escapes, tracing down my cheek. "You'll keep breaking my heart? Too late."

"Please." His voice cracks. "I can't watch you cry."

"Then you shouldn't have made me fall in love with you." The words rip out of me. "But here we are. You get to hurt me, but my tears are too much? That's not how this works. I can't compartmentalize my emotions into a nice tidy binder and file them away."

The silence hangs in the air, thick with everything he won't say.

I continue, "I have never felt the way I do when I'm with you. I thought I knew what love was, but God, I was so wrong. I burn for you, ache for you, and every cell in my body recognizes you. So whatever you're battling tonight? It's tearing me apart because that's what real love does—it binds you to someone so tightly that their pain becomes yours."

I step closer until there's barely a breath between us. His hands are still shoved in his pockets like he's physically restraining himself from touching me, but he doesn't back away. The air crackles with electricity, threatening to spark and consume us both.

"I love you, Matteo," I whisper. "And you love me too. Your mouth lies but your body can't. I see you're scared."

"I'm not afraid," he whispers weakly as if he's trying to convince himself.

"Liar." I inch closer. "You've spent your whole life running away from love. But it caught you anyway. You fell for me."

I'm so close that his hot breath is on my skin. Every muscle in his body is straining toward mine even as he holds himself back. The moonlight catches his face, illuminating the war in his eyes.

"See what you've done to me," I rasp, the words scraping my throat raw. "I'm ruined just like you wanted. For every other man, for my old life, for every notion I had about love. I'll never be the same because of you. Say something, dammit!"

He says nothing. The silence feels like a hand around my throat, squeezing until the last bit of hope dies. Tears spill over, each one burning like acid down my cheeks. The woman who plans everything, who has a backup plan for her backup plans, finally admits defeat.

"Right. Of course." My voice sounds empty. "I guess I'll add you to my collection of men who couldn't love me back."

I have to leave, right now. Each step away is like walking on broken glass. *Don't look back. Don't—*

His grip is a steel trap, locking around my wrist, yanking me back against his chest. His mouth comes down on mine with crushing force, stealing my breath, my thoughts, my sanity. The kiss tastes like goodbye and hello and everything in between. His fingers tangle in my hair, holding me like he's afraid I'll evaporate if he loosens his grip. I melt into him, my fingers gripping his shirt like an anchor.

"Tell me you love me," I beg between kisses. "Please. Tell me to stay."

His mouth claims mine again, harder, deeper, like he's etching himself into my soul. His tongue slides against mine as one hand grips my jaw. The other hand presses into my lower back until there's not even air between us, until I can feel his heartbeat hammering against mine.

"Katie," he says like it's a confession on his lips. "You're the beat of my heart, *mi amore*."

A panicked scream pierces the air, freezing my blood solid.

"What was that?" I breathe, stomach knotting with dread.

"Hurry," he says.

We sprint back to the gathering, fingers locked together, terror driving us forward. The crowd stands in a tight circle, gathered around something on the ground. No... not something. Someone.

"Jesus no," I gasp. There, unmoving in the center of the crowd, is Stan. Sweet, beloved Stan.

Beside him, Enrico's hands pump his chest in a desperate rhythm. My hands cover my mouth in horror as I watch Stan's lifeless body jostle limply with each thrust. Matteo takes over, his CPR movements precise, despite the fear that pales his face.

"Caterina!" The panic in Enrico's voice sends chills down my spine. *"Ambulanza! Non respira!"*

I catch Rose as her knees buckle.

One moment. And everything changes.

One heartbeat between love and loss.

CHAPTER NINETEEN

KATIE

Me: Any updates on Stan?

Me: Enrico and I got everyone checked into the hotel in Rome.

Me: Are you getting these texts?

Italian Stallion: Stan's pacemaker failed. He is stable now.

Italian Stallion: Thank you for helping Enrico.

Italian Stallion: I will see everyone tomorrow at breakfast.

Me: We need to finish our talk.

Italian Stallion: I have nothing else to say.

HE SAID *MI AMORE.*

Not *bella*, not *principessa*, not *cara mia*. No, *mi freaking amore.* My love. He looked me in the eye, kissed me like I held the key to his freedom, and said the words he's apparently never said to *anyone* else. And now— *What the hell?*

My phone's screen glows in the pre-dawn darkness, mocking me with its silence. I've reread Matteo's texts so many times the words have lost all meaning.

In a desperate attempt to regain some sanity, I do what I do best. I make a list.

Possible Reasons Matteo Monti is Ghosting Me:

1. Alien abduction *(Replaced by a very handsome extraterrestrial)*.

2. He's actually a spy, and my presence has compromised his latest mission *(Code name: Italian Stallion)*.

3. He won the Italian lottery and thinks I'm after his newfound millions.

4. He has a secret third nipple *(No. Scratch that. I'd definitely have noticed)*.

5. He's allergic to Americans, and the symptoms have just started kicking in.

6. He knows I overthink everything, so he fled before I could pitch turning Monti Tours into an international franchise.

7. Deep down, he's just an asshole.

8. My mother's "Team Jared" energy has cursed my love life.

9. He's secretly married to Lorenzo.

My normally pristine handwriting has devolved into aggressive scrawls. I'm a woman who's mainlined enough espresso to give a rhino heart palpitations.

I slam the binder shut, but the restlessness coursing through my veins demands action. The hotel room has become a cage.

From her bed near the window, Aunt Deb snores obnoxiously. She rolls over, mumbling something that sounds suspiciously like "Howie" before burrowing deeper into her silk sleep mask.

Great. We're both disasters in the romance department. At least she got a marriage proposal. All I got was an "I have nothing else to say" after the most intense declaration of my life.

The hotel's ancient radiator clanks on, startling me so bad my pen goes flying. It skitters across the floor as if it's trying to escape my descent into madness. I should probably follow its example, but instead, I'm hate-staring at my phone while mentally composing texts I'll never send.

Finally it's breakfast time, and I've been up since dawn, running on exactly three and a half hours of sleep and an unhealthy mix of caffeine and rage. I'm seated at a table with Aunt Deb, who's weirdly quiet this morning—probably still processing the whole Howie and the Boulder That Could Sink the Titanic proposal fiasco—but I can't focus on her.

My eyes are locked on the doorway with the intensity of a sniper, willing that infuriating man to appear and give me *something*. A smile. A wink. A *hey, sorry for being a feelings-phobic jackass.* Anything.

Spoiler alert: He doesn't walk in.

I need intel. Information. Data points I can organize into some semblance of sense.

Instead, I get Lorenzo, putting professional competitive eaters to shame at the breakfast buffet. His plate looks like he's preparing for hibernation, if bears hibernated on prosciutto and pastries.

I corner him between the bread basket and fruit display, planting myself in his path like a particularly determined traffic cone. "Lorenzo."

He acknowledges me with a grunt that somehow manages to convey both "good morning" and "please go away" in a single sound.

"Have you seen Matteo?"

"No," he grumbles, shoveling bacon onto his plate fast and furious.

I cross my arms. "Tell me, are all Italian men stupid assholes?"

"Sì," he replies without hesitation, his voice devoid of irony.

I blink. "Seriously?"

"Sì."

"Okay, well, do you know what's bothering him?"

"Sì."

My heart skips a beat. Finally some progress! "Will you tell me?"

He stops mid-bite. "No, piccola."

"Why not?"

"Some men, they carry world on shoulders. Until they ready to share weight..." He shrugs.

Then, as if he's just dropped some secret piece of wisdom, he inhales his pastry and walks away.

I stand there, shell-shocked, as he plops down at a table and digs into his buffet for one, utterly unfazed by the emotional bomb he just dropped.

What. The. Actual. Hell.

"Men," Aunt Deb mutters when I flop back into my seat, radiating frustration.

"Men," I echo, stabbing my croissant with unnecessary force.

For a brief moment, she smirks, her usual Aunt Deb sparkle flickering back to life. "If I didn't know better, I'd think you're in love with that Italian stud."

I scowl at her. "I'm not in love with him. I'm *in rage* with him."

"All shades of the same color, darling," she says, taking a sip of her coffee.

I glare at my plate, my chest tight with confusion and hurt and a tiny glimmer of hope I can't quite extinguish. Matteo Monti might have called me *mi amore*, but right now? He's *mi headache*. And I'm not leaving Rome without some damn answers.

"There she is! Katie! Katie!"

I freeze mid-stab into my half-dissected pastry. That voice. That voice belongs to— No. It couldn't be. My head swivels toward the entrance, and my stomach drops.

I blink. Once. Twice. "Mom?"

There, standing in the doorway, is my mother, Suzanne Crawford. Her impeccably highlighted blonde hair and country-club tennis tan radiate suburban perfection. But she's not alone. Oh no. Behind her is my entire family, lined up like suspects in a crime where the weapon was passive aggression.

My fork clatters against fine china as I take in the emerging catastrophe. My dad in his signature golf polo. My brother David, who probably squeezed in this family ambush between saving babies and walking on water. His perfect wife Emma and their Instagram-worthy children. And hovering at the edges like supporting characters in my personal rom-com gone wrong: Jared's parents?

"Surprise!" Mom's voice could shatter the crystal chandeliers. "We're in Rome!"

She yanks me from my chair and pulls me into a hug so tight I'm pretty sure one of my tits just got a mammogram. "Can you believe it? We're all here!"

"No," I manage, my voice strangled. "Really. I cannot believe you are all here."

I shoot Aunt Deb a desperate look, but she simply raises her coffee cup with a smirk. "You're on your own for this one, kiddo."

And then, as if Satan himself is determined to turn my life into a horror movie, I see him.

Jared.

Standing there in his neatly knotted tie covered in tiny dinosaur fossils. He's a man who missed the memo to stay in the past.

"Hey there, Katiebug." His smile is hesitant, familiar.

"Hi?" I say, the word tumbling out more like a question because my brain has gone offline.

"Oh, isn't this just wonderful!" my mom chirps, clearly oblivious to the fiery vortex of chaos she's unleashed. "I've been talking to Jared's mom, Barbara, and we both agreed it was time to hatch a plan to get you two back together. *Surprise!*"

I gape at her, my mouth opening and closing like a goldfish desperately searching for water. *Words? Where are the words?*

Jared takes a step closer, rubbing the back of his neck in that boyish, awkward way he used to when he'd forget my birthday. "Katie, listen. I... I'm sorry. I've missed you like crazy. I didn't reach out because I didn't know what to say after being such a jerk. But Katie, I still love you."

"And don't worry," Mom chirps, patting Jared's arm as though he's a prized show poodle. "I told him all about your tour guide fake-boyfriend scheme to get his attention."

"Yes, it worked!" Jared nods enthusiastically. "I was insanely jealous. When I saw those pictures of you with that guy, I thought I'd lost my shot completely. Then your mom reached out and told me your true feelings."

She said what now?

I stand, dumbfounded. Aunt Deb gives me an exaggerated thumbs-up, clearly enjoying the show.

"Okay." I finally find my voice. "But what are you all doing here? Why are you in Rome?"

My mom gives Jared a nudge that's about as subtle as Chester doing naked lunges on the beach.

And then? The entire Crawford-Wagner clan pulls out their phones and starts filming.

Jared drops to one knee.

"Oh shit." *Did I say that out loud?*

Aunt Deb whispers loud enough for me to hear, "Well, this just got interesting."

Chairs creak as the seniors lean forward in their seats. Mrs. Thomas actually pulls out opera glasses.

"Katherine Blair Crawford," Jared starts, pulling out a ring box. "I was an idiot. A big one. Losing you was the hardest thing I've ever endured. But we can fix it. Let's have a wedding in Rome! Be spontaneous! Will you marry—"

I lose track of the words. Matteo stands at the back of the room.

No. No no no no no.

He's just... standing there... hands shoved into his pockets... eyes steady and intense. He's zeroed in on me, but his expression is unreadable.

I'm frozen. I have no contingency plan for this.

"Oh, how romantic!" My mother squeals. "You've made her speechless! Of course she wants to! Jared, stand up, put the ring on her finger!"

Both mothers start clapping and cheering like they've just successfully merged two Fortune 500 companies. The room erupts in applause; the sound is a wall of static.

My eyes find Matteo's across the room. For a moment, agony flashes across his face, before he masks it with a bright smile. He claps loudly, shouting "Congratulazioni!" as though this isn't breaking both our hearts.

As if *mi amore* meant nothing at all.

Aunt Deb clears her throat, the devil's glint back in her eye. I know that look. It's her "I'm about to cause a scene and thoroughly enjoy myself doing it" look. "Jared, sweetheart," she says, her voice saccharine sweet, "you simply *must* meet Matteo. The tour guide who played such a pivotal role in getting our Katie back on the path to true love."

My head jerks toward her so fast I'm surprised my neck doesn't snap. I give her my best *what the actual fuck are you doing?* glare, but Deb just winks back. *Winks.* "No, that's really not—"

"Matteo! Be a dear and come meet Katie's fiancé!" Aunt Deb blurts out.

Oh God. Every step Matteo takes toward us feels like watching a slow-motion train wreck, and I'm caught in a surreal, out-of-body experience watching it unfold.

His face is carefully blank, but there's tension in his jaw that makes me want to either kiss it away or run screaming from the room. Neither seems appropriate with my entire family recording this disaster on their phones.

Deb, on the other hand, is in her element. She gestures grandly between them. "Matteo Monti, meet Jared Wagner. The man who dumped our Katie and broke her heart into a thousand tiny little pieces. And Jared, this is Matteo. The man who worked tirelessly to help put her back together and win you over again."

Kill me now. Just... please, universe, let me spontaneously combust into a pile of ash right here.

Jared extends a hand, looking sheepish but trying to be polite. "Uh, nice to meet you," he says, though his tone suggests he's not entirely sure if Matteo is friend or foe.

In a panic, I blurt, "My mom told Jared all about our fake-dating scheme."

Matteo's gaze is so intense it could set fire to an iceberg. "So glad it worked out. I know Katie had only one goal when she came to Italy, to win you back."

The emphasis he puts on "one goal" feels like being stabbed with Lorenzo's pastry fork. Repeatedly. In the heart.

"Well, yes, that was my plan but—"

I stop. *No.*

No more lies.

No more dodging.

I have to tell the truth.

I have to say it out loud.

"That was before I fell in love with—"

"Italy," Matteo cuts in smoothly, his smile never reaching his eyes. "Katie fell in love with Italy. Like everyone does. You will too, I'm sure."

He gives me a pointed look, daring me to contradict him. I'm too stunned to speak. The words are right there, but my tongue's on strike.

"And what a delight it has been! But alas, today is our last adventure together on this tour. I must round up our wonderful group. *Arrivederci!*" He turns to leave, adding over his shoulder, "Again, congratulazioni to you both. Katie, please leave a five-star review, per favore."

And with that, he walks away. Like I'm nothing. As if we're nothing. My chest aches, and it's not just from holding my breath.

Matteo reaches the center of the room and claps his hands. "Buongiorno! I have fantastico news about Stan. He is doing much better but still recovering. Therefore, he and Rose will not be with us today."

There's a collective sigh of relief from the seniors, but Matteo doesn't spare me a second glance as he continues. "And it appears that Katie and Deborah have made other plans today. But for the rest of you, we will meet in the lobby for our walking tour of Rome."

Is this how it ends? Matteo Monti tossing me aside like another tourist he sweet-talked into bed, then dismissed by checkout time? Everything we've shared so easily forgotten? Am I just one more forgettable stop for the tour guide and his love-'em-and-leave-'em itinerary?

My chest constricts; the ache spreading through me is a slow poison. No. This isn't us. Not after the way he kissed me, the way "mi amore" fell from his lips like a love spell. I can't reconcile *that* man with the one ignoring me now.

This can't be the end. I won't let it be.

"I'm still coming!" I shout. Heads swivel in my direction, and I can feel every pair of eyes in the room on me.

Jared frowns, his brow furrowing in that familiar, condescending way that used to make me feel small. "Katie, I thought we'd spend the day together."

"Katie, sweetheart," my mom chimes in. "We have to work on wedding details. So much to plan!"

I shake my head, my voice firm. "I already mapped today out in my binder. And you know how I am about my schedules."

Jared's hand finds mine. "Of course. I know you like to stick to your plans."

"I'm sorry," Matteo interjects, "but we don't have room for everyone in your group to join us."

"That's fine," Aunt Deb pipes up with unholy glee. "Jared can take my place."

The look I shoot her could incinerate her designer sunglasses, but she just wiggles her fingers as if she's conducting an orchestra of chaos.

"I'll hang back and help Suzanne with the wedding plans," she adds with faux innocence. "I've seen Rome plenty of times."

The room closes in. My brain, usually a well-oiled machine of backup plans and emergency protocols, is out of order. My heart pounds so hard I hear it in my ears.

Jared turns to Matteo, completely oblivious to the tension radiating off both of us. "Thanks, man," he says, clapping Matteo on the shoulder like they're old frat buddies. "Appreciate you making room for me to be with my girl."

"I aim to please," he says, his tone razor-sharp.

"Oh, he's *very* accommodating," Deb adds with a wicked grin. "Isn't he, Katie?" Then she winks at me again, completely unbothered by the fact that she's actively lighting my life on fire.

"Well," Jared says, turning to me with that smug, self-assured smile—once swoon-worthy, now rage inducing. "Guess it's settled. Ready for our big day in Rome, Katiebug?"

Katiebug. God, I hate that nickname. I used to think it was sweet, but now it's a leash, like he's trying to pull me back into a version of myself I've outgrown.

I force a smile, my brain still frantically searching for an escape hatch. "Actually, Jared—"

"Wonderful!" Mom says. "Deborah, you and I will start brainstorming wedding venues, and the lovebirds can enjoy their day together. Isn't this just *perfect*?"

"Perfect," I echo, my voice dripping with sarcasm that goes entirely unnoticed by my mother.

Jared beams at me, and I feel Matteo's gaze on me again, heavy and unreadable. I glance at him, desperate for a signal or subtle clue to know what he's thinking. But his face is a mask, his eyes distant.

"One hour till go time!" Matteo calls out, already turning away.

I watch him stride toward the door. "Oh!" I slap my hand against my chest. "My pen! Jared, I forgot my traveling pen upstairs."

"We can get you another one in the lobby," he offers, as if I'm some kind of pen harlot who'll write with just anything.

"No, you don't understand. This is my *special* pen. My lucky pen. The one I've been using the whole trip." I say, already backing away. "With the perfect grip and the .38-millimeter point that makes my lists look like calligraphy done by angels. I can't have a notebook filled with mismatched ink styles and color discrepancies. Be right back!"

I sprint out of the breakfast room like my cardigan's on fire, catching sight of Matteo's broad shoulders disappearing down the carpeted corridor. Without thinking—which is becoming an alarmingly frequent occurrence—I grab his arm and shove him into the nearest bathroom, locking the door.

"Katie, what—"

"I had no idea they were coming."

"You're lucky," he cuts in, voice flat. "To have family who loves you so much."

The hotel bathroom's fluorescent lights cast harsh shadows, making Matteo resemble a brooding Italian statue. A very sexy, very stubborn statue who's currently giving me his best *I'm a tough guy who doesn't have feelings* face.

"Nuh-uh. Don't make this about them." My palm connects with his chest, feeling his heart thundering beneath my touch. "This is about you running away from us."

"There is no us."

"Stop saying that." My voice catches on the lump in my throat. "Yes, there is."

"No, bella." The muscle in his jaw ticks—his tell when he's lying. "That is just the glow of vacation. Jared is real. He is the kind of man you want."

Every cell in my body rebels against his words. "No, he's not. And we're not talking about Jared or anything about that shitshow that just happened out there. We're talking about us."

"Again, bella." His voice is sandpaper. "There is no *us*."

I step closer, my hand finding his cheek. His stubble scratches my palm as he instinctively leans into my touch. "Last night you called me *mi amore.*"

For one blazing moment, his mask slips. Then he jerks away, leaving my hand burning in empty air.

"You misunderstood. I did not say *mi amore.*" His laugh sounds like breaking glass. "You don't speak Italian, bella. I said *mi attrai.* It means *you attract me.* It's just flirting, keeping things romantic. That's all."

"Wow, good to know that gaslighting is just as popular in Italy." My nails dig crescents into my palms. "So we're rewriting history now? Next, you'll tell me all those orgasms were just part of the standard tour package."

"You can't force this to be something it's not. You can't control everything, bellissima."

"And you can't pretend what's between us doesn't exist. You don't get to control how I feel about you."

"Life doesn't always work out giving you everything you want." He sighs, and something dark and wounded flashes in his eyes, a glimpse of the real pain he's hiding.

"You don't want to tell me what's really bothering you, fine." I soften my voice. "I know something happened. I figured out that much from Lorenzo. Let me in, Matteo. Let me help."

"Nothing's broken except this fantasy you've built." His jaw clenches. "You're the forever kind of girl. I'm the right-now kind of guy. I told you that from day one."

"That's bullshit. I'm not asking for marriage. I'm asking for you to be honest."

"You want honesty?" His eyes burn into mine. "It was just sex. Amazing sex. You were fun."

The words are bullets to my chest. "Is that really all I was? Just another tourist to fuck?"

"You wanted to feel desired." His voice could shred steel. "Mission accomplished. Vacation over."

"Not yet it isn't."

His hands fist at his sides. "Let's end this cleanly."

"No." I step closer, watching his control fracture.

"I don't want you."

Another step. "Your body betrays you."

"Katie—" My name sounds wrecked on his lips.

I press closer, until there's nothing between us but lies and want. His eyes drop to my mouth, hunger blazing in their depths.

"You want to kiss me right now."

"No." But his voice shakes.

I brush my lips against his jaw. "Yes, you do."

"Principessa—" It comes out like a plea.

"No." I silence him. "You want to play this the hard way, not tell me what's going on? Fine. I'm not going to make it easy for you to walk away from me." I take a step back. "Let me explain something about relationships since you've spent your entire adult life dodging them. Couples fight. They work out their problems. And then they kiss and make up."

My hand finds the door handle, but I pause, turning back to deliver one final blow. "And by the end of the day, you're going to tell me what's wrong, kiss me, and admit that you love me."

His head jerks up, his brow furrowing, and for a fleeting moment, his expression wavers. Hope? Guilt? Panic. Maybe all three? I don't wait to find out. If I stay one second longer, I'll do something reckless.

I yank the door open and storm out—my flats are tiny war drums slapping against the polished tile.

But the satisfaction of my dramatic exit is short-lived. As I strut down the hallway, I realize I have no plan. I'm basically a ten-year-old who just declared she's running away from home but forgot to pack snacks.

The air smells like Italian coffee and pastries, and for a second I consider abandoning my plan to win Matteo back and simply bury my feelings in cannoli. But no. I can't do that. I'm a woman with a mission. A very vague, half-baked mission, but a mission nonetheless.

What the hell are you doing, Katie?

Chasing after a man who told me I'm nothing but a vacation fling? Who basically stamped No Refunds on his heart and expects me to just accept it?

But then I remember how he looked at me last night. I was the center of his universe. I was *his*.

And damn it, I am his. He just won't admit it yet.

This whole morning has been a three-ring circus of emotions, and I'm done being the silent clown. My mom, Jared, Matteo—they've all decided what's best for me. But newsflash: It's my life. My decisions. My mess to make.

Ugh. Jared.

Who flies to another continent, ambushes their ex with a proposal, and expects a standing ovation? *Please.* Maybe if after six years he'd ever managed to find my clitoris I'd feel a tiny bit bad about using him to make Matteo jealous. But he didn't, so I don't.

These men think they can tell me how to feel? How to love? The only difference is, one of them makes my pulse throb in all the right places *(hint, it's not the one with the dinosaur tie collection)*.

Operation Win Back the Italian Stallion is officially in motion. Because if there's one thing Matteo Monti needs to learn, it's that Katie "Control Freak" Crawford doesn't give up.

Not on love.

Not on mind-blowing orgasms.

And definitely not on him.

CHAPTER TWENTY

MATTEO

ROME IS A CITY built on ruins and lost dreams. How fucking fitting.

The morning sun burns against my skin as I stand at the edge of the Trevi Fountain, listening to the endless crash of water that sounds too much like my own heartbeat. The marble gods and goddesses watch over the scene, probably wondering why the hell humans keep throwing perfectly good money into their bathtub.

Oceanus, the Titan God of the Earth, looms over his domain, his ancient, icy gaze piercing through me. I can feel his judgment cutting into my cowardice. My weakness.

I sold my soul this morning, signed it away to Italy Express with black ink that felt like blood. The contract is a death sentence in my back pocket. Less than twenty-four hours. That's all I have left before I become everything I swore I'd never be again—a corporate puppet leading soulless tours on a schedule driven by profit and greed.

My parents would disown me.

None of it matters. Not when Katie's thirty feet away, letting *him* wrap an arm around her waist for another worthless selfie.

Merda. My hands clench and unclench by my sides. Jared's playing the doting fiancé, positioning her just right, ensuring the light catches that massive diamond he surprised her with this morning.

The ring probably cost more than my entire bankrupt company is worth.

She glances over her shoulder, those green eyes finding mine like heat-seeking missiles. No smile. No pretense—just a silent promise that she was far from done proving me wrong.

After our confrontation in the hotel bathroom, she made it clear—she's not giving up without a fight. The vision of her, all fire and fury, lingers like a tattoo I never asked for. *By the end of the day, you are going to tell me what's wrong, kiss me, and admit that you love me.*"

Her defiance echoes in my head, but it collides with another image, one I'd rather forget—last night's emergency. Stan lay motionless in his hospital bed, machines keeping him alive, while Rose sat vigil, her thin fingers locked around his.

Not speaking. Not crying. Just... enduring. Loving with quiet devastation.

It's a love that I'm familiar with, the kind that destroys you, piece by piece until you're hollowed out—nothing but memories and sorrow. It's a pain I've lived with most of my life, one that hides in the shadows, waiting to strike when you least expect it.

Like right now. The memory of my parents' funeral floods in—two closed caskets, my ten-year-old hands clutching wilting roses. The priest's words reverberating off marble walls: "They died as they lived. Together."

Together. As if it was romantic instead of fucking tragic.

My tour group mills around the fountain, cameras clicking, voices chattering. I should be divulging the fountain's secrets. How it took thirty years to build. How it marks the end point of an ancient Roman aqueduct. How throwing a single coin means you'll return to Rome, two coins means you'll find love, and three means marriage *(No goddamn way I'm sharing that last one).*

Instead, I'm watching Katie fake smile for Jared's selfie while my lungs forget how to function.

I spent the whole night convincing myself to let Katie go. To push her away before she could burrow into my heart any deeper. Before I could hurt her with my failures—my bankrupt company, my mountain of debt, my inability to be the man she deserves.

Then this morning happened.

Jared.

That *idiota* kneeling in the middle of the hotel breakfast room like some kind of fucking cartoon prince, holding that ring box as if it was an apology. And Katie standing there, frozen, her hands clenching the hem of her dress.

And her face— *Dio mio, her face.*

Lost. Trapped. Her eyes darting around the room searching for an escape route. The panic in her eyes when they found mine... it gutted me.

I thought I'd feel relief. *Isn't this what I wanted?* For her to move on? To be with a man who could give her the stability I can't?

But instead, it felt as if someone had taken a sledgehammer to my chest, shattering every last piece of my heart. I stood there, clapping, pretending it didn't kill me to see her ex proposing to her. Pretending I didn't want to grab her, pull her into my arms, and beg her to choose me.

Forever isn't for failures. And that's what I am.

Better to end it now—save her from settling for this fucking mess. God knows she'll waste her love on me and I'll only disappoint her.

I force myself to look away, to focus on the fountain's endless cascade. If I can just get through this day.

Be professional.

Keep my distance.

Pretend my heart isn't being carved out with a dull blade.

"She deserves better than him," a deep, husky voice says beside me.

What the—

I turn to find Lorenzo settled against the fountain's edge, methodically unwrapping his daily prosciutto sandwich as if he hasn't just obliterated five years of mostly silent communication.

"You speak English?"

He takes a bite, a strip of meat dangling from the corner of his mouth. "Sì."

"How long?"

Another bite. A shrug. "Long enough."

My mind reels. "You speak two languages and all this time I've been talking to you like I'm playing charades. Do you know how many maps I've drawn in the dirt? The hand signals? The miming?"

"You talk with hands anyway. Why waste words?"

I shake my head. "Unbelievable."

Lorenzo's eyes track to where Katie stands with Jared, his weathered face softening. "She loves you."

"I know. But love isn't enough."

"Ha! Love is always enough. But you must be brave to choose it."

My throat feels too tight. "What if I'm not?"

He shrugs, but his eyes hold mine with surprising intensity. "Then you end up like me."

"What's that supposed to mean?"

He takes another slow bite of his sandwich, chews, swallows. "Old. Alone. Eating sandwiches. Watching young idiotas make same mistakes."

I huff out a humorless laugh. "Some mistakes aren't optional. They're inevitable."

"And some regrets follow you forever."

For all the years I've known him, he's been a man of few words, always keeping his thoughts and life to himself. And now, here he is, holding up a mirror I don't want to look into.

He stands, brushing crumbs from his shirt. Then he claps a heavy hand on my shoulder, leaving a perfect greasy handprint.

"Love," he says quietly, "is worth pain."

Whistling softly, he walks away, leaving me with the uncomfortable truth buzzing in my ears and the distinct scent of prosciutto in my nose.

"Matteo! We need your expertise!" Katie shouts.

Her voice cuts through the crowd with the force of a whip, and every muscle in my body snaps to attention.

Here we go.

"Yes, bella. How can I help?"

"Could you take our picture?" She holds out her phone, batting those long lashes. "We're having *such* trouble getting the right angle of the fountain."

Clueless Jared is already searching the area for the most picturesque spot, grinning like the picture will prove he's got it all. Meanwhile, I'm trying to calculate how many coins it would take to throw in the fountain to wish him away forever.

I take the phone, my jaw tight, and step closer to her. "I know what you're doing."

Katie tilts her head, all wide-eyed innocence. "I have no idea what you're talking about."

"You're messing with me. You want me to be jealous."

"Why would you be jealous," she whispers devilishly, "of my fiancé's hands all over me?"

And then she's gone, sauntering over to Jared. My molars crush together as I watch her place his hands on her waist, tilting her head, attempting to re-create the same sexy pose we did in Florence.

Except Jared is about as seductive as a sack of potatoes.

He's stiff as a board, hands hovering like he's trying to pet a porcupine without getting pricked. Katie's trying, bless her scheming heart, but the guy couldn't smolder if you lit him on fire. I snap a few pictures, but... it's not happening. You can't make spaghetti sultry.

From what Katie shared about him, I figured I was *superiore* in the bedroom. But witnessing this wet noodle firsthand? I'm the pussy *maestro*.

When she returns for her phone, I am prepared.

"Guess what I was just daydreaming about?" She steps closer, her emerald irises sparkling with devious intent. "That first photoshoot in Florence. How your hands felt sliding up my thighs. How I had to bite my lip to keep from moaning... how wet I was for you."

I am not prepared.

My dick throbs like a metronome keeping time with my racing heart.

"And now"—her voice, pure sex wrapped in honey—"you'll spend all day wondering if being near you, remembering your touch, is enough to soak my panties."

Dio Santo.

My breath seizes, the heat flooding my veins like lava. Before I can recover, she pulls back with a triumphant grin, daring me to respond.

Then she walks away, her hips swaying because she knows exactly how she's affecting me. Forcing my mind to remember every curve, every sound, every goddamn whispered plea.

That calculating, absolutely maddening woman.

***

I FUCKING HATE JARED.

I've never wanted to strangle someone with their own dinosaur tie before, but watching Jared ignore Katie for the umpteenth time today has me contemplating new hobbies.

The Colosseum dominates the landscape, a grand tribute to the battles fought here, while I'm losing my own war against the urge to commit tourist-cide. The warmth of the day amplifies the air, thick with centuries of dust and glory even as the tang of my own fury rages.

My tour group is now a walking gift shop, thanks to the relentless vendors prowling the Colosseum line like seagulls over a sandwich. Normally I'd roll my eyes at souvenir swords and overpriced magnets, but the excitement in their voices makes me bite my tongue—for now.

Katie, with her oversized, plastic battle helmet, is staging an impromptu gladiator performance in the heart of the arena. The seniors have formed a makeshift amphitheater around her and Chester and are now whooping and cheering like the world's most geriatric fight club.

And what a performance it is.

Jared, the *stronzo*, is so absorbed in his headset tour across the arena that he's missing the woman captivating us all.

"Behold my mighty blade!" She lifts her tacky sword to the sky. "Forged in the fires of... uh... that really hot place with all the fire!"

"Mount Vesuvius?" Chester says, brandishing a kid-sized trident made of foam.

"No, no—the other one! With the lava and the... you know what? Never mind. Prepare to die!"

"You'll never defeat Chester the Terrible!" Chester attempts a battle stance, but the poor guy looks more like he's passing a kidney stone. "I am invincible! Except for my left knee. And my lower back. And that weird clicky thing my shoulder does when it rains."

The Dawson sisters chant, "Fight! Fight! Fight!"

Jared still hasn't looked up from his audio guide. He's more interested in lusting after weathered rocks than his gorgeous fiancée.

Earlier at the gelato shop, he actually ordered for himself first—*pistachio*, like the boring *pezzo di merda* he is—then tossed his wallet at Katie as if she were a vending machine.

Then the pig finished his gelato and started chowing down on her strawberry cone without asking.

I can't shake the fantasy of tasting that sweet strawberry flavor still lingering on her lips. Even after she's gone, I know her strawberry scent will haunt me.

I catch her stealing glances at me between battle poses. She knows what she's doing—putting on a show, being adorable, making me fall more in love with her with every ridiculous battle cry.

"Is that all you've got?" she taunts through the slot in her over-sized plastic gladiator helmet. "I've battled lions fiercer than you, old man!"

"Your skills may be legendary!" Chester declares, slashing the air in a move that looks less deadly and more mosquito swat. "But can you handle... THIS?"

His "this" involves a lot of arm-waving before he bops her on the head with his foam trident. He retreats into a wobbly hip swivel that has me calculating the distance to the nearest hospital.

The seniors are eating it up. Cameras are snapping, someone's filming on their giant tablet, and Mrs. Thomas shouts "Finish him Katie-cus Maximus!"

Katie seizes the opportunity, delivering a fake fatal slow-motion blow that has Chester collapsing in a heap at her feet. She raises her floppy sword to the sky, victorious, before clutching her own chest and letting out a melodramatic gasp. "Plot twist! Chester the Terrible's blade was laced with poison. Alas, my wounds are fatal!" she says, staggering backward like a Shakespearean heroine meeting her tragic end.

"*¡Hasta la vista!*" she yells, collapsing to the ground dramatically and sticking out her tongue.

I laugh alongside everyone else, but inside, I long to scoop her up, kiss her, and tell her she's the best person I've ever met. Instead, I keep my face impassive, my steps steady, and stop just short of her "lifeless" body. My shadow falls over her.

"Once again, principessa, that's Spanish."

An eye pops open. "I know," she whispers. "Wanted to make sure you were paying attention."

She sticks her tongue out again and closes her eye—back to playing dead.

Dio Santo, the things I want to do to that tongue.

My gaze shifts to Jared, still nodding along to his headset—the human equivalent of beige paint drying. *How does he not see her?*

I know I'm not worthy of Katie's love, but there's no way in hell I'm letting her marry this boring asshole. My company might be fucked, but this problem I can fix.

"Attenzione!" I proclaim in my best ringmaster voice. "Time for the grand finale of our Roman holiday—Vatican City!"

Katie stands and brushes the dust off her sundress. *Cristo, if he wasn't here...*

As our group shuffles toward the bus, I fall into step beside Jared, inspiration striking.

"Oh, Jared, I feel terrible," I say, laying it on thick. "Katie was telling me about your passion for dinosaurs."

His head snaps around like a cat zeroing in on a laser pointer. *Got him.*

"The Museo Civico di Zoologia has this brand-new exhibit on Jurassic-era fossils. It's a multimillion-dollar facility, very high tech..."

His eyes glaze over with unadulterated fossil-lust.

"The Museo Civico?" He practically squeaks. "They have the most comprehensive collection of Mesozoic specimens in southern Europe! Their analytical approach to—"

"Sadly," I cut in before he can start a TED talk, "there is no time with our schedule. Even though it is very close."

Katie, my brilliant co-conspirator, jumps in as though we've rehearsed this. "Couldn't Jared go to the museum and meet us later?"

"Katiebug!" He turns to her with puppy-dog eyes that make me want to vomit. "Come with me! There's this fascinating study on coprolites—"

"Fossilized dung," Katie translates for my benefit.

"But I really wanted to see the Vatican," she says. "The Sistine Chapel, the art..."

"Well..." Jared fidgets with his dinosaur tie, torn between ancient poop and his supposed true love.

"You could meet up with us after," Katie suggests, already pulling out her phone. Her fingers fly across the screen. "Look, we're still sharing locations from... well, before. I can track you. You can track me. Just like always."

The "just like always" hits me hard. *Damn.* They never turned off their location sharing. Even after breaking up. Even after everything.

"You're the absolute best!" Jared chirps, planting a quick kiss on Katie's cheek.

"I promise I won't be too long," he says, already speed-walking toward the taxi stand.

"Take your time!" I shout.

"Did you seriously cockblock my fiancé with dinosaur bones?"

"Bella, if he'd rather spend time with extinct reptiles than your delicious mouth, he deserves his fate."

Finally her first true smile of the day. Score one for the Italian Stallion.

"Besides," I add, keeping pace with our cheerful seniors, "You like it when I'm *on top* of things."

The blush that spreads across her cheeks is worth every manipulative moment. Let Jared have his fossils. I've got plans for *this* living, breathing work of art.

Though I do say a quick prayer of thanks to those ancient lizards. Who knew dinosaurs would be such excellent wingmen?

***

WELCOME TO VATICAN CITY, the ultimate power flex. Built on centuries of guilt, gold, and a whole lot of questionable decision-making. Because nothing says "We're kind of a big deal" like having your own country.

And the Sistine Chapel? Sure, it's a masterpiece, a jaw-dropping work of art. But here's the kicker—Michelangelo was actually a sculptor who got strong-armed into being a painter. Mamma always claimed he was so pissed he painted his own face on the famous ceiling, giving the Pope the holiest "fuck you" in history. Papa argued no way, the man was an artist, not an idiota.

I'm on Team Mamma. Of course he did it.

But the clock is ticking. I don't have time to entertain such thoughts. I have to get Katie Crawford to stop her self-destructive game. Every time I try to make a move, a senior from my group appears—like Katie-deflector shields.

"What year was this painted?"

"Does the Pope have a favorite gelato flavor?"

"Do angels have belly buttons?"

Mrs. Thomas actually asked me if Michelangelo was "packing" under those robes. Then Chester piped in with, "I mean, four years painting a ceiling? The man had to be hanging more than brushes."

It's official. This tour gets a trophy for most penis jokes.

Now we're headed to a gift shop, which I usually avoid like the plague, but today? Today I'll let the seniors debate whether God bobbleheads are blasphemous if it gets me five minutes alone with Katie. Still, I'm not about to let these seniors spend their retirement funds on Vatican-approved trinkets when the shop around the corner sells the same glow-in-the-dark crosses for a third of the price.

But time's running out. Jared could walk back through that door at any minute, ready to steal Katie away. And once we're back at the hotel? It's over. The Crawford Family Circus will make sure I never get near her again.

"One hour till go time," I announce to my flock of holy shoppers. A chorus of agreement echoes back, and they disperse into the aisles as if they were dismissed by the Pope himself.

I stride toward Katie and take her hand. "Time to talk, bella."

The last time I pulled her away, I dragged her into a Hard Rock dressing room. My body was on fire then. Now... it's an inferno of need and desperation.

The moment we clear the gift shop doors onto the sidewalk, Katie spins to face me. "Well, well, well. Ready to stop being an idiot and admit you're in love with me?" She puckers those sinful lips, clearly thinking she's won.

My cock stirs at her boldness, but I force out, "Katie—"

"No?" She taps her chin thoughtfully, and Cristo, even that simple gesture is erotic torture. "Guess I'll try a different approach. Maybe take a nice, long swim at the hotel later."

Madre di Dio. She takes a step closer and trails a single finger down my chest.

"You remember my bikini? The black one with barely any fabric. You couldn't keep your eyes off me. And then it was your hands that couldn't get enough—"

"You can't marry him!"

Her seductive smile vanishes. "Excuse me?"

"Jared. You can't marry that stronzo."

"Oh, this should be good." Her eyes narrow to deadly slits. "Explain to me how you get to reject me but still control my life. I'm dying to hear that logic."

"He doesn't understand you!" I grab her shoulders, needing her to listen. "He barely acknowledges your existence. But I see you, Katie. The real you. The woman who makes my blood burn. Who challenges me to break every rule I've ever made."

This isn't how this was supposed to go. Every word is another reason why she belongs with me, not him.

"How can you marry someone who doesn't worship the ground you walk on?"

"God, stop acting like I'm some kind of prize, Matteo. You want to know the truth? I'm the office joke—the family disappointment. The friend everyone tolerates," she says, her voice splintering as she points to herself. "This? This obsessive, controlling, binder-loving mess? People mock me for it. They have my whole life. 'You're a *lot*, Katie. Too organized. Too intense...'" She swallows hard. "'Too much.'"

Her voice cracks. "You made me feel seen. Respected. Like my crazy was... beautiful. Surprise, surprise, you're no different—rejecting who I am and ripping my heart out as you abandon me."

My chest caves in. I need to tell her. Need to explain about the bank, the loan, how I've failed at everything except loving her.

"Matteo Monti! Still the ultimate ladies' man, I see!"

Fucking merda.

Antonio's voice slices through the bustling tourist chatter like judgment day, that red Italy Express polo blinding in the bright, noonday shine. Panic turns my blood to ice.

Not like this. She can't find out like this.

"I'm Antonio, and you are... an especially bellissima woman." His eyes crawl over Katie like slime, and my hands curl into fists.

"Katie Crawford," I grit out. "From my tour group."

"Best guide in the business, right?" Antonio's smile is all teeth.

"He thinks so." Katie's voice could freeze lava.

"She's not feeling well." I try to steer her away. "Needed some air—"

"Say no more!" Antonio starts to leave but turns back, twisting the knife. "Oh, and get ready to live in that gift shop. Just scored ten percent kickback on all Italy Express sales. We're going to be swimming in euros!" His grin widens. "It'll be old times all over again. See you tomorrow. Welcome back to the family, number one!"

The second he's gone, Katie detonates. "Tomorrow! I am such a fucking idiot. You never planned on us spending two weeks together."

She storms off, rushing into a nearby alley.

"Katie, wait! Please, Bella—"

"Don't." She whirls on me, tears making her eyes glimmer like broken glass. "Don't you dare 'bella' me. Every word you've said was complete bullshit."

"I need to explain. Please—"

"You warned me." Her laugh is bitter wine. "But I was too stupid to listen. I saw our future so clearly—but I was just another tourist in your bed, wasn't I? Go ahead, Matteo. Get back to fucking your way through Italy's tourist population."

"Katie—" I hold her face between my palms, catching the tears I caused. She shoves me away with enough force to send me to my knees.

And that's where I belong. On my knees before her, confessing my sins.

"Yesterday I lost everything." The words pour out like blood from a wound. "My company's bankrupt. You were right—I should have stuck to schedules instead of playing Fairy Godfather with those stupid Wish Cards. Now I have to crawl back to that snake Antonio."

Understanding dawns in her eyes. I'm humiliated, but I press on. "I'm a disaster. You deserve better. I can't even keep my parents' dream alive. I wanted you to stay, I promise. But there's no future with me."

"How can I believe you?" Her voice trembles.

"Because your heart knows me." I rise to my feet. "We're two halves of the same soul. I had a dream for us, to travel across Italy and create memories." I step closer, my hands shaking. "You've captured my soul, Katie Crawford. It's yours. Even when you leave Italy, you'll take it with you. If I could, I'd keep you forever because *ti amo, mi amore*. I do love you."

I crash my mouth to hers, pouring everything I can't say into the kiss. She tastes of tears and possibility, like the one dream that matters. Her fingers tangle in my hair as I back her against the wall. My hand cradles her head while the other grips her hip.

Our tongues dance, desperate and deep, as though we're trying to memorize each other.

"I have nothing," I rasp against her lips. "Nothing to offer except a heart that beats for you." I force steel into my voice. "Go back to Los Angeles. Marry Jared or don't. Just... let me go, *mi amore*."

"Why didn't you tell me?"

"I knew this was going to end, one way or the other. You deserve much more than what I can give. My life is in ruins, please Katie I—"

Movement catches my eye. *Fanculo all the way to hell.* Jared stands at the alley entrance. Silence. Finally he clears his throat. "So... not a fake boyfriend."

"I'm not her boyfriend." Each word is a knife in my own heart. "I'm a vacation fling. Her Italian souvenir."

I commit her to memory one last time—tears catching sunlight like diamonds, chest heaving with each breath, lips swollen from my kisses.

"Goodbye, Katie."

I walk away as I fall apart.

CHAPTER TWENTY ONE

KATIE

GROUP CHAT : CPK FOREVER

Petra: WTF! Your mom's having a social media MELTDOWN. Why is she posting that you're getting married in Rome? And now you're not? What the hell?

Cam: Should we be worried about all her "God's plan" and "Everything happens for a reason" posts?

Petra: Seriously, Katie. Answer or I'm calling the embassy.

Cam: We're here. Whatever you need. Even if it's drinking wine through FaceTime.

Me: Everything's fucked. I'm so fucked. My heart is... fucked.

Petra: Who should I murder? Dinosaur Boy or Italian Stallion? Or both? I'm flexible.

Me: Save your rage. They're not worth the jail time.
Cam: When are you coming home?
Me: First flight out. And when I get back, I'm burning
my passport.

ITALY CAN BITE ME. I'm so done with this whole damn country.

The sun is fucking irritating, poking through the hotel curtains like a nosy neighbor with nothing better to do. The digital clock on the nightstand blinks 12:00 over and over, acting like it doesn't know the time—which is appropriate since I've lost track of it too. I shut off my phone about three emotional breakdowns ago, hoping for a message from Matteo that never came.

I burrow deeper under my pillow fortress, but the sounds of Rome invade anyway. I can hear the hum of Vespas zipping down streets, the chatter of tourists, and the low, rhythmic tolling of church bells that somehow sound judgmental. It's as if the chimes are saying, "Quit being so dramatic, American!"

I squeeze my eyes shut, but it doesn't help. The memories linger: the rough stones of that alley wall against my back, Matteo's hands cradling my face—that kiss was like he was trying to pour his entire soul into me.

"Ti amo, mi amore."

I love you, my love.

And then he walked away.

I stood there like a statue, watching him leave. *Why didn't I yell, chase, beg—do something?* Every cell in my body wanted to go after him, to hold him, to force him to see that his struggles don't make him less worthy of love. But I couldn't move, not as the bitter truth pierced my hopeless heart.

He doesn't want me in his life.

He'd rather run than love me.

And then there was Jared.

After Matteo disappeared, Jared and I finally talked. Not the kind of fake, surface-level talk we'd perfected during our relationship, but the *real* kind that should have happened long before.

He apologized for the ambush proposal, admitting my mother's powers of persuasion rivaled only my own. I admitted that my obsession with planning and control isn't just about keeping things in check; it's my go-to coping mechanism for dealing with anxiety. And he owned up to being a lazy partner who'd gotten way too comfortable letting me sort his world into neat little boxes.

I returned his ring, wished him a lifetime of fossil-hunting happiness, and that was that.

My mother, predictably, went nuclear.

"You're making a huge mistake, Katherine!" She hyperventilated. "Marriage is the goal of life! Security. Stability! How could you throw all that away for a silly fling with some tour guide?"

For once, I didn't whip out a bullet-pointed argument to defend my life choices. I just looked at her and said, "Marriage is not the goal of my life, Mom. *I* am the goal of my life."

And then something miraculous happened.

My brother, David "The Favorite Child" Crawford, defended me. "Katie doesn't need someone else to validate her worth, Mom," he declared, becoming the protective big brother I'd forever wished for. "She's fully capable and destined for greatness. And anyone who can't see how special she is? They don't belong in her orbit."

My mom didn't say another word. Even Dad took my side and muttered something about how Jared's tie collection was "concerning."

In that moment, I opened my brain's binder to the section labeled How to Be Perfect and dismissed it as total crap. I'd spent years feeling the need to systematically prove that I was enough. But now?

Poof.

Gone.

I ripped it out, shredded it, and tossed it in the trash—tabs, dividers, and all.

That was yesterday, but it seems like a lifetime time ago. Today my family is wandering the streets of Rome, probably haggling over overpriced leather bags and taking selfies with random statues. And me? I'm... multitasking: turning hotel bedding into a first-class cocoon of sadness, debating which expensive room-service meal pairs best with misery, and googling how fast I can book a one-way ticket home.

Then a knock at the door.

Aunt Deb charges into the hotel suite like a champagne cork at a celebration.

"Up and at 'em darling! Your fairy godmother has arrived, armed with glitter, charm, and just enough fabulousness to banish this tragic little pity party!" She takes a dramatic sniff and recoils. "Sweet Mary and Joseph, it stinks like heartbreak and stale pasta in here."

She pulls back the curtains and opens the windows. Rome floods in—the sounds and smells of coffee and chaos and other people's lives.

"You're disrupting my den of despair," I mumble into my mattress.

She perches on my bed, her bangles clinking. "Now darling, you really must understand why I gave away my walking tour spot to your dinosaur-obsessed ex."

I emerge from my pillow fortress, my messy bun channeling Medusa's worst hair day. "Fine. Why did you do it?"

Her perfectly lined eyes soften. "I've known you since you were categorizing your baby blocks like a tiny CEO in training. Your brain's always been a powerhouse of problem-solving, but I could tell you needed more time."

"Yeah, well, fat lot of good that did. Jared found out anyway, and Matteo still left."

"So what are you going to do about it?"

"Give up? Accept defeat? Start a cat sanctuary?"

She laughs so loud they can hear it in the tunnels under the Colosseum. "Oh darling, that's the biggest load of bull I've heard since your mother argued that sensible shoes were sexy. You've never given up on anything you truly wanted. It's the thing about you I admire most. Took me decades to become that kind of woman—but you, my dear, were born ready to chase your dreams and make them real."

"Wow... thank you," I say, caught between surprise and pride. Then a question that's been nagging at me bursts out. "Why did you turn down Howie's proposal? Was it because you don't love him?"

"No, it's because I *do* love him."

"That makes no sense."

"Has your mother ever told you about the time I almost got married when I was young?"

"Mom pretty much sticks to the message 'Aunt Deb, the Cautionary Tale of Braless Spinsterhood.'"

"Ha! Well, your rigid grandparents wrote that particular script." A hint of melancholy flickers across her face, at odds with her luminous demeanor. "His name was Roger. We met at Berkeley—he was dynamic, passionate—leading protests against the Vietnam War. The type of man who could start a revolution with just his smile. Which he did—in my pants."

"Aunt Deb!"

"Oh please, as if you and your Italian Stallion weren't testing the structural integrity of every surface in Italy." She smooths her dress, but I catch the slight shake in her hands. "Anyway, it was the *Make Love, Not War* era, darling, and let me tell you—we took that slogan as a personal challenge. I learned positions that made *The Kama Sutra* look like a children's book."

She waves away my scandalized expression.

"We got engaged—had it all planned—a Golden Gate Park wedding filled with love, flowers, and just the right amount of rebellion to keep it interesting. But then your grandparents..." She hesitates, her features tightening. "Religious, old-fashioned, and about as flexible as a brick wall. They saw my young groom as a threat to everything they stood for. They made it clear: break up with the radical or lose my family."

"That's horrible."

"It was the sixties, Katie-kins. If you married the wrong person, or God forbid, didn't marry at all, people assumed you were defective or in a cult."

She dips her hand into her purse, a soft sigh escaping her lips, and reveals a worn-out set of dog tags. The same ones I saw during my Great Condom Heist at the nude beach.

"I was young and scared, so I chose my family," she says softly, as if reliving every moment. "Then he got drafted and I knew—God, I knew—I'd screwed up." She pauses, swallowing hard. "I wrote to him, begged him to believe I was sorry, that I'd been wrong. Told him I'd drop everything and everyone so we could build a life together, far away from anyone who disapproved."

"What did he say?"

"I'll never know. The letter came back marked DECEASED." She grips the tags as though they're the only thing keeping her from unraveling. "He died believing I chose fear over him. That I wasn't strong enough to risk it all for us."

Tears—ones I thought I'd exhausted—form again.

"I see the same fear in Matteo," she adds softly. "That terror of losing what you love. But sweetie, sometimes the biggest risk is not taking one at all."

"He's made it pretty clear he wants nothing to do with me. His company's bankrupt and he's..." I choke back a wave of emotion. "He's broken."

"Oh, you young people and your dramatic self-sabotage! You think love ever happens in the right conditions? It's about weathering the storms together. Preferably naked."

"Of course you make it about sex."

"What? Sex is an excellent cardio and emotional workout." She takes her hands in mine. "Now answer me this—does your heart sing for him? Do you want to spend every moment with him?"

"Yes," I whisper. "And yes."

"Even when he's being an idiot."

"Especially when he's being an idiot."

"Then that's your starting point. Build from there."

"I could say the same for you and Howie."

She arches one perfect eyebrow. "This is about *you* right now. Besides, there's only room for one wise auntie who dispenses life-changing wisdom."

I hurl myself at her in a smothering hug. "Thank you for bringing me on this trip, Aunt Deb. For teaching me that sometimes the best plans are no plans at all."

"Oh darling, I'm just thrilled I got to witness your sexual awakening! Though I recommend being a bit more discrete in wine cellars. They can be quite the echo chambers."

I nearly fall off the bed. "You heard that?!"

"Heard it? We were all slow clapping and cheering you on. Now tell me—was he the dynamo in the sheets I suspected? Because those hands..." She fans herself dramatically.

Heat floods my face. "Oh my God, I didn't know you could have that many orgasms!"

"I knew it! I want *all* the delicious details later, but right now you need to go. Tell that beautiful man you love him—bankrupt company and all."

"He knows I do. I've told him a million times."

"Then make it a million and one." All the theatricality drops from her voice. "Trust me, sweetie. You don't want to live with the regret I have. Pain like this..." She tenderly places Roger's tags back in her purse. "It stays with you forever."

She stands and all her jewelry jangles.

"Wait—stay and help me get all dolled up?"

"Oh darling, I would, but Howie and I have a couples massage before the ceremony."

"Ceremony?"

"What kind of love guru would I be if I didn't follow my own amazing advice?"

With the timing of a soap opera diva, she reaches into her purse and pulls out the massive sapphire engagement ring—it's even bigger up close—and slides it onto her finger with a flourish.

"Well, since you called off your wedding, I thought—why waste the opportunity of having the whole family here in Rome?" Her eyes sparkle with mischief. "Someone should get married."

She throws me a wink straight out of a Vegas showgirl's playbook. "Ceremony's at six. Shoes optional, orgasms mandatory!"

And then she's gone, her voice trailing into the hallway: "Coming, sugarplum! Mama's got plans for that massage table!"

From the hallway, I hear Howie's warm drawl. "Whatever you want, sweet tea."

I stare at the door, my heart doing something complicated in my chest. Because while I've been wallowing in my own romantic tragedy, my aunt—the woman who's spent fifty years running from love—just showed me what courage looks like.

It doesn't look like perfection. It doesn't look like guarantees or neatly tied-up endings. It looks like rolling the dice, closing your eyes, and betting everything you've got on love.

I throw off the covers and sit up so fast the room spins.

I blink, see my binder on the nightstand, and snatch it up. My pen's at the ready to make a list until my gaze lands on it...

The Wish Card.

It's still blank, tucked into the clear sleeve as though it has been waiting for this moment.

I slide it out, holding the little rectangle of possibility in my hand. My fingers brush the smooth surface, and a wave of clarity sweeps over me.

This is it.

I don't need a plan.

I just need one wish.

And I know exactly what it is.

***

I'M CLEAN. I'M DRESSED. I'm caffeinated.

In under an hour I transformed myself from heartbroken tourist to professional powerhouse. My hair's blown out, my red lipstick's applied, and I'm rocking my most confident sundress—the one that screams "I'm here to conquer the world and your heart *(and maybe your bed too)*."

Since Matteo is treating my texts as if they're coated in radioactive man-repellant, I decided to show him what happens when you ghost a woman whose idea of foreplay is problem-solving. So I've shown up at his workplace unannounced, like any self-respecting stalker *(I mean, determined woman)*.

Natural light floods the Italy Express corporate office—all gleaming glass and polished marble with red accents. Above the reception desk is a large, mounted TV screen that displays overly smiley tourists riding on Segways. The air-conditioning hits me like a polar bear's breath, and I swear my nipples could cut glass.

Personal memo: This thin sundress was not the power move I thought it was.

The receptionist—razor-sharp bob, perfectly manicured nails—wears a matter-of-fact smirk and is a corporate clone if I ever saw one. "*Buongiorno, signorina.* Do you have an appointment?"

"No." I flash my most dazzling smile. "But I have an urgent matter to discuss with Antonio."

"Antonio is very busy."

"He'll want to see me." I lean in as though I'm about to share government secrets. "It's about a serious legal issue with his number one tour guide."

Five minutes later, I'm face-to-face with Antonio himself. His overly styled helmet of hair and starch-laden red polo shirt tells me this is a guy who thinks looking slick equals being respected. He recognizes me as he says, "Ah, another one of Matteo's broken hearts."

The words hit like a slap, but I keep my composure. "Actually, I didn't get to finish my tour yesterday, and I really want to see more of Italy."

He snorts. "You look like a woman who wants to wring Matteo's neck."

Well, he's not entirely wrong about the neck-wringing part.

"I need to join Matteo's tour. Today."

"We don't do last-minute additions. Company policy."

Time to pull out the big guns. "Listen, I'd hate to have to leave a scathing review about how Italy Express isn't accommodating to its customers—especially one who works with high-profile clients."

His eyebrow does this thing that would make The Rock jealous. "High-profile clients?"

"Yes." I keep my voice steady, channeling my inner con artist. "Prominent celebrities."

"Which celebrities?"

My mind races. I don't technically know Reece Dare—social media's favorite prankster turned energy-drink mogul—but Cam practically lives in his back pocket as his videographer. And these are desperate times...

"Reece Dare, for one." I drop the name as if it's no big deal, even though my internal voice is screeching "Liar, Liar, sundress on fire!"

Antonio's eyes light. "Reece Dare? The YouTuber?"

"That's right."

"I don't believe you."

"Then I'll prove it," I tell Antonio, hitting FaceTime and praying Cam answers.

The screen rings once. Twice. "Pick up, Cam. Pick up," I mutter under my breath, my heart doing nervous backflips.

Finally her face appears, sunshine bright as usual. "¡*Hola*, Katie! What's up girlie?"

I want to blurt out how stunning she looks. My utility-belt-wearing, scrunchie-collecting friend has gone full island goddess. She's rocking a strapless dress that definitely wasn't bought with camera gear in mind. Her usual practical ponytail has been replaced with soft waves, complete with a flower tucked behind her ear.

Nope. Must turn on the professionalism. "Camila Morales, thank you for taking my call."

Her eyes do this little dance of confusion, but she matches my tone. "Of course, Miss Crawford. How can I help you?"

I angle my phone so Antonio has a clear view. "I'm here with Antonio from Italy Express. Can you please confirm that Reece Dare and I are working together on an upcoming event?"

MÉLISA RYUN

Cam's expression doesn't falter, but her eyes are screaming *Girl, what mess are you dragging me into?* "Absolutely. I'm with Mr. Dare right now. Let me grab him."

She turns the phone, and there he is—Reece Dare himself, in all his sun-kissed, slightly sweaty splendor, radiating dark-haired surfer Ken Doll energy—sculpted six-pack abs on full display.

"Reece," Cam says. "Can you confirm your upcoming meeting with Katie Crawford for the launch of your new energy drink?"

His confused puppy eyes would be adorable if my entire plan didn't hinge on his acting skills. "Oh, uh... yeah. Yes. Miss Crawford! Good to talk to you... again?"

Crap. That totally came out as a question. Hopefully, Antonio doesn't notice.

Instead, he practically levitates out of his leather chair. "Reece Dare! I love your videos. The one with the ostrich race? Genius!"

"Thanks, man. I appreciate it."

"If you're ever in Italy, we'd love to host you for a private, complimentary tour of the country."

"You know what? I might take you up on that. This Hawaii trip has been... mind-blowing."

Reece's eyes rake over Cam with the kind of fire that could set off sprinklers. I can feel the heat radiating through the screen before he says, "Nice talking to you, Miss Crawford."

Oh. My. God. That look. Coming from a man Cam refers to as Prickwad Douchewaffle. Why is he suddenly giving her *ruin-me-in-a-rainforest* energy?

Cam's face pops back into view, a flush spreading across her cheeks. *Is she getting lei'd in paradise?* "Thank you for calling."

"Yes, and I hope your trip is... satisfying." I try to keep the *spill the tea* out of my voice.

"LOTS to catch you up on later," she says with a smirk that promises scandalous details. "I suggest you watch tomorrow's video. *Hasta luego,*" she says before hanging up.

I study Antonio, who's still basking in the afterglow of his brush with YouTube fame.

"All right," he sighs, defeated but trying not to show it. "I'll add you to Matteo's tour. But promise me you'll get Reece Dare to come to Italy. It would be a dream come true."

"I'll see what I can do," I say, tucking away both my phone and my guilt about lying.

Antonio hands me a clipboard full of forms, which I sign without reading. My mind is already racing ahead.

I'm coming for you, Matteo Monti.

***

THE COLOSSEUM TEEMS WITH energy and excitement, but all I can focus on is my pounding heart and sweaty palms. Tour groups swarm every corner, snapping selfies, their voices blending into a chaotic hum of languages I don't recognize. The air smells of sunscreen, sweat, and overpriced gelato. Next to me, a group of teens are losing it over the bad Wi-Fi situation. Tragic. I mean, how will they share their $10 coffees with the world?

But none of that matters.

Because there he is. Matteo Monti. Red flag in hand, looking like a grumpy Italian snack in his red polo shirt. His khakis are pressed within an inch of their life *(who hurt you, khakis?)*, and his artfully messed-up hair has my fingers itching to mess it up more. That scowl on his face? It shouldn't make my lady bits tingle, but here we are.

I weave through the crowd like I'm playing human *Frogger*, dodging selfie sticks and overstuffed backpacks until I'm close enough to hear him. His voice carries over the headset receivers, low and gravelly, but there's no passion. He's listing off facts the same way he'd read the ingredients on the back of a cereal box.

"Built in 70 AD. Originally named the Flavian Amphitheater. Could seat up to fifty thousand spectators..."

Oh hell no. This is not my Matteo.

"Excuse me," I shout loudly. "But I didn't get my headphones."

Matteo's head snaps up, his dark eyes locking onto mine. His face flickers, for just a split second *(is that surprise? A hint of relief?)*, but then his scowl returns with a vengeance.

"Katie. What are you doing here?"

"I'm here for the tour. Obviously."

"You're not part of this tour."

"Oh, but I am." I grin, pulling my secret weapon out of my bag: the red shirt. "Ta-da! Official member of the Italy Express Red Shirt Brigade. Or should I say *brigata*? That's Italian for brigade, right? No? Still Spanish?"

"Bella. I don't have time for this."

"Oh, you've got time." I step closer, making sure his group is watching—because what's a public rejection without an audience? "I have no headphones. How can I possibly hear all the riveting information about gladiators and lions? I have questions. About their dietary habits. Their workout schedules. Their skincare routines."

He narrows his eyes. "This isn't the time or place."

"Then when, Matteo?" I challenge. "Because I've been texting you, calling you, trying to do this the easy way, but all I've gotten is silence. You've left me no choice but to join your lovely tour. I even brought snacks for everyone. But if you choose the hard way..."

The corner of his mouth twitches. He's fighting a smirk. "Why can't you just take no for an answer?"

"Not my style," I shoot back, tilting my head. "You know that."

He looks at me sternly and exhales, as if to say *I'm not playing your game*, and sharply turns back to his group. "We have five more minutes for pictures," he announces, "and then we'll visit the gift shop, where they're offering a discount on 'I Survived the Colosseum' mugs."

"So you're choosing the hard way. Fine, but remember, you asked for this. I just wanted to talk."

A flicker of concern crosses his stupidly handsome face. Good. He should be worried. Because the hard way? It's a public spectacle that'll probably get me banned from Italy forever and earn me my own special exhibit in the Embarrassing American Tourist Hall of Fame.

I step into the middle of the Colosseum's dusty floor and the crowd takes notice. I pull my portable speaker out of my purse and set it down, ready to drop the beat like it's the party of the century. My fingers fumble with my phone as I scroll through playlists.

"All right, Katie," I mutter to myself as I pull on the red shirt and adjust the feather boa I definitely didn't steal from Aunt Deb's luggage. "Time to channel your inner exotic dancer."

I hit *Play*.

The opening drumbeat of "Pour Some Sugar On Me" by Def Leppard ricochets off the large stone walls like a call to arms. Every confused tourist within earshot freezes mid-selfie and swivels in my direction.

No turning back now.

This is it.

Showtime.

On the front of my shirt, in hastily scribbled Sharpie letters, is the word *K-Tease*.

I strike my first pose, legs wide, boa trailing behind me like a sequined comet, and start gyrating my hips as if I'm spinning an imaginary hula hoop. The amphitheater echoes with the unmistakable sound of '80s glam metal—and suddenly, I'm eleven years old again in Mrs. Garrett's fifth-grade talent show, mortifying myself in front of my classmates.

Except this time there's no Mrs. Garrett to hold me back. And no talent show trophy to win. Just Matteo Monti, standing somewhere behind me, ready to either murder me or finally, *finally* talk to me.

My hips jerk left, then right, then freeze somewhere in between. It's not so much grapevine as a full-blown "get this spider off me" dance. Phones are popping up, recording my chaos, so I throw in a symbolic shoulder shimmy that says, "You're welcome, world."

Despite the music blaring, the Colosseum fills with the sound of people choking on their laughter.

But Spontaneous Katie doesn't care about dignity anymore. She bends her knees, throws her arms up, and attempts a spin that nearly takes out a family of four standing too close.

I drop to the ground—*yes, the ground*—and do what can only be described as the world's most uncoordinated body roll. I'm like a fish flopping on the deck of a boat. The boa gets caught in my hair, but I push through because Aunt Deb taught me: never break character, darling.

"Sweet baby Jesus, what am I looking at?" someone mutters in the crowd. *It's a valid question.*

I spring back to my feet—or try to. It takes two attempts and I flash everyone my cotton panties in the process. The boa, now more of a sad feather duster, gets tangled in my hair as I attempt to twirl it over my head like a lasso. It whips back and smacks me in the face, leaving me spitting out feathers.

Then I spot him.

Matteo.

He's standing a few feet away with the most bewildered expression I've ever seen.

I throw my arms wide, channeling all the false confidence I have, and shout over the music, "Are you not entertained?!"

"Katie," he snaps. "What. The. Hell."

"Just living my best life!" I attempt a high kick that barely clears my knee. "But I'll stop if you talk to me."

"No."

"Then buckle up, Monti. This routine's on repeat until my phone battery runs out. Which means every three minutes you'll see my finale which involves"—I pause for dramatic effect—"jazz hands."

His face twitches. "Jazz hands?"

"Never underestimate the power of jazz hands, Matteo." I fling the boa over my shoulder and attempt another high kick. "Did you know I can do the worm? I mean, I can't, but I'm willing to try. Right here. On this sacred, once-respected ground. In front of all these nice people with cameras."

The crowd's totally on board now. A group of college guys begins chanting "K-Tease! K-Tease!"

Matteo steps closer—he's either going to strangle or kiss me. "I'm at work. Besides, you're going to get us both arrested."

"Fine by me. You'll be forced to talk in jail." I twirl again, my movements so stiff and jerky I look like a malfunctioning robot. "Your choice, Italian Stallion. I can do this all day."

He groans, pinching the bridge of his nose. "You're insane."

"Says the man who won't stop me," I say, attempting a seductive shimmy; but I'm guessing it looks more like I'm being electrocuted in slow motion.

Matteo steps into my personal space, his eyes burning into mine. "Fine. You win. I'll talk to you. But for the love of God, turn off that music before the Colosseum bans Italy Express forever."

I snatch up my phone, killing the music mid-guitar solo, panting and sweaty but triumphant. "Thank God. Without a microphone stand, I was going to have to do my big ending by grinding on you."

That does it. Matteo laughs—a deep, sexy, throat-shaking laugh that makes my knees wobble. "You're ridiculous," he says, shaking his head.

"Ridiculously determined," I say, grinning up at him.

He crosses his unfairly muscled arms across his chest, and I have to suck back my drool. Post-dance cardio plus bicep exposure is a dangerous combination.

"All right, principessa, what can you say that hasn't already been said?"

I ignore his tone—because Matteo loves to pretend he's unbothered while secretly having all the feelings—and whip out my binder.

His eyes drop to it, and that mouth I want to kiss curls up. "Of course you brought that."

"What can I say? A girl likes to be prepared." I flip it open with a flourish, pulling out the Wish Card with nervous fingers. "I finally decided what I want for my wish."

"That tour ended, Katie."

"Just take it," I insist, shoving it at his chest.

His jaw tightens as he reads, then softens as he speaks the words aloud: "I wish for Matteo Monti to love me."

His gaze lifts to mine. A storm is brewing. "Katie, I already love you. You know that. That's not the problem."

"Yeah, I figured you would say that. I've made a plan to tackle your problems and show you how we can build a perfect future."

I thrust my binder at him as if I'm serving legal papers. He takes it, his expression caught between skepticism and curiosity as he flips through the pages. One. Two. Three. His movements grow more frantic. "What is this?" His eyes dart to mine, confusion written all over that beautiful face. "These pages are blank."

"Exactly," I say, stepping closer. "I don't want a perfect life anymore. I want the messy, unpredictable, slightly terrifying life with you. That's the point. I don't have a plan."

"You... want to wing it?"

"Yes. Bring on the chaos. The unknown. We'll figure it out together. Though maybe with a smidge better accounting practices."

"Katie... I don't know. I've never been in a relationship and—" He swallows hard. "I can't let you down."

I grab his hand and press it to my chest, directly over my hammering heart. "You don't have to promise me forever," I whisper. "I just need you to love me. The rest we'll figure out one day at a time."

His eyes lock onto mine, wide and vulnerable. "I don't deserve you."

"And I don't deserve you," I whisper back. "Yet somehow we found each other."

Something shifts in his expression, like a dam breaking. His hands cup my face, and then his mouth is on mine, hot and desperate and perfect. His kiss is a fierce, unbridled force of feelings impossible to contain, a thunderous roar that sweeps me off my feet and steals my breath away.

When he finally pulls back, resting his forehead against mine, his breath fans across my lips.

"But what if this goes horribly wrong?"

"What if it goes amazingly right?"

A smile tugs at his lips. "I guess if it does go wrong, we know who to blame."

"Lorenzo," we say together, chuckling.

"Are you sure you're not Italian?" Matteo says with a smile. "Because your stubbornness rivals Caterina's."

"I'll take that as a compliment."

"Oh, it was," he says, then shifts his voice to a sinful rumble. "And I expect to see that stubborn fire in my bedroom tonight. After the tour."

I raise an eyebrow, patting his chest. "Then you'd better get back to it, Italian Stallion."

His palms settle against my cheeks, his eyes tender and warm. "Katie, you are the most captivating creature I've ever beheld. I will make it my mission to be worthy of your love."

Before I can respond, he grabs my waist and lifts me off the ground, my legs instinctively wrapping around him. "And screw waiting," he growls, his lips brushing my ear. Louder, he announces, "Attenzione! One hour till go time!"

He holds me tight as he leans over and scoops up my dance gear and purse.

"Where are we going?" I ask, breathless and giddy.

"I thought I'd show you my Leaning Tower of Pisa."

"Oh really? Let me guess—it's rock-solid?"

"Only for you, *mi amore.*"

"Say it again."

"Mi amore."

His lips meet mine, and in that moment, I know two things: (1) Matteo Monti is my soulmate, and (2) I'm either getting a call... or my she-devil of an aunt slipped her "travel companion" into my purse.

Bzzzzzzzzzz!

EPILOGUE

MATTEO

1 YEAR LATER

"Buongiorno!" Katie and I chorus, warmly greeting the travelers inside our beloved four-wheeled disaster. The old girl got some upgrades—expensive tires, fresh paint, new seats—but that mysterious smell? It's either still haunting us or Lorenzo's prosciutto farts have gotten worse.

w"Before we begin our adventure today," I announce, catching Katie's eye with a playful wink, "we need your help getting this chariot of dreams moving."

My gorgeous girlfriend is effortlessly commanding attention in her way-too-adorable sundress that's making my blood run hot. Her blonde hair bounces with each little gesture, and her smile owns me. Then, because she's a menace, she throws me a flirty over-the-shoulder look that has my heartbeat thumping... below the belt.

Katie smirks, then takes the mic. "Everyone ready? Guida l'autobus, Lorenzo!"

They respond with a chorus of mangled Italian sounds and syllables. It's not pretty, but it does the job. Lorenzo, reigning champion of minimal cues, grunts and adjusts his signature newsboy cap before stomping on the gas. The bus lurches forward, sounding like a dragon gargling rocks.

We've come to appreciate her noises as the old girl's way of saying, "Buckle up, bambinos, this nonna's ready to party!"

Katie leans into me, her strawberry scent mixing with our ride's eternal eau de mysterious, and whispers, *"Tu me vuelves loca, Semental Italiano."*

You drive me wild, Italian Stallion.

Even with her terrible accent, my cock pulses at her phrase.

"Still Spanish, mi amore." I slide my hand to her hip, hidden from our audience.

"Oh is it?" She grins wickedly. "I didn't know."

Thing is. She's fluent in Italian now. Like, could sit down with the Pope and swap ravioli recipes fluent. She tackled it the way she does everything—with laser focus and enough enthusiasm to make the rest of us look lazy. And her absolute refusal to behave does things to me I can't begin to explain. I'm a goner for her. Completely and irrevocably hers.

Now we are studying French and Spanish together, expanding Monti Tours to welcome more international travelers. But my new favorite hobby is hearing her practice dirty talk in multiple languages. When she purrs those filthy phrases, I swear, I'm putty in her hands. My appreciation for linguistics has reached a whole nother level.

She kisses my jaw before speaking into the mic. "Everyone, check the pocket in front of your seats! You'll find our welcome packages along with a collapsible water bottle, local treats, and mineral sunscreen—because barbecue-chicken-skin-glow vibes are not the photos we're looking for in Verona."

This is my Katie—always thinking three steps ahead. She's revolutionized my touring company with these thoughtful touches. When we decided to manage the business together, she was true to her word about "making it up" as we went along. But once we agreed on a direction—Madonna santa—did she run with it.

I'll never forget the night she burst into our bedroom, wearing nothing but one of my shirts—hair wild, eyes blazing, and sexy determination that had my whole body at attention. She found the solution to reviving Monti Tours—premium pricing.

Unlike Italy Express with their cookie-cutter tours, we now offer a unique experience. Travelers submit their Wish Cards before booking, detailing their travel aspirations in Italy. Katie, spreadsheet sorceress that she is, calculates the exact cost to make that wish come true, right down to the last cannoli. Then the client decides if their heart's desire is worth the premium price tag.

Not a single complaint. In fact, we have repeat customers booking trip after trip because each vacation is completely different. My Katie didn't just save my company—she reinvented it as something unforgettable.

The seniors-only tours will always be our most beloved. There's a special charm in watching retirees embrace life with the enthusiasm of college kids on spring break—minus the body shots and terrible decisions. Well... minus the terrible decisions anyway.

This particular group holds an extra special place in our hearts. Several faces from that first chaotic tour where Katie and I met are back, proving that even mysterious bus smells can't keep a good tourist down.

Katie pulls out today's Wish Card, handing it to me with a genuine smile. "Matteo, please share what wish we're making come true today."

"Signore e signori," I project with a theatrical flourish, "today we journey to fair Verona, where our dear friend Chester wishes to pay homage to the famous statue of Juliet."

"By 'homage' he means cop a feel of those bronze knockers!" Chester yells from his seat, waggling his eyebrows. Today's funny shirt reads, STILL GOT THE MOVES, JUST NEED A LITTLE WD-40.

The bus passengers cackle with laughter.

"Mrs. Thomas and I are excited about our first bronze three-way. It's a ménage à trois where no one can complain about cold hands."

"Chester!" Mrs. Thomas swats his arm, but her blush says she's not really objecting.

Katie grabs the mic, eyes dancing. "Speaking of familiar faces, we are thrilled to welcome Mrs. Thomas again."

"Well, it was either sit at home watching soap operas or come hang out with you crazy people!" she shouts, her fingers intertwined with Chester's.

Their first trip brought them together, and now? They're inseparable.

I'm holding back the most exciting part of Chester's wish. Despite his jokester reputation, he's unironically planned a heartfelt, over-the-top proposal. I proofread his speech and it brought me to tears, especially the ending: "Forever starts here, with you and me."

Mrs. Thomas has no clue how romantic this man is under all that silliness.

Seeing them reminds me of the first time I held Katie's hand in Verona—on our first *real* date, when my fingers linked with hers and the whole world shifted into place. And now having her hand in mine feels like coming home.

Truth is, I wanted to call her mine after the experience on Lake Como. No, not *that* experience, not when my balls turned into frosticles. The turning point for me was when I snapped that first picture of her, and she embraced it. I felt like I earned a piece of Katie's trust, and I had to protect it. That day, something changed in me—a fierce desire to keep her heart safe.

And Katie stuck to her guns about taking things slow—which nearly killed me, by the way. But when she finally called me her boyfriend? Cristo, I almost combusted from pure fucking joy.

Turns out commitment is not an issue for me—I'd marry her tomorrow. But Katie is in no hurry for rings and white dresses. I get it. She's too busy living in our perfectly imperfect bubble of happiness.

Though sometimes my caveman brain needs just a bit of reassurance. Which is why, one day, my girlfriend did the most spontaneous thing ever—walked into a tattoo parlor and had my name inked inside a heart on her hip. Only I'm allowed to see it. Well, and occasionally half of Italy when she's rocking that dental floss bikini or we're running naked on the beach *(which happens way more often than my Catholic guilt is comfortable with)*.

My girl was adamant I ink her name on me too. I suggested my forehead *(go big or go home, right?)* She countered with my dick.

"That'll ensure," she purred, "everyone will know exactly who owns the real you."

We agreed to put her name over my heart where it belongs.

"And I spot some more troublemakers," Katie announces into the PA system. "Please welcome back our favorite fashion duo, the Dawson sisters!"

Margaret preens, silver curls bouncing with every gleeful tilt of her head. "We are here to raid Italy's hidden fashion treasures for our growing empire. Or as the kids call it, our 'online store.'"

"Turns out the internet shares the same impeccable taste as two stylish old broads," Agnes says. "Isn't that right, sister dear?"

"Where budget meets boujee!" Agnes says, whipping out PEN-NIES FOR PRADA business cards like confetti. "Italy's closet rejects are Gen Z's next obsession."

These women inspire the hell out of me. Their first tour lit a fire under them to start a whole new career. Their Wish Cards are no longer to find trinkets; now they're all about unearthing secret fashion shops tourists never see. And watching them dive headfirst into their dream, proving it's never too late to be bold and badass. It's a front-row seat to the best kind of magic.

KATHUNK!

Our vehicle hits a pothole that could swallow the Leaning Tower of Pisa.

"Mama mia! Hold on!" Lorenzo barks. *An actual full sentence? The apocalypse must be near.*

Suddenly everyone's bouncing and jerking like we're riding a mechanical bull through an earthquake. I grab Katie, yanking her against my chest as purses and water bottles go flying. Her soft curves mold against me, and even potential death by potholes can't stop my body from soaking her in.

I assume we've driven through the worst of it because our driver gives us a thumbs up.

"These ancient Roman roads could use some modern love," I say to our travelers.

Katie starts collecting scattered belongings, bending over to show me a playful peak of her cotton panties, and my mouth goes dry.

"Shit!" Katie shouts. She jerks up as if stung by something. "Really, Aunt Deb?"

Bzzzzzzzzzz!

Katie hands the vibrating lipstick-shaped device to her aunt.

"Darling, it's like American Express—never leave home without it," Deb says proudly. "And Katie-kins, you should include those in your welcome bags! What do you think, my Southern stud? Should we fund that particular business expansion?"

"Of course, sweet tea. Who doesn't enjoy a little pickle tickle between excursions?" Howie drawls.

These two haven't slowed down since their wedding. Their year-long honeymoon makes *Fifty Shades* look like a Nicholas Sparks novel.

"Everyone," Katie says boastfully, "please meet Deborah and Howie Dixon. They're not just valued guests; they're also the primary investors in Monti Tours."

"Without whom none of this would be possible," I add. "Let's give them a round of applause!"

The whole bus cheers. Howie grins ear to ear while Deb basks in the attention—a cat on a sun-warmed windowsill. Katie's brilliant idea to seek private financing saved us from those stuffy banks who tried poo-pooing our dream. With Howie's billions backing us, we're not just surviving—we're fucking crushing it.

"How about you invest some of those Dixon dollars in a bus that doesn't smell as if a skunk and a dumpster had a baby?" Chester shouts from the back.

"Sorry, amico." I caress our battle-scarred dashboard. "This old girl, she's family."

Katie snatches the mic from my hand. "Time to get this party started!"

I hit the music button, and the opening drums of "Pour Some Sugar On Me" blast through our freshly upgraded speakers. The disco ball—*yes, I kept that promise*—sends rainbow lights spinning across the bus interior like a kaleidoscope, turning our rolling disaster into a legitimate party venue. She may still smell, but dammit now she's got style.

And then my bellissima, brilliant, slightly unhinged girlfriend launches into her signature K-Tease performance. Her hips start doing this thing that should honestly require a permit. The seniors lean forward like they're watching the Second Coming, except instead of Jesus, it's Katie Crawford bringing sexy back one questionable dance move at a time.

"Work it!" Aunt Deb shouts. "Remember what I taught you—swing those hips like you're trying to hypnotize a cobra."

Katie attempts a sultry shimmy but looks more like she's being attacked by bees. *God, I love this woman.*

Just when I think I can't possibly love her more, she proves me wrong.

The feather boa becomes a dangerous weapon as she twirls it overhead, nearly taking out Mrs. Thomas's latest perm. But nobody cares because witnessing Katie Crawford doing the K-Tease is like watching a beautiful disaster in slow motion—you can't look away.

"That's it, baby girl." My auntie jumps up, proud choreographer of this beautiful chaos. "Show them my signature moves. Thrust those hips with a little more *oomph*—that's how I snagged my Howie!"

Deborah distributes feather boas to our cheering crowd as though she's Oprah. "You get a boa! And you get a boa! Everyone gets a boa!"

The seniors are living their best lives, waving their new accessories like victory flags.

Katie and Deb sync up their moves, and the guests go wild, absolutely loving it *(I'm pretty sure the original choreography had much less seat grinding)*. Or maybe it did. This is Aunt Deb we're talking about.

SCREECH!

Our tour vehicle swerves sharply—Lorenzo's too busy watching the show in his mirror to notice we are drifting into oncoming traffic.

"Eyes on the road!" I shout.

His response? Mining for nose gold like he's hoping to strike it rich.

Some things never change.

"Su-*ZANNE*!" Deb sashays over to where Katie's mom sits ramrod straight. "Show these youngsters where Katie got her irresistible moves."

Katie's mother shakes her head, lips pursed like fun is an infectious disease. "Deborah, really. I don't think—"

"Come on, Mom," Katie calls out. "Remember what we talked about? Being more spontaneous?"

Then it happens. Suzanne Crawford, queen of country-club brunches and perfectly coordinated tennis outfits, stands up. She adjusts her silk blouse, takes a deep breath like she's about to dive into shark-infested waters, and starts... moving.

"That's it, Suzy Q!" Deb whoops. "Show Katie how to twerk it."

David Senior claps along, beaming at his wife and daughter like the lucky man he is. The passengers on the bus lose their shit as three Crawford women attempt to make Def Leppard proud.

I still remember the Great Italian Standoff, as we now call it. When Katie told her mom she was staying in Italy, Suzanne went through all five stages of grief in about thirty seconds. There were tears, accusations about throwing away her future, and at least three keynote speeches about the benefits of living in Los Angeles.

But sometimes distance brings people closer. Now Suzanne Face-Times us so often that I know her tennis schedule by heart. Her Pinterest board description reads: "My daughter lives in Tuscany and yours doesn't," which makes her country-club friends green with envy.

This Christmas, I'm flying to Los Angeles with Katie—my first real holiday since losing my parents. She's already got a five-page checklist of magical holiday moments we *must* experience together. Yesterday she ordered us matching Christmas sweaters, complete with light-up reindeer noses. Embarrassing? Yes. But I'd wear a musical sweater every day of my life to be part of this new family.

Katie attempts another spin, the boa creating a feathery tornado around her. Her jazz hands could guide planes safely to landing, and Cristo, I've never seen anything sexier.

I catch her eye and mouth, "I love you."

Her face lights up as she mouths back, "I love you too."

Speaking of love stories that last a lifetime, we're short a couple of familiar friends this tour. Stan and Rose are off being international jet-setters. Last month, they were in Japan—I saw pictures of them at Lake Kawaguchiko with their grandkids. Another lake checked off his bucket list.

The familiar skyline of Verona appears on the horizon, and my stomach growls. That little pizzeria where I took Katie on our first official date is calling my name. The same one where she lectured me for forty-five minutes about the superior qualities of California Pizza Kitchen and had to eat her words (and half my pizza).

For her twenty-sixth birthday, Katie's besties—Petra and Cam—outdid themselves. They shipped frozen CPK pizzas across the Atlantic *(and probably lived on ramen noodles for six months to afford the shipping)*. But watching Katie bounce in her seat as she forced me to try BBQ chicken pizza? I would've paid double.

Look, I'll never admit this out loud, but it wasn't terrible. Don't get me wrong—Italian pizza is still superiore in every way, but I finally understand why Katie and her friends love CPK. The pizza isn't just food—it's the cornerstone of their best moments together.

I haven't met the infamous Petra and Cam in person yet, but I feel I already know them. Katie's weekly FaceTime sessions are like watching a reality show where three best friends try to coordinate time zones and life crises across continents.

Here in Italy though, Katie's officially found her new BFF. She and Caterina are practically glued together—or more accurately glued to their phones since they text as often as they breathe. Most of our free time is spent at the vineyard, where Katie's revolutionized their inventory system with something she calls "emotional wine categorization."

Little Luca, Caterina and Enrico's baby boy, owns every heart in a fifty-mile radius. That kid's inherited his papa's charm and his mama's sass—he's going to be a holy terror when he starts walking. Katie adores him but has made it crystal clear that she is in no rush for our own bambinos. She loves our life exactly as it is. And so do I... for now.

Those *quality control inspections* of the wine cellar are a regular thing for us. And mysteriously, we always finish with way less clothing than when we began. If those barrels could talk... let's just say some escapades are best kept in the basement. Our naughty little secret.

I can't tear my eyes away from Katie as she shimmies down the aisle—she's changed me, changed us, so much so, that every time I think I've hit peak happiness, she finds a way to raise the bar. I reach for Mamma's old Nikon—now the keeper of our most precious memories.

Through the lens, I wait to capture Katie's silly dance moves for what they are.

Charming. Playful. Sexy as hell. *CLICK.*

Others join in. The Dawson sisters attempt *(and fail)* the Electric Slide. *CLICK.*

Chester flaunts his "signature move" which is... enthusiastic knee wobbling I guess. *CLICK.*

Mamma, Papa, you'd be crying with laughter right now.

They would have absolutely adored Katie. I know it.

They also would love how we spend our days exploring and sharing the hidden corners of Italy. But the real marvel? It's in those quiet moments between adventures. How she curls into me at night, her strawberry scent fusing with whatever pasta feast we demolished for dinner.

The passion between us burns hotter than a Vegas summer, but now it's got layers, like a good tiramisu. I crave her like a drug—from her excited chattering about new tour ideas to that laugh that's pure charm. Hell, even when she teases me for walking into a wall when her ass is distracting. And those little sighs she makes—biting into the perfect carbonara or seeing our tourists fall head over heels for Italy. She's a damn masterpiece, and I'm hooked.

The music changes to a lively Italian folk song, and Katie claps along, a human espresso shot, jolting everyone awake with her boundless energy.

Suddenly she's facing me, and her wide smile dares me to catch up to her enthusiasm. "Dance with me, tour guide, before I write you up for workplace negligence."

"You can't," I say, setting down the camera and pulling her close. "I'm *il capo*, principessa. The boss."

"Co-boss," she says, smashing her breasts against me. "And your moves need serious evaluation."

I take her hand, leading her in a dance that's half waltz, half whatever-the-hell-we're-making-up. We twirl along the narrow walkway, backed by the most spirited, off-time clappers on the planet.

We roll into Verona, and—merda—there she sits. The bright red, overpriced eyesore that is the Italy Express bus.

Antonio's still operating his cookie-cutter operation, but karma's a beautiful thing. These days their TripAdvisor page reads like a horror novel. The number one scathing review I love most: "Spent more time in souvenir shops than actual Italy. My authentic Italian experience was buying a Made in China Leaning Tower of Pisa key chain."

The best part? Their disappointed customers keep finding us, begging for real adventures steeped in culture.

Katie catches me smirking. "Stop gloating and help me wrangle our dancing queens off this bus."

"Just admiring the competition, amore. Or should I say, lack thereof?"

"Your ego is showing."

"You love my big ego."

"I tolerate your ego. I *love* the size of your big eggplant."

I pull her into me and whisper, "I'm going to do filthy things to that dirty mouth of yours tonight."

To hell with waiting. I cup Katie's face in my hands and pour everything I'm feeling into this kiss—all the love, the gratitude, the pure joy of having this incredible woman in my life. Her lips are soft and eager against mine, and the little sigh she makes hits me like Italian sunshine.

Our passengers break into applause. "Now that's *amore*!" Howie calls out. "Though you might want to save some of that fire for after the tour, Romeo."

"Get it, baby girl!" Aunt Deb shouts.

Neither of us cares that we've got an audience of seniors who will absolutely turn this into today's main discussion topic. Sorry, Juliet's balcony—you've been demoted to second most-romantic sight in Verona.

My hands slide to Katie's waist, memorizing this moment. Sometimes I hold her this tight because I still can't believe she's real.

I'll admit, sometimes that fear still lingers. The fear that this—*us*—is too good to last. That one day I'll wake up and this beautiful, maddening woman will be gone, leaving me with nothing but memories and the faint scent of strawberries.

But not today.

Today I'm just a man who found his home in a woman who carries emergency highlighters in her purse. Before Katie, I thought I was living. I wasn't. I was existing, floating through life with no purpose beyond the next tour, the next fling, the next distraction. Now? Every day with her is an adventure.

When we finally come up for air, we're both panting like we've climbed the stairs to the Colosseum. Twice. Her lipstick is smeared, her hair's a mess, and Cristo, she's never been more breathtaking.

"Well," she says, her voice husky, "that was unexpected."

I grin, running my thumb along her cheek. "Unexpected? I've been planning that kiss for at least thirty seconds."

"Thirty whole seconds? Impressive. What's next, color-coded schedules?"

"Don't get your hopes up."

Her hands slide up to my chest, her smile softening. "Matteo," she says, "I love you so much it actually hurts my brain."

"Good," I say, stroking her cheek. "I'm so hopelessly, completely, wildly in love with you."

Her grin turns wicked. "Phew. Because after that tattoo, you're officially stuck with me. I don't know anyone else named Matteo."

I laugh, leaning down to brush another kiss across her lips.

"All right, you horny teenagers!" Chester bellows. "Save some action for Juliet's statue. Those bronze boobies aren't going to fondle themselves."

We step off the bus together, her hand warm in mine as Verona welcomes us like an old friend. Life with Katie isn't predictable—it's a constant surprise of sticky notes and stolen kisses, a mix of highlighted itineraries and spontaneous adventures. But watching her try to organize my chaos while creating her own? That's the kind of perfect I never knew existed.

***

Find out what happens with Cam and Reece in their grumpy sunshine vacation romance: **Hawaii Can Suck It**

hey there, bella!

Ring? Check. Romantic vineyard? Check. A perfectly planned proposal? Uh, not quite. See how Matteo's big gesture for Katie takes a hilariously unexpected turn.

Don't miss the laughs in this
FREE BONUS EPILOGUE!

Scan code or visit:

MELISARYUN.COM/BONUS

MORE BOOKS BY MÉLISA RYUN

AUTHORS' NOTE

Hey Lovelies!

Fun fact from your favorite married romcom duo: *this* was the very first book we wrote together. And oh, what a wild, espresso-fueled, gelato-sticky adventure it's been!

We wrote this story during a huge transitional time in our lives. After spending over a decade making families laugh on YouTube with our daughters, we decided it was time to step into a new phase of our creative journey. Think of it like moving from a delightful, colorful Vespa to a shiny, unpredictable Ferrari—exciting, terrifying, but 100% worth the ride.

We've always been writers, but until now, it's mostly been screenwriting (one day, we'll share our Hollywood horror stories over a glass of wine). But this? Writing romance novels together? It's a dream we've always whispered.

Here's the plot twist: we'd saved up for an anniversary trip to Italy—a bucket list dream. But instead of indulging in pasta and gondola rides, we took that money and put it toward our *real* dream: becoming full-time writers together. So, while Katie and Matteo were sipping vino and dancing under the Tuscan sun, we were at our kitchen table, pouring our hearts into their story and dreaming of the day we'd get to share it with you.

Funny thing about the fabulous seniors in this book—that part was inspired by real life! Back in our twenties, we went on a cheap casino/buffet bus tour to celebrate an anniversary. Get this, we were the *only* people under seventy. And let us tell you, those seniors were WILD. We became everyone's honorary grandchildren for three unforgettable days of card games, hilarious stories, and unsolicited life advice. We've never forgotten that trip, and we hope we've honored their unshakable zest for life in our novel.

This book is our love letter to fabulous senior citizens everywhere. Age doesn't define us—*we* define us. The limits we think exist? We put them there. No matter where you are in life, you can carry the spirit of these seniors with you. Be bold. Be adventurous. And when the time comes, may we all be as fearless as Aunt Deb in our seventies, dancing on the beach in nothing but courage and a smile.

Love, laughter, and a busload of thanks, *MéLisa & Ryun*

And darlings, isn't it Aunt Deb's turn to go viral? Please leave us a fabulous AMAZON REVIEW!

ACKNOWLEDGEMENTS

To our readers, thank you for hopping on the bumpy bus ride of love and laughter with Katie and Matteo through Italy. You are the heart of every page. We couldn't do this without you. We cherish every review, every comment, and your always-spot-on book recs!

To the friends and mentors who've supported us, inspired us, and laughed with us along the way—we're so lucky to have you in our corner.

- All Write Well

- Author Ever After

- TCP Authors

- Valerie Humbard

- Joquena and Renee Lomelino

To the incredible writers of the romance community—thank you for being the queens of steam. Your stories inspire us and your hustle keeps us grinding. We bow down.

ABOUT THE AUTHORS

MéLisa Ryun is our combined pen name, and we're a husband-wife duo who've been finishing each other's sentences (and steamy scenes) for nearly 30 years. We left the glitz of Hollywood for the glitter of Vegas. Despite calling Sin City home, we say what happens in Vegas should definitely not stay in Vegas—not with our scorching hot romcoms.

We spend our days in a death match of yoga and joke-writing. Living out our happily-ever-after while making silly social media videos together. **Snark. Swoon. Spice!**

VISIT MELISARYUN.COM
FIND US ON SOCIAL MEDIA @MELISARYUN